The Structure of Defoe's Phrasal Verbs

An Exploration into Defoe's Language of Fiction

The Structure of Defoe's Phrasal Verbs
An Exploration into Defoe's Language of Fiction

Kazuho MURATA

KEISUISHA
2018

copyright©Kazuho MURATA
Printed in Japan

ALL RIGHT RESERVED. No part of this work may be reproduced, redistributed, or used in any form or by any means without prior written permission of the publisher and copy-right owner.

Published by KEISUISHA co., ltd.
1-4 komachi naka-ku Hiroshima 730-0041 JAPAN
ISBN978-4-86327-426-6   C3097

To the Memory of Professor Hiroyuki Ito

Acknowledgements

This book is dedicated to the late Dr. Hiroyuki Ito. While studying under him at Kumamoto University, I learned the importance and pleasure of "close and sensitive reading" of works of English literature with great concern for the use of language, the core of his teaching being based on the spirit of "philology" or love of words. Professor Ito would very often impress upon us that we, as Japanese students, should always consult the *Oxford English Dictionary* when discussing and studying English literature. The present work is, therefore, partly my sincere response to this teaching, for the reader will find in the following pages frequent references to this superb dictionary. Professor Ito had been anxiously awaiting the publication of this book, but to my regret, last year he passed away before its publication. Without his long-term guidance and encouragement, this research would have *never* been completed. I am deeply obliged to him.

The present book is a completely revised version of my doctoral dissertation presented to Kumamoto University in 2014. Dr. Sadahiro Kumamoto, professor at Kumamoto University, was a supervisor for my doctoral project. In my formulation of the findings in my earlier studies on Defoe's phrasal verbs (during the period 2000-2013), he advised me to pay special attention to the "structure" of phrasal verbs and consult *The Structure of Chaucer's Rime Words* (1964), a classic book by the late Dr. Michio Masui; Prof. Ito was one of his students. Although phrasal verbs and rhyme words are different linguistic phenomena, the emphasis on the "structure," namely "how phrasal verbs are built up and employed," was found to be very helpful. Even after I was granted a PhD, Professor Kumamoto continued to assist me with the revision process to develop my dissertation into book-form, sometimes through long enthusiastic discussions at a coffee shop. I wish to express my heartfelt thanks to him.

Though not so directly as the two teachers mentioned above, there are many people to whom I would like to give my gratitude, for supporting this book. Among them is Professor Risto Hiltunen; if I had not read his interesting article on phrasal verbs (1994), the present research would not have developed so smoothly. Professor Matsuji Tajima, who invited me to give presentations and write short essays for the Japanese Association for Studies in the History of the English Language, chiefly organized by him; this experience helped me develop as a scholar. Professor Masahiko Agari, who, perhaps just a little impressed at my oral presentation at Kumamoto University in 2012, encouraged me to start writing a doctor's thesis as soon as possible. Professor Masanori Toyota, who has inspired me since my student days through his lectures and books. And Professor Richard Gilbert, who has given me excellent insights from the very beginning of my study on phrasal verbs. I am also grateful to the late Professor Chiyoshi Yamada for kindly sparing his time to read Shakespeare with me, and his one-on-one guidance over the course of seven years, after finishing my graduate course, up until his passing.

In 2005-2006, I stayed at Cambridge as visiting scholar of the University of Cambridge. During my stay, I had a great opportunity to have a couple of meetings with Professor Sylvia Adamson; she gave me invaluable advice on my research project on Defoe's phrasal verbs. In Cambridge, besides attending lectures and classes at the Faculty of English, I was usually in the University Library. Whenever I became tired of reading (or rather trying to read) tons of books and articles, I

Acknowledgements

looked absent-mindedly out the window and thought of my past, present and future. After which, I never failed to *walk meditating back* home through the various college campuses and historic streets of Cambridge. My Cambridge experience has no doubt broadened my mind as well as my perspective for studying English literature. In that sense, I am greatly indebted not only to Professor Adamson and the University staff but also to the University itself and the city of Cambridge.

In addition, I wish to express my gratitude to all the fellow members of the Kumamoto English Stylistics and Philology Circle established by Prof. Ito, in particular, Masahiro Hori and Tomoji Tabata; their energetic activities have motivated me. Moreover, I want to express my sincere thanks to the faculty and students of the National Institute of Technology, Ariake College, where I have been working since 1993. Among them, my fellow colleagues, Hiroshi Yakiyama and Kenji Mito have given me great encouragement to continue my studies and Richard Grumbine kindly read, commented on, and carefully edited earlier drafts of this book. And Kaoru Takahashi, president of the college, granted generous financial support for this project. Furthermore, I would like to thank Mr. Itsushi Kimura, president of Keisuisha Co., Ltd., for having undertaken this publication, and Ms. Tokiko Kimura and Ms. Kyoko Fukumoto of the Keisuisha staff, for their editing, rescuing me from many careless mistakes. Of course, responsibility for any surviving errors is mine alone.

Finally, I heartily thank my family: my wife, Noriko, who has devotedly supported my work, and my daughter, Izumi, whose wonderful smile never fails to give me great cheer and encouragement.

Fukuoka, Japan
March 2018

Kazuho Murata

Contents

Introduction 1

Chapter 1 The Syntactic Structure of Intransitive Phrasal Verbs 23
1.1 The Simple Pattern "Verb + Particle" 33
    1.1.1 Fronting of the Particle
1.2 Adverbial Insertion: the "Verb + *Adverbial* + Particle" Pattern ... 48
1.3 The Composite Pattern "Verb + *-ing* (Present Participle) + Particle" 66
1.4 Towards a "Phrasal-prepositional Verb": the Structure of "Verb + Particle + Preposition" 78
    1.4.1 The Use of *Upon* in Defoe's Fiction
    1.4.2 Idioms or Set Phrases
    1.4.3 Hybrid Formation
1.5 Gerunds 99
    1.5.1 Groups with a Determiner
    1.5.2 Groups Lacking a Determiner
1.6 Conversion of Intransitive Phrasal Verbs into Nouns (or Adjectives) 112

Chapter 2 The Syntactic Structure of Transitive Phrasal Verbs 119
2.1 The Pattern "Verb + Particle + Object" (VPO) 129
    2.1.1 The Simple Pattern
    2.1.2 Phrasal Verbs as a Reporting Verb

2.2 The Pattern "Verb + Object + Particle" (VOP) 136
    2.2.1 The Pattern "Verb + *Personal Pronoun* + Particle"
    2.2.2 The Pattern of "Verb + *Reflexive Pronoun* + Particle"
    2.2.3 The Pattern "Verb + *Non-personal Pronouns* + Particle"
    2.2.4 The Division of Object by the Particle: As Special Cases of the VOP Pattern

2.3 The Fronting of the Particle: the Pattern "Particle (+ Subject) + Verb + Object" (PVO) 156

2.4 The Pattern "Object (+ Subject *or To*) + Verb + Particle" (OVP) ... 157
    2.4.1 The OVP in the Main Clause
    2.4.2 The OVP in the Subordinate Relative Clause
    2.4.3 The OVP in the *To*-Infinitive Construction

2.5 The Pattern of "Verb + (Indirect) Object + Particle + (Direct) Object" (VOPO) 165
    2.5.1 The VOPO Pattern
    2.5.2 Additional Patterns: VOOP, VPOO and OVOP

2.6 Passive Construction 169
    2.6.1 With *Be*-Verbs
    2.6.2 The Passive Progressive
    2.6.3 Without *Be*-Verbs
    2.6.4 Adjectival Use

2.7 Gerunds 188
    2.7.1 The VPO Pattern
    2.7.2 The VOP Pattern
    2.7.3 The OVP Pattern
    2.7.4 Passive Construction
    2.7.5 The Pattern Distribution in the Gerund Construction: Statistical Summary

2.8 Adverbial Insertion: the "VP [adv] O" and "VO [adv] P" Patterns... 204

2.8.1 The "VP [adv] O" Pattern
2.8.2. The "VO [adv] P" Pattern and the "V [adv] P" Pattern
2.9 The Composite Pattern of "V and VPO" or "V and VOP" 218
2.10 Distribution of Syntactic Patterns in Transitive Phrasal Verbs ... 221
 2.10.1 Choice between VPO and VOP

Chapter 3 Semantic and Stylistic Analysis of Phrasal Verbs: Six Aspects 231

3.1 Coordinated Use with Other Verbs: the "A and B (and C ...)" Pattern 231
 3.1.1 Cohesive Relation in the "A and B" Coordination
 3.1.2 Synonymous Relation in the "A and B" Coordination
 3.1.3 Coordinated with Words or Phrases of Different Word Class
3.2 Inversion and Particle Fronting for Stylistic Effect 244
3.3 The Function of Particles in Psychological Contexts 250
 3.3.1 The Function of Particles in Intransitive Phrasal Verbs
 3.3.2 The Function of Particles in Transitive Phrasal Verbs
 3.3.3 Orientational Metaphors: *Down* and *Up*
3.4 Descriptions of the Sea: With Special Reference to Nautical Terms
 256
 3.4.1 Descriptions of Navigation
 3.4.2 Descriptions of Scenery
 3.4.3 The Role of Absolute Participial Construction
3.5 The "Redundant" Use of Particles 269
3.6 Repetition and Synonym: the Case of *Shut Up* 274
 3.6.1 Repetition of *Shut Up*
 3.6.2 Synonyms for *Shut Up*

Conclusion 287

Appendices 297
References 305
index 311

Introduction

The rise of the English novel as a new literary form is generally considered to have been established by writers in the early eighteenth century; in particular, Daniel Defoe (1660 or 1661-1731) and Samuel Richardson (1689-1761) have played an important role. In terms of innovation of the "novel" (which etymologically means a "new" type of prose fiction), these two writers and their works have been discussed and studied from a variety of angles (e.g. social, thematic, literary, linguistic, etc.). When Defoe's "novels," specifically several fictional works from *Robinson Crusoe* (1719) to *Roxana* (1724), are exclusively focused on, the reader will likely feel that each and every action or movement by characters like Robinson Crusoe or Moll Flanders is described far more vividly and realistically than that in the previous fiction, for example, John Bunyan's *The Pilgrim's Progress* (1678, 1684) or Aphra Behn's *Oroonoko* or other short stories (1688-96). When analyzed linguistically, such descriptions of their actions naturally center on the predicate of a sentence. After examining the predicate's constituents, I have found that in Defoe's works "phrasal verbs" consisting of a verb and an adverbial particle such as *run away* or *take up* are used not only with high frequency but also with great diversity (which might be called syntactic, semantic and stylistic diversity). However, the relation between Defoe's language and his use of phrasal verbs has not been explored to date; actually, to the best of my knowledge, this issue has *never* been touched upon. Therefore, it is worth investigating, first from syntactic, and then semantic and stylistic viewpoints, how Defoe exploited phrasal verbs in composing his "new" fictional works. Neither (1) Defoe's language and style nor (2) the phrasal verbs of Defoe's era, namely in the eighteenth century, have been thoroughly examined. Let us take a quick look at earlier studies concerning each of these two topics.

Defoe, a journalist and political pamphleteer, and later a novelist in early eighteenth-century England, represents "one of the great examples of colloquial diction in English Literature" (Jespersen 1992 [1924]: 27). Over the last century, the "colloquial" aspects of Defoe's prose style have been noted by numerous writers and scholars.[1] In reflecting upon his colloquial style, Defoe's unique "loose" sentence-structure has often been referenced (cf. Furbank and Owens 1986: 125-133; McIntosh 1998: 88-94). On the other hand, research on Defoe's vocabulary, with particular focus on "the phrasal and idiomatic use of words,"[2] remains both sparse and fragmentary.[3] In this regard, I would like to give careful consideration to a remark made by Dobrée (1990 [1959]: 51) that in "the new colloquialism of phrase rather than of diction ... Defoe was a pioneer."[4] This remark could imply Defoe's idiosyncratic use of "phrasal" verbs.[5]

In addition, as regards Defoe's innovative use of language as the "novel" writer, Watt (1957a: 29), by constantly comparing Defoe with Richardson, regards "the break which Defoe and Richardson made with the accepted canons of prose style" as "the price they had to pay for achieving the immediacy and closeness of the text to what is being described."[6] Watt then goes on to make a generalization: "With Defoe this closeness is mainly physical, with Richardson mainly emotional" (p. 29). As a means of expression which linguistically represents "physical" closeness in Defoe's novels, a "phrasal verb" could be regarded as one of the most definitive examples, chiefly because this type of verb is intrinsically physical, "charged with energy and muscular associations" (Smith 1947 [1925]: 263).[7]

On the other hand, phrasal verbs such as *put off*, consisting *mainly* of dynamic, monosyllabic verbs of native origin and spatial adverbs, are "now part and parcel of the English language" (Hiltunen 1994: 129). In the context of the historical development of English, Kennedy (1967 [1920]: 11) demonstrates the tendency "toward the elimination of the verb with unstressed, inseparable particle and the gradual increase of the verb-adverb combination."[8] That is, while old compound verbs such as *forgive* and *understand*, both of which are still in common use, have become obsolete, multi-word verbs, including verb-adverb combinations such as *give up* have been growing increasingly productive and diverse, practically on a daily basis. In fact, phrasal verbs in present-day English are widely dealt with, not only in linguistic monographs (cf. Bolinger 1971; Fraser 1976, etc.), but also in dictionaries for the verbs under consideration (cf. *Cambridge Phrasal Verbs Dictionary* [2nd Edition] 2006; *Collins COBUILD phrasal Verbs Dictionary* [3rd Edition] 2012, etc.), and in various learning materials (cf. McCarthy and O'Dell 2004; 2007, etc.). Nevertheless, historical research on phrasal verbs has not yet been fully conducted, excepting a short monograph by Kennedy (1967 [1920]).[9] In particular, Akimoto (1999: 221) has stated that "little mention has been made of phrasal verbs in 18th and 19th century English. ... Books on the history of English also keep silent about verb-adverb combinations in the 18th century in particular." The first major presentation of multi-word verbs (including "verbo-nominal combinations" like *take care* as well as phrasal verbs) is found in Claridge (2000), who presents a thorough investigation of the 1640-1740 period, based on the *Lampeter Corpus*. There is a significant limitation to this research, however, as the corpus contains only rather formal writings on topics such as law, politics, science, and religion. Taking into account the general view (cf. Hiltunen 1994; Akimoto 1999; Biber et al. 1999: 408-409) that phrasal verbs are more frequently employed in informal writing such as drama, fiction and letters, there is ample need for further research on phrasal verbs in the eighteenth century, or rather in the novels or fictional works in this period.

In order to demonstrate Defoe's frequent use of phrasal verbs, a quantitative comparison between phrasal verbs in Defoe and his contemporaries is presented below. This comparison is based on the approach to "phrasal verbs" developed by Hiltunen (1994: 129-140). His approach (which will be considered more in detail later) focuses on seven adverbial particles: *away, back, down, forth, off, out,* and *up,* and treats those cases in which any of the seven adverbial particles combines with a lexical verb, as a "phrasal verb."[10]

Table 1 presents the occurrences (or tokens) of the seven particles (which co-occur with lexical verbs) in Defoe's seven novels or fictional works, and also compares these with John Bunyan's *The Pilgrim's Progress*, Aphra Behn's *Oroonoko* and other five short stories,[11] Jonathan Swift's *Gulliver's Travels*, and Richardson's *Pamela*:

Table 1. Frequency of Occurrence of Seven Particles

*title	PP **(1678, 1684)	Behn (1688-1696)	RC (1719)	MC (1720)	CS (1720)	MF (1722)	JPY (1722)	CJ (1722)	Rox (1724)	GT (1726)	Pamela (1740)
***total words	104,693	84,500	122,091	102,298	111,348	137,004	93,929	125,330	133,982	102,254	224,780
up	237	113	360	241	243	234	275	236	258	190	411
out	161	84	250	161	158	213	153	192	219	112	276
away	75	32	149	96	175	138	114	172	128	24	213
off	36	45	116	144	108	138	59	114	130	49	81
down	97	49	180	63	93	86	72	99	80	98	285
back	112	20	80	52	74	96	42	83	94	31	53
forth	23	10	0	1	4	1	1	0	1	1	7
total of seven	741	353	1,135	758	855	906	724	896	910	505	1,326
per 1,000 words	7.08	4.18	**9.29**	**7.40**	**7.67**	**6.61**	**7.62**	**7.14**	**6.79**	4.93	5.89

*The abbreviations of the texts are: *PP* = John Bunyan's *The Pilgrim's Progress* (including the second part); Behn = Aphra Behn's Fiction (including *Oroonoko* and five other works) based on Oxford World's Classic; *RC* = *Robinson Crusoe*; *MC* = *Memoirs of a Cavalier*; *CS* = *Captain Singleton*; *MF* = *Moll Flanders*; *JPY* = *A Journal of the Plague Year*; *CJ* = *Colonel Jack*; *Rox* = *Roxana*; *GT* = *Gulliver's Travels*. **The number (below the title) enclosed by parentheses stands for the publication year. ***In counting the total number of words, the preface to each work is excluded. In addition, the *JPY* text contains several bills of mortality: these tokens (i.e. words and figures) are likewise excluded from the word count.

The number of particle occurrences in Table 1 corresponds exactly to those of "phrasal verbs." Comparing the frequency per 1,000 words, the total of these seven particles in any of Defoe's seven works is revealed to be more frequent than those in Aphra Behn's Fiction, *Gulliver's Travels* and *Pamela*. On the other hand, Bunyan is relatively close to Defoe, though the distribution pattern of the particles is quite different; *forth* is hardly used either by Defoe or Swift.[12] The similarity between the two writers (Bunyan and Defoe) is likely associated with a remark made by Watt (1957b: 199) that "Defoe's prose contains a higher percentage of words of Anglo-Saxon origin than that of any other well-known writer, except Bunyan." Moreover, the lower frequency in *Pamela* suggests that Richardson's "emotional" closeness in his novels, as Watt points out, might not be directly connected with his use of phrasal verbs. In any case, via such a comparison, Defoe's frequent use of phrasal verbs in his novels can be appreciated, to some degree.

The diversity of phrasal verbs employed by Defoe must also be mentioned. In particular, the range and diversity of syntactic structures in Defoe's phrasal verb use is rich and varied. In his "novel" descriptions, Defoe manages to make the best of both elements, "verb" and "particle." More specifically, by separating these two elements (sometimes as far as possible) as well as sticking them together, he seems to have attempted to create a variety of nuances or shades of meaning, in the context; probably he should be considered to have introduced a "new" mode of writing in his own way. Let us look at a few examples from each of typical syntactic patterns.

In intransitive use, first of all, many of phrasal verbs occur in a very simple pattern of "Verb + Particle" such as *we* **hurry'd away**, (*CJ* 275) or *the Weather* **clear'd up**, (*RC* 9), but sometimes, Defoe likes to front the particle, such as **away** *he* **went** *like the Wind*, (*RC* 240) or **away runs** *Friday*, (*RC* 294). Secondly, Defoe often inserts adverbials between the verb and the particle, such as *I* **resolv'd to run** <u>quite</u> **away** *from him.* (*RC* 6) or [*Friday*] **went** <u>close</u> **up** *to him*, (*RC* 292), and sometimes these inserted adverbials are long, like *he* **walk'd**, <u>talking with another Man of the same Cloth</u>, **back** *again, just by me*; (*Rox* 85). Thirdly, Defoe employs the pattern of "Verb + -ing + Particle" like *all on a sudden I found the Earth* **come crumbling down** *from the Roof of* *my Cave*, (*RC* 80). This pattern seems to contain two "phrasal" verbs of not only *come down* but also *crumbling down* in a deep structure. Fourthly, intransitive phrasal verbs are often followed by prepositional phrases like I **went away** <u>to the Hill</u>, (*RC* 183), but among such cases the relationship of "Verb + Particle + Preposition" is so close and strong that such a three-word verb could be treated like a one-word "transitive" verb like *I* **came in** <u>with</u> (= "overtook") *him, hearing the Noise*; (*MC* 170).

In transitive use, as the object is an essential formative element, the relation between "Verb + Particle" and the object must be dealt with. From a syntactic viewpoint, attention is always paid to the position of the object. Generally speaking, two main patterns are used: first, the pattern of "Verb + Particle + Object" (VPO) like *I* ***pull'd off*** *my Clothes*, (*RC* 48) and, second, the pattern of "Verb + Object + Particle" (VOP) like *I* ***gave*** *this Attempt* ***over*** ... (*RC* 128). Defoe seems to prefer the VOP pattern to the VPO, and as evidence thereof he sometimes puts a very long object between the verb and the particle, like *I began to work my Way into the Rock, and* ***bringing*** *all the Earth and Stones that I dug down* ***out*** *thro' my Tent*, (*RC* 60) or [the Gentleman] ***took*** *the Cloth, and the Remains of what was to Eat,* ***away***; (*Rox* 63). Of course, not *all* instances of transitive phrasal verbs belong to these two patterns. Defoe often also uses the pattern of "Object + (Subject or *To*) Verb + Particle" (OVP) like <u>The Trees that</u> *I* ***cut down***, *were lying to rot on the Ground.* (*RC* 129) or *I have no* <u>Cloaths</u> *to* ***put on***, (*CJ* 126). Fourthly, Defoe sometimes employs two (direct and indirect) objects in the use of phrasal verbs, like [he] ***gave*** <u>me</u> ***back*** <u>an exact Inventory of them</u>, (*RC* 33) or *Then I pull'd out his Watch and* ***gave*** <u>it</u> <u>him</u> ***back***, (*MF* 155). Fifthly, transitive phrasal verbs are often used in the passive voice, like *the Masque was* ***thrown off***, (*MC* 270) or *with my Heart as well as my Hands **lifted up** to Heaven, ... I cry'd out aloud*, (*RC* 96). In this case, the subject of the passive voice is virtually the object of the active voice. In addition, some of the passive instances serve as an adjective like *so I ... look'd like a **cast-off** Mistress,* (*Rox* 182).

Thus, in order to provide a comprehensive picture of Defoe's use of phrasal verbs, we should examine how Defoe exploits and manipulates phrasal verbs and describe as accurately as possible, on a syntactic basis, the variety of instances from the above passages.

Further, the stylistic expressiveness of phrasal verbs will be intensively discussed. Defoe had already made effective use of phrasal verbs in political pamphlets written in his early career. One instance is taken from *The Shortest Way with the Dissenters* (1702), one of his most noted pamphlets, which contains passages where religious matters are often discussed through the use of phrasal verbs to convey concrete and vivid images:[13]

> when our Church shall be **swallowed up** in Schism, Faction, Enthusiasme, and Confusion; (105) / till the Spirit of Whiggism, Faction, and Schism is **melted down** like the Old-Money! (103) / there [i.e. in Scotland], they made entire Conquest of the Church, **trampled down** the sacred Orders and suppressed the Episcopal Government, with an absolute, and, as they supposed, irretrievable Victory, (101)

In the passages cited above, *swallow up*, *melt down*, and *trample down* are typical instances of phrasal verbs. In the next pamphlet example, the metaphorical use of the image of a plant is quite unique:

Introduction

> This is the time to **pull up** this <u>Heretical Weed of Sedition</u>, that has so long disturb'd the Peace of our Church, and poisoned the good Corn. (104)

Here a religious idea, as the words *Heretical* and *Sedition* suggest, is compared to plants or weeds. Through the simple everyday image of pulling up the weeds, Defoe's ironic, satirical idea of demolishing a religious revolt or mutiny of *Sedition* is made vivid and effective.[14] The plant imagery is further developed, as follows:

> 'You had an Opportunity to **root out** this cursed Race from the World, ...' (105) / the Contagion will be **rooted out**. (107) / THIS Obstinacy must be **rooted out** with the Profession of it! (108) / the Posterity of the Sons of Error may be **rooted out** from the Face of this Land, for ever! (109) [cf. *OED* s.v. root, *v.* 7. a. "To pull, dig, or take *out* by the roots; hence *fig.*, to extirpate, exterminate, destroy." *c* 1450~]

Root out, which occurs four times in this pamphlet, is a phrasal verb evoking a vivid and tangible image. This transitive phrasal verb is combined with abstract nouns as objects (or subjects in passive voice) tinged with negative implications, as with *Obstinacy* or *Contagion*. Thus, a series of phrasal verbs in this short pamphlet act as a dynamic metaphor, throwing Defoe's satirical intention into relief. In addition, the combination between monosyllabic dynamic verbs and adverbs of direction, such as *root out* and *pull up*, produces a motion-picture effect which Jespersen (2010 [1960]: 594) refers to as "kinematographic [i.e. cinematographic],"[15] in many descriptions. Such an effect can often be observed in the use of phrasal verbs; in particular, in action scenes in Defoe's novels.

It is necessary to give a precise definition of "phrasal verb," because it has not always been applied consistently among linguists and grammarians.[16] The definition in the present study is mainly based on the classification by Quirk et al. (1985):

> Three Types of Verb-Particle Combinations (Quirk et al. 1985: 1150-1167):
> (1) **phrasal verb** (e.g. *drink up*): "verb + (adverbial) particle"
> (2) **prepositional verb** (e.g. *dispose of*): "verb + preposition"
> (3) **phrasal-prepositional verb** (e.g. *get away with*): "verb + (adverbial) particle + preposition"

The term "phrasal verb" here is chiefly applied to verbs of Type (1), but a problem also arises. Quirk et al. confine their treatment of "phrasal verbs" to idiomatic combinations which "behave as a single unit" (p. 1150), and distinguish such combinations from "free combinations in which the verb and the adverb have distinct meanings" (p. 1152). It can be observed that there exist two distinct groups in this type: *give in* ['surrender'] and *put off* ['postpone'], in a figurative sense, versus *come in* or *go out* in the literal sense. Both groups of combinations are however closely related, in that figurative or idiomatic meanings have been developed through a metaphor or image, from literal meanings. Moreover, since idiomaticity is a matter of degree, there are no clear-cut boundaries between "idiomatic" and "non-idiomatic" phrasal verbs (i.e. free combinations). Therefore, it is nearly impossible to divide all the instances of verb-adverb combinations in Defoe's texts into the two distinct groups. Consequently, in this study, undue attention will not be given to such a distinction, and all cases of such combinations will simply be considered "phrasal verbs."[17]

Furthermore, verbs of Type (2), "prepositional verbs," are completely excluded from our discussion, but verbs of Type (3), "phrasal-prepositional verbs," are included, as in the case where a "phrasal verb" is combined with a preposition, such as "*get away + with.*" This distinction (i.e. concerning exclusion and inclusion) is not arbitrary. The main reason why "prepositional verbs" should be clearly distinguished from "phrasal verbs" (and so will not be discussed here) lies in the difference in style or register between these two types of verbs. According to Brinton and Traugott (2005: 126), "In contrast to phrasal verbs ["consist[ing] of a small set of post-verbal particles, *up, down, off, out, over, through, away, on,* and *along,* which typically collocate with native, monosyllabic verbs" (p. 123)], prepositional verbs consist of a larger set of prepositions, which collocate with Romance as well as native verbs." As a result, prepositional verbs in present-day English, which "are relatively common in academic prose," "do not have the same informal overtones as phrasal verbs" (Biber et al. 1999: 415). On the other hand, "phrasal-prepositional verbs" seem to present different problems than "prepositional verbs," when analyzing multi-word verbs in Defoe's texts (as well as other writer's texts in the early eighteenth century). It has been found that a pattern in which a verb is followed by two particles (the first an adverb and the second a preposition) in Defoe can be included in Type (1), for two reasons: diachronic and synchronic, as will be explained.

From a diachronic perspective, attention is paid to the fact that the *Oxford English Dictionary* on CD-ROM (henceforth, *OED*), based on historical principles, describes (most) verbs of Type (3) as a subentry of verbs of Type (1), not Type (2), as in the treatment of *put up with* (*OED* s.v. put, *v.* 56. **put up**, p. (b).), indicating that such a type, concerning three-word verbs, is historically derived from a verb-adverb combination. In addition, in the process of development of multi-word verbs, Denison (1998: 223) states that "The phrasal-prepositional verb has been gaining ground" in Late Modern English (i.e. in the period 1776-1997) and "has moved in on the territory of the transitive phrasal verb," citing the case where *put up* 'endure' (1573 [*OED* year of first instance]) has been replaced by *put up with* (1755). Taking into consideration Denison's statement, the extensive use of phrasal-prepositional verbs seems to have begun somewhat later than the period of Defoe's writing career (*c*.1690-1725).[18]

Next, from a synchronic viewpoint, some linguists or grammarians point out a remarkable similarity between verbs of Type (3) and Type (1) in present-day English. Biber et al. (1999: 424) mentions, "Although phrasal-prepositional verbs are similar to prepositional verbs in their valency patterns, their register distribution is more similar to phrasal verbs"; "phrasal verbs and phrasal-prepositional verbs are notably rare in academic prose." It follows that verbs of Type (3) are "largely restricted to informal English" (Quirk et al.: 1160). These observations lead to the insight that, in pursuit of Defoe's colloquialism, verbs of Type (1) and Type (3) should be treated on equal terms.[19]

Since a "phrasal verb" is here defined as "the combination of any lexical verb with an adverbial particle (optionally plus a preposition)," the next matter to be discussed concerns the range of "adverbial particles" under consideration. The criteria in this research for identifying a phrasal verb in Defoe's texts is whether or not an adverbial particle is syntactically and semantically related to any lexical verb occurring in the same sentence or context; not whether a verb is related to any particle. As Bolinger (1971: 17-18) puts it, "Though the particle class is unquestionably far smaller than the verb class, deciding exactly what words it contains is harder than one might imagine."

Therefore, it is worth considering how different types of particles have been investigated in previous studies concerning phrasal verbs.

(a) The Case of Hiltunen (1994)
As "belong[ing] to the most productive elements forming phrasal verbs in contemporary English" (p. 129), Hiltunen exclusively focuses on the following seven particles:

away, back, down, forth, off, out, up.

Hiltunen's approach is based on the *Helsinki Corpus of English Texts*, and has been proven highly effective for observing the general trend in the use of phrasal verbs during the period 1500-1700, and describing characteristics of those verbs between different text types in the corpus. Application of Hiltunen's approach to the investigation of phrasal verbs in Defoe has yielded interesting findings, as partly demonstrated above. Nonetheless, extracting the most significant features of those verbs related to the language of Defoe, in a survey based on a mere seven particles, imposes a serious limitation. Given that this is true, what should be added to the seven particles? For example, Hornby (1955: 192) mentions that "The most important [particles] are: *up, down, **in**, out, **on**, off, away, back.*" Here, *forth* is excluded, but *in* and *on* are included. In researching Defoe's use of phrasal verbs it will be shown that these two particles are essential elements.

(b) The Case of Kennedy (1967 [1920])
In his pioneering work on phrasal verbs, Kennedy deals with 16 "prepositional-adverbs" (p. 9), as follows:

> about, across, around (or round), **at**, by, down, ***for***, in, off, on, out, over, thru, to, up, **with**.

Of interest here is the exclusion of *away*. This is probably because Kennedy assumes *away* never functions as "preposition," however this particle is among the most productive elements among all phrasal verbs. In addition, there is the highly problematic issue that the particles *at, for*, and *with* are included as adverbs. Kennedy gives these instances of "verb-adverb combinations": "*come at* 'to reach or gain,' *get at* 'to reach,' *look at* 'to view'" (p. 19). Here *at* in these three examples is no doubt a preposition. Moreover, as regards what Quirk et al. call "phrasal-prepositional verbs," Kennedy, mentioning that "Occasionally the verb-combination comprises two adverbial particles (my emphasis added) instead of just one," cites the following examples: *catch up with* 'to overtake'; *fall in with* 'to accept'; ... *stick up for* 'to defend' (p. 32). Although Kennedy regards two particles in the sequence "(fall) in with" or "(stick) up for" as adverbs, the second particles (i.e. *with* and *for*) are, in effect, prepositions. In this connection, these three particles should be removed from the list of adverbial particles.

(c) The Case of Fraser (1976)
Fraser suggests the 16 "formatives" which "have been observed to function as a particle with at least one verb" (p. 5):

> **about, across**, along, **around**, aside, *away, back,* **by**, *down, forth,* **in**, *off,* **on**, *out,* **over**, *up.*

The particles in bold type are not included in the list of (a). Unlike

Kennedy's list, each can function as an adverb.

(d) The Case of Claridge (2000)
As "possible particles in phrasal verbs" (p. 46), Claridge lists the following 35 particles:

> **aback, aboard,** *about,* **above,** *across,* **after,** **ahead,** *along,* **apart,** *around,* **ashore,** *aside,* **astray, asunder,** *away, back,* **behind,** *by,* **counter,** *down, forth,* **forward(s),** *home, in, off, on, out, over,* **past,** *round, through, to,* **together,** *under, up.*
> [The particles in bold type are not included in the list of (c).]

Claridge first admits "This is not a complete list" (p. 47). With Cowie and Mackin's list (to be discussed later) under purview, Claridge removes about twenty particles from their list as "irrelevant for the present analysis" (p. 46), and establishes her own list. Based on the 35 particles in the list above, Claridge studied phrasal verbs in the *Lampeter Corpus*. As a result, she demonstrated that "24 particles as formative elements" are used in this corpus (p. 124).

(e) The Case of Cowie & Mackin (1975)
With their intention of compiling a "Dictionary of Current Idiomatic English," Cowie and Mackin present a more complete and extensive (though not exhaustive) list of 56 particles:

> *aback, aboard, about, above,* **abreast,** *abroad, across,* **adrift,** *after,* **aground,** *ahead,* **aloft,** *along,* **alongside,** *apart, around, aside, astray, away, back,* **backward(s), before,** *behind,* **below, between, beyond,** *by, counter, down,* **downhill, downstairs,** *forth, forward(s), home, in,* **indoors, in front, inside, near,** *off, on,*

15

on top, *out*, **outside**, *over*, **overboard**, *past*, *round*, *through*, *to*, *together*, *under*, **underground**, *up*, **upstairs**, **without**.

The 23 particles in bold type are not contained in the list of (d), and *ashore* and *asunder* in Claridge are missing here. This brief review suggests that no complete list has yet been developed.

With a view to accomplishing the primary mission of finding pivotal characteristics in Defoe's language and style, it seems most relevant to focus on a limited number of select particles, as opposed to an attempt to create a full and comprehensive list of all particles. From the Cowie and Mackin list, or even Claridge, certain particles can be removed for the present study.[20] Seen in this light, Fraser's selection of 16 particles in list (c) appears reasonable and practicable, in that this list encompasses the most frequent and important particles of not only phrasal verbs in present-day English but also phrasal verbs in Defoe.

In accordance with the above arguments, the aim of the present research is to reveal the syntactic and semantic structure of the phrasal verb in Defoe's novels, and to elucidate the genius of his language of fiction. At the same time, this quest is intended to clarify, as far as possible, the actual usage of phrasal verbs in the early eighteenth century. In order to disclose the syntactic structure of phrasal verbs in more precise detail, it is necessary to divide all instances of such verbs into two distinct classes based on whether each is "intransitive" or "transitive." This book is comprised of three chapters. In Chapter 1, the syntactic structure of intransitive phrasal verbs will be investigated; Chapter 2 will examine the syntactic structure of transitive phrasal verbs; and Chapter 3 will, based on the linguistic results obtained in the previous two chapters, explore semantic and stylistic features unique to the use of those verbs, including six main topics: (1) coordinated use

Introduction

with other verbs, (2) inversion and particle fronting for stylistic effect, (3) the function of particles in psychological contexts, (4) descriptions of the sea, (5) the "redundant" use of particles, and (6) repetition and synonym. Concluding Remarks will summarize the main points presented in the previous three chapters and offer insights into Defoe's language and style through the use of phrasal verbs.

Finally, **the texts used** in this study are as follows: J. Donald Crowley ed. *Robinson Crusoe* (Oxford University Press, 1983), James T. Boulton ed. *Memoirs of a Cavalier* (Oxford University Press, 1991), Shiv K. Kumar ed. *Captain Singleton* (Oxford University Press, 1990), G. A. Starr ed. *Moll Flanders* (Oxford University Press, 1981), Louis Landa ed. *A Journal of the Plague Year* (Oxford University Press, 1998), Samuel Holt Monk ed. *Colonel Jack* (Oxford University Press, 1965), and John Mullan ed. *Roxana* (Oxford University Press, 1996). In addition, the texts by authors other than Defoe are: W. R. Owens ed. Bunyan's *The Pilgrim's Progress* (Oxford University Press, 2003), Paul Salzman ed. Behn's *Oroonoko and Other Writings* (Oxford University Press, 2009), Herbert Davis ed. Swift's *Gulliver's Travels* (Basil Blackwell, 1965), and Thomas Keymer and Alice Wakely eds. Richardson's *Pamela; or, Virtue Rewarded* (Oxford University Press, 2001). Citations in this book are from the above texts. Page references are in parentheses, and all emphases are mine; italics in citations are original.

notes

[1] In providing a brief survey of how Defoe's style has been viewed historically, it seems appropriate to begin with a quote from Sir Walter Scott, in 1810: "It is greatly to be doubted whether De Foe could have changed his colloquial, circuitous, and

17

periphrastic style for any other, whether more coarse or more elegant" (reprinted in Rogers 1972: 75). Scott's statement has been influential in labeling Defoe's style as "colloquial," as from this point forward, his "colloquial" style has been widely and controversially discussed by literary critics. There has been, in particular, consistent debate as to whether Defoe is a one-style (i.e. a colloquial and "awkward style") writer, or on the contrary, a versatile and skilled writer. It has been pointed out that the "one-style" argument is inextricably connected with the first-person narrative which Defoe employed in writing his fiction. In fact, "the ghost of Moll Flanders or some other fictional character of Defoe's is haunting the argument [concerning Defoe's style]" (Furbank and Owens 1986: 126). That said, subsequent studies, particularly by James (1972), Starr (1974), and Furbank and Owens (1986), have attempted to newly argue for, and illustrate aspects of, Defoe's stylistic versatility. In consequence, Richetti (2005: 96) offers a concise and insightful summary of existing arguments and counter-arguments on Defoe's style: "His colloquial manner is a strategy, only one of his various styles and tones, although perhaps his most frequent and effective mode." As a research issue to be investigated, it seems essential to specify more precisely what Richetti terms "colloquial manner" from a linguistic viewpoint, especially in that the term "manner" may lack specificity.

[2] As for the English language during the three hundred years between 1485-1785, Partridge (1969: 67) states that "The aspect of syntax most significant for style is the phrasal and idiomatic use of words, which grammarians have tended to neglect, …"

[3] A significant exception is a brief but detailed analysis of *Moll Flanders*' language by McIntosh (1986: 22-36). As "the most vulgar of Defoe's many voices" (p. 22), the three principal categories of usage, "colloquialisms," "solecisms," and "archaisms," have been discussed.

[4] For the purpose of greater accuracy, Dobrée's remark in his observations on "Defoe To 1710" (i.e. in his journalistic career) is quoted verbatim: "But what is interesting from the point of view of literature is the new manner, the new colloquialism of phrase rather than of diction—for Tom Brown and Ned Ward had the latter—a run of everyday phrase which Swift was to catch and to better. In this, as in so many other things, Defoe was a pioneer" (my emphasis added).

[5] This connection regarding style has been mentioned by Nevalainen (1999: 423): "the phrasal verb largely belongs to the colloquial idiom in Early Modern English [i.e. in the period 1476-1776]." Furthermore, it is worth mentioning that in *Style in Fiction* (2nd ed.) by Leech and Short (2007) a new suggestion has been added to a checklist of stylistic categories: that scholarly researchers should "look out for phrasal verbs and how they are used" (p. 63). This remark is not found in the

equivalent passage in the first edition (Leech and Short 1981: 77). This recent addition being a sign that the significance, as a stylistic element, of the verbs in question has been recognized among scholars in the quarter-century after its first publication (1981), has further reinforced my own interest in the relation between Defoe's style and his use of phrasal verbs.

[6] In his invaluable study of these two writers and Henry Fielding, Watt (1957a: 10-11), dealing with realism "as the defining characteristic which differentiates the work of the early eighteenth-century novelists from previous fiction" (p. 10), states that "the novel's realism does not reside in the kind of life it presents, but in the way it presents it" (p. 11). Thus, his emphasis on *how* the novel is described, rather than on *what* the novel describes, suggests the possible existence of what might be termed the "language of realism."

[7] In his pioneering studies of English idioms, Smith (1947 [1925]: 251) mentions: "phrasal verbs like *to pull through, to keep up*, (originally enclosed in quotation marks) are kinaesthetic metaphors, arousing imagined sensations of muscular effort"; these verbs consist of dynamic verbs "which express movement or attitudes of the body" plus the adverb and preposition.

[8] Likewise, Sinclair (1991: 68) mentions that "the whole drift of the historical development of English has been towards the replacement of words by phrases, with word-order acquiring greater significance."

[9] This book includes the section "theory and history of verb-adverb combination in English" (pp. 11-18) and makes a brief historical survey on the verbs in question from the Old English period. It must be noted that in the recent monograph, Thim (2012) finally managed to explore the English verb-particle construction from a historical and cross-linguistic perspective.

[10] The treatment of these "adverbial" particles presented here is the same as those in my previous studies (Murata 2000-2014). Cases where particles function as prepositions (e.g. *the Tears ran down his Face* (*RC* 258)) are completely excluded. Likewise, the phrase *out of* is excluded as a preposition (e.g. *she went out of the Room* (*MF* 161)). In addition, there are several cases where two particles are juxtaposed by "and" or "or," such as "up and down." According to the *OED*, some of the cases can be regarded as set phrases:

> [he] rose instantly and plunged **up and down** as if he was struggling for Life; (*RC* 30) / Asfor the Way which I propos'd to my self to go **in and out**, for I left no Avenue; (*RC* 161) / Here we took up our Station, cruising **off and on**, to see if we could meet any Ships going to, or coming from the *Buenos Ayres*, (*CS* 164) [cf. *OED* s.v. off and on, *advb. phr.* 2. *Naut.* "On alternate tacks, away from and towards the

shore." *a* 1608~]
These compound phrases can be treated as a single unit and are thus a separate category. They are not included in the counts for the items that make up the compound phrase. For example, "up and down" is not included in the counts for "up" or "down."

[11] Behn's other five works are as follows: *The Fair Jilt, Memoirs of the Court of the King of Bantam, The History of the Nun, The Adventure of the Black Lady,* and *The Unfortunate Bride.*

[12] In comparing the *Lampeter Corpus* with the *LOB Corpus*, Claridge (2000: 128) mentions that "*Forth* is a victim of linguistic fashion, so to speak; it is nowadays perceived as archaic and/or formal." According to her monograph (Claridge: 126-127), *forth* appears only 18 times in the contemporary English corpus (*LOB*) while it occurs 196 times in the Early Modern English corpus (*Lampeter*). In this regard, the scarcity of *forth* in Defoe and Swift, who belong to Early Modern English, attracts attention.

[13] Citations from *The Shortest Way with the Dissenters* are based on W. R. Owen ed. Volume 3: DISSENT from *Political and Economic Writings of Daniel Defoe* (General Editors: W. R. Owens and P. N. Furbank), 8 vols. (Pickering & Chatto 2000).

[14] In this pamphlet, Defoe, the dissenter, takes a diametrically opposite stance. According to Richetti (2005: 21), "Defoe intended this pamphlet as ironic mimicry of High Church polemics, a satiric exercise in which his rendition of the incendiary rhetoric of the conservative clerical antagonists of the dissenters such as the notorious Anglican firebrands, Dr. Henry Sacheverell and Charles Leslie, was meant to reveal its untenable extremism."

[15] With respect to monosyllabism in English, Jespersen (2010 [1960]: 594) argues that such "short words" can be understood "only in connexion with other words." And the "comprehension becomes, if I may say so, <u>kinematographic</u>: we have no time to see the single picture in itself, but perceive it only in combination with what comes before and after and thus serves to form <u>one connected moving picture</u>" (my emphasis added) (p. 594).

[16] Some linguists or philologists, like Halliday (1994) or Blake (2002 and 2004), call all cases of the combination of verb plus particle (in cases of both prepositions and adverbs) "phrasal verbs," while others prefer to use different terms such as "verb-adverb combination" (Kennedy 1967 [1920]), "verb-particle combination" (Fraser 1976) or "prepositional verb" (Huddleston and Pullum 2002).

[17] Claridge (2000), who likewise treats both "idiomatic" and "literal" combinations as phrasal verbs, mentions as follows: "Literal phrasal verbs are the core from

which figurative types are ultimately derived" (p. 47).

[18] In accordance with Denison's view, Beal (2004: 84) points out that "*put up with* has a first citation of 1755 in the *OED*, but is not included in Johnson's *Dictionary* until the 1765 edition, ..." This fact might support my treatment of this type of verb.

[19] Claridge (2000) made a clear differentiation between verbs of Type (1) and Type (3) in her study of multi-word verbs in 1640-1740. While her exhaustive study of multi-word verbs is an outstanding achievement, at least as far as her treatment of "phrasal-prepositional verbs" is concerned, there seems to be a problem. See Murata (2010) for a more detailed analysis.

[20] For example, *home* in Cowie & Mackin (as well as in Claridge) is obviously different in quality from common particles such as *out, in, off*. Many of the particles given denote a particular direction or spatial orientation, but are themselves implicit and context-dependent; here, the implicitness inherent to such particles contributes to a wide variety of use and meaning of phrasal verbs using such particles. On the other hand, *home* in *I **went Home** that Evening greatly oppressed in my Mind* (*A Journal of the Plague Year*; p. 12) is far more explicit in denoting its specific goal (i.e. going "to one's place of residence" (Cowie & Mackin: 135). In relation to the problem discussed, the overly explicit *upstairs/downstairs, downhill, indoors, on top, underground*, etc. seem inappropriate as formative elements of phrasal verbs. In addition, *upstairs* and *downstairs* are always written in two-word form (i.e. *up stairs* or *down stairs*) in Defoe. For example, in *A Journal of the Plague Year*, two variations between "up stairs" (two instances) and "up the stairs" (three instances) appear. This evidence suggests that *upstairs* or *downstairs* still have not been established as a "particle" in Defoe's era.

Chapter 1
The Syntactic Structure of Intransitive Phrasal Verbs

Defoe's use of intransitive phrasal verbs is very revealing and a powerful rhetorical device which adds impact and flair to his work, making it more pointed, vivid, and lively. The following is an examination of intransitive phrasal verbs as used by Defoe in his seven major novels. The primary questions are: (1) how many different types of phrasal verbs are employed, (2) how frequently these phrasal verbs are used, (3) the types of phrasal verbs which most frequently occur, and (4) which of the 16 particles are most frequently employed in the formation of intransitive phrasal verbs.

As for question (1), the combination of a verb and a particle, such as *he **went away*** or *I **came back***, is treated as a "phrasal verb." However, in cases such as *he **came running back***, from a structural point of view, it is very difficult to determine whether the particle (i.e. *back*) is *more closely* related to the main verb (i.e. *came*) or the present participle (i.e. *running*). As a result, the syntactic pattern consisting of "Verb + (-*ing*) Present Participle + Particle" will be considered as a "composite" pattern, and instances in this pattern are to be distinguished from others. As a matter of practical convenience, the syntactic pattern such as *he **went away*** is by contrast termed a "simple" pattern.

First, the types of intransitive phrasal verbs used will be presented. As for the use of "type": for example, *come back* is itself "one" type, regardless of how many times it is used. In order to grasp the individual characteristics of phrasal verbs in each of the works, as well as the general tendency in Defoe's use of those verbs, the frequency according to each work is shown in Table 1, below:

Table 1. Types of Intransitive Phrasal Verbs

works (total words)	RC (122,482 words)	MC (102,360)	CS (111,346)	MF (137,174)	JPY (93,929)	CJ (125,342)	Rox (134,078)
phr. vbs	195	132	189	118	98	161	115
"simple" pattern	(190)	(129)	(179)	(117)	(97)	(158)	(113)
"composite"	(5)	(3)	(10)	(1)	(1)	(3)	(2)
(lexical vbs)*	(89)	(61)	(91)	(57)	(46)	(79)	(55)
one type vs. two-or-more types*	51 (58%) vs. 38 (42%)	38 (62%) vs. 23 (38%)	58 (64%) vs. 33 (36%)	38 (66%) vs. 19 (34%)	29 (63%) vs. 17 (37%)	52 (66%) vs. 27 (34%)	36 (65%) vs. 19 (35%)

* The figures are exclusively limited to instances of the "simple" pattern; instances of the "composite" pattern are excluded here.

Robinson Crusoe contains the most different types of intransitive verbs (195 types: 190 "simple" and 5 "composite"), the significance of which is assessed in Table 1. The following list covers *all* the types of intransitive phrasal verbs in *RC*:

> List 1: Types of Intransitive Phrasal Verbs in *RC*
> [The "simple" pattern: "Verb + Particle"] (listed in alphabetical order)
> blaze *up*; break *away, out, in* (3); burn *out*; burst *out*; call *out*; clamber *up*; clear *up*; climb *up*; close *in*; coast *along*; <u>come *away, back, down, off, out, up, about, along, in, on, over* (11)</u>; cry *out*; draw *back, in* (2); drive *up*; **drop *down***; ebb *away, out* (2); face *about*; **fall *down*, *off, out,***

24

Chapter 1 The Syntactic Structure of Intransitive Phrasal Verbs

in (4); flutter *away*; fly *away, up* (2); get *away, back, off, out, up, in, over* (7); give *back*; go *away, back, down, off, out, up, about, along, by, in, on, over* (12); grow *up*; hang *down, up* (2); hasten *away, back* (2); join *in*; jump *away, down, up, about, in* (5); keep *off, in* (2); kneel *down*; launch *out*; lay *down, up* (2); lean *up*; leave *off*; let *down*; lie *down, off, out, by* (4); look *back, out, up, about, on* (5); make *out, on, over* (3); march *away, down, off, out* (4); move *off*; pass *on, over* (2); plunge *in*; point *up*; pull *off, in* (2); put *out, in* (2); ramble *about*; reach *back*; ride *up*; **rise *up***; roll *down*; row *away, up* (2); run *away, back, off, out, up, about, in, on* (8); rush *out, in* (2); sail *by, on* (2); scramble *away*; scud *away*; seek *out*; send *up*; set *off, out, in* (3); sheer *off*; shine *in*; shoot *out, up, over* (3); shuffle *along*; **sink *down***; sit *down, up* (2); slip *off*; spring *up*; stand *away, off, out, up, by, in, over* (7); start *away, up* (2); steer *away*; step *back, down, out, up* (4); stir *away, out, up* (3); stoop *down*; straggle *about*; stretch *away, out, over* (3); stroll *away*; swim *away, off, about, over* (4); take *out*; thrust *in*; travel cross; tumble *down*; turn *about*; veer *out*; venture *back, out, in, over* (4); walk *back, off, out, up, about, on* (6); wander *about, off, out* (3); wear *off, out* (2); wheel *about*; work *out, on* (2); [out of 89 lexical verbs, **190 types** of phrasal verbs]

[The "composite" pattern: "Verb + *-ing* + Particle"]

come crumbling *down*; come pouring *in*; come running *back, in* (2); go bleeding *off*; [**5 types**]

[195 types in total]

The figures in parentheses represent the number of the types of phrasal verbs generated from the verb in question; phrasal verbs lacking a number indicate that the verb involved generates only one type of intransitive phrasal verb. To be more specific, the first two items in the list, "blaze *up*; break *away, out, in* (3)," show that *blaze* forms "one" type of *blaze up*, while with *break*, the "three" types of *break away, break out, break in* occur as an intransitive phrasal verb in *RC*.

Of particular interest are the combinations—*fall down, drop down*, or *sink down* (in bold letters) in List 1—which suggest that these verbal elements denote downward movement, just as "down" does. On the other hand, "rise" in *rise up* denotes an upward movement, just as "up" does. These redundant combinations could be an effective way to help describe Defoe's fiction, taking into consideration the statement by Hampe (2002: 196) that such seemingly-redundant combinations "are a lot more vivid than their simple counterparts" (i.e. *fall down* vs. *fall*).[1]

Most of the verbs in List 1 are dynamic, monosyllabic verbs of native origin. The exceptions are *clamber, crumble, flutter, hasten, ramble, scramble, shuffle, straggle, travel, tumble, venture,* and *wander*; all of which are disyllabic; trisyllabic cases are not observed here (and rarely seen in Defoe). On the other hand, there are fewer Romance verbs (as typified with verbs of Latin origin) : *launch, march, travel, veer, venture,* etc. The disyllabic verbs or Romance verbs just mentioned are however not particularly lengthy words. What is to be noted here is that these verbs all denote, more or less, something "dynamic," rather than static, in their conceptual meanings.

A glance at Table 1 confirms three points: (i) out of the **89** lexical verbs, **190** types of phrasal verbs of the simple pattern (apart from five "composite" types) are generated; (ii) among the 89, 51 verbs (57%) form only one type of phrasal verb, while the other 38 verbs (43%) generate two or more types of phrasal verb;[2] (iii) the most prolific and versatile verbs are *go* (12 types), *come* (11), *run* (8), *get, stand* (7).

The most frequent verbs forming intransitive phrasal verbs are presented in Table 2:

Chapter 1 The Syntactic Structure of Intransitive Phrasal Verbs

Table 2. The Top Five Most Prolific Verbs

	RC	MC	CS	MF	JPY	CJ	Rox
1	go (12 types)	go (12)	come, go (11)	go (13)	go (12)	come, go (12)	go (11)
2	come (11)	come (9)		come (11)	come (11)		come (9)
3	run (8)	get (8)	run, stand (7)	run (8)	run (7)	get, look, stand, walk (7)	get, run (6)
4	get, stand (7)	march (7)		look (7)	get, look, walk (4)		
5		fall, ride, run (5)	get (6)	get (5)			stand (5)

Table 2 reveals that both *go* and *come* play a vital role in producing types of intransitive phrasal verbs throughout the seven works. These two verbs are the typical instances of "pure" intransitive verbs that do not take an object (cf. Quirk et al. 1985: 1169). As will be evidenced in later discussions, *go* and *come* are not only used most frequently through Defoe's seven texts, but also serve as essential elements for the structure of intransitive phrasal verbs in his works. Among others, *get, run,* and *stand* are also productive. Defoe's seven works each have distinctive characteristics in terms of the story and subject matter, since the story mainly unfolds in a desert island in *Robinson Crusoe* or in the society in London in *Moll Flanders*. Nonetheless, the basic material (i.e. verbal elements) of which intransitive phrasal verbs in each work are composed is remarkably similar across the board.

Question (2), how frequently these phrasal verbs are used, is examined next. The frequency of occurrences of intransitive phrasal verbs is presented in Table 3:

Table 3. Frequency of Intransitive Phrasal Verbs

works (total words)	RC (122,482 words)	MC (102,360)	CS (111,346)	MF (137,174)	JPY (93,929)	CJ (125,342)	Rox (134,078)
phr. vbs (tokens)	661	561	582	608	397	675	568
frequency per 1,000 words	5.39	5.48	5.23	4.43	4.23	5.39	4.23
one occurrence vs. two-or-more occurrences	99 (52%) vs. 91 (48%)	63 (49%) vs. 66 (51%)	**105 (59%)** vs. 74 (41%)	47 (41%) vs. **69 (59%)**	45 (46%) vs. 52 (54%)	80 (51%) vs. 78 (49%)	59 (52%) vs. 54 (48%)

Text volume differs from work to work. Therefore, a comparison of the frequency per 1,000 words will be employed. *RC, MC, CS,* and *CJ* generally belong to one group, while *MF, JPY* and *Rox* to a different group. Broadly speaking, the former group consists of an adventure story by a male narrator and the latter group, *MF* and *Rox* are mock-romances told by a female narrator (though both are quite different in character), while *JPY* is fictional reportage written in a partly-documentary style. The frequency gap per 1,000 words might be due to differences in the narratives, but here a more specific discussion on this matter will be avoided.

Another important concern is the distinction between one occurrence and two-or-more occurrences. *CS* and *MF* are diagonally opposite to each other in Table 3. This demonstrates that *CS* shows the widest variety of intransitive phrasal verbs, while *MF* has the strongest tendency in depending upon the repetition of certain phrasal verbs.

As for question (3), the types of phrasal verbs which most frequently occur, these are presented in Table 4:

Chapter 1 The Syntactic Structure of Intransitive Phrasal Verbs

Table 4. The Top Five of the Most Frequently Used Phrasal Verbs

	RC	MC	CS	MF	JPY	CJ	Rox
1	come back (33)*	come up (60)	come up (29)	go on (42)	go away (36)	go away (49)	go away (54)
2	go out (32)	fall in (32)	go away, go back (27)	go away (40)	break out (21)	go on (48)	come in, go on (31)
3	go away (26)	go on (20)		come back (34)	come up (20)	come up, come in (30)	
4	come up (23)	come in (19)	go on, stand away (25)	come in, go out (31)	come out (19)		sit down (26)
5	go back (21)	draw up, fall on, run away (18)			go about (18)	sit down (27)	come over, go back (23)

* The figure in parentheses indicates the number of occurrences.

Most of the phrasal verbs in the above table are composed of *come* and *go*. Exceptions are *fall in, draw up, fall on, run away* in *MC, stand away* in *CS, break out* in *JPY, sit down* in *CJ* and *Rox*. These phrasal verbs are closely associated with the narrative in each work (and some of them will be examined later).

Next, the frequency of occurrences of *come*- and *go*-phrasal verbs in the additional six works is presented in Table 5:

Table 5. Frequency of *Come*- and *Go*-Phrasal Verbs

	RC	MC	CS	MF	JPY	CJ	Rox
come-phr. vbs	107 (16%)*	136 (24%)	112 (19%)	155 (25%)	86 (22%)	161 (24%)	131 (23%)
go-phr. vbs.	154 (23%)	**69 (12%)**	139 (24%)	200 (33%)	130 (33%)	195 (29%)	188 (33%)
both in total	261 (39%)	205 (37%)	251 (43%)	355 (58%)	216 (54%)	356 (53%)	319 (56%)
other phr. vbs		*fall*-phr. vbs 65 (12%)	*stand*-phr. vbs 52 (9%)				

* The percentage shows the ratio of the total occurrences of intransitive phrasal verbs.

As mentioned, Defoe's use of intransitive verbs heavily depends on *go* and *come*. Interestingly, this tendency becomes stronger in his four later novels.

In addition, *MC* has far fewer instances of *go*-phrasal verbs; this work presents a reverse phenomenon, in that *go*-verbs occur less frequently than *come*-verbs. This seems to be closely associated with the relatively high frequency of *fall*-phrasal verbs, which, as seen in the use of *fall in* and *fall on* in Table 4, act mainly as military terms, unique to *MC*. Also, *CS* shows a relatively high frequency of *stand*-phrasal verbs. As exemplified in *stand away* in Table 4, this group of phrasal verbs is chiefly found in the abundance of nautical terms employed in *CS*. (*Fall-* and *stand*-phrasal verbs will be discussed later.)

Finally, as for question (4), which of the 16 particles are most frequently employed in the formation of intransitive phrasal verbs, the data is shown in Table 6:

Chapter 1 The Syntactic Structure of Intransitive Phrasal Verbs

Table 6. The Top Five Most Prolific Particles

	RC	MC	CS	MF	JPY	CJ	Rox
1	out (33 types)	out (18)	up (29)	out (21)	out (20)	away (23)	out (18)
2	up (29)	away (16)	away (27)	up (14)	away, up (14)	out (22)	up (17)
3	in (20)	off, up (15)	out (23)	off, in (12)		up (20)	in (13)
4	away (19)		off (20)		on (9)	about (17)	away, back (12)
5	off (18)	in (14)	in (18)	away, down (10)	in (8)	in (16)	
others	down (17), about (13), back (11), over (10), on (9), along, by (4), across (= cross) (1), forth, aside, around (0)	back (11), down, on (10), about (8), over (7), around (= round), by (2), along (1), forth, aside, across (= cross) (0)	down (15), about (10), back, on, over (9), along (4), around (= round), by (2), forth, aside (1), across (= cross) (0)	on (9), about (7), over (6), back (5), around, by (4), along (2), forth, across, aside (0)	down, about (6), off (5), back, over (4), along, by (3), around (1), forth, aside, across (0)	on, down (14), off (10), over (8), back (6), by (5), along (3), forth, around, across, aside (0)	down, on (9), off (8), over (7), about (5), along (2), by (1), forth, across, around, aside (0)

Table 6 reveals that *out* is ranked first (most-frequently used) in five of the works. Hence *out* is the most productive particle when Defoe makes intransitive phrasal verbs. Among the other particles, *up, away*, and *in*, are always within the top five in the examined works. Surprisingly some particles are rarely used: *forth, across, aside*, and *around*. Most of these four particles are *never* used in the seven works.

Scrutiny of the Tables in the overview section reveals the general picture of intransitive phrasal verbs in Defoe. There are however numerous linguistic phenomena yet to be discussed and analyzed from a syntactic point of view. The next sections will present a more in-depth examination of those verbs.

The number of occurrences of intransitive phrasal verbs includes a wide variety of grammatical forms, with respect to the verb as a formative element. Namely, the phrasal verbs under discussion are used in the present tense, past tense, and present and past participles, infinitive (both *bare* and *to*), and gerund (or verbal noun). In addition, several are converted into different parts of speech (or word classes), such as nouns or adjectives. *All* cases are included in the frequency counts in the Table lists above.

Furthermore, some phrasal verbs function as (part of) the predicate of either the main or subordinate clauses in a sentence, such as: *he **went back*** or <u>*when*</u> *I **came back***. These are typical instances of the finite group. On the other hand, others are in a nonfinite group. For those belonging to the nonfinite, it is possible to point out four grammatical subcategories: (1) the *to*-infinitive, (2) the *-ing* participial clause, (3) the gerund, and (4) the bare infinitive after causative verbs or perception verbs (and the present participle after perception verbs). The cases where phrasal verbs are used as gerunds, however, should be discussed separately (Section 1.5) because many of these gerunds contain unique structures.

Phrasal verbs are used with structural regularity and diversity in Defoe's fiction. The following sections will delve more deeply into the structure of these verbs.

Chapter 1 The Syntactic Structure of Intransitive Phrasal Verbs

1.1 The Simple Pattern "Verb + Particle"

Intransitive phrasal verbs in Defoe are often not followed by any word, as in (i) *when I* **came back**, (*RC* 54). This is the simplest form of the simple pattern in the finite use. Defoe makes full use of the simplest form of those verbs. Such phrasal verbs are used in the following grammatical forms, in order to compose his fiction (namely, to describe physical or mental behaviors by fictional heroes or heroines, or the scenes where they are): (ii) the progressive (e.g. *as he was* ***going away***, (*CJ* 140)); (iii) the bare infinitive which comes after auxiliary modal verbs, (e.g. *I might be sure no more* would **come down**. (*RC* 74)); (iv) the *to*-infinitive (e.g. *so I turn'd to* **go away**, (*RC* 205)); (v) (part of) an adverbial participial clause, by which intransitive phrasal verbs are usually utilized in the present participial (-*ing*) form,[3] (e.g. *so* ***stepping back***, *I open'd the Door*, (*CJ* 192)); (vi) bare infinitives which occur after a perception verb and its object, (e.g. *I* saw *about ten or twelve Ears* [i.e. of barley] **come out**, (*RC* 78)); (vii) a present participial (-*ing*) in the same syntactic situation as in (vi) (e.g. *as I* felt *my self* ***rising up***, (*RC* 45)); (viii) bare infinitive which follows a causative verb and its object (e.g. *he* let *me* ***come away***, (*MF* 339)).

Let us look at additional instances in the (i) to (viii) patterns:

> (i) as soon as ever my Fire **blaz'd up**, I heard another Gun, (*RC* 186) / the Weather **clear'd up**, (*RC* 9) / thus I lay 'till the Water **ebb'd away**, (*RC* 52) / Nothing was done, but the Treaty **broke off**, (*MC* 227) / few of the Garrison **got away**, (*MC* 80) / they were satisfied the *Indians* **fled away**, (*CS* 207) / the Night before we **set out**, (*CS* 84) / I **sunk down** when they brought me News of it, (*MF* 282) / those Thoughts **wore off**, and I declin'd seeing him again, (*MF* 235) / till the Moment

33

they **dropt down**, (*JPY* 82) / the Decrease **went on**, (*JPY* 225) / as we **pass'd along**, (*JPY* 34) / we **hurry'd away**, (*CJ* 275) / her fallen Flesh **plump'd up**, (*CJ* 259) / she **swoon'd away**, (*Rox* 22), etc.

(ii) The Night was **coming on**, (*RC* 299) / the Top of my Cave was **falling in**, (*RC* 80) / one of them ... hollow'd for the rest who were **straggling about**, (*RC* 253) / as we were **marching on**, (*MC* 128) / as the Party was **drawing out**, (*MC* 88) I was just **getting up**, (*MC* 176) / if a hundred Lions or Tygers were **coming along**, (*CS* 89) / the Boatswain ... told me the Boat was **going off**, (*MF* 307) / he was just **fainting away**. (*MF* 103) / all People expected he would besiege *Exeter*, where the Queen was newly **lying in**, (*MC* 220) [cf. *OED* s.v. lie, $v.^1$ 24. a. "To be brought to bed of a child" *c* 1440~], etc.

(iii) I might **coast along**, as I did on the Shore of *Africk*, (*RC* 198) [cf. *OED* s.v. coast, *v*. 4.b. *intr*. "To sail by or along the coast;" 1555~] / they should **come back** perhaps with two or three hundred of their Canoes, (*RC* 237) / none of the neighbouring Garrisons durst **stir out**; (*MC* 208) / there would be no Order, and several of the Men might **drop away**, (*CS* 261), etc.

(iv) the Violence of the Heat was too great to **stir out**; (*RC* 114) / the King halted, and Commanded to **draw up**. (*MC* 88) / I faced about and began to **march off**; (*MC* 94) / The Weather began now to **clear up**, (*CS* 102) / the Northern Monsoons being perhaps by that time also ready to **set in**. (*CS* 198) / [I] call'd upon him to **come back**, (*MF* 153) / I had not so much as the least inclination to **leave off**; (*MF* 221) / when the Dead-Carts began to **go about**, (*JPY* 59) / on the other Hand they desir'd the People to **keep off**, (*JPY* 142) / and thus they prepared to **set out**. (*JPY* 125) / we gave time to the *French* Cavalry to **come up**, (*CJ* 214) / the Girl ask'd her to **walk in**. (*Rox* 319), etc.

Chapter 1 The Syntactic Structure of Intransitive Phrasal Verbs

(v) [I] hallowing aloud to him that fled, who **looking back**, was at first perhaps as much frighted at me, (*RC* 203) / several of the Officers rid clear away, **coasting round**, and got to London, (*MC* 165) / Sir *John* **stepping up**, met the King coming down some Steps into a large Room ... (*MC* 57) / **setting out** when the Sun was about the Solstice, ... we had found the Benefit of it in our Travels. (*CS* 98) / the Horses **going on**, overthrew the Cart, and left the Bodies, (*JPY* 179) / I heard some body Hallow to me; and **looking about**, I saw *Will* running after me: (*CJ* 72), etc.

(vi) He <u>heard</u> them **come in**, and began to be a little in a Rage, (*CJ* 201) / in a few Minutes more we <u>perceived</u> their Boat **put off**; and as soon as the Boat put off, the Ship struck, and came to an Anchor, as was directed. (*CS* 217) [cf. *OED* s.v. put, *v.* 46. n. (a) *intr. Naut.* "To leave the land; to set out or start on a voyage; also, to leave a ship, as a boat." 1582~] / The Fellow follow'd diligently to the Gate of an Inn in *Bishopsgate-Street*, and <u>seeing</u> him **go in**, (*Rox* 219), etc.

(vii) I thought I <u>saw</u> my Ruin **hastening on**, (*Rox* 11) / as we <u>saw</u> it [= the infection] apparently **coming on**, (*JPY* 16) / we observ'd the People running on a sudden, as to <u>see</u> some strange Thing just **coming along**, (*CJ* 100) / but he <u>heard</u> a Noise of People **coming on** as if it had been a great Number, (*JPY* 130) / till he <u>heard</u> the Noise of the Coach **going on** again, (*CJ* 63) / [In the relative clause] *here*, says he, *is the same young Rogue, <u>that</u> I told you I <u>saw</u>* **Loitering about** *t'other Day when the Gentleman lost his Letter Case*, (*CJ* 28), etc.

(viii) then you shan't be deny'd, *said I*, <u>let</u> me **get up**. (*MF* 181) / come, *says he*, <u>let</u> us **go away**? (*CJ* 101) / he <u>bad</u> me **Lug out**; (*CJ* 20) [cf. *OED* s.v. lug, *v.* 5. b. *absol.* or *intr.* "to pull out money or a purse." 1684~] / at which, *Amy* run first, and I after her, and <u>bid</u> the QUAKER **come up** as soon as she had let them in. (*Rox* 282) / I <u>made</u> *Friday* and the Spaniard **go out** one Day, (*RC* 247)

35

/ this <u>made</u> us **lye by**, wishing to see them put to Sea, (*CS* 146) / he would endeavour to <u>have</u> them **stand in**, (*CS* 12) [cf. *OED* s.v. stand, *v.* 95. **stand in**. e. *Naut*. To direct one's course towards the shore. (See sense 36.) *c* 1595~], etc.

NOTES:

According to (iii): Phrasal verbs sometimes occur in the form of a past participle with an auxiliary *have* after auxiliary modal verbs, as with *he would have come back in half an Hour*, (*CJ* 49). This case implies that the proposition expressed by the phrasal verb *come back* was not fulfilled, namely that he *did not* come back in half an hour. Other similar cases are:

so that if I <u>would have</u> **gone away**, I could not, and I continued ill three or four Days, (*JPY* 13) / she had persuaded me to go on, when I <u>would have</u> **left off**: (*MF* 284), etc.

(iv): Concerning a "choice between the infinitive and participle constructions," Quirk et al. (1985: 1191) state that "As a rule, the infinitive gives a sense of mere 'potentiality' for action, as in *She hoped to learn French*, while the participle gives a sense of the actual 'performance' of the action itself, as in *She enjoyed learning French*."[4]

(v): Sometimes such verbs, by following *having* or *being* as an auxiliary verb, occur in the form of the past-perfect tense (or the progressive tense, on rare occasions), such as *having fallen in* or *being got over*. The participial clause in *so **stepping back**, I open'd the Door*, (*CJ* 192), *stepping back* (cited above), gives additional and detailed information (indicative of dynamic movement) to the main clauses (i.e. *I open'd the Door*).[5]

(vii): The use of the present participle apparently gives a more vivid and lively description than that of the bare infinitive, because the *-ing* form emphasizes "progress" or "continuation" of movement, where the bare infinitive implies "completion."

(viii): The pattern "*let* + object + phrasal verb" is often used in an imperative mood in the dialogue between characters. On the other hand, the use of the causative verb *bid* chiefly describes "indirect" speech acts (denoting "To ask pressingly" or "To command, enjoin" (*OED*)).

1.1.1 Fronting of the Particle (e.g. *away he went,* (*RC* 239))
Defoe makes great use of a syntactic pattern in which the particle is "fronted" (i.e. occurs before the verb as well as the subject) like *away he went,* (*RC* 239). Such a manipulation of word-order seems to be directly connected with and essential to the language of Defoe's fiction. This is an important variation of the "simple" pattern, and needs to be considered.

Claridge (2001: 264), dealing with an instance of particle fronting (... *up came a Foot-man in a gentile Livery,*) from the *Lampeter Corpus* (i.e. a collection of non-literary prose covering the 100-year period from 1640 to 1740), states that this syntactic pattern "is not very common, and usually only found in narrative contexts." Her statement suggests that such fronting tends to occur generally in story telling such as fiction. She further goes on to mention that "The fronting of the particle is a simple narrative device, making the action more vivid by indicating a sudden, unexpected or surprising event" (p. 264).[6] As for the syntax of particle fronting, when the subject is a personal pronoun, Defoe usually chooses the word-order of "Particle + Subject + Verb" as in *away he went*.

Additional cases of the simple pattern are given:

> ... so **away** he **went** like the Wind; (*RC* 240) / so **down** he **sits**, (*RC* 294) / **away** we **marched**; (*MC* 129) / For as soon as they saw us coming, **away** they **run** as above. (*CS* 55) / **Away** he **runs**, as if he had a glad Message to carry, (*CS* 237) / the Boy said, *yes Madam, very welcome*, and **away** I **came**. (*MF* 200) / **Away** I **went**, and coming to the House I found them all in Confusion, you may be sure; (*MF* 205) / ... and **away** he **runs** swift as the Wind: (*MF* 195) / ... and **away** I **walk'd** as fast as I could; (*MF* 266) / so in the Morning they took up their Tent and loaded their Horse, and **away** they **travelled** all together. (*JPY* 134) / and **away** he **came** to look for me; (*CJ* 70) / and **away** we **Gallop'd** together as fast as the Horse would well go; (*CJ* 89) / WITH this **away** he **went**, (*CJ* 110) / and **away** we **went**, (*CJ* 110) / and **in** he **goes**, (*CJ* 43) / so, without giving me Time to answer her, **away** she **goes**. (*Rox* 222) / **Away** I **run**; (*Rox* 319), etc.

As the passages cited above illustrate, this type of phrasal verb in Defoe tends to occur in the middle (or end) of, rather than at the beginning, of a sentence.

In the following citation, the present-participle *Dancing* follows the verb *turns*:

> If I am hang'd there's an End of me, *says she*, and **away** she **turns** Dancing, (*MF* 275)

Chapter 1 The Syntactic Structure of Intransitive Phrasal Verbs

The fronted particle *away* is no doubt connected with *turns*; here the phrasal verb *turn away* is varied. Yet, is it possible to ensure that the particle is *not* related to the subsequent *Dancing* at all? The issue of the pattern "Verb + *-ing* + Particle" will be further examined in Section 1.3.

The next pattern includes a preposition, such as ***away*** they ***went*** to the Woods (*RC* 299). (The pattern "Verb + Particle + Preposition [+ Noun Phrase]" will be discussed more in-depth later in Section 1.4). Additional cases are:

> **away** we **march'd** to the Place, (*RC* 207) / **away** he **run** to his Gun, (*RC* 296) / **up** he [= a bear] **scrambles** into the Tree, (*RC* 295) / ... and **away** they **stroll'd** about the Country again; (*RC* 253) / **Away** we **go** to *Leeds* by three several Ways, (*MC* 207) / **away** we **went** for *Newark*; (*MC* 232) / so **back** we **came** again to the Golden River, (*CS* 96) / **away** he **went** for *Surat*. (*CS* 250) / **AWAY** she **comes** to me and tells me this Story; (*MF* 230) / ... and **away** she **runs** from me out of her Wits, (*MF* 205) / ... and **away** I **walk'd** into the Street. (*MF* 266) / and **away** he **comes** after me. (*CJ* 93) / so **down** she **goes** to him, (*CJ* 109) / so **away** he **runs** to *Lombard-Street*, (*CJ* 21) / and **up** I **run** to *Amy*, (*Rox* 297) / I took up a great Firebrand, and **in** I **rush'd** again, with the Stick flaming in my Hand; (*RC* 177) / So **away** he **hops** with his Crutch, (*MC* 208) / and **away** I **went** with them at all hazards; (*CJ* 223), etc.

Adverbials here are indicative of direction (e.g. *Northwards*) and follow the verb element (of a phrasal verb), as in:

> and **away** they **marched** Northwards. (*MC* 255) / the Climate was so hot, that we did not attempt to salt up any more, ... and

> **away** we **stood** Southward crossing the Line, (*CS* 204) [cf. *OED* s.v. stand, *v.* 87. b. *Naut.* "To sail or steer away (from some coast, quarter, enemy, etc.)" 1633~]

In the second passage cited above, ***away we stood*** in *CS* is a stylistic variation in the use of *stand away* as a nautical term, one of the most frequent and significant phrasal verbs in *CS*.[7] Here, *stand* acts as a dynamic rather than stative verb.

When the subject is not a personal pronoun, but a common noun or a proper noun, in accord with the suggestion by Quirk et al. (1985: 522), the inversion of "verb + subject" occurs after the position of a particle, such as ***out rushed*** *three monstrous Wolves*, (*RC* 292).

Other instances of the simplest form are:

> ... **away runs** *Friday*, (*RC* 294) / ... **away runs** the Maid; (*MF* 205) / ... **out rush'd** a Horse, with a Saddle, (*RC* 299) / **Away goes** *Will*, and watches, and waits about the Place, (*CJ* 47) / in the middle of which, **up comes** my honest good QUAKER, and put an end to our Discourse: (*Rox* 291) / While the poor Woman was telling this dismal Story, **in came** the Gentlewoman's Husband, (*Rox* 22)
> [cf. with a prepositional phrase] **AWAY goes** the old Lady to her Daughters, (*MF* 51) / and **down comes** another Gentleman from him, (*CJ* 48) / So **away goes** *Amy* for *Roan*. (*Rox* 216)

As regards a type of inversion, *Moll Flanders* has three cases where the personal pronoun *I* is used as a subject; this word order is apparently considered deviant:

> ... and **away comes** I with the two Children and the Bundle. (*MF*

205) / ... and **away came** I with my Bundle; (*MF* 206) / **AWAY went** I, and getting Materials in a publick House, I wrote a Letter from Mr. *John Richardson* of *New-Castle* to his Dear Cousin *Jemey Cole*, in *London*, (*MF* 240)

The results of the particle fronting are summarized in Table 7, below:

Table 7. Frequency of Occurrences of Particle Fronting

	RC	MC	CS	MF	JPY	CJ	Rox	total
particle fronting	12	6	10	24	1	23	12	88
(PSV)*	(9)	(6)	(10)	(19)	(1)	(21)	(8)	(75) (85%)
(PVS)**	(3)	(0)	(0)	(5)***	(0)	(2)	(4)	(13) (15%)

* PSV = "Particle + S + Verb"; ** PVS = Particle + Verb + S; *** Three "deviant" instances in *MF* are included.

A glance at Table 7 reveals a large discrepancy between the higher counts of *MF* and *CJ*, and the minimal counts of *JPY*. Based on the assumption that the pattern of particle fronting gives a (fictional) narrative a dynamic and dramatic force, it is possible to say that while the narratives in *MF* and *CJ* are remarkably dramatic, the narrative in *JPY* is the least dramatic. This suggests that *JPY* is written in a style suitable for non-fiction rather than fiction.

In addition, when particle fronting is used, the word order of "Particle + Subject + Verb" is predominant (85%) with the subject always being a personal pronoun. In this connection, the three deviant instances, such as ***away comes*** *I* in *MF* attract attention. There is a strong possibility that Defoe intentionally makes Moll Flanders, as an unintelligent narrator, use this form in order to give the reader a realistic feel.

Next, the types of intransitive phrasal verbs in this pattern and their frequencies are observed in Table 8:

Table 8. Particle Fronting: Types of Phrasal Verbs

	RC	MC	CS	MF	JPY	CJ	Rox
phr.vbs	8	4	5	7	1	10	6
occurrences of each type of phr. vbs	go away (3)*, run away, rush out (2), march away, rush in, scramble, sit down, stroll away (1)	go away, march away (2), hop away, run away (1)	go away (4), run away (3), come back, fall down, stand away (1)	go away (10), come away (6), run away (3), walk away (2), come out, come in, turn away (1)	travel away (1)	go away (10), come away (3), come down, go in (2), come out, gallop away, go down, run away, scour away, walk away (1)	go away (6), run away (2), come out, come up, come in, run up (1)

* The figure in parentheses indicates the number of occurrences.

Interestingly, *MF* has the largest number of instances of fronting (24 occurrences), but the least variety of phrasal verbs (7 types) compared with those in *RC* (8 types) and *CJ* (10 types). It can be pointed out that the fronting pattern in *MF* largely depends on the repetition of *go away* and *come away* (both occur 16 times).

Go away is the most frequently fronted, occurring 35 times in total (40%); the second-most frequent is *run away* (12 times: 14%).

The most common fronted particles are presented in Table 9:

Chapter 1 The Syntactic Structure of Intransitive Phrasal Verbs

Table 9. Particle Fronting: Most Common Particles

	RC	MC	CS	MF	JPY	CJ	Rox
1	away (4 types: 7 occurrences)	away (4: 6)	away (3: 8)	away (5: 22)	away (1: 1)	away (6: 17)	away (2: 8)
2	out (1: 2)		back, down (1: 1)	out, in (1: 1)		down (2: 3)	up (2: 2)
3	up, down, in (1: 1)					in (1: 2)	out, in (1: 1)
4						out (1: 1)	

Even a cursory glance reveals that the use of *away* is predominant when compared to other particles; of the total 88 instances of particle fronting, phrasal verbs with *away* are used 69 times (78%). This suggests that Defoe likes to use the fronting pattern of "*away* + pronominal subject + *go* (or its equivalent dynamic verbs)."

Another aspect to be highlighted here is the use of what Jespersen in *Modern English Grammar* (henceforth *MEG*): Vol. IV calls the "dramatic present" (p. 19). That is, within the past-tense narrative the fronting pattern tends to appear in the present tense, as in:

> WHEN he had got it, he came out to me, who stood but at the Door, and pulling me by the Sleeve; run *Jack*, says he, for our Lives, and **away** he **Scours**; (*CJ* 43) [cf. *OED* s.v. scour, v.[1] 1.b. "To move rapidly, go in haste, run. Chiefly with *advs*., indicating the direction, etc."]

In the passage cited, the past tense (i.e. *came* and *stood*) suddenly changes to the present tense (*says*) by inserting the dialogue "run *Jack*." Bear in mind that ***away*** he ***Scours*** also appears in this context.

43

As Jespersen (*MEG* IV: 19) suggests concerning the use of dramatic present, "the speaker, as it were, forgets all about time and imagines, or recalls, what he is recounting, as vividly as if it were now present before his eyes." This instance can be considered a typical case of the dramatic present. The occurrences of the dramatic present which utilize particle fronting are summarized in Table 10:

Table 10. Particle Fronting: Frequency of Occurrences in the Dramatic Present

	RC	*MC*	*CS*	*MF*	*JPY*	*CJ*	*Rox*	total
occurrences of fronting	12	6	10	24	1	23	12	88
(dramatic present)	(3)	(2)	(1)	(10)	(0)	(7)	(5)	(28)* (32%)

* The use of *run* as in "**away** we **run** up the Hill" (*CS* 26) is counted as a past form rather a present form (cf. *OED* or Lannert (1910)).[8]

Surprisingly, about one third of the total occurrences of particle fronting are in the dramatic present. The combined use of particle fronting with the dramatic present undoubtedly achieves double "dramatic" effects in those descriptions in which it occurs.

NOTES:

As far as the works by the authors other than Defoe are concerned, in *The Pilgrim's Progress* (by Bunyan), there are four instances of the particle fronting, all of which occur in the past tense, as in:

> So **away** he **went**, (16) / These three Villains set upon me, and I beginning like a *Christian* to resist, they gave but a call and **in came** their Master: (125) / So **in** I **went**, thinking all was well: (174) / So **on** they **went**, and *Joseph* said, (228)

Chapter 1 The Syntactic Structure of Intransitive Phrasal Verbs

Behn's fiction contains its six instances, which are always used in the past tense, as well:

Down they **came**, and saluted like gentlemen, (130) / but **away** she **flew**, big with the empty title of a fantastic king, (131) / the coach was got ready, and **on** they **drove** to the playhouse. (134) / Striving through wild amazement to run from such a scene of horror as her apprehensions showed her, **down** she **dropped**, (208) / and **away** Home they **came**: (135) / The House was alarm'd, and **in came** poor Celesia, (208)

In *Gulliver's Travels*, there are only two instances of the particle fronting, both in the past tense:

I set him gently on the Ground, and **away** he **ran**. (31) / for a whole Troop of old ones came about us at the Noise; but finding the Cub was safe, (for **away** it **ran**) and my Sorrel Nag being by, they durst not venture near us. (265)

In *Pamela*, 27 instances of particle fronting can be found in the intransitive use of phrasal verbs. *All* of them, which are of great interest in relation to Defoe's, are given below in order of appearance:

... **in comes** my young Master! (12) / And **away** I **tripp'd**, as fast as I could; (49) [cf. *OED* s.v. trip, *v*. 1. *intr*. "To move lightly and nimbly on the feet;" *c* 1386~] / *And **away went** I, with a Curchee and Thanks. (50) / ... **in stept** my Master, (55) / **out rush'd** my Master, (63) / and **in** I **stept**, and was ready to burst with Grief; (102) / And at last **away** he **drove**, Jehu-like as they

45

say, out of the Court-yard; (102) [cf. Jehu, king of Israel, is "famous for driving his chariot furiously." (according to *2 Kings* 9) (*OED*)] / for **in came** the Coachman with the Look of a Hangman, (105) / And **away** he [= Jacob the gardener] **walk'd**, to another Quarter, out of Sight. (127) / *just as I was taking a Spring to get up, and **down came** I, and received such a Blow upon my Head, (171) / *and **away limp't** I! (171) / And **up** he **came**! (182) / And **in** I **went**. (224) / *And **away** the Woman **went**, (224) / So **down** I **went**, (244) / So **away drove** the Chariot! (245) / and **down** I **went** that very Moment. (281) / So **down I came**. (294) / and **down** I **sunk**. (294) / and **in** I **jumpt**, without touching the Step, (398) / *And he mounted, and *Colbrand* said, Don't be frighten'd, Madam; nobody shall hurt you.—And shut the Door, and **away** *Robert* **drove**; (398) / *he said, What bold body dares disturb my Repose thus? and open'd the Door. **In rush'd** she; (416) / And **away** she **went** down Stairs, in a great Hurry. (425) / And **away** he [= Mr. Longman] **went**. (461) / Then **in came** *Harry*, and *Isaac*, and *Benjamin*, and the two Grooms of this House, and *Arthur* the Gardener, (467) / and **away** she **tript**, after the others. (477) [cf. *OED* s.v. trip, *v*. 3. *intr.* "To go, walk, skip, or run with a light and lively motion;" ? *a* 1400~] / and **in** she **came**, in a Moment. (478)

A close examination of the instances cited above suggests the following four points:

i) In *Pamela*, there is only one case in which the verb is used in present tense, in " ... **in comes** my young Master!" (12); this is the first appearance of particle fronting in this work. In the other 26 cases, the verbs appear in the past tense. Consequently, the frequency gap in the choice of the present tense between Defoe (28 cases of 88: 32%) and Richardson (1 case of 27: 4%) reflects a difference of

46

narration style. Namely, in Defoe's works, since the "past" events are principally narrated and recorded,[9] the sudden intervention of the present tense is quite effective in giving a sense of reality to the passage. On the other hand, in *Pamela*'s narration, which mainly focuses on the "present" (or, to be more precise, "recent past") events,[10] the author might have felt that the use of the present tense is not as necessary for a realistic narrative.

ii) As for the use of particles, Defoe makes heavy use of *away* (69 instances of 88: 78%), while Richardson's instances are characterized by a relatively balanced use of them: *away* (11 instances: 39%), *in* (9: 32%), *down* (5: 18%), *out, up, off* (one occurrence respectively).

iii) With verbs, in Defoe, *go* and *come* are almost exclusively used. In *Pamela*, *go* and *come* are used seven times each, *drive* three times, *rush, step, trip* twice, *jump, limp, pull, sink, walk* once. Thus, a greater variety of verbs can be used in particle fronting.

iv) Interestingly enough, there are six cases marked with an asterisk (21.4%), as in "And **away went** I" (50) or "And **away** the Woman **went**" (224); as seen above, these are not in normal word order. In Defoe, only three cases are exclusively in *Moll Flanders*. In *Pamela*, Richardson makes the heroine use as many as six instances. Incidentally, a careful look at their corresponding parts in the 6th edition reveals that the six instances in question remain unrevised. That Richardson as "an inveterate reviser" (Blewett (2001: xi) has not touched them until the 6th edition leads to the following assumption: Richardson did not feel the necessity to "elevate or correct the language"[11] as far as the word-order in the six instances

47

is concerned. It would be crucial to investigate the linguistic phenomena and the author's real intention.[12]

To conclude this subsection on particle fronting, it is worth considering an interesting statement made by Charleston (1960: 153). According to her, "When the prepositional adverb is given front position, the whole phrase becomes lively, which is usually the effect of some feeling in the speaker—<u>friendliness, liveliness, jollity</u>, etc." (my emphasis added). There is no doubt that this syntactic pattern makes the whole phrase "lively" and gives the reader "some feeling in the speaker," but, as far as the instances in Defoe's fiction and *Pamela* are concerned, favorable feelings such as "friendliness" or "jollity" cannot be detected at all. Rather, unfavorable feelings like "surprise" or "fear," as well as speed and agility of action, seem to be conveyed. Charleston's observation has been based on materials by 19th- and 20th-century novelists such as Conrad, Greene, Kipling, and Maugham. Thus, the use of the particle fronting seems to be greatly affected by the artistic tastes of the period.

1. 2 Adverbial Insertion: the "Verb + *Adverbial* + Particle" Pattern

Since a phrasal verb, whether used intransitively or transitively, functions as a "verb," it is important to look into the syntactic relation between two-word verbs and "adverbials." Phrasal verbs in the simple pattern are often postmodified by adverbials. As in (i) *We all **turn'd out** <u>immediately</u>;* (*CS* 25), the "Verb + Particle + *Adverbial*" pattern is usually observed. In addition, sometimes adjectives follow phrasal verbs, like (ii) *till they* **fell down** Dead, (*JPY* 168); the past-participle form of verbs with a passive meaning comes after phrasal verbs, as in (iii) *so I had none of the Absolution, by which the Criminal confessing,* ***goes away*** comforted; (*Rox* 265); the *-ing* present participle form of verbs occurs after a phrasal verb, like (iv) *I ...* **came back** musing *with myself what Course I might take ...* (*RC* 98). Note: in (ii) and (iii), *dead* and *comforted* act as a subject complement.

Additional instances in the (i) to (iii) patterns are given as follows; instances in the (iv) pattern will be discussed separately in Section 1.3:

(i) this Rumour **died off** again, (*JPY* 1) / I **swoon'd away** twice, one after another, (*MF* 289) / I **stood off** very boldly, I told him that tho' my Cargo of Tobacco was damag'd, yet that it was not quite lost; (*MF* 109) / I **wander'd about** very uncomfortably, (*RC* 111) / I therefore diverted the present Discourse between me and my Man, **rising up** hastily, (*RC* 219) / The King **coming in** seasonably to the Relief of his Men, routs *Middleton*, (*MC* 221) / we **went on** very sociably together. (*RC* 35) / how many [of "Earthen Vessels"] crack'd by the over violent Heat of the Sun, being **set out** too hastily; (*RC* 120) / [as *to*-infinitive] the Prince ordered me to **come off** so privately, (*MC* 197) / my Heart began to **look up** more seriously, than I think it ever did before, (*MF* 336), etc.

(ii) Sometimes a Man or Woman **dropt down** Dead in the very Markets; (*JPY* 78) / till they **dropp'd down** stark Dead, (*JPY* 163) / Another [person] **run about** Naked, (*JPY* 21) / he **fell down** as dead as a Stone, (*MC* 176) / now the Weather **set in** hot, (*JPY* 6), etc.

(iii) so our Men **came back** again very well satisfied for that time. (*CS* 74) / I seem'd like an old Piece of Plate that had been hoarded up some Years, and **comes out** tarnish'd and discolour'd; so I **came**

out blown, and look'd like a cast-off Mistress, nor indeed, was I any better; (*Rox* 182) / [as *to*-infinitive] They began to **rise up** a little surpriz'd, (*JPY* 160), etc.

In Defoe's works, however, adverbials (not only ordinary adverbs such as *softly, gently, gravely*, etc., but also noun phrases or prepositional phrases as adverb-equivalent, such as *a great way* or *with all his might*) may occur between a verb and particle, as with ***went** softly **back*** or ***go** a great Way **out***. This is an interesting phenomenon, when seen from the structural viewpoint of a phrasal verb.

Quirk et al. (1985: 1167) state that "An adverb (functioning as adjunct) can often be inserted between verb and particle in prepositional verbs, but not in phrasal verbs" (my emphasis added), comparing the use of a prepositional verb *call on* [= 'visit'] with that of a phrasal verb *call up* [= 'summon']: "*They called angrily on the dean*" vs. "**They called angrily up the dean*" (*unacceptable). It is important to keep in mind, however, that phrasal verbs as defined by Quirk et al. exclusively refer to "idiomatic" verbs. Regarding the idiomaticity of phrasal verbs, Palmer (1987: 227) makes an interesting point that "In general, the more closely related semantically are the verb and adverbial particle of a phrasal verb, the less likely they are to be separated." He goes on to mention that "An ordinary adverb may much more easily separate the elements of the phrasal verb if it is not idiomatic" (Palmer 1987: 228), giving instances such as "*The troops marched briskly in*" vs. "**The troops fell briskly in*" (*unacceptable). It must be admitted that linguistic insights, as noted above, concerning phrasal verbs in contemporary English, do *not always* directly apply to these same verbs in the early eighteenth century. This is not to say that such insights do not apply whatsoever; sometimes they may offer

Chapter 1 The Syntactic Structure of Intransitive Phrasal Verbs

an informative perspective. This section, therefore, examines (1) what kinds of adverbials are inserted, and (2) with which types of phrasal verbs this pattern occurs.

According to their different meanings, inserted adverbials might be roughly divided into several groups: degree, space (and distance), time (and frequency), manner, etc.

(a) Degree Adverbials (e.g. *till I came quite up to him*, (*Rox* 71))
This first group contains "degree" adverbials: the typical instance of degree adverbials is *quite*, as in *they came quite up* (*RC* 266). This adverb modifies the following particle *up* and makes the whole phrasal verb *came up* more dynamic. *Quite* is inserted into intransitive phrasal verbs a total of 18 times in Defoe's works. Several instances are cited below:

> I resolv'd to **run** quite **away** from him. (*RC* 6) / [I] **work'd** quite **out** and made me a Door to come out, (*RC* 67) / our Ship was **gone** quite **away**, (*CS* 21) / till we **got** quite **up** into Fenchurch-street, (*CJ* 43) / her Appetite sunk and **went** quite **away**, (*CJ* 241) / till I **came** quite **up** to him, (*Rox* 71), etc.

Other adverbials in this degree group include *so, a little, much, more, higher, well, very well, clean*:

> for tho' I **went** so **away**, (*Rox* 88) / it [= "this Book"] hitch'd at the Pocket-hole, or stop'd at something that was in the Pocket, and **hung** a little **out**, (*CJ* 54) / it would necessarily oblige me to **go** much **about**, (*JPY* 88) / the Air, and the shaking of the Coach made the Drink he had **get** more **up** in his Head than it was before, (*MF* 225) / I found the Roof **rose** higher **up**, (*RC* 178) / we **got** well **in** again, (*RC* 20) / and with this my Affairs

51

> went <u>very well</u> on. (*CJ* 155) / had any Creature jump'd at them [= stakes], unless he had gone <u>clean</u> over, (*CS* 99) [cf. *OED* s.v. clean, *adv*. II Of degree. 5 "*wholly, entirely, quite, absolutely*." And 5. a "with verbs of removal, and the like." *a* 1000~]

There are also cases where a different adverbial is added to the degree adverbial, such as *also quite* and *first a little*:

> the Apprehensions of its being the Infection went <u>also quite</u> away with my Illness, (*JPY* 14) / I made <u>first a little</u> out to Sea full North, (*RC* 190) [cf. *OED* s.v. make, *v*.¹ 91. m. *intr*. "To go, start, or sally forth;" 1558~]

The degree adverb, *clear*, attracts attention, and occurs three times in *MF* and *CJ*, respectively. As the *OED* suggests, this adverb is used especially "where there is some notion of getting clear of obstructions, or of escaping" (*OED* s.v. clear, *adv*. 5b). No doubt, *clear* emphasizes the following particles of *off* and *away*, and consequently serves to vividly describe criminal actions such as robbery:

> I found means to slip a Paper of Lace into my Pocket, and come <u>clear</u> off with it, (*MF* 256) / the Woman they had taken, ... got <u>clear</u> away in the Crowd; (*MF* 246) / I had made a Prize of a Piece of very good Damask in a Mercers Shop, and went <u>clear</u> off myself; (*MF* 221) / they had time enough to get <u>clear</u> away, and in about an Hour *Will* came to the Rendezvous; (*CJ* 57) / [he] got <u>clear</u> away with them [= "15 or 16 *l*. in Goods"]; (*CJ* 96) / [they] stole about a Hundred weight of Pewter, and went <u>clear</u> off with that too, (*CJ* 66)

(b) Space and Distance Adverbials (e.g. *the Tyde* ebb'd <u>so far</u> out, (*RC*

Chapter 1 The Syntactic Structure of Intransitive Phrasal Verbs

48))
The second group of adverbials, those associated with "space and distance," can be represented by the adverb, *far*, and its variants:

> but [I] never **went** far **out**, (*RC* 137) / I charged them not to **go** far **off** from the Sea Coast, (*CS* 178)

This adverb is also used in an emphatic form, as with *so far*:

> the Tyde **ebb'd** so far **out**, (*RC* 48) / it was not safe for me to keep too close to the Shore for the Breach, nor to **go** too far **off** because of the Stream. (*RC* 138) / the Thieves were sure to be **gone** far enough **off** when they had allarm'd the Country; (*MF* 187)

Moreover, the comparative form of *far* is also used:

> I plainly saw the Current again as before, only, that it **run** farther **off**, (*RC* 151) [cf. *OED* s.v. run, *v.* 75. b "Of water, etc.: To flow off or away." 1707~] / we must **stand** farther **off**: (*RC* 22) / they **drew** farther **off**. (*MC* 78) / so the Ships which had Families on Board, remov'd and **went** farther **off**, (*JPY* 112) / unless she had **gone** farther **off** too than she did, (*CJ* 207)

Farther is repeated between verb and particle, as follows:

> this Noise of the *Indians* **went** farther and farther **off**, (*CS* 207)

In the following passage, *a little*, a degree adverb, modifies *farther*:

with a great deal of Difficulty [I] **got** <u>a little farther</u> **in**, (*MC* 27)

The near-synonym, *further*, in the sense of "At a greater distance in space" (*OED* s.v. further, *adv*. 4), is used as well:

> this made them paddle and shove the Boat away as well as they could, as they lay, to **get** <u>further</u> **off**. (*CS* 236) / In one of these [huts], which was a little one, and **stood** <u>further</u> **off**, (*CS* 34) / they seemed to be the better furnish'd for Travelling, and had it in their View to **go** <u>further</u> **off**; (*JPY* 133)

A little is added to this adverb, as in:

> after we were **gotten** <u>a little further</u> **off** of their own Country, (*CS* 64)

As illustrated in the above instances, *far* and its variants tend to occur before the particle *off*.

As antonymous to *far*, the adverb *close* is inserted between *come* or *go* and *up*, as seen here:

> [*Friday*] **went** <u>close</u> **up** to him, (*RC* 292) / The Armies **coming** <u>close</u> **up**, the Wings engaged first. (*MC* 244) / All this while the Foot on both Sides were desperately engaged, and **coming** <u>close</u> **up** to the Teeth of one another with the clubbed Musquet and Push of Pike, (*MC* 160) / Our Gunner ... had a great Mind to have **gone** <u>close</u> **up** to one of the outermost of them, (*CS* 83)

The insertion of the two words *close almost* suggests a more subtle distance as in:

a thick Wood **came** <u>close almost</u> **down** to the Sea: (*RC* 231)

Noun phrases such as *a great* (or *a long* or *some other*) *Way* are used adverbially as well:

I was oblig'd to **go** <u>a great Way</u> **out** to Sea to double the Point. (*RC* 138) / After I had tyr'd my self thus with **walking** <u>a long way</u> **about**, and so eagerly, (*MF* 192) / the Coaches **went** <u>some other Way</u> **back** to *Lyons*; (*Rox* 101)

Words and phrases indicating a specific direction and distance, such as *North, three Steps*, and *5000 Miles*, are also inserted. These adverbials serve to make the meaning of the following particles more specific:

they intended to have **gone** <u>North</u> **away** to *Highgate*, (*JPY* 133) / I had not **gone** <u>three Steps</u> **in**, (*RC* 177) / I could ha' done this as well in *England* among my Friends, as ha' **gone** <u>5000 Miles</u> **off** to do it among Strangers and Salvages in a Wilderness, (*RC* 35)

(c) Time and Frequency Adverbials (e.g. *We **went** <u>frequently</u> **out** with this Boat a fishing*, (*RC* 20))

The third group consists of "time and frequency" adverbials, which includes some of the *-ly* adverbs, such as *immediately, frequently, seasonably, daily*, and *yearly*:

he ... **came** <u>immediately</u> **back** to me, (*RC* 233) / unless the Winds by a kind of Miracle should **turn** <u>immediately</u> **about**. (*RC* 43) [cf.

OED s.v. turn, *v.* 65. b. "To reverse one's position or course; to turn so as to face or go in the opposite direction: = turn round, 79 b. Now rare." 1303~] / We **went** frequently **out** with this Boat a fishing, (*RC* 20) / ... those Dragoons, who **came** seasonably **in**, (*MC* 159) / our Men **went** daily **out** a Hunting, (*CS* 22) / two Thousand eight Hundred Pounds **coming** Yearly **in**, of which I did not spend one Penny, (*Rox* 188)

As with the instances of *immediately* cited above, the insertion of *apace* suggests the speed of action denoted by the phrasal verb, i.e. "walking away":

[she] turns back, and **walks** apace **away** from her: (*Rox* 314)

On the other hand, *long* emphasizes the duration of "holding out":

his Majesty loath to be cooped up in a Town which could on no Account **hold** long **out**, (*MC* 266)

Other instances of "time and frequency" adverbials are:

but [I] **came** always **back** without any Discovery, (*RC* 170) / had I not **gotten** first **up** upon this Hill, (*RC* 138) / I resolv'd to **go** no more **out** without a Prospective Glass in my Pocket. (*RC* 164) / I **come** now **back** to my own History, (*CS* 249) / I asked him ... when we **came** first **up** with them? (*CS* 163) / unless it was thus, that a Man should, as it were **run** just **up** to the Top, (*CS* 210) / I **going** still **on** with the Particulars, (*MF* 228) / I **ventured** so often **out** in the Streets, (*JPY* 77) / **going** then **back** to *France*, he was yet uneasie, (*Rox* 226)

Chapter 1 The Syntactic Structure of Intransitive Phrasal Verbs

Also, noun phrases denoting "time and frequency," such as *every Day* and *two or three times*, are inserted:

> the Crouds which now **came** every Day **in** to his Standard, were incredible. (*MC* 147) / [he] **rid** every Day **out** to the Forest a Hunting, (*Rox* 11) / she **look'd** two or three times **up** at me, (*Rox* 123)

The following is a case where two elements, *one Day* and *all*, are combined:

> we **went** one Day all **out** to Sea in her together, (*CS* 26)

(d) Manner Adverbials (e.g. *they came boldly out*, (*MC* 231))
This fourth group deals with adverbials relating to "manner"; many instances of *-ly* adverbs such as *softly, boldly, bravely*, etc., belong to this group. The "manner" adverbials likely modify whole phrasal verbs rather than the following particles. Cases in point are numerous:

> they **came** boldly **out**, (*MC* 231) / he was **going** directly **back** to the Coast of Brasil. (*RC* 42) / The Bear was **walking** softly **on**, (*RC* 294) // He **gallops** bravely **up** to his Adversary, (*MC* 131) / we had Leisure enough to **ride** gently **back**: (*MC* 9) / We **marched** slowly **on** ... (*MC* 102) / the Imperial Soldiers **went** unwillingly **out**; (*MC* 110) // we might **come** safely **back** again. (*CS* 80) / we **went** merrily **on** for the Coast of Ceylon, (*CS* 218) [cf. *OED* s.v. merrily, *adv*. 3. "With alacrity; hence, with reference to inanimate things, briskly." 1530~] / so we resolv'd, ... to **look** diligently **out** for Food. (*CS* 113) / he **look'd** gravely **up** at me, (*CS* 159) / [we] **marched** boldly **up** to them; (*CS* 52) // the Sister

57

and the younger Brother **fell** grievously **out** about it; (*MF* 21) / I wanted to **get** quietly **away** from *Ipswich*. (*MF* 266) / I **got** softly **out**, (*MF* 226) / I **went** boldly **in** and was just going to lay my Hand upon a piece of Plate, (*MF* 269) // so others got out by bribing the Watchmen, and giving them Money to let them **go** privately **out** in the Night. (*JPY* 57) // it would be fire in my Flax if I should mingle it with what I had now, which was **come** honestly **by**, (*CJ* 157) / she **came** readily **in**, but blush'd mightily, (*CJ* 246) / I would have you leave it for the present, and **go** quietly **away**. (*CJ* 203) / all **going** merrily **on** for *London*, (*CJ* 111) / nor are those poor young People so much in the wrong, as some imagine them to be, that **go** voluntarily **over** to those Countries, (*CJ* 174) / the *Jew* **came** impudently **back**, into the Room, (*Rox* 114) / there was, and would be, Hours of Intervals, and of dark Reflections which **came** involuntarily **in**, (*Rox* 48) / [cf. the "composite" pattern] the Horse ... **came Trotting** gently **on** by himself, (*CJ* 93)

It should be noted that some *-ly* adverbs do not belong to this group. For instance, *fairly* and *thorowly* (i.e 'thoroughly') have to do with "degree" rather than "manner," as in:

though the Wind blew very hard, yet it [= the Wood] **burnt** fairly **out**; (*RC* 186) [cf. *OED* s.v. burn, *v.*[1] 2. c. "quasi-refl. and pass."] / I **fell** thorowly **out** with her: (*Rox* 312)

Strait (i.e. 'straight') might belong to the manner adverbials:

it [= the plague] did not **come** strait **on** towards us; (*JPY* 14)

As a prepositional phrase, *with all his might* describes the manner of his "swimming off":

> [he] **swam** <u>with all his might</u> **off** to those two who were left in the Canoe, (*RC* 236)

A participial clause, *talking with* ... , is also inserted. A rather long *-ing* clause suggests the manner in his "walking back":

> he **walk'd**, <u>talking with another Man of the same Cloth</u>, **back** again, just by me; (*Rox* 85)

A phrasal verb with the *-ing* clause inserted (i.e. ***walked** talking ... **back***) is completely different from the composite pattern of *he came running back* (as will be examined in Section 1.3), because in this instance *talking* and *back* cannot be combined.

(e) Others
There are adverbials which do not belong to these four groups; *not* and *thus* are each inserted once, respectively:

> I spent all that Evening there, and **went** <u>not</u> **back** to my Habitation, (*RC* 99) / **Wandring** <u>thus</u> **about** I knew not whither, I pass'd by an Apothecary's Shop ... (*MF* 191)

Here, a one-word adjective, *lame*, is inserted. The adjective seems to function as the subject complement:

> tho' I **came** <u>Lame</u> **off**, (*CJ* 221)

59

Two prepositional phrases, *with us* and *all our Cargo*, and one clause, *as I said*, occur between verb and particle, as in:

> [MY Governess] **went** with us **Round** into the *Downs*, (*MF* 319) / we **went** with all our Cargo **over** to *Maryland*. (*MF* 330) / Upon this we **marched**, as I said, **on** to *Burton*, (*MC* 237)

Finally considered is the use of *all*, which occurs between the verb and particle 12 times in total. It is appropriate to interpret *all* as in *they flew all away* as a kind of (reflexive) pronoun, rather than an adverb, because this word is inserted only when the subject is a plural noun, or a word with plural meaning (e.g. *the Family* **went** *all* **away**); when it is a singular noun (e.g. *I, he*, or *the man*), *all* never occurs. Some instances of *all* are given below:

> when they grew older they **flew** all **away**, (*RC* 76) / these [men] **came** all **down** to the Water's Edge, (*CS* 221) / they [= wild animals] **went** all **off**, (*CS* 90) / the Men ... **jumpd** all **back** again into their Boat, (*CS* 156) / [Dutchman says] they would immediately **come** all **running down** to the Shore, (*CS* 234) / while the Family **went** all **away** in the Evening, (JPY 53) / so we **came** all **away** good Friends, (*CJ* 80), etc.

Next, the frequency of adverbial insertion in the seven works is summarized next in Table 11:

Table 11. Adverbial Insertion: Frequency of Occurrence (or Tokens)

	RC	MC	CS	MF	JPY	CJ	Rox	total
adverbial insertion (tokens)	40 (6.1%)	18 (3.2%)	27 (4.6%)	22 (3.6%)	14 (3.5%)	26 (3.9%)	13 (2.3%)	160 (3.9%)
types of adverbials	24	16	19	19	13	15	13	119
total occurrences of intransitve phr. vbs	659	559	582	608	396	675	568	4,052

The adverbials inserted in each of the seven works are:

In *RC*:

    i) degree: *quite* (5), *fairly, higher, well, first a little* (1)

    ii) space and distance: *far*-type (9)* [*far* (1), *so far* (2), *too far* (1), *farther* (5)], *a great way* (3), *close, close almost, three steps, 500 miles* (1)

    iii) time and frequency: *immediately* (2), *always, frequently, first, no more* (1)

    iv) manner: *directly* (4), *softly* (2), *with all his might* (1)

    v) others: *all, not* (1)

    [24 types] *The number in parentheses indicates that of occurrences.

In *MC*:

    i) degree: *clear* (1)

    ii) space and distance: *close* (2), *farther, a great way, a little farther* (1)

    iii) time and frequency: *immediately* (2), *every Day, slowly, now, long, seasonably* (1)

    iv) manner: *boldly, bravely, unwillingly, gently* (1)

    v) others: *as I said* (1) [16 types]

In *CS*:

    i) degree: *quite* (3), *clean* (1)

    ii) space and distance: *far*-type (6) [*further* (2), *far, farther, a little further, farther and farther* (1)], *close* (1)

    iii) time and frequency: *daily, first, just, now, one Day all* (1)

    iv) manner: *boldly, diligently, directly, gravely, merrily, safely* (1)

    v) others: *all* (5) [19 types]

In *MF*:

    i) degree: *clear* (3), *clean, quite, more* (1)

    ii) space and distance: *far enough, a long Way* (1)

    iii) time and frequency: *frequently, immediately, quickly* (1)

    iv) manner: *directly* (2), *boldly, grievously, quietly, softly, still* (1)

    v) others: *all, thus, with us, with all our Cargo,* (1) [19 types]

In *JPY*:

    i) degree: *much, quite, also quite, so often* (1)

    ii) space and distance: *farther, further, North* (1)

    iii) time and frequency: *immediately* (1)

    iv) manner: *boldly, directly, privately, strait* (1)

    v) others: *all* (2)   [13 types]

In *CJ*:

    i) degree: *quite* (6), *clear* (3), *a little, well* (2), *very well* (1)

    ii) space and distance: *farther* (1)

    iii) time and frequency: (0)

    iv) manner: *boldly, gently, honestly, merrily, quietly, readily, voluntarily* (1)

    v) others: *all* (3), *lame* (adjective) (1)   [15 types]

In *Rox*:

    i) degree: *quite, thoroughly, so* (1)

    ii) space and distance: *some other way* (1)

    iii) time and frequency: *first, yearly, then, every day, apace, two or three*

times (1)
iv) manner: *impudently, involuntarily, talking with another Man of the same Cloth* (1)
v) others: (0)   [13 types]

A close inspection of Table 11 and the adverbials listed above shows that adverbial insertion occurs most prominently in the first text, *RC*, while in the last, *Rox*, adverbials are least-frequently inserted. Yet as regards the types of adverbials, there is no great discrepancy between the works. *CJ*, for example, contains 15 types out of a relatively frequent 26 instances, but *Rox* shows 13 types out of 13 instances; the 13 adverbials are each different. Thus, in the works whose "variety degree" of the type is lower—a repetition of the same adverbial can be observed—as seen in the use of *quite* occurring six times in *CJ*.

The types of phrasal verbs associated with adverbial insertion also deserve attention; the phrasal verbs used in *RC* are listed in alphabetical order:

burn out (1)*, *come back* (3), *come down* (1), *come up* (1), *ebb out* (1), *fly away* (1), *get up* (1), *get in* (1), *go back* (3), *go off* (3), *go out* (4), *go up* (1), *go in* (2), *keep off* (1), *lie off* (2), *make out* (1), *ride up* (1), *rise up* (1), *run away* (1), *run off* (1), *shine in* (1), *stand off* (2), *swim off* (1), *travel cross* (1), *turn about* (1), *walk up* (1), *walk on* (1), *work out* (1) [28 types] *The number in parentheses indicates that of occurrences.

This list reveals the frequent use of what Quirk et al. (1985: 1150) term "free combinations" (phrasal verbs which retain the literal meaning of both verb and particle), such as *fly away*, *shine in* and *run away*; all indicating dynamic movement, rather than idiomatic phrasal verbs. There are 18 instances of *come*- and *go*-phrasal verbs (8 types), which make up 45% out of the total 40 instances. Among this list, *lie off* is fairly unique, in that it denotes a state rather than a movement, as seen here:

> it [= the "stranded Vessel"] **lay** <u>so far</u> **off**, (*RC* 46) / [cf. *OED* s.v. lie, *v*.¹ 25. **lie off**. a. *Naut.* "Of a ship or boat: To stand some distance away from the shore or from some other craft." 1596~] / except some Rocks which **lay** <u>a great Way</u> **off**, (*RC* 53)

Types of phrasal verbs associated with adverbial insertion in Defoe's other works are summarized in Table 12:

Table 12. Types of Phrasal Verbs Associated with Adverbial Insertion

	RC	*MC*	*CS*	*MF*	*JPY*	*CJ*	*Rox*
occurrences of adv. insertion	40	18	27	22	14	26	13
types of phr.vbs	28	15	18	17	8	20	10
come- and *go-*phr. vbs. (types: occurrences)	8 types: 18 occurrences (45%)	7:9 (50%)	10:18 (67%)	8:11 (50%)	6:12 (86%)	11:16 (62%)	5:8 (62%)
others (types: occurrences)	20 types: 22 occurrences (55%)	8:9 (50%)	8:9 (33%)	9:11 (50%)	2:2 (14%)	9:10 (38%)	5:5 (38%)

Phrasal verbs in the six works other than *RC* are as follows:

In *MC*:

> <u>come out</u> (1)*, <u>come up</u> (2), <u>come in</u> (2), *draw off* (1), *gallop up* (1), *get off* (1), *get in* (1), <u>go back</u> (1), <u>go out</u> (1), <u>go in</u> (1), <u>go on</u> (1), *hold out*

(1), *march on* (2), *ride away* (1), *ride back* (1) [15 types] *The number in parentheses indicates that of occurrences.

In *CS*:

<u>*come back* (2)</u>, <u>*come down* (1)</u>, <u>*come up* (3)</u>, <u>*go away* (1)</u>, <u>*go back* (1)</u>, <u>*go off* (5)</u>, <u>*go out* (2)</u>, <u>*go up* (1)</u>, <u>*go on* (1)</u>, <u>*go over* (1)</u>, *jump back* (1), *look out* (1), *look up* (1), *march up* (1), *run down* (1), *run up* (1), *stand off* (2), *come running down* (1) [18 types]

In *MF*:

<u>*come off* (1)</u>, <u>*come up* (2)</u>, *fall out* (2), *get away* (2), *get out* (1), *get up* (1), <u>*go back* (1)</u>, <u>*go off* (3)</u>, <u>*go in* (1)</u>, <u>*go on* (1)</u>, <u>*go over* (1)</u>, <u>*go round* (1)</u>, *turn round* (1), *wander about* (1), *walk out* (1), *walk about* (1), *wear off* (1) [17 types]

In *JPY*:

<u>*come up* (1)</u>, <u>*come on* (1)</u>, <u>*go away* (5)</u>, <u>*go off* (2)</u>, <u>*go about* (2)</u>, <u>*go out* (1)</u>, *run down* (1), *venture out* (1) [8 types]

In *CJ*:

<u>*come away* (1)</u>, <u>*come back* (1)</u>, <u>*come off* (1)</u>, <u>*come by* (1)</u>, <u>*come in* (1)</u>, <u>*come on* (1)</u>, *get away* (2), *get up* (1), *get over* (1), <u>*go away* (4)</u>, <u>*go down* (1)</u>, <u>*go off* (2)</u>, <u>*go on* (2)</u>, <u>*go over* (1)</u>, *hang out* (1), *hollow out* (1), *look back* (1), *look out* (1), *slip down* (1), *come trotting on* (1) [20 types]

In *Rox*:

<u>*come back* (1)</u>, <u>*come up* (1)</u>, <u>*come in* (3)</u>, *fall out* (1), <u>*go away* (1)</u>, <u>*go back* (2)</u>, *look up* (1), *ride out* (1), *walk away* (1), *walk back* (1) [10 types]

A careful look at Table 12 reveals that the widest variety of phrasal verb types is found in *RC*, while *JPY* contains the fewest. Furthermore, the frequency of *come-* and *go*-phrasal verbs in *RC* is lower than those in the other works (compare 45% in *RC* with, for example, 86% in *JPY*).

Although, as mentioned above, phrasal verbs associated with adverbial insertion tend to retain the literal meaning of verb and particle, a few phrasal verbs possessing a figurative meaning do exist among those listed above. One of them is *fall out*, which occurs twice in *MF*, with one instance in *Rox*:

> they frequently found Fault with me, and sometimes **fell** quite **out** with me, (*MF* 33) / the Sister and the younger Brother **fell** grievously **out** about it; (*MF* 21) / all my Rage turn'd against *Amy*, and I **fell** thorowly **out** with her: (*Rox* 312) [cf. *OED* s.v. fall, *v.* 94. d. "To disagree, quarrel." 1562~ ; 94. e. **fall out with**: "to quarrel with." 1530~]

As the *OED* suggests, *fall out* (*with*), meaning "to quarrel (with)," seems to have been established as a set phrase or idiom in Defoe's era. The instances cited above, in which three different intensive adverbs are inserted into an idiomatic *fall out*, may serve as evidence that linguistic insights by Quirk et al. (1985: 1167) as well as others are not always applicable to observations concerning phrasal verbs in Defoe, or early eighteenth-century English.

1.3 The Composite Pattern "Verb + *-ing* (Present Participle) + Particle"

Defoe sometimes uses the pattern "Verb + *-ing* (as a present participle)

+ Particle," such as *when he came running back* (*RC* 230). The *-ing* participle, at first glance, seems to be an adverbial, like "came (running) back." There is, however, more to this pattern than meets the eye. The pattern "Verb + *-ing* + Particle" in Defoe's fiction provides an interesting case when analyzed from a structural viewpoint.

A crucial question that must be answered when trying to understand this three-word pattern is to which of the two verbs the particle is more closely related, as this affects the meaning. In (*he*) *came running back*, is the particle, *back*, more closely related to one of the two verbs, *came* or *running*? Generally, *come back* and *run back* are both "common" phrasal verbs. In any case, it is difficult to identify a "phrasal verb" (i.e. a "two-word" verb) in a three-word pattern. Therefore, as mentioned in the beginning of Chapter 1, instances of this composite pattern are excluded from those of the simple pattern. The reason for using the nomenclature "composite" is explained below.

Three-word phrases have yet to be seriously examined. However, the two-word construction of "verb + *-ing*" has been discussed by grammarians. Sweet (1955 [1898]: 122) is one of the earliest to conduct a full analysis of this construction. He remarks: "When the present participle is added to an intransitive verb, it is logically partly in a kind of apposition to the verb, and at the same time qualifies the subject." Regarding these two examples, *he came running* and *the fog came pouring in at the window*, he goes on to state: "*came* is so subordinated in meaning to the participle that it is felt almost as an auxiliary" (p. 122). Thus, it is plausible to assume that the *-ing* participle (i.e. *running* and *pouring*) has a more verbal character than the main verb (i.e. *came*)—these verb combinations seem to resemble an auxiliary plus lexical verb pattern, suggesting that this is really past progressive tense with *came* replacing the more usual *be* verb.

Returning to Defoe's instance of *came running back*, based on the analysis presented above, *back* is more closely related to the immediately preceding participle, *running*; hence *run back* could be regarded as a phrasal verb. Yet, it remains to be seen whether the particle has something to do with the main verb. Here is another instance of the basic type occurring in *RC*, which is a more complicated issue:

> several others [of wolves] were wounded, and **went bleeding off**, (*RC* 298)

If the same analysis is applied here, the three-word phrase *went bleeding off* ought to contain *bleed off* as a phrasal verb. However, *bleed off* is quite uncommon, in comparison with *go off*. Is it possible that *bleeding* in an adverbial use happens to occur between *go* and *off*, [go (bleeding) off]? If so, why was the word-order of *go off bleeding* not chosen?

In order to enhance the uniqueness of the composite pattern "V + -*ing* + P," the pattern "V + P + -*ing*," which sometimes occurs in Defoe's text, will next be examined. Several instances of this pattern are:

> [a] I ... **came back** musing with myself what Course I might take ... (*RC* 98) / so we were all produc'd, some [boys] **came out** rubbing their Eyes, and scratching their Heads, (*CJ* 10)
> [b] [we] were **sat down** musing what we should do; (*RC* 260) / we could see them, by the little Light there was, **run about** wringing their Hands like Men in Despair; (*RC* 266)
> [c] He [= a lion] **started up** growling at first, (*RC* 28)

The pattern "V + P + -*ing*" in the above passages seems quite similar

Chapter 1 The Syntactic Structure of Intransitive Phrasal Verbs

to "V + -ing + P," but from a structural viewpoint these patterns are quite different, in that in [a] *muse back* or *rub out* are unacceptable; the combinations between the main verb and the particle, e.g. *come back* and *come out* in [a], are exclusively regarded as phrasal verbs. As for the structural difference of the patterns "V + -ing + P" and "V + P + -ing," findings are drawn from a survey of the instances above. In [a] and [b], the present participles *musing* (twice), *rubbing, scratching,* and *wringing,* all of which are transitive, by taking their objects, build up rather longer verb phrases: *musing ... what Course I might take, rubbing their Eyes,* and *wringing their Hands.* In [c], *growling* as an intransitive verb is used alone, but *start up,* meaning "To rise suddenly" (*OED* s.v. start, *v.* 13a) is considered to be more "idiomatic," in comparison with "literal" phrasal verbs containing *come* or *go.* These seem to be the main reasons why the *-ing* participles in [a] to [c] do *not* occur between the main verb and the particle.

Here, another instance of the "V + P + -ing" pattern is presented:

The QUAKER **came in** smiling, (for she was always soberly chearful) ... (*Rox* 291)

The alternative word order of *come smiling in* might also be possible, but the choice of the "V + P + -ing" pattern seems to comply with the principle of "end focus."[13] Namely, the parenthetical statement, in which the Quaker is described to be "always soberly chearful (i.e. cheerful)," is strongly connected with the immediately preceding word *smiling.*

In the "V + -ing + P" pattern there are two exceptional cases. One is in [d] (in relation to [e]):

69

[d] The Fire and Noise [of the gunshot] amazed all their Women and Children, and frighted them out of their Wits, and they **ran staring and howling about** like mad Creatures. (*CS* 76)

[e] they **run about** <u>yelling, and skreaming</u>, like mad Creatures, (*RC* 234)

In both passages, *run about* and the adverbial phrase *like mad Creatures* are used. But in [d] *run about* follows the end focus principle, and in [e] *yelling, and skreaming* does. Namely, in [d] the action or movement of running "about" is emphasized, while in [e] the manner of "yelling and screaming" while running about is the focus. This syntactic differentiation seems to have some affinity with the choice of "Verb + Particle + Object" (VPO) and "Verb + Object + Particle" (VOP) in the use of transitive phrasal verbs; this problem will be discussed in Chapter 2.

The other case occurs in a rather deviant word order, which has already been discussed in Section 1.2:

he **walk'd**, <u>talking with another Man of the same Cloth</u>, **back** again, just by me; (*Rox* 85)

The choice of *walk'd talking ... back*, not *walk'd back talking ...* might suggest that the action of "walking back" rather than the manner of "talking" is emphasized.

Next, instances of the composite pattern other than *come running back* and *go bleeding off* are offered:

when the Scouts **came galloping in**, the Men were in such Disorder, (*MC* 127) / they **run screaming away** as if they were bewitched. (*CS* 53) / they **run screaming away** as in a Fright. (*CS*

Chapter 1 The Syntactic Structure of Intransitive Phrasal Verbs

68) / the Steward or the Overseer of the Plantation **came riding by**, (*CJ* 126) / two Gentlemen on Horseback **came riding-by**, having over-taken the Coach, and pass'd it, and went forwards towards *London*. (*Rox* 217)

In the passages cited above, *scream away* in *run screaming away* (used twice) is uncommon, in comparison with *run away*. On the other hand, in *come riding by* (also used twice), the instance from *Rox* is recorded as *came riding-by*. The "fondness for hyphenation" in the text of *Roxana* "probably represents a quirk on the part of a compositor" (Furbank 2009: 293). Even if true, it is also the case that this anonymous compositor, a contemporary of Defoe (in 1724), had previously noted the close relation of *ride by* in the three-word phrase.

In the following passages, a prepositional phrase follows the composite phrasal verb:

while we **went spooning away** large with the Wind, (*CJ* 274) [cf. *OED* s.v. spoon, *v.*[1] 1. *intr.* "In sailing, to run before the wind or sea; to scud. Also with *away*. (Common in 17th cent.)" 1576~ ; The *OED* cites this passage.] / The Prince ... **came galloping away** in the Dark to the Place, (*MC* 195) / he being a good Swimmer, **came swimming over** to this Side. (*MC* 89) / they [= *Indians*] would **come flying out** at the Top. (*CS* 211) / it [= "the Force of the Powder"] **came roaring out** there as out of the Mouth of a Cannon; (*CS* 213) / Upon the Noise of these Guns, Abundance of Men **came running down** to the Shore, (*CS* 179) / we were most of us laid down upon our Matts to Sleep, when our Watch **came running in** among us, (*CS* 90) / an ignorant weak poor Man, ... **went piping along** from Door to Door, (*JPY* 90) / Had not the kind QUAKER, in a lucky Moment, **come running in** before them, (*Rox* 282), etc.

71

The first instance, *go spooning away*, is of great interest, in that the *OED* cites this passage for the definition of the verb *spoon*, adding the syntactic information of "with *away*." Hence, the *OED*'s editors admit the syntactic (and semantic) relation of *spoon away* as a phrase.

Between the "verb + *-ing*" and the "particle," the manner adverb, *gently*, is inserted (already cited in Section 1.2):

> He had not got half thro' the Town, but the Horse having some how or other got loose, **came Trotting** <u>gently</u> **on** <u>by</u> himself, and no body following him; (*CJ* 93)

All, probably as a reflexive use (i.e. "*all* of them"), occurs between the verb and the present participle:

> [Dutchman says] they would immediately **come** <u>all</u> **running down** <u>to</u> the Shore, (*CS* 234)

This pattern also is used in a relative clause:

> the Fury of the Sea, <u>which</u> **came pouring in** <u>after</u> me again, (*RC* 46)

In the following passages, the "composite" pattern follows perception verbs, such as *find* or *see*, and their objects:

> all on a sudden I <u>found</u> the Earth **come crumbling down** <u>from</u> the Roof of my Cave, (*RC* 80) / we were surprised about an Hour after, to <u>see</u> them [= wild animals] **come thundering back**

Chapter 1 The Syntactic Structure of Intransitive Phrasal Verbs

again <u>on</u> the other Side of us, (*CS* 88) / at length we <u>found</u> the Land break off, and **go trending away** <u>to</u> the West Sea, (*CS* 205) [cf. *OED* s.v. trend, *v*. 4. *intr*. "To turn off in a specified direction; ... to run, stretch, incline, bend (in some direction), as a river, current, coast-line, mountain-range, territory, stratum, etc." 1598~] / I <u>saw</u> the Milleners Maid, and five or six more **come running out** <u>into</u> the Street, (*MF* 257)

Among the instances which have been offered so far, there are some cases where the relationship between the *-ing* participle and the particle is very close, such as "(come) riding by" or "(go) spooning away"—and other cases where the relationship seems to be tenuous, as with "(go) bleeding off" or "(run) screaming away."[14] If *ride by* or *spoon away* in the three-word verb are regarded as phrasal verbs, it follows that *bleed off* or *scream away* can be also regarded as phrasal verbs. Yet, a single use of the latter (e.g. *the wolves **bled off*** or *they **screamed away***) might have differed from the conventional use of phrasal verbs (or rather be beyond the limit of expression) in the early eighteenth century.

In contemporary English, such phrasal verbs have become more available. Cowie and Mackin (1975: xxiii) explain the phenomenon where verbs that inherently do not indicate movement, through a combination of the particle, develop into verbs of movement:

> Such verbs as **puff, steam, stump** and **zoom** combine freely with a number of particles and prepositions of *direction* (e.g. **across, along, back**) to form such expressions as **puff across** (the bridge), ... **steam into** (Newcastle), ... Characteristically, these combinations are equivalent in meaning to a verb of motion + a particle of *direction* + an adverbial phrase of *manner*. Thus **puff across** = move across sending out smoke etc. and/or panting

noisily.

Defoe, of course, did not (or *could not*) use such phrasal verbs as *puff across*. However, the "verb + *-ing* + particle" pattern might be considered a forerunner of the phrasal verbs such as *puff across*.

Thus, looking at these instances in Defoe leads to an awareness that the pattern of "*-ing* + particle" occurs in a "stable" environment where the main verb (i.e. *come* or *go*) can share the same particle with the *-ing* participle. In this sense, *come* or *go*, as Sweet wisely suggests, might also be capable of serving as an "auxiliary" verb to the *-ing* participle. On this point, it could be argued that the three-word verb in question is in the "composite" form, consisting of two phrasal verbs: the *-ing* + a particle and the main verb + *the same* particle. The co-existence of two phrasal verbs here might be indicated, if not at a syntactic, then semantic level. If so, the structure of *he came running back* is represented as follows:

he [came back] + [running back]

Here, *running back* adds specific and realistic detail to the description of *come back*. So perhaps *running* functions both as an adverbial to the stable phrasal verb *come back* and as the verb in a second phrasal verb, *running back*. This additional implied meaning makes the description more vivid. The verbs *came* and *running* are providing more than just tense information. They are each also making a semantic contribution. This analysis is similarly applicable to all other composite instances.

The final instance, which is quite different from the others already described, needs to be considered in greater detail. In this case, the main verb is neither *go* nor *come*, but *stand*:

they ... **stood edging in** <u>for</u> the Shore, (*CS* 216) [cf. *OED* s.v. edge, *v*.[1] 5. *intr*. "To move edgeways; to advance (esp. obliquely) by repeated almost imperceptible movements. Also with advs. *aside, away, down, in*, etc. Chiefly *Naut*." 1624~]

This passage is cited by the *OED*. As suggested by the *OED* definition of the verb *edge*, the editors admit the phrasal value of *edge in*, but seemingly do not recognize (or they ignore) the influence of *stand in*. In the analysis presented here, *stand edging in* is the composite expression of *stand in* plus *edging in*. It is important not to overlook the fact that *stand*-phrasal verbs are used very frequently (52 times as shown in Table 5) in *Captain Singleton*, and among them, *stand in* occurs ten times. One is given here:

we **stood in** <u>for</u> the Shore with all the Sail we could make. (*CS* 37) [cf. *OED* s.v. stand, *v*. 95. e. *Naut*. "To direct one's course towards the shore." *c* 1595~]

In both passages, in which *they* and *we* refer to the crew of a ship, nautical navigation is equally described. A comparison between the above two instances confirms that *stand edging in* (*for the Shore*) is a more precise and detailed expression of *stand in* (*for the Shore*).

The results of the composite pattern are summarized in Table 13:

Table 13. The Composite Pattern: Types and Occurrences

	RC	MC	CS	MF	JPY	CJ	Rox	total
occurrences of composite phr.vbs	5	3	13*	1	1	3	3	29
(types of the composites)	(5)	(3)	(10*)	(1)	(1)	(3)	(2)	(21)**
come -ing types	4	(3)	6	1	0	2	2	(15)**
go -ing types	1	0	1	0	1	1	0	3
others	0	0	*run -ing* (2)*, *stand -ing* (1)	0	0	0	0	3

* One exceptional instance (i.e. *ran staring and howling about*) is included. ** *Come running in* occurs in *RC*, *CS*, and *Rox*, and *come riding by* in *CJ* and *Rox*. Such overlapping cases are each counted as one type, respectively.

There is a discrepancy in frequency between *CS* (and *RC*) and the other works. It is interesting to note that there is only one instance of this pattern in *MF*, the narrative which is the most "dramatic" in terms of frequent particle fronting. This pattern is closely related to the situational context of the narrative. The grammatical subjects of the composite pattern often have inhuman attributes, such as *wild animals* **come thundering back**, *wolves* **went bleeding off**, *the earth* (i.e. soil) **come crumbling down**, *the Fury of the Sea ...* **came pouring in**, and *the Land ...* **go trending away**. Or, the subjects are non-Englishmen as in *Friday* **came running in**, *the old Dutchman* **came running down**, or *they* (i.e. uncivilized people) **run screaming away**. Thus, this composite pattern is likely to be used to vividly describe extraordinary scenes, which Londoners of those days would have rarely if ever seen in daily life.

Examined next is a main verb of the composite type. Of the 21 distinct combinations, *come* forms 15 of them (71%); *go* only 3; *run* two, and *stand* one. The frequency gap between *come* and *go* suggests a correlation with descriptions of the "extraordinary scenes" just mentioned. The primal sense of *come* expresses "movement towards or so as to reach <u>the speaker</u>" (*OED*), and that of *go* expresses "a movement *away from* <u>the speaker</u>" (*OED*). In this discussion, the "speaker" in the *OED* definitions could be substituted for the narrator in Defoe's fiction. That is, the descriptions accompanying *come -ing*, by the proximity of something (undesirable), are likely to affect (or pose a risk to) the narrator.[15] Conversely, the descriptions with *go -ing*, due to the distancing of something, might relieve the narrator, as seen in *wolves* **went bleeding off**.

As for combinations with present participles, *running* is used in five, *galloping* in two, and the other 14 participles each occur only once.

Concerning the types of particles, *in* occurs in four types, *away* and *out* in three types, *back* and *down* in two types, *about, along, by, off, on, out,* and *up* each occur once. There is no particular preference shown in the use of particles.

NOTES:
In other works than Defoe's fictions, there are four instances in *The Pilgrim's Progress* and two in the Behn fiction:

> [from *PP*] they [= "three Sturdy Rogues"] ... **came galloping up** with speed: (121) / *Ignorance* he **came hobling after**. (141) / *Obstinate* **went railing back**, (27) / so she looked white, and **came trembling away**, (268) cf. the Women was in a very great

> scuffle, the children also **stood** <u>crying</u> **by**. (184)
> [from Behn] which they took, and looked on us round about, calling still for more company; who **came swarming out**, all wondering, and crying out: 'Tepeeme', (53) [cf. *OED* s.v. swarm, v.¹ 2. *intr.* "To come together in a swarm or dense crowd; to collect, assemble, or congregate thickly and confusedly; to crowd, throng; also, <u>to go or move along in a crowd</u>." c 1386~] / Wildvill missing his bride, and hearing the loud shriek, **came running down**, and entring the room, sees his Bride lie clasp'd in Frankwit's arms. (207-208)

As for the use of the *-ing* participle, verbs of movement like *gallop, hobble* or *swarm* are used while *rail* and *tremble* do not indicate movement by themselves; they belong to what Dixon (2005: 124) calls "corporeal verbs."

On the other hand, *Pamela*, as far as its first edition is concerned, contains no instance of "composite" pattern. This is an interesting phenomenon, because Richardson might have considered that such expressions are not needed in describing the physical or outer world in which the heroine Pamela is placed; in other words, phrasal verbs of "composite" pattern might not be suitable for depicting Pamela's emotional or inner world.

1.4 Towards a "Phrasal-prepositional Verb": the Structure of "Verb + Particle + Preposition"

When phrasal verbs occur in the pattern "Verb + Particle + Preposition (+ Noun Phrase)," the prepositional phrase (i.e. a preposition plus NP) can function as a key element in the structure of the "phrasal verb" as

Chapter 1 The Syntactic Structure of Intransitive Phrasal Verbs

a two-word verb. These combinations sometimes eventually develop into idiomatic three-word verbs, or what Quirk et al. (1985) refer to as a "phrasal-prepositional verb."

Viewed from a syntactic perspective, intransitive phrasal verbs are roughly subdivided into two types: "V + P," and "V + P + Prep. (*mainly* indicative of *direction*) + NP." By examining instances of *come-* and *go-*phrasal verbs in *RC*, the difference in function between the two types is considered:

> [a] when I **came back**, I found no Sign of any Visitor, (*RC* 54) / I **went in** to fetch my Perspective Glass, (*RC* 249)
> [b] we **came back** to our Castle, (*RC* 208) / I **went away** to the Hill, (*RC* 183)

Phrasal verbs in [a] have a tendency to omit locative specification, for instance, *I went in* implies "into my Hutch"; such a specification is understood from the context. In this respect, the use of such "simplified" phrasal verbs is considered extremely implicit and context-dependent.

On the other hand, the instances in [b] are more detailed and explanatory than those in [a], in that the prepositional phrases (i.e. *to our Castle* and *to the Hill*) make the goal of the actions denoted by the phrasal verbs specific.

Note that these two types coexist in the same text and complement each other, depending on the context. That is, intransitive phrasal verbs can sometimes be simplified, as in instances in [a], and sometimes need elaboration, as in [b].

Also note the three-word verb type where a phrasal verb is not so structurally related to its following prepositional phrase:

[c] Nov. 3. I **went out** with my Gun ... (*RC* 71) / I **went out** with my Dog, (*RC* 76)
[d] the *Spaniard*, and the old Savage the Father of *Friday*, **went away** in one of the Canoes, (*RC* 248)
[e] so they made no stay here, but **went off** again with all possible Speed, (*RC* 160)

The prepositional phrases highlighted above, all are adverbials, expressing "accompaniment" in [c], "means (of transportation)" in [d], and "manner" in [e]. Although they add specific information to the predicate in each passage, they are not necessarily essential for the structure and meaning of the phrasal verbs themselves.[16]

In the same vein, a prepositional phrase as an adverbial (esp. of manner) often occurs after a phrasal verb (as in the instance of [e] cited above), as in:

he **burst out** with a strange kind of Passion, (*RC* 16) / a great Piece of the Top of a Rock ... **fell down** with such a terrible Noise, (*RC* 80) / I **started up** in the greatest hast imaginable, (*RC* 185) / nothing but a scalding Sand, which, as the Wind blew, **drove about** in Clouds, (*CS* 79) / The rest of the Negroes **rose up** in a Hurry, (*CS* 70) / Her Mother ... **shriekt out** in such a frightful Manner, (*JPY* 56) / the passionate Creature **flew out** in a kind of Rage, (*Rox* 270) / Tho' I **hung back** with an awkwardness that was really unfeign'd, (*Rox* 223), [as *to*-infinitive] he came near enough to **jump down** on his Feet, (*RC* 296) / I resolv'd the next Morning to **set out** with the first of the Tide; (*RC* 190) / they were entirely routed, lost most of their Horses, and were forced to **come away** on Foot; (*MC* 252) / they set us all to Work, to **go off** in our Boats, (*CS* 42). etc.

Chapter 1 The Syntactic Structure of Intransitive Phrasal Verbs

Instances of the "V + P + Prep. (+ NP)" pattern, in which the prepositional phrase seems to be more closely related to the "verb + particle" portion, are sorted below according to their prepositions, in alphabetical order:

(i) *against*:

Hereford which had **stood out** against the whole Army of the *Scots* was surprized by six Men . . . (*MC* 259) / if no Body **came in** against him, he hop'd he should be clear'd; (*MF* 301) / [he told me] that there would abundance of People **come in** against him. (*MF* 281) / as I **stood up** against the corner of the House at the turning into the Alley; (*MF* 195), etc.

(ii) *among*:

she **fell in** among a Gang of Thieves, (*CJ* 258) / the Actors **fall out** among themselves, (*MC* 225) / when we **came in** among the *Spice* Islands themselves, (*CS* 191) / when it was done, who would **venture up** among such a Troop of bold Creatures as were there? (*CS* 209) / six or seven of them [= wolves] fell, or rather **jump'd in** among us, (*RC* 301) / the Infection **got in** among them and made a fearful Havock; (*JPY* 115), etc.

(iii) *at*:

so we **put in** at a little House, (*CJ* 94) / ... and that Vice **breaks in** at the breaches of Decency, (*MF* 126) / the Vice **came in** always at the Door of Necessity, (*MF* 128) / they were poor distressed People from *London*, who ... had fled out in time for their Lives, and ... had first **taken up** at *Islington*, (*JPY* 141) [cf. *OED* s.v. take, *v.* 93. (d) *absol.* or *intr.* "To take up one's quarters, lodge, 'put up'. *Obs.* 1626~; the *OED* citing 1724 De Foe Mem. Cavalier (1840) 14, I was ... forced to take up at a little village.] /

my Heart beat as if it wou'd have **jump'd out** at my Mouth; (*Rox* 284) / [as *to*-infinitive] as if they look'd for a Creek to **thrust in** at for the Convenience of Landing; (*RC* 251) [cf. *OED* s.v. thrust, *v.* 3. a. *intr.* "To push or force one's way, as through a crowd; to crowd *in*; to make one's way or advance as against obstacles;" *c* 1330~], etc.

(iv) *by*:

as the Current of the Ebb **set out** close by the South Point of the Island; (*RC* 190) / When he [= *Friday*] went in to him [= his father], he would **sit down** by him, (*RC* 238) / they **kept on** by the Banks of it, (*CS* 178) / he came and **sat down** by my Bedside, (*Rox* 295), etc.

(v) *for*:

We **sailed away** for the Cape of *Good Hope*, (*CS* 168) / I **cry'd out** for Help; (*Rox* 124) / We **look'd out** very narrowly for some River, or Creek, or Bay, (*CS* 220) / [as *to*-infinitive] we set sail, ... with Design to **stretch over** for the *African* Coast, (*RC* 41) [cf. *OED* s.v. stretch, *v.* 11. "*Naut.* To sail (esp. under crowd of canvas) continuously in one direction. Also with advs." 1687~] / my desire to **venture over** for the Main increased, (*RC* 124) / we were obliged often to **seek out** for Food. (*CS* 67) / at length he resolved to **go away** for the *Bermudas*. (*CJ* 175) / [after the verb of perception] I presently saw a Boat at about a League and half's Distance, **standing in** for the Shore, (*RC* 249), etc.

(vi) *from*:

a great Quantity of Earth **fell down** from the Top and one Side, (*RC* 74) / we **plied away** from them to Windward, (*CS* 149) [cf. *OED* s.v. ply, *v.*² II. In nautical and derived uses. 6 intr. "To beat up against the wind; to tack, work to windward." 6. b. "with *about, off*

Chapter 1 The Syntactic Structure of Intransitive Phrasal Verbs

and on, to and again, up and *down*, and the like." *c* 1595~] / they **ran about** from one Neighbours House to another; (*JPY* 34) / Capt. *Jack*, in this time fell into bad Company, and **went away** from us, (*CJ* 11) / [as *to*-infinitive] Our next Consideration was to **get away** from this cursed Place, (*CS* 23) / [after the verb of perception] I thought I felt a little Breeze of Wind in my Face, **springing up** from the S.S.E. (*RC* 140), etc.

(vii) *in*:

we **hanker'd about** in *Castle-Alley*, and in *Swithins-alley*, and at the Coffee-house-doors. (*CJ* 42) [cf. *OED* s.v. hanker, *v.* [1]. *intr.* "To 'hang about', to linger or loiter about with longing or expectation. Now dial." 1601~] / The Whore **sculks about** in Lodgings; (*Rox* 132) / [progressive] as we were **strouling about** in *West-Smithfield*, on a Friday, (*CJ* 56) / so I **sat down** in my Chair, and lighted my Lamp, (*RC* 93), etc.

(viii) *into*:

The Families, ... **fled away** into the Country, (*JPY* 73) / the Coachman that had taken me up was **getting up** into the Box, (*MF* 257) / I **launch'd out** into a new World, as I may call it, in the Condition (as to what appear'd) only of a poor nak'd Convict, (*MF* 312) / In this Manner I **set out** into the World, (*Rox* 7) / he might not be surpriz'd with it, and **fly out** into any Passions and Excesses on my account, or on hers; (*MF* 98) / How did my Blood **flush up** into my Face! (*Rox* 300) / [as *to*-infinitive] now I was to **launch out** into the Ocean, (*RC* 189) / it [= the crop] could get no Time to **shoot up** into Stalk. (*RC* 116) / I had nothing before me, but to **fall back** into the same Misery that I had been in before. (*Rox* 39), etc.

(ix) *on*:

... where the Apothecary's Apprentice, as I suppose, was **standing up** on the Counter, with his Back also to the Door, (*MF* 191) / I never **lay down** on my hard Lodging, (*CJ* 167) / one Party of them **comes up** on my Wing, (*MC* 250) / our Dragoon **goes in** on this Side to meet him; (*MC* 89) / I **look'd back** on the Life I had led, with the utmost Contempt and Abhorrence; (*Rox* 127) / [as *to*-infinitive] I was forc'd to **lye down** on the Ground to repose, (*RC* 69) / When we came to **look down** on the other Side of the Hills ... (*CS* 92), etc.

(x) *out of*:

I **got up** out of my Cabbin, (*RC* 11) / so we **jog'd away**, crossing the Fields, out of the Path towards *Tottenham-Court*; (*CJ* 64) / I would have **got up** out of my Chair, but was so Weak I could not for a good while; (*MF* 47), etc.

(xi) *through*:

he **walk'd up** thro' the Room only to see the Place both then, (*CJ* 29) / He did not run, but **shuffl'd along** a pace thro' the Crowd, (*CJ* 20) / I walk'd away, and turning into *Charter-house-Lane*, **made off** thro' *Charter-house-Yard*, into *Long-Lane*, (*MF* 239) / so we **went up** thro' all the Rooms, (*Rox* 33) / Major *Jack* became as dexterous a Pick-pocket as any of them, and **went on** thro' a long variety of Fortunes, (*CJ* 16), etc.

(xii) *to*:

I ... **clamber'd up** to the Top of the Hill, (*RC* 201) / BUT I **hasten on** to my own History, (*CJ* 215) / if once we **push'd on** to the Coast, (*CS* 132) [cf. *OED*. s.v. push, *v.* 7. a. *intr.* "To make one's way with force or persistence (as against difficulty or opposition). With various adverbs and preps.; esp. ***to push on***, to

Chapter 1 The Syntactic Structure of Intransitive Phrasal Verbs

press forward, to advance with continued effort." 1718~] / [as *to*-infinitive] his Lordship was gathering his Forces to **come up** to him; (*MC* 235) / Sir *William Balfour*, ... was forced to **wheel about** to his own Men; (*MC* 159) / they began (in time) to **grow up** to a dangerous Height, (*MF* 92) / so I had nothing to do, but to **go-away** to *London*, (*Rox* 163) / [after the verb of perception] seeing a glimpse of some Body **running over** to the Shop, I had so much presence of Mind, (*MF* 269), etc.

(xiii) *towards*:

they **went off** towards the Shore, (*CS* 225) / I **goes on** towards the Ale-house, (*MF* 239) / I **rambl'd about** towards the Place, (*MF* 321) / we were **driving back** towards *London*; (*Rox* 217) / [as *to*-infinitive] I ... endeavoured to **make on** towards the Land as fast as I could, (*RC* 44) [cf. *OED* s.v. make, v.¹ 90.b *intr.* "To go forward, proceed; to hasten on." 1608~ ; The *OED* cites this passage] / we were obliged to **stand away** towards the Coast of *Africa*, and the *Cape Guarde Foy*, (*CS* 176) / [after the verb of perception] we saw about a hundred [wolves] **coming on** directly towards us, (*RC* 298), etc.

NOTES:

According to (viii): The instances of *into* are worth commenting on. Unlike *to* as in *I came back* to *his House* (*Rox* 120), the preposition *into* tends to refer to "a space or thing having material extension" (*OED* s.v. into, *prep.* 1a), not a mere goal, as with ***get up*** *into the Box* or ***launch out*** *into the Ocean*. As well, this preposition is used in more abstract and figurative descriptions, as seen in ***set out*** *into the World* or ***fall back*** *into the same Misery*. Further, this preposition refers to (sudden) changes in the emotion of characters, as in ***fly out*** *into any Passions*. Especially, (*How did*) *my Blood* ***flush up*** *into my Face* is

85

of great interest, in that this description captures both physical and emotional aspects of the heroine.

(xi): Note the difference between *walk up thro' the Room* and *go on thro' a long variety of Fortunes* in the passages cited above; the former is (merely) physical and spatial description, while the latter is figurative.

1.4.1 The Use of *Upon* in Defoe's Fiction

The preposition *upon* plays a crucial role in describing action and behavior in Defoe's fiction. For example, it is used to describe immediate physical actions, as in:

> after he **sat down** upon the Bed. (*JPY* 71) / I was no sooner **stepp'd down** upon the firm Ground, (*RC* 80) / She blush'd and **look'd down** upon the Ground, (*CJ* 247)

The last instance *look'd down upon* actually denotes her "eye" movement (which also hints at her "inner" state of mind, partly in relation to "blushing"), rather than immediate contact with the ground.

The phrasal verb *look back*, which usually describes the (penitential) mentality of the protagonists, is more frequently followed by *upon* than *on*. In his seven works, Defoe employs *look back upon* 27 times and *look back on* 10 times in total,[17] as in:

> Now I **look'd back** upon my past Life with such Horrour, (*RC* 97) / I **look'd back** upon my Wickedness with Abhorrence, (*Rox* 129) [cf. *OED* s.v look, *v.* 32. *intr.* b "To direct the mind to something that is past; to think on the past. Const. *into, on, upon, to.*" 1599~] (cf. he had **look'd back** on the Crime he had

committed, with some Regret, (*Rox* 226))

The instances of the three-word verb (including *upon* or *on*) cited above most obviously act as a form of psychological expression. Although *upon* and *on* can be alternatively exchangeable in this context, the reason why Defoe prefers *upon* might have to do with the expressiveness of the "disyllabic" preposition; *upon* can be considered more dynamic than the monosyllabic *on*). It follows that *upon* is frequently used in the descriptions of a wide range of violent actions, as in:

> the Enemy had **broke in** upon him in two Places, and had routed one Troop, (*MC* 250) / Our Party in the Head of the Lane taking the Advantage of this Mistake of the Enemy, **charged in** upon them, and routed them entirely. (*MC* 206) / a Serjeant with 12 Dragoons **thrust in** upon the Out-Centinels, and killed them without Noise. (*MC* 103)

The three different phrasal verbs with *upon*, each of which occurs only once, equally describe fierce attacks on the battlefield in *Memoirs of a Cavalier*; the fierceness can be inferred from the coordinated verb phrases, such as *routed them entirely* or *killed them*. These expressions might be considered a stylistic variation of *fall in upon* (and *fall on upon*), which occur ten times (and six times) in *MC*, as in:

> *Gustavus Horn* commanded the left Wing of the *Swedes*, and having first defeated some Regiments which charged him, **falls in** upon the Rear of the Imperial right Wing, and separates them from the Van, (*MC* 61) / some Regiments ... **falls on** upon *Tilly*'s main Battle, and defeated Part of them, (*MC* 61)

87

As shown in Table 5, the verb *fall* is the most formative of the verb elements (apart from *come* and *go*) in *MC*; most of the phrasal verbs with *fall* act as military terms in this work.

Excepting the military context, the three-word verbs with *upon* (more specifically *in upon*) have a strong tendency to describe some sort of violent attack in Defoe's fiction. Here are some instances:

> the Captain ... **ran in** upon him, and knock'd him down, (*RC* 265) / [personification] the Plague rag'd so violently, and **fell in** upon them so furiously, (*JPY* 129) / I was in a great Surprize, and started to run, but one of them **clap'd in** upon me, and got hold of me, (*CJ* 77) / *Will* a Nimble strong Fellow **flew in** upon him, and with Struggling, got him down, (*CJ* 63) / when I first **broke-in** upon my own Virtue, (*Rox* 156) / All these Thoughts, and many more, **crowded in** so fast, I say, upon me, that I wanted to give Vent to them, and get rid of him, (*Rox* 230), etc.

The last instance from *Rox* is an interesting case where a descriptive mode of the "attack" develops into a psychological expression. The parenthetic phrase *I say* (i.e. between *crowded in* and *upon*) suggests that the three-word sequence (Verb + Particle + Preposition) is idiosyncratic.[18]

1.4.2 Idioms or Set Phrases

The case where *sit down* is followed by a preposition *before* in *MC*, which occurs eight times, seems to give this phrasal verb a particular shade of meaning unique to a military context. Here are two out of the eight instances, in comparison with the common instances of *sit down* with *upon* or *by*:

Chapter 1 The Syntactic Structure of Intransitive Phrasal Verbs

>the Army marched Westward, and **sat down** <u>before</u> *Gloucester* the Beginning of August. (*MC* 182) / The King, ... **sits down** <u>before</u> *Banbury*, and takes both Town and Castle, (*MC* 164) [cf. *OED* s.v. sit, *v*. 23. c. (b) "To encamp *before* a town, etc., in order to besiege it; to begin to a siege." 1607~]
>cf. after he **sat down** upon the Bed. (*JPY* 71) / he came and **sat down** by my Bed-side, (*Rox* 295)

As seen in the *OED* definition, the co-occurrence of *sit down* with *before* develops into a military term in the sense of "To encamp (*before* a town)" or "to begin to a siege" in the passage above, though the *OED* has not recorded the three-word combination as "a (military) phrase."

Thus, some instances of the "three-word" verb have the potential to serve as what Quirk et al. (1985) call "phrasal-prepositional verbs" (as defined in the Introduction). It is difficult to determine whether, and how, the unity of such a three-word verb was found to be both strong and cohesive in such an early-eighteenth-century text. However, a close examination of the *OED*, especially its treatment as a "phrase," and the date of its first (or earliest) citation, would help solve such a problem.

Typical instances of the three-word verbs recorded as a "phrase" in the *OED* are given in alphabetical order:

bear down upon:
>when we spy'd a large Ship to the Northward, **bearing down** directly <u>upon</u> us; (*CS* 216) [cf. *OED* s.v. bear, *v*. 37. b. *Naut*. and *gen*. ***to bear down upon***: to proceed (esp. with force) towards. 1716~]

come in for:
>*Waller*'s Men, willing to **come in** <u>for</u> the Plunder, a thing their

89

General had often used them to, quit their Post at the Pass, (*MC* 220) / the first time we always let a raw Brother **come in** <u>for</u> full share, (*CJ* 41) [cf. *OED* s.v. come, *v.* 63. o. "*to come in for*: to be included among those who receive a share of anything; to receive incidentally." 1665~]

come in with:

In this Pickle, with the Enemy at his Heels, I **came in** <u>with</u> him, hearing the Noise; (*MC* 170) [cf. *OED* s.v. come, *v.* 63. n. "*to come in with*: <u>to overtake</u>; to meet; to fall in with." *Obs.* 1557~ ; The *OED* cites this passage.]

come up with:

About three in the Afternoon he **came up** <u>with</u> us, (*RC* 18) / We **came up** <u>with</u> the Enemy's Leaguer about Break of Day, (*MC* 235) / had we had a Day before us, we should certainly have **come up** <u>with</u> her, (*CS* 147) / Well, says he, and will he **come up** <u>with</u> us dost thou think? (*CS* 150), etc. [cf. *OED* s.v. come, *v.* 74. c. "esp. *to come up with*, to come so as to be abreast of, <u>to overtake</u>; <u>to reach</u>."]

cry out of:

our Man **crying out** loud <u>of</u> this Violence, (*CS* 51) / they wou' d **cry out** <u>of</u> the Cruelty of being confin'd; (*JPY* 170) [cf. *OED* s.v. cry, *v.* 21. b. "Const. *against, at, on, upon* (persons or things objected to); *for* (something wanted); *to cry out of*, to complain loudly or vehemently of (a matter)." *c* 1385~]

fall in with:

I might **fall in** <u>with</u> some Christian Ship, (*RC* 198) [cf. *OED* s.v. fall, *v.* 91. "**to fall in with**. a. To come upon by chance, light upon, meet with, get into company with." 1594~]

Chapter 1 The Syntactic Structure of Intransitive Phrasal Verbs

look out for:

[I] **lookt out** <u>for</u> a Voyage. (*RC* 16) / We **look'd out** very narrowly <u>for</u> some River, or Creek, or Bay, (*CS* 220) [cf. *OED* s.v. look, *v*. 40. e. "*to look out for*: to watch or search for; to be on the look-out for; to await vigilantly." 1669~]

make up to:

they spread their Antients, and **made up** <u>to</u> us in a Line as if they would fight us, (*CS* 186) [cf. *OED*, s,v, make, *v*.¹ 96. n. *intr*. (a) "To advance in a certain direction; now only in *to make up to*, to draw near to, approach." 1595~]

run away with:

how they had **run away** <u>with</u> the Ship, (*RC* 275) / This Boat, and Provisions they **ran away** <u>with</u>, and sail'd North to the bottom of the Bay, (*CJ* 117) [cf. *OED* s.v. run, *v*. 72. c. "*run away with*: (a) To depart surreptitiously with, to carry off (something)." 1624~]

set up for:

they had no more to say to me, than to Jest with me, and tell me that the little Gentlewoman might **set up** <u>for</u> her self if she pleas'd. (*MF* 16) [cf. *OED* s.v. set, *v*.¹ 154. mm. "*to set up for*. (a) to set up for oneself, to start on a career on one's own account." 1622~]

take up with:

nay, be any thing, be even an Old Maid, the worst of Nature's Curses, rather than **take up** <u>with</u> a Fool. (*Rox* 8) [cf. *OED* s.v. take, *v*. 93. z. "*take up with*. (Cf. *take with*, 75 a-c.) (a) To associate with (a person); to begin to keep company with; to consort with (esp. with a view to marriage); to become friendly with, to form a relationship with." *a* 1619~]

The instances above include some cases which are now "obsolete" in contemporary English, as the *OED* suggests. These include: *come in with* or *cry out of.*

In the list of the "three-word" verbs, some of them could be paraphrased by "one-word" transitive verbs as seen in the *OED*'s definition; *come in with* and *come up with* could be paraphrased by *overtake* or *reach*. In this connection, an interesting instance of *run away with*, however, from a different work by Defoe, *The Farther Adventures of Robinson Crusoe* (1719) is given below:

> [the ship] was **run away** with by a reprobate Crew that were on Board" (*RC* 2: p. 161 in the Pickering & Chatto Edition)

This is the only instance where the three-word verb under consideration can be found; it is employed in the passive form. Defoe no doubt treats this three-word verb as if it is one-word "transitive" verb. The passivization of such multiple-verbs, as Palmer (1987: 239) suggests, can "display their unity."

NOTES:

In *Pamela*, the three-word verbs, *run away with, break in upon,* and *look out for*, are used in the passive voice. Their instances are cited in comparison with the active ones:

run away with:

> [in the passive] he need not have caus'd me to be **run away** with, (138) / For not being contented when I was **run away** with, in order to ruin me; (201) / [cf. as a gerund] upon my being in that

strange manner **run away** with, (138)
[in the active] said she, here's a charming Creature! would not she tempt the best Lord in the Land to **run away** with her! (107) / Could I think that a Brother of mine would so meanly **run away** with my late dear Mother's Waiting-maid, (257)]

break in upon:
[in the passive] when some of my Brother Rakes, such as those we were **broke in** upon, ... (369) [cf. *OED* s.v. break, v. 53. c. "To infringe *upon* or interfere with; to interrupt or disturb suddenly or unexpectedly." 1657~] / let me be consign'd to Penitence for my past Evils: A Penitence however, that shall not be **broken in** upon by so violent an Accuser. (434) / I was displeased to be **broken in** upon, after your Provocations, by either of you; (442) [in the active] they will not offer to **break in** upon my Conditions, (369) / she [= Pamela] has, unbidden, **broken in** upon me, and must take the Consequence of a Passion, (435) / Now, had you not **broken in** upon me, while my Anger lasted, (443)

look out for:
[in the passive] And then, next, after we have, perhaps, half broken their Hearts, a *Wife* is **look'd out** for: (444)
[in the active voice] he won't **look out** for any other Place; (462)

The idiomatization (or idiom formation) of such three-word verbs developed over the course of two decades.

1.4.3 Hybrid Formation

Like *we **came back** to our Castle*, (*RC* 208), the structure inherent in a three-word verb has been shown to consist of the "V + P" combination and its following prepositional phrase (i.e. [come back] + [to NP]).

Nonetheless, this structural analysis does not apply to all cases. In *Roxana*, an instance of *burst out* (*into*) is first to be considered:

> I **burst out** into Tears, without speaking a Word for a Minute; (*Rox* 135)

In this passage, the structure of *burst out into tears* is difficult to analyze, as the two set phrases, *burst out* and *burst into* (*tears* or *laughter*), are used differently in the same text:

> when she beckon'd to her Maid to withdraw, and immediately **burst out** in crying, (*Rox* 253) / it made me **burst** into Tears, and I cry'd vehemently for a great while together, (*Rox* 16)

Thus, *burst out into tears* can be easily construed as an emphatic form of *burst into tears*, though its structure cannot be strictly determined as "[burst out] + [into tears]."

Interestingly, Claridge (2000: 107) points out that the *Lampeter Corpus* of Early Modern English Tracts contains certain "probabl[e] nonce formations" which are "still more graphically to be seen than usual"; she gives three instances (the following citations from her book are abbreviated, for convenience):

> (1) And [I] **sent in for** Captain Stoakes, ...
> (2) but if we will **look back into** the Examples of former Ages, ...
> (3) there are Men who ... are **calling out for** new Methods of Vengeance, ...

According to Claridge's analysis, all three instances "are actually

Chapter 1 The Syntactic Structure of Intransitive Phrasal Verbs

the prepositional verbs *send for, look into* and *call for*, with an extra adverbial particle added"; in (1) *in* "serves as a directional marker" and in (3) *out* "has an intensifying function" (p. 107). She argues moreover that such three-word collocations are "hybrid formations" that "show a willingness to make use of a whole pile of particles for the sake of greater expressiveness," as being distinct from "a more 'traditional' make-up, such as *fall in with, given over to* or *live up to*" (p. 107).

A similar analysis can be conducted for Defoe. In practice, *burst out into tears* might better be considered a "hybrid formation," in which both *burst out* and *burst into* seem to be included; the structure of the three-word verb is more likely represented as [burst (out) into tears].

As for *send in for* in the instance (1) given by Claridge, similar though more complex cases of the "hybrid formation" can be observed in Defoe's use of *send up* and *send away*. It should be noted that the *OED* does not address the verb *send* intransitively. For example, in the usual usage, e.g. *I sent for a doctor*, the *OED*, based on historical principles, regards its use as belonging to "absolute uses" (cf. *OED* s.v. send, *v.*[1] 9. **send for** —. a. "To send a messenger or message for"; 1338~). Namely, the part of "a messenger or message" in the *OED* definition, which virtually acts as the object of *send*, is omitted as tacitly understood (or considered unimportant). In terms of the collocation of *send for*, Defoe apparently adds the particles, *up* and *away*, flexibly, as follows:

[a] Well, says I, I will **send** <u>for</u> them **up**, and talk with them for you; (*RC* 275) / When the Captain was gone, I **sent** <u>for</u> the Men **up** to me to my Apartment, (*RC* 276) /

[b] My Landlord, an Officious tho' well-meaning Fellow, had **sent**

95

away <u>for</u> the Neighbouring Clergy Man; (*MF* 182)

[c] upon the Emperor's Ban, the Protestants **send away** to the King of *Sweden* <u>for</u> Succour. (*MC* 41) / Now *Essex* **sends away** to the Parliament <u>for</u> Help, (*MC* 221)

In [a], *up* occurs after "*send for* (+ NP)," in [b] *away* comes between *send* and *for*, and in [c] *away* plus the prepositional phrase occurs between *send* and *for*. These five instances of a three-word verb can be considered a stylistic extension "for the sake of greater expressiveness" of the prepositional verb *send for*,[19] rather than the case where a prepositional phrase (i.e. *for* + NP) is added to the phrasal verbs *send away* or *send up*.

Next, a seemingly "ambiguous" three-word verb, *fall in among*, is considered; it is used four times in *Colonel Jack*. Instances are presented in their order of appearance:

[d] indeed they scourg'd him so severely, that they made him Sick of the Kidnapping Trade for a great while; but he **fell in among** them again, and kept among them as long as that Trade lasted, for it ceased in a few Years afterwards. (*CJ* 12)

[e] they wandered thro' the Woods, till they came into *Pensilvania*, from whence they made shift to get Passage to *New-England*, and from thence Home; where **falling in among** his old Companions, and to the old Trade; he was at length taken and hang'd, about a Month before I came to London, which was near 20 Years afterward. (*CJ* 118)

[f] the Horse [i.e. "the horse soldiers, cavalry" (*OED* s.v. horse *n.* 3b)] advanc'd first to Charge and they carried all before them Sword in Hand, receiving the Fire of two Imperial Regiments of Curiassers, without firing a Shot, and **falling in among** them, <u>bore them down</u> by the strength of their Horses, putting them

Chapter 1 The Syntactic Structure of Intransitive Phrasal Verbs

into Confusion, (*CJ* 219)
[g] [She told] that she wanted Bread, and those Wants and Distresses brought her into bad Company of another Kind, and that she **fell in among** a Gang of Thieves, (*CJ* 258)

In the above passages, where *fall in among* occurs, the instance in [f] seems quite different from the other three, especially given that the passage is the description of a battlefield. Here, *fall in among*, as *bore* (*them*) *down* (i.e. 'overwhelmed') suggests, probably refers to a violent attack against the enemy. The *OED*, though not dealing with this three-word collocation as a "phrase," provides an interesting instance as one of the citations of *fall in*:

cf. They ... **fell in among** a company of Spanish soldiers ... who immediately fired at them. (1697 W. Dampier *Voy.* (1698) I. 247 [*OED* s.v. fall *v.* 88. d. "to rush in with a hostile intention"])

Judging from this limited context, the meaning and structure of *fall in among*, in the above passage, is the same as that in [f]. Accordingly, as regards *fall in*, as seen in [f], the sense of "to rush in with a hostile intention" is appropriate to the context; therefore, the structure can be represented as "[fall in] + [among NP]."

On the other hand, three instances in [d], [e] and [g] are distinctly different in terms of meaning and structure from that in [f]. What is common among these three instances is the object of the preposition *among*. As *a Gang of Thieves* in [g] explicitly suggests, the objects are equally indicative of "bad company"; it is helpful here to keep in mind that *Colonel Jack* is written in a *bildungsroman* form of narrative.[20] Thus, the verb *fall* itself in [d], [e] and [g] may possess a negative moral connotation (e.g. "To yield to temptation, to sin" [*OED* s.v. fall, *v.* 22a]). As such, in order to gain better understanding of this three-word verb, it is necessary to observe it in a broader context (i.e. in a wider context than the single sentence).

A close reading of the text of *CJ* leads to an awareness that prior to [d], the two-word verb *fall among* is used in the following passage:

> In this manner we liv'd for some Years, and here we fail'd not to **fall among** a Gang of naked, ragged Rogues like ourselves, (*CJ* 9) [cf. *OED* s.v. fall v. 35. a. "To come by chance into a certain position. Now chiefly in phrase (of biblical origin), ***to fall among*** (thieves, etc.)" *c* 1175~]

The phrase following *fall among* (i.e. the object of *among*), *a Gang of naked, ragged Rogues*, carries a connotation of bad company, as well. The *OED* treats *fall among* as a phrase "of biblical origin," citing the passage in Luke x. 30 translated by Wyclif: "Sum man cam doun fro Jerusalem in to Jerico, and **felde among** theuues (i.e. thieves). [So 1535 in Coverdale; 1611 in A.V.]." In addition, the notation [So 1535 in Coverdale; 1611 in A.V.] denotes that this phrase has been handed down via the history of Bible translation into English; this is *the* traditional phrase. Near the beginning of this novel, Defoe uses just such a biblical phrase and, in a similar context a few pages later, slightly modifies the phrase: *fall among* (p. 9) => *fall in among* (p. 12). During this process of modification, a no less interesting two-word verb occurs:

> *Capt.* Jack, in this time **fell into** bad Company, and went away from us, (*CJ* 11)

Although the *OED* does not specifically define *fall into* as a "phrase," [21] this expression certainly serves as a context-dependent synonym of *fall among*. Thus, Defoe uses *fall among* only once, through the use of its synonym (*fall into*), and alters it to become *fall in among*, which is employed two more times, in [e] and [g]. This is a very interesting phenomenon, because *fall in among* in [d], [e] and [g] can be analyzed as a nonce formation in which the adverb, *in*, is a directional marker inserted between *fall* and *among*: [fall (in) among]. At a deeper and more contextual level, this three-word phrase can be regarded as a composite, or mixture, of its preceding two-word verbs, *fall among* and *fall into*. Rather than being limited to the familiar biblical (therefore more archaic) phrase *fall among*, Defoe might have been attempting to create a more dynamic and realistic phrase by adding the spatial adverb *in*, making effective use of the three-word framework.

1.5 Gerunds

Defoe often uses phrasal verbs "like a noun." When a two-word verb, not one-word one is employed like a noun, more syntactic difficulties arise. To shed light on the issue, the the gerund, or "a nominal *-ing* form with verbal properties" (Denison 1998: 268) will be examined. Although the gerund and the present participle both have the same *-ing* form, their functions completely differ. Present participles are generally more dynamic than their gerund counterparts which tend to be more static—compare *before they **were coming over*** and *before their **coming over***. Present participles, gerunds, and nouns can be thought of as existing on a continuum of verbal expression with participles having the most verbal nuance and nouns with none or nearly none—compare *before their **coming over*** and, for example, *before their **arrival***.

Instances of the gerund in the use of intransitive phrasal verbs can be divided into two main groups: a group of instances with a determiner (such as *my* or *the*) as with *before their **coming over*** (*Rox* 5), and a group of those lacking a determiner: *upon some sudden Occasion of **going out*** (*RC* 219). The former group can be considered more nominal, for a determiner essentially acts as an index of nouns. Furthermore, some of the instances possessing a determiner, especially "*the* V-*ing* + P," functionally differ from the instances lacking determiners (the relation between the definite article and *-ing* phrasal verbs will be discussed in further detail in Chapter 2).

1.5.1 Groups with a Determiner

i) The Determiner as a Personal Pronoun (e.g. *before his **going away***, (*MF* 290))

First, instances with a determiner are examined. Those cases where the determiner is a personal pronoun such as *at my **coming back**, I shot at a great Bird* ... (*RC* 53) will first be discussed. Most instances occur after a preposition:

> whereupon *Tilly*, to be provided for the King at his ***coming over***, falls to work in a Wood right against the Point, (*MC* 90) / Our Passage into the Lane being narrow, gave us some Difficulty in our **getting out**; (*MC* 205) / The first Piece of News they told us after the short History of their **coming away**, was, that our Companion was on board, (*CS* 20) / The next Day, which was the tenth from our **setting out**, (*CS* 86) / a knowledge of the Occasion and Reason of my **coming over**, (*MF* 329) / before his **going away**, (*MF* 290) / he stops short the last time of his

100

Chapter 1 The Syntactic Structure of Intransitive Phrasal Verbs

> **coming by**, (*CJ* 141) / <u>Upon</u> my **coming in**, she ask'd for the Ladies, (*CJ* 191) / she made such Preparations <u>for</u> her **lying in**, (*CJ* 194) / my Father was in very good Circumstances <u>at</u> his **coming over**, (*Rox* 5) / yet I cou'd not bear the Thoughts of his **going away** neither; (*Rox* 159) / my Spouse and I had taken Measures <u>for</u> our **going-off**; (*Rox* 274) / they depend <u>upon</u> our **going over**, (*Rox* 295), etc.

In the gerund constructions under discussion, the *-ing* form of *lie in* in *MF* and *Rox* is also observed:

> the extraordinary Expences <u>of</u> my **Lying Inn** (*MF* 117) / <u>in</u> my **Lying Inn** (*MF* 118) / every thing necessary <u>to</u> my **Lying-in** (*Rox* 77) / with the Circumstance <u>of</u> my **Lying-in** (*Rox* 77) [cf. *OED* s.v. lying-in, a. "The being in childbed; accouchement." *c* 1440~]

The *OED* entry gives "lying-in" as a headword, separate from the verb entry for "lie." In this regard, *lying in*, as cited above, might be excluded from this discussion as a compound noun. However, *lie in* is also used as a (phrasal) verb, in the same texts, for example: *she acquainted the Parish Officers that there was a Lady ready to **lye in** at her House*, (*MF* 117), and *She hop'd I wou'd stay and **Lye-in** at her House* (*Rox* 283). Hence, it is possible to construe that *lying in* in Defoe acts as a gerund, whose origin stems from *lie in*.

Adjectives can also be added to the *-ing* phrasal verb with a determiner, as in:

> when I received a very dangerous Thrust in my Thigh, rather occasioned by my <u>hasty</u> **running in**, than a real Design of the Person; (*MC* 16) / tho' not so well as we were provided in our

101

first **setting out**; (*CS* 119)

Some instances of the gerund occur as the object of certain verbs, such as *expect, watch, prevent, secure*, as in:

> yet the Ship having thus struck upon the Sand, and sticking too fast for us to expect her **getting off**, (*RC* 43) / we hauled our Main-Sail and Fore-Sail up in the *Brails*, lower'd the Top-Sail upon the Cap, and clewed them up that we might lye as snug as we could, expecting their **coming out**; (*CS* 147) /... a Party of the Enemy's Horse who stood to watch our **coming out**. (*MC* 107) / several Counsels were held about Ways to prevent its **coming over**; (*JPY* 1) / the locking up the Doors of Peoples Houses, and setting a Watchman there Night and Day, to prevent their **stirring out**, or any coming to them; (*JPY* 48) / Having thus secur'd my **going away** the next Day, (*Rox* 302)

The gerund construction with a determiner functions as a subject of the sentence, as follows:

> his **walking out** to see the Town, was not to satisfie his Curiosity in viewing the Place; (*CJ* 87) / Madam, *says she*, your **Lying-In** will not cost you above 5 *l.* 3 *s.* in all, (*MF* 166)

In the perfective form (i.e. *being* + PP), only one instance occurs:

> they put a Stop to this Work upon the News they had of our being **come in**. (*CS* 180)

ii) The Determiner as Personal Pronoun with a Prepositional Phrase

Instances with a prepositional phrase also mainly occur after a preposition, as in:

> As I had once done thus in my **breaking away** <u>from</u> my Parents, (*RC* 38) [cf. *OED* s.v. break, *v*. 50.c *intr*. [from 36.] "To start away with abruptness and force; to go off abruptly; to escape by breaking from restraint. Also fig." 1535~] / The King, at his **coming up** <u>to</u> this Town, sends me with my little Troop, (*MC* 94) / we employed our selves in things necessary for our **going off** <u>to</u> Sea; (*CS* 164) / after our **Putting out** <u>to</u> Sea, (*CS* 220) [cf. *OED* s.v. put, *v*. 48. j. (a) *Naut*. "To send or take (a vessel) out to sea. rare." (b) <u>*intr*. "To go out to sea; to set out on a voyage.</u> (Said of a vessel, or person.)" 1590~] / Upon his **coming up** <u>to</u> them, (*MF* 51) / she had prepar'd everything in order to her **going over** <u>with</u> me <u>to</u> *Holland*; (*Rox* 328), etc.

Sometimes adverbials (including prepositional phrases) follow the gerund:

> for as to my **coming back** <u>again</u>, (*CS* 189) / my Store [of powder] being now within the Quantity of one Barrel; so neither could I be sure of its **going off** <u>at any certain Time</u>, (*RC* 168) [cf. *OED* s.v. go, *v*. 85. c "Of firearms, explosives: To be discharged, explode." 1579~] / I am speaking now of People made desperate, by the Apprehensions of their being shut up, and their **breaking out** <u>by Stratagem or Force</u>, (*JPY* 55) / by their **wandring about** <u>with the Distemper upon them</u>, (*JPY* 53)

The *to*-infinitive follows the gerund with a determiner (only once):

> our Travellers had no need to be afraid of their **coming up** <u>to</u>

103

disturb them; (*JPY* 131)

In the following passage, the gerund form serves as a subject:

> my **coming back** as it were into Life again, might not be a returning to the Follies of Life ... (*MF* 290)

There are also cases in which the gerund occurs as the object of certain verbs, i.e. *delay* and *hasten*:

> to be with Child again by him, which to be sure would have prevented, or at least delay'd my **going over** to *England*. (*MF* 90) / for it happen'd just after I was marry'd, and serv'd to hasten my **going over** to *Holland*; (*Rox* 271)

iii) Cases When the Determiner is Not a Personal Pronoun
When the determiner is an indefinite pronoun *a*, the following instance occurs:

> yet it was more suitable to me, and what had more of Art in it, more room to Escape, and more Chances for a **coming off**, if a Surprize should happen. (*MF* 254)

In such a case, adjectives, such as *sad* and (*thorough*) *serious*, can be added to the gerund, as in:

> so this Scene of my Life may be said to have begun in Theft, and ended in Luxury; a sad **Setting out**, and a worse Coming home. (*CS* 138) / he was not altogether insensible of it, even then;

Chapter 1 The Syntactic Structure of Intransitive Phrasal Verbs

but nothing that amounted to <u>a thorough Serious</u> **looking up** to Heaven: (*CJ* 163)

Next, to be examined are gerunds introduced by the definite article, *the*. It occurs ten times in combination with a gerund, as in:

even till <u>the</u> **going down** of <u>the Sun</u>, (*RC* 103) / <u>The</u> **growing up** of <u>the Corn</u>, ... had at first some little Influence upon me, (*RC* 89) / in <u>the</u> **shooting out** of <u>the Cart</u>, (*JPY* 62) / it being just at <u>the</u> **shutting in** of <u>the Day</u>, we soon lost Sight of them, (*CJ* 298) [cf. *OED* s.v. shut, *v*. 15. **shut in**. e. *intr*. "Of the day, evening, etc.: To close in, grow dusk. Also of the days: To shorten." 1623~] / the Ship had fresh Way, but a great Sea rolling in upon us from the N.E. which we afterwards found was <u>the</u> **Pouring in** of <u>the Great Ocean</u> East of *New Guinea*. (*CS* 194)

What these five instances cited above have in common is that the gerund form of phrasal verbs is followed by the prepositional phrase (i.e. *of* + NP). Here the underlined noun phrases, *the Sun, the Corn, the Cart, the Day*, and *the Great Ocean*, all denote the notional subject of the gerund, respectively. Consequently, these five gerund phrases have the basic structure of "the Sun goes (or went) down," "the Corn grows (or grew) up," "the Cart shoots (or shot) out," "the Day shuts (or shut) in," and "the Great Ocean pours (or poured) in," etc. Since gerunds are inherently "timeless" expressions, there is no fully adequate paraphrase concerning their tense.[22]

An adjective (i.e. *constant*) modifies a gerund just once:

<u>the constant</u> **rushing in** of <u>the Water</u>, (*RC* 191)

This case has the same basic structure as the above five, and can roughly be paraphrased as "the Water *constantly* rushes (or rushed) in."

The other three instances (of the ten) are in the use of *breaking out* in *JPY*:

> in the first **breaking out** of the Distemper, (*JPY* 72) / At the first **breaking out** of the Infection, (*JPY* 221) / the first **breaking** of it [= "the Plague"] **out** in a House in *Long-Acre*, (*JPY* 194)

In these three cases, the adjective *first* is added to the gerund. The noun phrase functioning as the object of the preposition, *of*, is also understood to be the subject of the gerund. Here, when a personal pronoun (e.g. *it*) is used in the last instance, the syntax or word order of the gerund is changed; *the ... **breaking of it out***. This phenomenon seems closely related to the syntax of transitive phrasal verbs (i.e. *he **picked up** a book* vs. *he **picked** it **up***), as will be discussed later in Chapter 2.

As for determiners other than the articles *a* and *the, no* is also used, as in:

> Dec. 24. Much Rain all Night and all Day, no **stirring out**. (*RC* 75) / Nay, *says she*, ... there's no **going back** now; (*MF* 200) / there was then no **stirring out** into the Country, (*JPY* 114)

Moreover, when the determiner is a common noun or a proper noun, the apostrophe (indicating possession) is added, as *with the Plague's **going off**, (JPY* 114). Other similar cases are:

> when the News of his Majesty's **coming down** was positively

known, (*MC* 146) / as it happened just upon <u>Gustavus Horn's</u> **coming up**; (*MC* 116) / the King of *Hungary* seeing the Duke's Men as it were wavering, and having Notice of <u>Horn's</u> **wheeling about** to second him, falls in with all his Force upon his Flank, (*MC* 116) [cf. *OED* s.v. wheel, *v*. 3. *Mil*. a *intr*. "Of a rank or body of troops: To turn, with a movement like that of the spokes of a wheel, about a pivot (pivot n. 2), so as to change front." 1579~]

In the following passages, the noun phrases without an apostrophe, i.e. *Peoples* and *any Evil*, seem to function as a determiner of the gerund:

Then I entered into the manner of <u>Peoples</u> **going over** to those Countries to settle, (*MF* 157) / where we could have the least apprehensions of <u>any Evil</u> **breaking out** upon us; (*CJ* 263)

These two instances are rather ambiguous in terms of the structure, in that the *-ing* form can be construed as a present participle; in such a case, both noun phrases are understood to be postposed by the *-ing* participial adjectives.

1.5.2 Groups Lacking a Determiner
i) The Simple Pattern (e.g. *he talk'd of **going away***, (*MF* 113))
As with cases possessing a determiner, the simple form of the gerund without a determiner mostly occurs after a preposition:

upon some sudden Occasion of **going out**; (*RC* 219) / By this resolute way of **coming on** he carried many a Town in the first heat of his Men, (*MC* 86) / The King was in some Passion at his Men, and rated them for **running away**, (*MC* 83) / The next

> Motion therefore was about **going back**, (*CS* 203) / At **going off**, I called a Council of all the Officers in the Ship, (*CS* 262) / there might be a way of **coming back** before I went, (*MF* 302) / he talk'd of **going away**, (*MF* 113) / the Water being too High at the usual Place of **going over**, (*CJ* 97) / he very Gravely comes up to the Horse, hits him a Blow or two, and calls him Dog for **running away**; (*CJ* 93) / as to **going away**, I had prepar'd every thing for parting; (*Rox* 119) / I cou'd not think of **going away**, (*Rox* 328), etc.

The gerund construction follows after certain verbs:

> I receiv'd this last part with some tokens of Surprize and Disorder, and had much ado, to <u>avoid</u> **sinking down**, (*MF* 56) / but she <u>declin'd</u> **going in** there, (*CJ* 237) / Others <u>proposed</u> **going back**, and getting a great Gun out of the Ship, (*CS* 209)

ii) The Case with a Prepositional Phrase (e.g. *the Thought of* **getting over** <u>to the Shore</u>. (*RC* 124))

Numerous instances of the gerund construction lacking a determiner are also used with PP (consisting of a preposition indicating *direction* and a noun), as seen in the above-cited instance. Additional instances are given:

> I was by this Time so fix'd upon my Design of **going over** <u>with</u> him <u>to</u> the Continent, (*RC* 226) / we found we had pull'd off to Sea instead of **pulling in** <u>for</u> the Shoar; (*RC* 20) / Of **venturing over** <u>to</u> the Terra Firma, (*RC* 136) / we had dismounted several of their Guns by **firing in** <u>at</u> their Forecastle, (*CS* 152) [cf. *OED* s.v. fire, *v.*[1] 13. a. *intr.* or *absol.* "To discharge a gun or other fire-arm; to shoot. Const. *at, upon, into*, etc." *c* 1645~] / Friend, says he, I

108

Chapter 1 The Syntactic Structure of Intransitive Phrasal Verbs

understand the Captain is for **sailing back** to the *Rio Janiero*, (*CS* 153) / since I talk'd of **going back** to *England*, (*MF* 337) / he discover'd many times his inclination of **going over** to *Virginia* to live upon his own; (*MF* 84) / it will certainly make them think not of sparing what they have only, but of **looking up** to Heaven for support, (*MF* 191) / [I] was at the very point of **sinking down** out of the Chair I sat in: (*MF* 38) / they were with great difficulty kept from **running out** into the Fields and Towns, (*JPY* 128) / once or twice I was upon the Point of **breaking in** upon them, (*CJ* 226) / whereas now, *says* Sir *Robert*, by the Humour of **living up** to the Extent of their Fortunes, (*Rox* 167) / this put me many times, upon **looking-back** upon things past. (*Rox* 214), etc.

A variety of adverbials, including a prepositional phrase, often follow *-ing* phrasal verbs:

I could not bear the Thoughts of **going back** again. (*CS* 79) / Immediately all the House rose up, and paid me a kind of a Compliment, by **removing back** every way to make me room, (*Rox* 175) / Nov. 4. This Morning I began to order my times of Work, of **going out** with my Gun, (*RC* 72) / I was quite Sick of **going out** in a Beggar's dress, (*MF* 254) / Here I wrote these Memoirs having to add, to the Pleasure of **looking back** with due Reflections, (*CJ* 307) / the rest of the Men said the same, being a little weary of **beating about** for above three Months together, (*CS* 175) [cf. *OED* s.v. beat, *v.*¹ 19. a. *Naut.* (*intr.*) "To strive against contrary winds or currents at sea; to make way in any direction against the wind. *to beat about*: to tack against the wind." 1677~] / After **Sailing on** N.W. by N. with a fresh Gale at S.E. about six Days, we found ... (*CS* 33), etc.

Occasionally, the *to*-infinitive follows a gerund construction, as in:

Now the King saw his Mistake, in not continuing his March for London, instead of **Facing about** <u>to fight</u> the Enemy at *Edgehill*. (*MC* 174) / we might haul home the Sheets without **going up** <u>to loose</u> them, (*CS* 148)

In the following passages, *a* ought to be construed as a preposition (cf. *OED* s.v. a, *prep.*[1] 13), rather than an indefinite article:

but I saw him <u>a</u> **coming in** about half an Hour. (*CJ* 46) / [He says] *are not we then <u>a</u> **running away** <u>from</u> her?* (*CS* 147)

It can also be seen that nominal -*ing* phrasal verbs follow certain verbs, such as *forebear, decline, justify*, and *give over*, as a phrasal verb:

yet I could not <u>forbear</u> **getting up** <u>to</u> the Top of a little Mountain ... (*RC* 69) / nor did the People <u>decline</u> **coming out** <u>to</u> the public Worship of God, (*JPY* 208) / he could not justifie **going off** of the Island, (*CJ* 284) / [having] <u>given over</u> **looking out** <u>to</u> Sea to see if I could spy a Ship, ... I began to apply my self to accommodate my way of Living, (*RC* 67)

Only one instance of the nominal -*ing* phrasal verb occurs after an adjective, *busy*, as in:

We were no sooner on Shore here, and all very <u>busy</u> **looking out** for a Piece of Timber for a Top-Mast, (*CS* 146)

As for the case of "busy -*ing*," the *OED* explains that "the prep. is now commonly omitted [i.e. from the original "busy in -*ing*"], so that the

110

vbl. n. becomes indistinguishable from the pr. pple." (cf *OED* s.v. busy, *a*. 1c).

The use of gerund is summarized in Table 14:

Table 14. The Gerund: Frequency of Occurrence

	RC	*MC*	*CS*	*MF*	*JPY*	*CJ*	*Rox*	total
gerund	21 (3.2%)	18 (3.2%)	29 (5%)	23 (3.8%)	20 (5.1%)	22 (3.3%)	26 (4.6%)	159 (3.9%)
with a determiner	(9)	(10)	(12)	(12)	(13)	(9)	(18)	(83)
without determiners	(12)	(8)	(17)	(11)	(7)	(13)	(8)	(76)
total occurrences of intransitve phr. vbs	661	561	582	608	397	675	568	4052

Taken together, phrasal verbs functioning as the gerund are very infrequently used (about 4% of the total). Nevertheless, it has been observed that there is a great diversity of expressions which use phrasal verbs in a nominal (less dynamic and more static) sense.

Although the frequency-counts of Table 14 do not seem to reveal any specific feature, the totals found in *JPY* may suggest that its language tends towards the nominal style; this tendency becomes far more conspicuous in the gerund use of transitive phrasal verbs.

Finally, the frequencies of *come-* and *go-*phrasal verbs used as gerunds are given below:

Table 15. The Gerund: *Come*- and *Go*-Phrasal Verb Frequency of Occurrence

	RC	MC	CS	MF	JPY	CJ	Rox	total
gerund	21	18	29	23	20	22	26	159
come- and *go*-phrasal verbs	7 (33%)	8 (44%)	16 (55%)	16 (70%)	11 (55%)	11 (50%)	18 (69%)	87 (55%)
come-phr. vbs	(1)	(7)	(4)	(6)	(5)	(7)	(3)	(33)
go-phr.vbs	(6)	(1)	(12)	(10)	(6)	(4)	(15)	(54)

Rather surprisingly, more than half (55%) of all instances of the gerund use of intransitive phrasal verbs consists of *come*- and *go*-phrasal verbs; *go*-phrasal verbs occur 54 times and *come*-verbs 33 times. The earlier works (*RC* and *MC*) have less instances of these verbs, but the heroine-narrator novels (*MF* and *Rox*) show a much higher frequency. In any case, the figures in this Table suggest that Defoe fairly often uses very common phrasal verbs in the gerund.

1.6 Conversion of Intransitive Phrasal Verbs into Nouns (or Adjectives)

Apart from the gerund or verbal noun, there are very few instances of phrasal verbs used as a completely different word class. Therefore, special attention will be paid to all cases.

First, *Memoirs of a Cavalier* contains 17 instances of *run away*, and three of these are used as a different word class, as follows:

> [a] their own **run-away** Brethren (*MC* 116) [*OED* s.v. runaway, II *attrib*. or as *adj*. 3. a "Having run away; given to running away;

fugitive;" 1548~ ; this passage is cited in the *OED*.]
[b] We immediately attacked them, . . . and forced them at last to a down right **Run-away**, (*MC* 231) [*OED* s.v. runaway, *n.* 2. a. "An act of running away;" The *OED* cites this passage as its earliest illustration.]
[c] they stood their Ground, and having rallied the **Run-aways** of both the other Parties, (*MC* 254) [*OED* s.v. runaway, n. 1. a. "One who runs away; a fugitive, a deserter." *c* 1515~]

Run away is used as an adjective in [a] and a noun in [b] and [c]. But the two instances as a noun are rather different in meaning. *Run away* in [b] refers to "An act of running away," while the plural form in [c] obviously denotes "One who runs away." According to the *OED*, the uses of *run away* in [a] and [c] were already in existence in Defoe's era, but it is worth noting that the use in [b] is this dictionary's earliest instance.

As for the cases where a phrasal verb as a noun refers to the person who commits its verbal action, the following two, *stander-by* and *hanger-on* are cases in point:

here I experienced the Truth of an old English Proverb, *That* **Standers-by** *see more than the Gamesters.* (*MC* 29) [cf. *OED* s.v. stander, 2. stander-by. a. "One who stands by; one who looks on and abstains from interfering; one who stands aside from or has no concern in (a game, a quarrel, etc.);" 1545~]

this it seems, was a Contrivance of one of my Female **hangers-on**, (*Rox* 172) / I added, that I had no **hangers-on**, that shou'd trouble him; (*Rox* 249) [cf. *OED* s.v. hanger², 5. **hanger-on**. a. "A follower or dependant (familiarly and often disparagingly)." 1549~]

Next, *Colonel Jack* has one instance of *come out* as a noun:

> we were awaken'd in the Dead of the Night <u>with</u> **come out** *here*, (*CJ* 10)

This is likely a nonce-use. In this context, *come out* [*here*] might be paraphrased as "a shout by which somebody tells us to come out here." The rest are the following:

> [d] many Families found Means to make **Salleys out**, and escape that way after they had been shut up; (*JPY* 57) [cf. *OED* s.v. sally, *n.*¹ 1. "A sudden rush (out) from a besieged place upon the enemy; a sortie; esp. in the phrase *to make a sally*." 1560~ ; the *OED* citing Bunyan's *Holy War* (1905) 380 The Captains . . . of the Town of Mansoul agreed, and resolved upon a time to make a **salley out** upon the camp of Diabolus.
> [e] [we] kept a **Look out** upon the Hill. (*CS* 193) [cf. *OED* s.v. look out, look-out, *n.* 1. "The action (occas. the faculty or the duty) of looking out. *lit.* and *fig.* Chiefly in phrases *to <u>keep</u> (rarely to take) <u>a</u> (good, etc.) <u>look-out</u>; to be, place, put on or upon the look out*; orig. *Naut.* 1748~]
> [f] then I gave a great **Cry-out**, and fell a-scolding in my Way, (*Rox* 97) [cf. *OED* s.v. cry, *n.* 15 Combined with an adv., as **cry-out**, the act of crying out, exclamation, outcry. 1814~]

In [d], based on the *OED* definition and citation of Bunyan's *Holy War* (1682), it is possible to infer that *make salleys out* is a more vividly verbal variation of the set phrase *make a sally*, and here pairing of the particle, *out*, with *salleys* gives the phrase a greater sense of direction or movement.

On the other hand, in [e] and [f] (*keep a*) ***look out*** and (*give a*)

Chapter 1 The Syntactic Structure of Intransitive Phrasal Verbs

cry-out can be considered instances prior to the *OED* first-citation (the years 1748 and 1814, respectively). In fact, such a phenomenon (of a phrasal verb converted into a noun) is relatively new.[23] Defoe has always (excepting a single instance, in [f]) used the old compound-noun of *outcry*, as in:

> *Amy* then seeing him so perfectly deluded, made a long and lamentable **Outcry**, (127) [cf. *OED* s.v. outcry, *n*. 1. "The act of crying out" 1382~]

notes

[1] In terms of the relation between redundant-combinations and the simple verbs (e.g. *fall down* and *fall*), Hampe (2002: 196) states: "the use of the particle makes this kind of dynamic perception of a static scene much more explicit, which enhances the expressivity of the passage" (my emphasis added).

[2] A look at Table 1 suggests that the figures in types of phrasal verbs show a close correlation with those in types of lexical verbs. That is, *RC* and *CS* with a relatively higher frequency of lexical verb-types contain a greater variety of intransitive phrasal verbs, while those verbs in *JPY, MF* and *Rox* with a lower frequency of verb-types are less various. But the distinction between the one type and the two-or-more types is remarkably similar throughout the seven works.

[3] The instances discussed in this section are strictly distinguished from the use of post-modification in the *-ing* participle, as with: "not only of the Wars then **going on**, but also of the Wars in *Oliver's* time, (*CJ* 11)" and in "they were no more to me than a Picture **hanging up** against a Wall (*CJ* 188)." These can be regarded as having adjectival rather than adverbial force. In actual usage however, post-modification in intransitive phrasal verbs is extremely rare. Other examples are:

> as to Ships **coming in** from Abroad (*JPY* 217) / upon one or two stops of the Ships **coming up** (*JPY* 221) / I was like a Passenger **coming back** from the *Indies* (*Rox* 243).

[4] What is here referred to as a "participle" is treated as a "gerund" in the present study.

[5] As Quirk et al. (1985: 1124) states: "In *-ing* clauses, verbs used dynamically tend to suggest a temporal link, and stative verbs a causal link"; the *-ing* phrasal verbs

cited above, all in dynamic use, definitely have a temporal (rather than a causal) relation to the main clause.

[6] Quirk et al. (1985: 522), referring to instances such as *Down they flew* (which are syntactically the same as the instance form *RC* just cited), states: "As predication adjuncts, they [i.e. direction adjuncts] have a dramatic impact and a rhetorical flavour in that position [i.e. the "front" position]." Although it remains uncertain whether Defoe's instances are tinged with a "rhetorical flavour," the word-order of *away he went* offers no doubt a more "dramatic impact" to the reader than the normal word-order of, for example, *he went away*.

[7] As Table 5 shows, *stand away* is ranked as the fourth most-frequent phrasal verb, and is used 25 times in this work.

[8] As for the distribution between *ran* and *run* as a past form in *Robinson Crusoe*, Lannert (1910: 68) states that "The preterite *run* ... is much commoner (forty instances), while *ran* is only met with twenty-one times."

[9] Defoe's fiction is primarily written in the form of autobiography. According to Mullan (1998: 268), "Defoe's narrators look back in amazement at their lives, ... Though protagonist and narrator are one and the same person, there is a gap between them. Invariably, the protagonist is a sinner, the narrator a penitent."

[10] Davis (1983: 182-183), mentioning that Richardson's real innovation is what he called "spontaneous writing," makes the point: "What was significant and unique in this new method of spontaneous writing was the ability to recapture recent time past and to forcibly decrease the interval between event and transcription" (my emphasis added).

[11] Richardson revised *Pamela* eight times during his lifetime. Throughout the course of such revision, for example, "had broke (or wrote)" has been changed to "had broken (or written)"; "says I" or "thinks I" has been changed to "said I" or "thought I." A large percentage of such editorial changes were "designed to elevate or correct the language" (Eaves and Kimpel 1967: 64). As for the relation between the revision of *Pamela* and the use of phrasal verbs, see Murata (2003).

[12] Although such study can be categorized as sociolinguistics, what must be kept in mind in discussing the language of *Pamela* is that most of the letters and journals in this work are seemingly written by a fifteen-year old servant girl, Pamela.

[13] Leech (2006: 37) explains "end focus" as follows: "The principle by which elements placed towards the end of a phrase, clause or sentence tend to receive the focus or prominence associated with new information."

[14] Verbs such as *bleed* or *scream* can be classified into what Dixon (2005: 124) calls "corporeal verbs" which deal "with bodily gestures."

[15] As beyond the scope (i.e. of the 16 particles) of this study, this interesting case is

Chapter 1 The Syntactic Structure of Intransitive Phrasal Verbs

observed: "a raging Wave, Mountain-like, **came rowling a-stern** of us, ..." (*RC* 44) [cf. *OED* s.v. astern, *adv*. 2. b. "astern of: in the rear of (a ship). "]

[16] As for adverbials following certain verbs, Dixon (2005: 31) presents two types of criteria. One is an "inner adverbial" that "is semantically linked to the reference of the verb," as in *He sat <u>on a chair</u>, She carried the pig <u>to market</u>*, and *She stared <u>at the picture</u>*; here the verbs "demand a spatial adverbial." And the other criterion is an "outer adverbial": these "do not have the same sort of semantic link to the verb," as with *John kissed Mary in the garden*. Here, the adverbial can be "moved to initial position" as in *In the Garden John kissed Mary*. Though prepositional phrases following phrasal verbs in Defoe cannot be rigidly classified into these two types (i.e. *inner* or *outer*), this dichotomy is very helpful. If this can be applied to Defoe's instances, *I went away <u>to the Hill</u>* would be called an "inner" adverbial and [they] *went out <u>in one of the Canoes</u>* an "outer" adverbial.

[17] Among the 27 occurrences, *look back upon* is used 7 times in *RC*, once in *MC*, 5 times in *MF*, 7 times in *CJ*, and 7 times in *Rox*. On the other hand, among the 10 occurrences, *look back on* is employed only 4 times in *MF*, once in *CJ*, and 5 times in *Rox*. Thus, it is interesting to notice that the use of *on* is almost exclusively (nine out of the ten instances) limited to female narration.

[18] McIntosh (1986: 25) states: "*I say* (originally enclosed in quotation marks) has the additional effect of reestablishing the speaker's presence and heightening a sense of social immediacy, somewhat as "you know" does in twentieth-century colloquial English."

[19] Here, since *for* is always a preposition, *send for* is not a phrasal verb; see the definition of multi-word verbs in the Introduction.

[20] Richetti (2005: 261) states that "*Colonel Jack* is a proto-Bildungsroman or novel of education. ... *Colonel Jack* features the hero's adventures as a thief, a soldier and deserter, as an indentured servant and then an overseer and planter in Virginia, but the center of the narrative is his progress to an increasingly sophisticated grasp of the moral and social issues that surround his adventures."

[21] *Fall into*, in effect, is given eight different senses as a phrase (*OED* s.v. fall, *v*. 63. a-h), but none of the definitions are relevant to this context.

[22] As works prior to Defoe's fiction, *PP* and Behn's fiction contain instances of the same kind occurs, as in:

By <u>the **going up**</u> of <u>the Fire</u> we are taught to ascend to Heaven, by fervent and hot desires. (*PP*: 217) [=> the Fire goes (or went) up] / by <u>the **going away**</u> of <u>the Gentlemen</u> that were at the Grate, (Behn: 162) [=> the Gentlemen go (or went) away]

[23] Sørensen (1988: 150), on the basis of the data by Lindelöf (1937), states: "when

we come to the 19th century, the type [of conversion of phrasal verbs into nouns] begins to grow very popular."

Chapter 2
The Syntactic Structure of Transitive Phrasal Verbs

Transitive phrasal verbs by definition must take objects. Defoe manages to use these objects in combination with verbs and particles in a wide variety of ways to achieve his many literary objectives. An overall picture of transitive phrasal verbs in Defoe will be presented in a manner similar to Chapter 1. Considering the seven works of Defoe, four fundamental questions will be examined: (1) how many different types of phrasal verbs are employed, (2) how frequently phrasal verbs are employed, (3) what type of phrasal verbs most frequently occur, and (4) which of the 16 particles are most frequently employed in the formation of transitive phrasal verbs.

As for question (1), the types of transitive phrasal verbs are seen in Table 1; for example, *take up* is itself one "type," regardless of how many times it is employed:

Table 1. Types of Transitive Phrasal Verbs

works: (total words)	*RC* (122,482 words)	*MC* (102,360)	*CS* (111,346)	*MF* (137,174)	*JPY* (93,929)	*CJ* (125,342)	*Rox* (134,078)
trans. phr. vbs	239 *(195)	172 (132)	197 (189)	203 (117)	154 (98)	203 (161)	185 (115)
lexical verbs	127 *(89)	91 (61)	116 (91)	99 (57)	79 (46)	102 (79)	101 (55)
one type vs. two-or-more types	85 (67%) vs. 42 (33%)	63 (69%) vs. 28 (31%)	83 (72%) vs. 33 (28%)	60 (61%) vs. 39 (39%)	49 (62%) vs. 30 (38%)	60 (59%) vs. 42 (41%)	67 (66%) vs. 34 (34%)

* The number in parentheses indicates the types of intransitive phrasal verbs.

In comparison with the types of intransitive phrasal verbs marked with an asterisk (*), transitive phrasal verbs have a wider variety of types in *all* works. By definition, "transitive" phrasal verbs must take an object and Defoe emphasizes the role of these objects through his more frequent use of transitive phrasal verbs,[1] in composing his seven fictions. The predominance of transitive types over intransitive is particularly noticeable in *MF* and *Rox*: *trans.*=203 *vs. intr.*=117 (in *MF*) and *trans.*=185 *vs. intr.*=115 (in *Rox*); CS shows the least noticeable difference of 197 *vs.* 189. It follows that verbal elements of transitive phrasal verbs are more variable than those of intransitive phrasal verbs.

On the basis of *RC*, which contains the greatest number of types of phrasal verbs, the significance of the results of Table 1 is assessed. The following list covers all types of transitive phrasal verbs in *RC*; the notation of this list is the same as that displayed in the intransitive list in Chapter 1:

List 1: Types of Transitive Phrasal Verbs in *RC* (arranged in alphabetical order)

bar *up*; barricado *round*; bear *down, on* (2); beat *down, out* (2); block *up*; blow *up*; botch *up*; break *down, off, up* (3); breed *up*; bring *away, back, down, off, out, up, in, on, over* (9); burn *out, up* (2); bury *in*; call *away, off, out, in* (4); carry *away, back, down, off, out, up, on* (7); cast *away, down, off, up* (4); cheer *up*; choke *up*; choose *out*; clear *away, up* (2); close *up*; cook *up*; cover *over*; cry *out*; cut *away, down, off, out, up* (5); deliver *up, over* (2); dig *away, down, up* (3); drag *out*; draw *back, up, in* (3); drive *off, out, up, in* (4); dry *up*; eat up; eke *out*; entice *away*; fence *round, in* (2); fetch *back*; fill *up*; find *out*; fire *off*; fit *out, up* (2); fleet *off*; float *out*; force *in*; furbish *up*; gather *up*; get *down, off, out, up, along, on, over* (7); give *back, up, in, over* (4); grant *away*; hale *up, in* (2); hand *out*; hang *out, up* (2); have *on*; hearten *up*; heap *up*; heave *up*; help *off, up*

Chapter 2 The Syntactic Structure of Transitive Phrasal Verbs

(2); hoise *up*; hoist *out*; hold *out, up* (2); hunt *down*; hurry *away, about, along, on* (4); jam *in*; keep *down, off, out, up, in* (5); knock *down, up* (2); launch *off, out* (2); lay *down, out, up, aside, cross, by* (6); lead *away, up, along, in* (4); leave *off*; let *down, out* (2); lift *off, up, in, over* (4); live *out*; lock *up*; lower *down*; make *up*; mark *out*; minute *down*; nurse *up*; order *out*; pack *up*; paddle *along*; pen *in*; pick *up*; pile *up*; pluck *up*; pour *in*; prop *up*; pull *off, out, up, in* (4); push *on*; put *off*, out, *in, on* (4); raise *up*; ride *out*; rip *up*; rub *out*; run *out, in* (2); send *away, off, out, up, in, over* (6); serve *out*; set *down, out, up, aside, in, over* (6); shake *off, out* (2); shoot *off*; shut *up*; single *out*; sit *down*; speak *out*; splinter *up*; stir *up*; stretch *out*; swallow *up*; sweep *away*; take *away, back, down, off, out, up, in* (7); tear *up*; tell *over*; thrash *out*; throw *away, down, out, in, over* (5); thrust *off, aside, in, on* (4); tie *up*; toss *up*; tread *down*; trim *up*; turn *away, down, off, up, about* (5); veer *out*; venture *out*; waft *over*; wear *off, out* (2); whelm *down*; work *out, up, on* (3); wrap *up*; wrench *up*; write *down*; [out of 127 lexical verbs, **239 types** of phrasal verbs]

As in the case of intransitive phrasal verbs, many transitive phrasal verbs in the above list consist of "dynamic, monosyllabic verbs of native origin," such as *beat, blow, break, breed, bring, burn, bury, choke, drag, fetch, give*, etc. However, Romance verbs are also used: not only monosyllabic ones (e.g. *bar, block, cheer, cook, grant, order, nurse, pile, serve*, etc.), but also disyllabic ones (e.g. *carry, cover, entice, furbish*), the trisyllabic *deliver*, and even the quadrisyllabic *barricado* (of Spanish origin). In addition, *splinter* is of Dutch origin, and *rip* of uncertain (Flemish?) origin. Thus, lexical verbs used as transitive phrasal verbs are etymologically less "native" than the intransitive verbs, at least in *RC*.

A closer look at Table 1 and List 1 demonstrates the following three points: (i) out of 127 different verbs, 239 types of transitive phrasal verbs are formed;[2] (ii) among the 127 verbs, 85 types (67%)

121

form only one type of phrasal verb, while the other 42 types (33%) generate two or more types of phrasal verbs; (iii) the most productive verbs are *bring* (i.e. which generates 9 types of phrasal verbs), *carry, get, take* (7 types), *lay, send, set* (6 types), and it has been shown that *come* and *go* develop 11 and 12 different types of intransitive phrasal verbs, respectively.

The most prolific verbs in forming transitive phrasal verbs in each work are shown, in Table 2:

Table 2. The Top Five Most Prolific Verbs

	RC	*MC*	*CS*	*MF*	*JPY*	*CJ*	*Rox*
1	bring (9 types)	bring (9)	send, take (8)	bring (10)	bring, carry (8)	bring, carry (9)	bring (9)
2	carry, get, take (7)	beat (7)		carry, put (8)			carry, put, take (7)
3		draw, fetch, take (6)	carry (7)		lay (7)	put, take (7)	
4				take (7)	put, take, turn (6)		
5	lay, send, set (6)		bring, throw (6)	call, cast, pull, set (6)		give, send (6)	give, send (6)

As seen in the above Table, *bring, carry* and *take* are considered among the most productive verbs throughout the seven works; apart from *CS*, *bring* is always the most frequently used.

Question (2), how frequently transitive phrasal verbs are used, is next examined. The frequency of occurrences (or tokens) of transitive phrasal verbs in Defoe's seven works is presented in Table 3:

Table 3. Frequency of Transitive Phrasal Verbs

	RC	MC	CS	MF	JPY	CJ	Rox
trans. phr. vbs	745 *(661)	487 (561)	498 (582)	581 (608)	533 (397)	563 (675)	632 (568)
frequency per 1,000 words	6.09 *(5.39)	4.77 (5.48)	4.46 (5.23)	4.23 (4.43)	5.67 (4.23)	4.49 (5.39)	4.71 (4.23)
one occurrence vs. two-or-more occurrences	122 (51%) vs. 117 (49%)	95 (55%) vs. 77 (45%)	106 (54%) vs. 91 (46%)	113 (56%) vs. 90 (44%)	81 (53%) vs. 73 (47%)	103 (51%) vs. 100 (49%)	87 (47%) vs. 98 (53%)

* The number in parentheses indicates the cases of intransitive phrasal verbs.

As well as in intransitive phrasal verbs, *RC* shows the highest frequency of transitive phrasal verbs (6.09 occurrences per 1,000 words) among the seven works. The second-most frequent (5.68) is found in *JPY*, which shows the lowest frequency in intransitive use. Interestingly, as seen in this Table, in *RC*, *JPY*, and *Rox* transitive phrasal verbs occur more frequently than intransitive ones; in the other four works, intransitive phrasal verbs are used more frequently. As regards the number of types of phrasal verbs, it has been observed that transitive types have more variation than intransitive, in all works. This strongly suggests that in *MC*, *CS*, *MF*, and *CJ*, (certain types of) intransitive phrasal verbs tend to be repeated more frequently than transitive verbs. Next, as for the one occurrence *vs.* two-or-more occurrences of transitive phrasal verbs, *Rox* exclusively shows more than 50% of two-or-more occurrences (once: 47% *vs.* twice-or-more: 53%). This indicates that (some types of) transitive phrasal verbs in this work are more repeatedly used than in the other six works.

Concerning question (3), the type of phrasal verbs which most frequently occur, the data is presented in Table 4:

Table 4. The Top Five Most Frequent Transitive Phrasal Verbs

	RC	MC	CS	MF	JPY	CJ	Rox
1	take up (55 times)	draw up (27)	take up (28)	take up (31)	**shut up (123)**	take up (29)	find out (41)
2	give over (25)	take up (20)	take in (24)	find out (26)	take up (20)	carry on, pull out (18)	take up (32)
3	carry away, set up (22)	beat off (17)	set up (18)	pull out (21)			put off (28)
4		give over (14)	give over (15)	make up (16)	lock up, set down, set up (14)	carry away, make up (14)	give up (22)
5	find out (21)	carry on, cut off (13)	take away (10)	take away (14)			pull out (16)

The most striking feature of this Table is the high frequency of *shut up* in *JPY*, which is by far the most frequently used (123 instances) among the seven works. Despite the fact that *JPY* is the smallest corpus among the seven texts (see Table 1), *shut up* occurs more than twice as frequently as *take up* in *RC* (55 times). On the other hand, *take up* is such a common and versatile phrasal verb that it may be used in many contexts; in fact it is *always* ranked number one or two in Table 4. In stark contrast, *shut up* seems to be limited to a specific context, as it is used only once in *RC*, in the case of *I **shut** it* [= "that Light"] ***up***, (*RC* 210). In this sense, the use of *shut up* in *JPY* deserves a closer investigation, with reference to factors of its high frequency, and the relation of the phrasal verb with the subject matter in this work. (This issue will be discussed at length in Chapter 3.) As for the others in the table, *find out*, *give over*, *set up* and *pull out*, which are all ranked in the top five in three of the works, these are among the more common

Chapter 2 The Syntactic Structure of Transitive Phrasal Verbs

transitive phrasal verbs like *take up*, while the most-frequent is *draw up* in *MC*, which is always used in a military context, in the sense of "To bring into regular order, as troops" (*OED* s.v. draw, *v*. 89f). This could be looked upon as a phrasal verb unique to a particular work,[3] as in the case of *shut up*.

Here the versatility of *take up*, which is the most frequently-used phrasal verb in *RC*, including intransitive verbs (the most frequent intransitive *come back* occurs 33 times), needs further elaboration. As exemplified in *come-* and *go*-phrasal verbs, intransitive phrasal verbs in Defoe, as has been pointed out, tend to be used in a literal sense, however *take up* is a highly polysemous phrasal verb. This is evidenced by the fact that the *OED* gives 56 different meanings to this phrasal verb (cf. *OED* s.v. take, *v*. 93). Several instances are cited next in order to demonstrate that *take up* in *RC* is employed with at least two or more meanings. The following passages, which are divided into four groups, show that the phrasal verb in each of the passages means not only something determinedly literal in [a] but also something transferred [b] to [d]:

> [a] I immediately stept to the Cabbin-door, and **taking up** my Gun fir'd at him, (*RC* 25) / I **took up** a great Firebrand, (*RC* 177)
> [b] I **took up** my Lodging, (*RC* 47) / I **took up** my Country Habitation. (*RC* 152)
> [c] These two whole Days I **took up** in grinding my Tools, (*RC* 83) / These Thoughts **took** me **up** many Hours, Days; (*RC* 157)
> [d] I must go back to some other Things which **took up** some of my Thoughts. (*RC* 60) / my Head was ... **taken up** in considering the Nature of these wretched Creatures; (*RC* 197)

The difference of meaning in *take up* originates from the (semantic) relation with its objects. For example, *Gun* and *Firebrand* in [a] are the concrete objects which the characters can "lift" (*OED* s.v. take, *v.* 93a) with their hands; while, from [b] to [d], in terms of whether they can be physically lifted, the objects seem to lose their concreteness and shift to something more abstract. It turns out that the more a certain phrasal verb takes a variety of objects, the wider the range of meaning in the phrasal verb can be.

As for the final question (4), which of the 16 particles are most frequently used in forming types of transitive phrasal verbs, the data is shown in Table 5:

Table 5. The Top Five Most Prolific Particles

	RC	MC	CS	MF	JPY	CJ	Rox
1	up (67 types)	up (45)	up (55)	up (44)	up (35)	out (43)	up (51)
2	out (45)	out (31)	out (38)	out (39)	out (30)	up (42)	out (34)
3	down, off (24)	off (19)	away (22)	off (23)	down, off (17)	off (24)	off (23)
4		away, down (16)	down (19)	away (19)		away (21)	away (17)
5	in (23)		off (18)	down, in (16)	away, in (13)	down (18)	down (14)
others	away (16), over (11), on (10), back (6), along (4), aside (3), about, round (2), cross, by (1), forth (0)	in (11), on, over (8), back (7), round (5), about (4), aside, by (1), forth, across, along (0)	in (14), back (9), over (6), along (4), about, aside, on (3), round (2), forth (1), across, by (0)	back (14), on (11), over (9), about (6), along (3), aside (2); by (1), forth, across, around (0)	back (8), over (6), on (5), along (4), about (3), round, aside, by (1), forth, across (0)	back, in, over (13), on (8), along (4), about (2), aside, by (1), forth, across, around (0)	in (12), back, over (10), on (6), by (3), along (2), forth, about, aside (1), across, around (0)

126

A glance at Table 5 shows that the distribution of the 16 particles of the transitive types is quite variable, while that of the intransitive types is less so with each particle having a more similar distribution as seen below when comparing the figures in the transitive list in *RC* with those in the intransitive list from Chapter 1 (see Table 6, p. 31): *out* (33 types), *up* (29), *in* (20), *away* (19), *off* (18), *down* (17), etc., in order of frquency.

What is most prominent among the particles listed above is the high frequency of *up*, which is ranked number one in all works except *CJ*. However, *out* is ranked number one in *CJ*, and number two in the other six works. Thus, *up* and *out* have been found to be very productive in forming transitive phrasal verbs. An intensifying or aspectual force inherent in the two particles may add emphasis or a nuance of completion to simple transitive verbs. Here, the expressiveness of *up* is touched upon. Based upon the results of Table 5, *up* in *RC*, by co-occurring with 67 different verbs, generates 67 types of transitive phrasal verbs (28% in total). Some of instances of these verbs are given below:

> I ***barr'd** it [= the door] **up** in the Night, (*RC* 208) / When I had done this I ***block'd up** the Door of the Tent with some Boards within, (*RC* 55) / I might ***botch up** some such Pot, (*RC* 119) / it [= the grain of corn] had been **burnt up** and destroy'd. (*RC* 79) / I gave him a Dram (out of our Patroon's Case of Bottles) to ***chear** him **up**: (*RC* 24) / all the In-side of the Ship was ***choack'd up** with Sand: (*RC* 84) / the 14th of April I ***closed** it [= "my Wall"] **up**, (*RC* 79) / I found Ways to ***cook** it [= food] **up** without baking, (*RC* 79) / it almost spoil'd some of them, and almost ***dry'd up** their Milk. (*RC* 158) / my Wall joyn'd to the Rock, was all ***fill'd up** with the large Earthen Pots, (*RC*

151) / I ***furbish'd up** one of the great Cutlashes, (*RC* 167) / whatever we may ***heap up** indeed to give others, we enjoy just as much as we can use, (*RC* 129) / how I was a Prisoner ***lock'd up** with the Eternal Bars and Bolts of the Ocean, (*RC* 113) / we ***pick'd up** two more English Merchants also, (*RC* 289) / I had the Seiling to ***prop up**, (*RC* 74) / [he] ***ripp'd up** his Wastcoat to feel if he was not wounded, (*RC* 211) / But I ***shut it** [= "that Light"] **up**, (*RC* 210) / I expected every Wave would have ***swallowed** us **up**, (*RC* 8) / the Trees were ***torn up** by the Roots, (*RC* 81) / I set my Dog to guard it in the Night, ***tying** him **up** to a Stake at the Gate, (*RC* 116) / we had gotten as much Land cur'd and ***trim'd up**, as we sowed 22 Bushels of Barley on, (*RC* 246) etc. [The phrasal verbs marked with an asterisk (*) indicate that its verb elements co-occur exclusively with *up* in *RC*.]

The particle *up* in the passages cited above is mostly used in the sense of "To or towards a state of completion or finality. (Frequently serving merely to emphasize the import of the verb.)" (*OED* s.v. up, *adv*.[1] 18.), rather than in the literal sense of "towards a higher place or position." Without the aid of the particle *up*, each of the lexical verbs, such as *bar*, *block*, *botch*, *burn* or *choke*, might express what is meant in the context (to some extent). Hence, the addition of *up* is no doubt intended to complete and enhance the meaning of the verbs. Such an addition of the monosyllabic stressed *up* seems to make the passage in which it is used more rhythmic, vivid and dynamic than the version without the particle, especially as seen in examples like *barr'd it up*, *chear* (i.e. *cheer*) *him up*, and *cook it up*, etc.

Next, the syntactic structure of transitive phrasal verbs will be analyzed. Perhaps the most crucial difference between intransitive and transitive verbs concerns whether or not they possess objects. Thus, an

Chapter 2 The Syntactic Structure of Transitive Phrasal Verbs

examination of the way transitive phrasal verbs take their objects will be the next matter examined.

Generally speaking, transitive phrasal verbs occur in two main patterns: "Verb + Particle + Object" (VPO) like *I **pull'd off** my Clothes*, (*RC* 48) and "Verb + Object + Particle" (VOP) such as *I **gave** this Attempt **over*** ... (*RC* 128).

However, transitive phrasal verbs in Defoe do not always occur in only these two patterns. There are two more patterns which need to be considered. One is the pattern of "Object (+ Subject) + Verb + Particle" (OVP), in which the relative pronoun as an object comes before (a subject and) a phrasal verb like *for my Corn, which I always **rubb'd out** as soon as it was dry* ... (*RC* 144). The other is the pattern of "Verb + (Indirect) Object + Particle + (Direct) Object" (VOPO), in which a phrasal verb takes two objects, such as [*he*] ***gave*** me ***back*** an exact Inventory of them them ... (*RC* 33). These two do not necessarily apply to any of the two main patterns, VPO and VOP—and neither does the "passive construction," in which the object is moved to the subject position by means of passive voice, as with *I was **lifted up** by the Waves* ... (*RC* 45). Hence, such syntactic patterns (OVA, VOPO and Passive Construction) will be separately described, below.

Finally, the distribution of the two main patterns, VPO and VOP (according to Defoe's seven works) must be examined. Additionally, it will be necessary to investigate the fundamental difference between the two patterns.

2.1 The Pattern "Verb + Particle + Object" (VPO)

When the object is not a personal pronoun (e.g. *me*, *them* and *it*), the pattern of "Verb + Particle + Object" (henceforth VPO) predominates in Defoe; conversely, personal pronouns (except for several cases of reflexive pronouns) *always* occur in the pattern of VOP (at least, in Defoe).

2.1.1 The Simple Pattern (e.g. *I pull'd off my Clothes,* (*RC* 48)
There are cases where no word follows the object, as seen in the above instance. This is the simplest form of the VPO pattern. Similar cases, in which noun phrases as the object consist of a determiner (e.g. *the, my,* or *some*) and a noun, are given:

> before we **hal'd in** our Sail, (*RC* 22) / the Parliament **cried up** their Victory, (*MC* 163) / This, I say, **took away** all Compassion; (*JPY* 115) / The Major **lug'd out** the Goods, (*CJ* 13) [cf. *OED* s.v. lug, *v.* 3. trans. "To pull along with violent effort; to drag, tug (something heavy). Also with *advs.*"; The *OED* cites this passage.] / When we **clos'd up** our Wedding-Week, (*Rox* 249) / if she **gave away** that Power, (*Rox* 149) / when I had **wrought out** some Boards, (*RC* 68), etc.

Instances in the form of *to*-infinitive are also numerous:

> I was going to **give over** my Enterprise, (*RC* 138) / I had no Plow to **turn up** the Earth, (*RC* 118) / the House refused to **lengthen out** the Time. (*MC* 228) / we durst not break our Order to **seek out** our Friends, (*MC* 64) / we got some Cattle here to **eke out** our Provisions, (*CS* 146) / I now began to **cast up** my Accounts; (*MF* 127) / by which I got time to **throw off** my Disguise, (*MF* 216) / before it went far enough to **burn down** the Houses; (*JPY* 242) / Nor was he ever once seen to **lift up** his Eyes, (*JPY* 120) / I began to **draw in** my Effects, (*Rox* 254) / he resolv'd to **lay**

Chapter 2 The Syntactic Structure of Transitive Phrasal Verbs

down his Trade; (*Rox* 10) / As I resolv'd to **put off** the Voyage, (*Rox* 280), etc.

In the use of the present participial (-*ing*) construction:

I walk'd about on the Shore, **lifting up** my Hands, (*RC* 46) / **pulling out** my Glass, I look'd, and saw plainly the Place where they had been, (*RC* 207) / I barr'd it [= the door] up in the Night, **taking in** my Ladders too; (*RC* 208) / . . . and **laying up** every Corn, I resolv'd to sow them all again, (*RC* 79) / . . . and then **searching up** the Stream, we found Gold there too; (*CS* 130) / **taking up** a Bundle, he made Signs to us, (*CS* 60) / **sending out** a Scout, he brought us Word a Party of the Enemy was at Hand. (*MC* 230), etc.

In the case following a perception verb or a causative verb and its object:

I told him, I could not but laugh to <u>see</u> us **spinning out** our Time here for nothing; (*CS* 213) / The Captain of this Gang <u>seeing</u> some of our Men **making up** their Hutts, (*CS* 38) / he <u>bad</u> me **hold out** my Hand (*CJ* 36) / so I <u>bid</u> him **take off** the Saddle, (*MC* 69) / [I] <u>bad</u> him **put up** his Finger; (*MC* 69), etc.

In the following passages, the object is a longer phrase:

I **furbish'd up** one of the great Cutlashes, (*RC* 167) / I now **gave over** any more Thoughts of the Ship, (*RC* 58) / so I **mark'd out** a larger Piece of Land, (*RC* 213) / Time **wears out** the Memory of it; (*Rox* 153) / his two Fellow Travellers **laid aside**

131

their Design of going to *Waltham*, (*JPY* 140) / we **eat up** all the Scraps of what we had left, (*CS* 106) / I was **cutting down** some thick Branches of Trees, (*RC* 176) / because I wou'd be sure not to go too publick, but so as to **take away** all Possibility of being seen, (*Rox* 275), etc.

Among those cases where the prepositional phrase follows the object, some cases exclusively modify the object, as in *Time however, and the Satisfaction I had ... began to **wear off** my Uneasiness about them*; (*RC* 166); "my Uneasiness about them" acts as a unit of meaning. Thus, noun phrases as an object in the VPO pattern tend to be long and elaborate. Additional instances are:

I fell on my Knees ... , resolving to **lay aside** all Thoughts of my Deliverance by my Boat, (*RC* 141) / nor had we any Way to **gather in** a Stock of Provisions for the passing this Desart, (*CS* 110) / I would have made an excuse to you, to have **put off** our Voyage to *Ireland* for some time, (*MF* 152) / he order'd me to **put up** a Bill for Letting Rooms, (*Rox* 33) / when a Woman had been weak enough to **yield up** the last Point before Wedlock, (*Rox* 152), etc.

The long object contains a relative clause (including the case where a relative pronoun is omitted), as in:

for a good while I **left off** the wicked Trade that I had so newly taken up; (*MF* 198) / she always **melted down** the Plate she bought, (*MF* 201) / I **run out** the little Money I had left, in Cloths and Subsistance, (*CJ* 103) / I **threw away** the only Opportunity I then had, (*Rox* 161) / [as *to*-infinitive] they began to **lay aside** all suspicious Thoughts of the People that dwelt thereabouts, (*CS* 239) / I shall not **take up** any of the little Room I have left here, (*CS* 201) / tho' I resolved to **leave off** the wicked Course I was in. (*CJ* 83), etc.

The simple pattern "Verb + Particle + Object" is often followed by a prepositional phrase, as with *he **lifted up** his Eyes to Heaven*, (*JPY* 106). Similar instances are given:

[*against*] therefore they had no more Cause to **take up** Arms against their Sovereign, (*MC* 193: two more instances of *to take up Arms against*) / [*behind*] he **puts back** the Horse behind a great white-Thorn Bush, (*CJ* 90) / [*between*] they **set up** a long Pole between them and us, (*CS* 27) / [*from*] [I] made a shift to **carry off** a gold Watch from a Ladies side, (*MF* 263) / [*out of*] he **drew away** his Cannon and Baggage out of *Dennington* Castle, (*MC* 225) / because the Rage of the Floods always **works down** a great deal of Gold out of the Hills; (*CS* 135) [cf. *OED* s.v. work, *v.* 15. "To move (something) into or out of some position, or with alternating movement (to and fro, up and down, etc.):" 1617~ ; The *OED* cites this passage.] / [*to*] I **stretch'd out** my Hands to it with eager Wishes. (*RC* 139) / my Girl **puts in** a Word to the Sister, (*Rox* 284) / [*towards*] he **cast up** his Eyes towards me ... (*MF* 297) / [*upon*] the Dragoons ... **poured in** their Shot upon those that were passing the Bridge: (*MC* 53) [cf. *OED* s.v. pour, *v.* 3. "to discharge in rapid succession or simultaneously, as missiles;" 1599~] / when the King **drew up** the whole Army upon the Field of Battle, (*MC* 64) / [*with*] I **block'd up** the Door of the Tent with some Boards within, (*RC* 55) / we **carried away** near 150 Prisoners, with 500 Horses (*MC* 154), etc.

The *to*-infinitive comes after the VPO pattern, as in:

they **brought over** four Prisoners to feast upon; (*RC* 207) / he **flung down** his Angle to meet him, (*CS* 243) / I walk'd about the Shore almost all Day to **find out** a place to fix my Habitation, (*RC* 71) / they agreed to **draw up** Propositions for Peace to be sent to the King. (*MC* 227) / We resolved ... to **look out** a proper Harbour to bring the Ship into, (*CS* 215) / if I could but come to **lay up** Money enough to maintain me: (*MF* 120), etc.

In the following passage, a phrasal verb in the *to*-infinitive form is followed by a second phrasal verb in the *to*-infinitive:

the Captain stay'd to **Pickle up** five or six Barrels of Beef to **lengthen out** the Ships Store. (*MF* 319)

2.1.2 Phrasal Verbs as a Reporting Verb (e.g. *the Boy **cry'd out**, Master, Master, a Ship with a Sail, (RC 32)*)

Some transitive phrasal verbs, such as *cry out* and *call out*, can serve as a reporting verb to introduce direct (or indirect) speech. Two different uses of *cry out* are next considered:

[a] the Moment he **cry'd out**, they fir'd; (*RC* 257) / she fell backward upon the Floor, and **cry'd out** most terribly, (*CJ* 230)
[b] one of our Men early in the Morning, **cry'd out**, *Land*; (*RC* 42) / I **cry'd out**, *Lord be my Help*, (*RC* 91)

In [a], *cry out* is no doubt used intransitively, though arguably in [b] it is used transitively, in that the following (originally) italicized words or phrases, *Land* and *Lord be my Help*, which indicate the exact words that the characters utter, can function as direct objects of *cry out*. In this sense, the combination of *cry out* as a reporting verb in [b] with the

Chapter 2 The Syntactic Structure of Transitive Phrasal Verbs

utterances in the form of direct speech (though as a convention of this era quotation marks are not used) fits perfectly into the pattern of VPO. Here are additional instances of *cry out*:

> he hears me, and **crys out**, *No shoot, no shoot*, (*RC* 295) [I] **crying out**, I was undone, undone, (*RC* 69) / the Woman **cried out**, *God bless them*, (*MC* 211) / the Foot, who were engaged in the Streets, **crying out**, *Horse, Horse*. (*MC* 241) / the Carpenter, ... **cried out**, *a Sail, a Sail*. (*CS* 25) / the Family being alarm'd **cried out** *Thieves*, (*MF* 209) / when she **cried out** *a Pickpocket*, (*MF* 211) / when they saw him they **cryed out**, *that's he, that's he*; (*MF* 246) / I **cry'd out**, *WELL, I know not what to do, Lord direct me!* and the like; (*JPY* 12) / the People **cryed out** *there's Jack*, (*CJ* 80) / one of the Gentlemen **cry'd out**, *Roxana! Roxana!* (*Rox* 176), etc.

The passages cited above show that the objects of *cry out*, namely the "reported" phrases or clauses, often contain a repetition of a certain word or phrase, for instance: *No shoot, no shoot, Horse, Horse, a Sail, a Sail*, and *Roxana! Roxana!*, etc.

As well, *call out* introduces direct speech as a reporting verb, as in:

> he **called out**, *Hey! where am I?* (*JPY* 91) / nor could he **call out** *stop Thief*, (*CJ* 56) / the Captain **calls out**, *stop the Horse*, (*CJ* 93) / no-body rose up to dance, but all **call'd out** *Roxana, Roxana*; (*Rox* 180) / but they all **call'd out** *Roxana* again; (*Rox* 180)

Cry out sometimes takes a *that*-clause as an object. In this case, the phrasal verb introduces "indirect speech," as in:

our Negroes, who were in the Front, **cry'd out**, that they saw a White Man; (*CS* 119) / she cry'd and took on like a distracted Body, wringing her Hands, and **crying out** that she was undone, (*MF* 283)

In the same vein, *put in* serves as a reporting verb introducing indirect speech:

at length the other People who were present, **put in**, that they should give Security to him, (*CJ* 51) / Two or three times the QUAKER **put in**, That this Lady *Roxana* had a good Stock of Assurance; (*Rox* 290) [cf. *OED* s.v. put, v.¹ 45. g. *trans*. "To interpose (a blow, shot, etc.; a word or remark; also with the actual words as obj., usually preceding); to intervene with;"]

2.2 The Pattern "Verb + Object + Particle" (VOP)

Instances in the "Verb + Object + Particle" (henceforth VOP) pattern are identified by the following three distinct options:

(i) O = a personal pronoun
(ii) O = a reflexive pronoun
(iii) O = others (i.e. nouns except personal and reflexive pronouns)

2.2.1 The Pattern "Verb + *Personal Pronoun* + Particle" (e.g. *These things, and the Approach of Night,* ***called*** *us* ***off****,* (*RC* 297))

When a phrasal verb takes a personal pronoun as a direct object in

Chapter 2 The Syntactic Structure of Transitive Phrasal Verbs

Defoe, the phrasal verb *always* occurs in the VOP. A "personal" pronoun exclusively refers to *me, us, you, thee, her, him, them,* and *it* as "neuter"; the possessive forms, such as *mine* or *yours* does not occur in this pattern, except for one case (e.g. *every one should give him as much as would **make** his **up** just as much as any single Share of our own,* (*CS* 128)). The simplest form of this pattern is the case with no word attached, as in the above instance.

Other similar cases are:

> for I always kept it [= "my Frigate"] sunk in the Water, I **brought** it **out**, (*RC* 255) / the Chimera of the *Germans* **put** them [= "our Generals"] **by**, (*MC* 28) [cf. *OED* s.v. put, $v.^{1}$ 41. d. "To prevent (a person) from attaining or carrying out something; to divert from. *Obs*." *a*.1586~ ; The *OED* cites this passage.] / now Captain *Bob*, says he, where's your Prince, so I **called** him **out**, (*CS* 65) / till nothing but Desperation **sent** them **away**; (*JPY* 96) / when the Gentleman heard of me, he **call'd** me **in**, (*CJ* 39) / *Amy*, who was an indefatigable Girl, **found** him **out**; (*Rox* 87) / [past participle] in short, Amy had **made** her **away**; (*Rox* 325) / I expected every Wave would have **swallowed** us **up**, (*RC* 8) / [in a relative clause] we had 1000 Dragoons, which **helped** us **out**. (*MC* 235) / it was he the Captain that **carryed** us **away** (*CJ* 114), etc.

The cases where a phrasal verb occurs in the form of *to*-infinitive are numerous:

> I gave him a Dram (out of our Patroon's Case of Bottles) to **chear** him **up**: (*RC* 24) / the Body halted to **bring** us **off**, (*MC* 250) / the *Imperial* Army was enough to **hasten** me **away**, (*MC* 50) / we were obliged to **give** it **over**, (*CS* 192) / I began to take

upon me a little to **hearten** them **up**, (*CS* 54) / the careless Boys had forgot to **take** it [= "a silver Tankard"] **away**. (*MF* 199) / it was so much the more difficult to **bring** them **along**; (*JPY* 174) / the Family had either Time to **send** them **out**, (*JPY* 74) / just as a Fellow offer'd to **pick** her **up**. (*CJ* 14) / I had Power to **put** her **away**; (*CJ* 239) / but she had no Breath to **take** it [= "a Glass of Wine"] **in**, (*Rox* 253), etc.

In the use of participial construction, the following cases can be seen:

I carry'd him and his two Men into my Apartment, **leading** them **in**, just where I came out, (*RC* 258) / *There*, says she, (**ushering** him **in**) *is the Person who, I suppose, thou enquirest for*, (*Rox* 223)

In the following passage, the *-ing* clause occurs in the same manner as seen in the instances above, but its use is rather loose, in that the sense subject of *fitting it up* is *Workmen*, not *I*:

I found there were Workmen at work, **fitting** it [= the house] **up**, as I suppose, for a new Tennant; (*Rox* 89)

Phrasal verbs in the VOP pattern are often followed by prepositional phrases, especially including *to, into, from, upon*:

we **drove** him **back** to London in a very little while. (*MC* 150) / the high Tide had **floated** her [= the ship] **off** to Sea. (*CS* 156) / he **cut** them [= the old coins "beaten out"] **out** into the Shape of Birds and Beasts: (*CS* 28) / he has **dragg'd** me **over** into a strange Country, (*Rox* 90) / so the Crowd did, as it were **Thrust**

Chapter 2 The Syntactic Structure of Transitive Phrasal Verbs

me **away** from her, (*MF* 259) / I heard one of them say aloud to another, **calling** them **off** from the Boat, (*RC* 253) / they **set** him **up** again upon his Horse, (*MC* 210) / the Wind and the Sea had **toss'd** her [= the boat] **up** upon the Land, (*RC* 48) [cf. The *OED* cites this passage. (*OED* s.v. toss, *v.* 15. a)], etc.

Prepositional phrases containing *with*, which do not indicate direction, follow the particle, as in:

I **knock'd** him **down** with my Cane at one Blow; (*CJ* 243) / [I] **rubb'd** it [= the ear of the corn] **out** with my Hands; (*RC* 117) / though she easily saw the Disorder I was in, she **turned** it **off** with admirable Dexterity, (*MC* 33) / she **Bred** me **up** very carefully with her own Son, (*CJ* 5), etc.

In the following passages, prepositions *as* and *for* introduce a noun phrase, or an adjective, as object complement:

I **run** her **down**, as some scandalous Woman; (*Rox* 290) [cf. *OED* s.v. run, *v.* 73. j. "To disparage, defame, or vilify." 1668~] / not only the *Imperialists* but the Protestants themselves **gave** them **up** as lost: (*MC* 47) / I **gave** them **over** for lost; (*CS* 180) [cf. *OED* s.v. give, *v.* 63. f. "To abandon the hope of seeing, finding, overtaking, etc. Also, *to give over for (dead, lost):*" Obs. 1674~]

The last instance cited above, as the *OED* suggests, develops into a set phrase or an idiomatic expression.

The object of the preposition comes before the *to*-phrasal verb, as in:

what Trade she would please to **put** him **out** to? (*Rox* 192) / he had a Watch word to **let** them **in** by; (*CJ* 65)

This pattern contains instances in which adjectives as the complement of the object, *tame* and *alive*, come after the particle:

> I endeavoured to **bread** them ["wild Pidgeons"] **up** tame, (*RC* 76) / ["a large old He-Goat"] was so fierce I durst not go into the Pit to him; that is to say, to go about to **bring** him **away** alive, (*RC* 145)

(a) An "Empty" *It*

Numerous instances of phrasal verbs above-cited include the use of the "neuter" personal pronoun *it*. For instance, as seen in *I went up with the Ladder to the Top, and then **pull'd** it **up** after m*e (*RC* 79), *it* no doubt refers back to *the Ladder*. Notwithstanding, there are some cases where it is difficult to ascertain what *it* refers to, in the given context.

As for the use of *it* as an object, Rissanen (1999: 260) makes the interesting observation that "This pronoun has been used as a highly indefinite 'empty' object since Old English. In Middle English, the instances are few, but in Early Modern English the construction is common, particularly with phrasal verbs (my emphasis added; Rissanen goes on to cite two instances from Shakespeare: as *hold it out* and *make it up*).[4] It is in fact difficult to determine whether or not *it* is in some cases actually "empty." Therefore, based not only on the context, but also on the *OED*'s historical treatment of these (phrasal) verbs, some uses of phrasal verbs which might contain an empty *it*, such as *hold it out, fight it out*, and *make it up*, are next considered. It can be seen that

Chapter 2 The Syntactic Structure of Transitive Phrasal Verbs

hold it out is employed in many of the works, as follows:

> I was covered again with Water a good while, but not so long but I **held** it **out**; (*RC* 45) / his Man had the Plague, and died in two Days; my Man **held** it **out** well. (*MC* 29) / we stood away fair West, and **held** it **out** for about twenty Days, (*CS* 205) / the other Gentlemen sat down to Play; the Musick **held** it **out**; and some of the Ladies were dancing at Six in the Morning. (*Rox* 176) / [past participle] all I had, and all he had before, if he had any thing worth mentioning, would not have **held** it **out** above one Year. (*MF* 61) [cf. *OED* s.v. hold, *v*. 41. j. *intr*. "To maintain resistance, remain unsubdued; to continue, endure, persist, last. (Also formerly †*to hold it out* in same sense.)" 1598~]

As documented by the *OED*, *hold it out* has a (historically) close affinity with the intransitive *hold out*. In fact, it is not wide off the mark to interpret the instances cited above intransitively in each context.

In a similar vein, *it* in *fight it out* and *make it up* in the following passages can also be interpreted as "empty"; the *to*-infinitive instance (which seems of greater relevance) is also presented in order to make the argument more persuasive:

> the resolute Garrison, with the brave Baron *Falconberg*, **fought** it **out** to the last, (*MC* 45) / though they knew all was lost would take no Quarter, but **fought** it **out** to the last Man, (*MC* 62) / so I resolved they should **fight** it **out** among themselves, (*MC* 27) / the Physicians said two or three times, they could do no more for me, but that they must leave Nature and the Distemper to **fight** it **Out**, (*MF* 42), [cf. *OED* s.v. fight, *v*. 8. "*to fight out*: to settle (a dispute) by fighting, to fight to the end; often *to fight it out*." 1548~]

141

> I found this was a little too close upon him, but I **made** it **up** in what follows; (*MF* 39) / I came away with my Money, and having taken Six-pence out of it, before I **made** it **up** again, (*CJ* 26) / and so he told me, and that he would **make** it **up** in other things: (*Rox* 70) / upon the whole he told me very honestly that if I would take his Opinion, he would Advise me to **make** it **up** <u>with</u> them; for that as they were in a great Fright, and were desirous above all things to **make** it **up**, (*MF* 249), [cf. *OED* s.v. make, *v.*[1] 96. 1. *(c) intr.* (also often ***to make it up***). "To be reconciled after a dispute; to become friends again." 1669~; 1749 Fielding Tom Jones vii. v, I beseech you ... that you will endeavour to <u>make it up with</u> my aunt.]

Such an empty *it* might be seen when phrasal verbs are used as nautical terms,[5] as with *lead away*:

> we **led** it **away**, with the Wind large, to the *Maldivies*, (*CS* 185) [cf. *OED* s.v. lead, *v.* 18. b. "*Naut.* ***to lead it away***: to take one's course."]

The *OED* cites this passage as its sole illustration. Although the *OED* never refers to an intransitive meaning of *lead out*, in the same work can be observed an intransitive instance in nearly the same sense, as with *they seemed to **lead away** to the Northward a great Way*, (*CS* 113). This indicates that *lead it away* and an intransitive *lead away* can be used alternately in the same text.

In the following passages, the use of *beat it up* seems to be of the same nature as the case of *lead it away*:

> We took this Advantage, and stood away for *Carthagena*, and from thence with great Difficulty **beat** it **up** at a Distance from

under the Shore for St. *Martha*, (*CS* 145) / We were at Sea above two Months upon this Voyage, **beating** it **up** against the Wind, (*CS* 197) / [as a gerund] the Mate was for **beating** it **up** to Windward, and getting up to *Jamaica*, (*CJ* 295), [cf. *OED* s.v. beat, $v.^1$ 19. a. "*Naut.* (*intr.*) To strive against contrary winds or currents at sea; to make way in any direction against the wind."]

Although the three-word phrase *beat it up* is not mentioned at all, the *OED* gives the verb *beat* in nautical contexts the following definition: "To strive against contrary winds or currents at sea; to make way in any direction against the wind" (*OED* s.v. beat, $v.^1$ 19a), Further, this dictionary records that the "intransitive" phrasal verb *beat up* in the same meaning has appeared since 1720 (i.e. "*esp. to beat up* against the wind. 1720 Lond. Gaz. No. 5827/1 He beat up to Windward." (*OED* s.v. beat, $v.^1$ 19b). Thus considered, *beat it up* is probably an emphatic form of an intransitive phrasal verb *beat up* and seems to be tinged with an intransitive character.

2.2.2 The Pattern of "Verb + *Reflexive Pronoun* + Particle" (e.g. *I stept into the Cabbin and sat me down*, (*RC* 32))

Reflexive pronouns in Defoe are often used without "self." Jespersen (*MEG* III: 284) mentions that *I buy me clothes* can be considered to mean "buy to (for) myself"; *me* is grammatically the reflexive pronoun as a dative or indirect object. Among such instances, Jespersen, citing the passage from Defoe's *Robinson Crusoe* (*I made me a large tent*), points out that such a reflexive use is "frequent in Defoe." Reflexive pronouns lacking "self" are also used as an accusative, direct object. This use is closely associated with phrasal verbs occurring in the "V + *Reflexive Pronoun* + P" pattern, to be discussed. First considered is the reflexive use of *sit down*, which interestingly occurs in coordination with another verb phrase, as follows:

> I clamber'd up the Clifts of the Shore, and **sat** me **down** upon the Grass, (*RC* 46) / I stept out, and **sat** me **down** upon a little rising bit of Ground, (*RC* 190) / the Men came up close to us, and **sat** them **down** on the Ground, (*CS* 117) [cf. *OED* s.v. sit, *v.* V. *refl.* and *trans.* 32. *refl.* To seat (oneself). b. With *down*. (The more frequent use.) *c* 1450~]

Sit down is usually used intransitively; Chapter I has recorded that this phrasal verb is used intransitively, as with *after he **sat down** upon the Bed* (*JPY* 71). As such, what might be the difference between reflexive (and transitive) versus intransitive use? The four instances of *sit me* (or *them*) *down* (cited above) are coordinated with the intransitive dynamic verb phrases *step into*, *clamber up*, *step out*, and *come up* (*to*) in each of the passages; note that the instances of the reflexive *sit down* all occur in the place of B in the coordination pattern "A and B."

In *MF*, on the other hand, the reflexive use of *sit down* occurs in the place of A, as follows:

> I **sat** me **down** and cried most vehemently; (*MF* 192) / I **sat** me **down** and look'd upon these Things two Hours together, and scarce spoke a Word, (*MF* 153)

A close observation of the six total instances cited reveals that the reflexive *sit down* seems to be less spontaneous and more controlled and intentional than the intransitive *sit down*.

The reflexive uses of *lay down* and *dress up* tend to occur in coordination with another verb phrase:

they committed themselves to God's keeping, and **laid** them **down** to Sleep. (*CS* 247) / so I **lay** me **down** again, and slept the rest of the Night quietly enough. (*CJ* 74) / I **laid** me **down** flat on my Belly, on the Ground, (*RC* 182) / Having thus heard the Signal plainly, I **laid** me **down**; (*RC* 272)[6]

I ... **drest** me **up** in the Habit of a Widow, and call'd myself Mrs. *Flanders*. (*MF* 64) / The next Day I **dress'd** me **up** again, (*MF* 257)

Next, the reflexive pronoun with "self" is considered. Interestingly, in the reflexive uses of *sit down*, *lay down*, and *dress up* the "self" forms appear as well:

at other Times I **sat** my self **down** contented enough without her [= "my Boat"]. (*RC* 149) / No, No, Mrs. *Betty*, pray sit still *says he*, and so **sits** himself **down** in a Chair over-against me, (*MF* 47) / he only found he had **laid** himself **down** to ease his Limbs; (*RC* 240) / I had **dress'd** myself **up** in a very mean Habit, (*MF* 238) / so the next Day I **dress'd** myself **up** fine, and took a Walk to the other End of the Town; (*MF* 256) / I went and **Dress'd** my self **up** in this Livery, (*CJ* 74)

Is there any significant difference in meaning or intention between, for example, *sit me down* and *sit myself down*? Or is this just a variation? Jespersen (*MEG* III: 325) suggests that some reflexive pronouns as an object may be taken to be "emphatic" pronouns in apposition to the nominative; these pronouns tend to become redundant and the transitive verbs accompanying them approach the status of an intransitive verb.[7]

In practice, it is difficult to distinguish whether a reflexive pronoun in instances of this pattern functions as an "emphatic" pronoun, or an actual object. In this light, instances of phrasal verbs with "self" in the simple pattern are next presented:

> [I] found the Weight of the Wreck had **broke** itself **down**, (*RC* 84) / before we found the Captain, who though very weak by the loss of Blood, had **raised** himself **up**, (*MC* 64) / *William* ... told me, he wanted to talk seriously with me a little; so we **shut** our selves **in**, (*CS* 255) / we did not **tye** our selves **down** when to march, (*CS* 73) / I **set** myself **out** too, as well as a Widows dress in second Mourning would admit; (*MF* 250) / some not able to bear the Torment, threw themselves out at Windows, or shot themselves, or otherwise **made** themselves **away**, (*JPY* 76) [cf. *OED* s.v. make, *v.*¹ 84. a *trans*. "To put (a person) out of the way, put to death; also, to put an end to (a person's life)". *Obs*. Common in 16-17th c. *refl*. 1581~] / But an Accident **thrust** itself **in** here, (*Rox* 318) / [as *to*-infinitive] [I] had more Presence of Mind when I was to **bring** my self **off**. (*MF* 220), etc.

The cases in which prepositional phrases follow phrasal verbs with *self*-reflexive pronouns are given:

> I **cast** my self **down** again <u>into</u> the deepest Gulph of human Misery that ever Man fell into, (*RC* 38) / I **fitted** my self **up** <u>for</u> a Battle, (*RC* 253) / Accordingly I **let** my self **down** <u>into</u> the Water, (*RC* 57) / so the People **let** themselves **down** <u>out of</u> their Windows, (*JPY* 53) / every one of them **gave** themselves **over** <u>for</u> dead Men, (*CS* 219) / as we had observ'd, as above, how the Men made no scruple to **set** themselves **out** <u>as</u> Persons meriting a Woman of Fortune, (*MF* 77) / the Watermen on the River above the Bridge, found means to **convey** themselves **away** <u>up</u> the River as far as they cou'd go; (*JPY* 151) / So possible is it for

Chapter 2 The Syntactic Structure of Transitive Phrasal Verbs

us to **roll** ourselves **up** in Wickedness, (*Rox* 69), etc.

There are some interesting cases where the reflexive pronoun occurs after the particle (i.e. in the VPO pattern). The most remarkable case is *give up*. In *Moll Flanders*, this phrasal verb with a reflexive pronoun occurs four times (including two instances of gerund) in the VPO pattern:[8]

> Thus I **gave up** myself to a readiness of being ruined without the least concern, (*MF* 26) / I told her as I had Reason to do, That I would **give up** myself wholly to her Directions, (*MF* 77) / [as a gerund] No Man of common Sense will value a Woman the less for not **giving up** herself at the first Attack, (*MF* 75) / which choice was now **giving up** her self to another in a manner almost as scandalous as hers could be. (*MF* 144) [cf. *OED* s.v. give, *v.* 64. d. *trans.* "To devote entirely to; to abandon, addict *to*. Chiefly with reflexive pron. as obj."; 1604~]

Among other instances of the reflexive use of *give up*, only one *to*-infinitive instance occurs in the VPO pattern in *A Journal of the Plague Year*:

> In a Word, People began to **give up** themselves to their Fears, (*JPY* 171)

Excepting these five instances, all others of *give up* occur in the VOP pattern. In particular, the five instances in *Roxana* mark a sharp contrast with those in *MF*:

> [I] ruin'd my Soul from a Principle of Gratitude, and **gave**

myself **up** to the Devil, (*Rox* 38) / I **gave** myself **up**, as above. (*Rox* 44) / he was the most obliging Gentlemanly Man, and the most tender of me, that ever Woman **gave** herself **up** to; (*Rox* 45) / I **gave** myself **up** to a Person, (*Rox* 65) / she was no better or worse than the Servant among the *Israelites*, ... who by that Act, **give** himself **up** to be a Servant during Life. (*Rox* 148)

Thus, the four instances of *give up oneself* in *MF* (and one in *JPY*) might be deviant, perhaps due to an unintelligent narrator, Moll; recall that the intransitive *away comes I* occurs exclusively in *MF*. However, as far as the *self*-reflexive pronoun is concerned, it might be possible that the position of the *self*-pronoun in the use of phrasal verbs (i.e. VOP or VPO) has not yet been fully fixed, in comparison with the case of personal pronouns, such as *it* or *me*.[9]

2.2.3 The Pattern "Verb + *Non-personal Pronoun* + Particle" (e.g. *the Stream **took** the other Soldier **away**,* (*MC* 89))

On the basis of his survey on the Helsinki Corpus, consisting of written texts between 1500-1700, Hiltunen (1994: 133) states that the VPO pattern "is the predominant one if the object is nominal." He goes on to demonstrate that "Among the total of 851 examples, there were only 30 cases where a nominal object ... intervened between the verb and the particle" (pp. 133-134). Thus, in the period of Early Modern English, when phrasal verbs take nouns other than personal and reflexive pronouns as an object, the VPO is generally assumed to be a standard pattern. Nevertheless, numerous instances of transitive phrasal verbs in Defoe also occur in the VOP pattern. In that sense, instances of this pattern are described here as accurately as possible.

According to the "length" of the object, namely *how many words* it consists of, instances of phrasal verbs in the pattern under

Chapter 2 The Syntactic Structure of Transitive Phrasal Verbs

consideration are given. When the object is one word, it is often a proper noun, as in:

>Upon this I **call'd** *Friday* **in**, and bid him lie close, (*RC* 249) / down comes another Gentleman from him, and **taking** *Will* **aside**, ask'd him what he had said about it? (*CJ* 48) / I think it was to **put** Powder **in**, (*RC* 77) / but now I had a Cabbin and room to **set** things **in**, (*MF* 316)
>[with a prepositional phrase] in order to **bring** *Friday* **off** from his horrid way of feeding, (*RC* 210) / above four Year, which was long enough to **send** Word **in**, to a Wife or Family, from any Part of the World. (*Rox* 90) / [he said] That he had perswaded the King of his Country to **send** Boats **off** to the Rock or Island, (*CS* 202) / ... to some of those She-Butchers, who **take** Children **off** of their Hands, (*Rox* 80) / I did not **send** *Amy* **up** under thirteen or fourteen Days, (*Rox* 309), etc.

In the following passage, *that* is a demonstrative pronoun, not a personal one:

>none knows how far to **carry** that **back**, (*JPY* 192)

Many objects are two-word noun phrases consisting of mainly "determiner + noun," as in:

>[two words]
>I **threw** this Stuff **away**, (*RC* 77) / the Horse in the fall **kept** the Collonel **down**, (*MC* 63) / but I could not **carry** my List **on**, (*JPY* 237) / The Man ... **sent** the Cart **away**; (*JPY* 152) / it seems she **slipt** the Lock **back**. (*CJ* 248) / then talking merrily enough, he

catch'd his Words **back**; (*Rox* 186) / [William says] Do with him, as he would do with us, **cut** his Head **off**. (*CS* 229) / [as *to*-infinitive] It was our good Fortune to **get** our Ship **off** that very Night, (*CS* 229) / we agreed to **lay** that Thought **aside**, (*CS* 93) / He was going to **send** the Letter **away**; (*CS* 275) / he made an Excuse to **send** his Man **away**, (*MF* 28) / The People have good Reason to **keep** any Body **off**, (*JPY* 123) / they ought either never to **put** their Pocket-books **up** at all, (*CJ* 45), etc.

[with a prepositional phrase]
God wonderfully **sent** the Ship **in** near enough <u>to</u> the Shore, (*RC* 66) / [we] **brought** 80 Prisoners **back** <u>to</u> *Worcester*. (*MC* 240) / the King **draws** his Forces **down** <u>into</u> the North, (*MC* 135) / till they almost **pull'd** the Cloths **off** <u>of</u> his Back, (*CJ* 28) / wherefore I **sent** the Sloop **away** <u>under</u> *Spanish* Colours, (*CJ* 283) / I had a great high shapeless Cap, ... to **shoot** the Rain **off** <u>from</u> running into my Neck; (*RC* 149) / Some of the Servants ... had much ado to **keep** their Hands **off** <u>of</u> me, (*MF* 242) / she agreeing never to **return** the Child **back** <u>to</u> me, (*MF* 177) / Prithee *says he*, don't go to **sham** your Stories **off** <u>upon</u> me, (*MF* 47) / the Fellow awaked, and struggled a little to **get** his Head **out** <u>from</u> among the dead Bodies, (*JPY* 91), etc.

In fact, in the employment of the *-ing* adverbial construction Defoe makes heavy use of the VOP pattern. When the object in the VOP pattern is a non-personal pronoun, it is often a two-word phrase consisting of determiner plus noun (as in the above instance):

and then **putting** the Fire **out**, I preserv'd the Coal to carry Home; (*RC* 177) / and so **putting** the Powder **in**, I stow'd it in Places as secure and remote from one another as possible. (*RC* 73) / Having **knock'd** this Fellow **down**, the other who pursu'd with him stopp'd, (*RC* 203) / having **taken** the Ladder **out**, I

climb'd up to the Top of the Hill, (*RC* 249) / and having **taken** the Substance **out**, I did not think the Lumber of it worth my concern; (*MF* 266), etc.
[with a prepositional phrase]
setting more Posts **up** with Boards, in about a Week more I had the Roof secur'd; (*RC* 75) / ... and **taking** the Bundle **up** into my Chamber, I began to examine it: (*MF* 206), etc.

[three words]
the Stream **took** the other Soldier **away**, (*MC* 89) / I had scarse **shut** the Coach Doors **up**, (*MF* 257) / so they **help'd** the poor Fellow **down**, (*JPY* 91) / I **had** my own Diamond-Necklace **on**, (*Rox* 247) / He had **read** his two Books **over** so often, (*CS* 242) / [as *to*-infinitive] Mrs.— desires the favour of her to **take** the two Children **in**; (*MF* 206) / All the Instructions I pretended to give *William*, was, if possible, to **get** the old *Dutchman* **away**, (*CS* 231) / [as participial construction] The Prince, ... kept at a Distance from the Enemy, and **fetching** a great Compass **about**, brings all safe into the City, and enters into *York* himself with all his Army. (*MC* 199), etc.
[with a prepositional phrase]
I **drew** my little Troop **in** among those Trees, (*RC* 300) / [he] **drove** Sir *Richard Greenvil* **up** into *Cornwall*, (*MC* 220), etc.

The following passages contain the personal pronouns *them* or *it*, but owing to the attachment of *some of* and *any of* to them, these four instances belong to the "non-personal" type:

I was forced to **pull** some of them [= stakes] **up** again. (*RC* 153) / the Weather was so hot, that we could not promise our selves to **salt** any of it [= "some good Beef"] **up** to keep; (*CS* 171) / so that the County was very uneasy, and had been oblig'd to **take** some of them **up**. (*JPY* 148) / he had gone so far as to seize my Goods, and to **carry** some of them **off** too. (*Rox* 25)

In the following passages, the object consists of four or more words:

[four words]

I **had** my formidable Goat-Skin Coat **on**, (*RC* 253) / In the Year Sixty Five, Which **swept** an Hundred Thousand Souls **Away**; (*JPY* 248) / The other Generals, ... drew off by Degrees, **sending** their Cannon and Baggage **away** first, (*MC* 92) / he takes it for an Affront, and **sets** all his other Business **aside** to pursue his Revenge; (*RC* 293)

[with a prepositional phrase]

[I] **brought** three great Fir Planks **off** from the Decks, (*RC* 84) / I **rais'd** a kind of Wall **up** against it of Turfs, (*RC* 67) / we **hauled** our Main-Sail and Fore-Sail **up** in the Brails, (*CS* 146) / if he would **carry** me and Captain *Jack* **back** to *England*, (*CJ* 117) / if he would have **carryed** me, and my Brother **back** again to *England*, (*CJ* 124) / We wish'd now we had **brought** some Bows and Arrows **out** with us, (*CS* 70) / [as *to*-infinitive] he thought to **take** her and her Kinswoman **along** with him this Voyage, (*Rox* 275)

[five words]

I **held** this wicked Scene of Life **out** eight Years, (*Rox* 188) / tho' she **had** little more than her Shift [= 'a woman's 'smock' or chemise' (*OED* s.v. shift, *n.* 10a)] **on**, (*JPY* 165) / Being thus prevailed upon by our own Reason to **set** the Thoughts of that Voyage **aside**, (*CS* 29) / I found myself so refresh'd with **having** a Pair of warm Stockings **on**, (*CJ* 15)

[with a prepositional phrase]

I had **shook** a Bag of Chickens Meat **out** in that Place, (*RC* 78)

Chapter 2 The Syntactic Structure of Transitive Phrasal Verbs

/ yet he ought to think I did not **bring** a great deal of Money **out** with me; (*MF* 336) / I fix'd my Umbrella also in a Step at the Stern, like a Mast, to ... **keep** the Heat of the Sun **off** of me like an Auning; (*RC* 137) / he must **draw** the Stench of the Plague **up** into his own Brain, in order to distinguish the Smell! (*JPY* 203)

[six words]
we should certainly have **taken** the Skin of this monstrous Creature **off**, (*RC* 297) / the King was perswaded to make one Step farther; and that, I confess, was unpleasing to us all; and ... that was **bringing** some Regiments of the *Irish* themselves **over**. (*MC* 192)
[with a prepositional phrase]
I **piled** all the empty Chests and Casks **up** in a Circle round the Tent, (*RC* 55) / the Mizen Top-sail Braces ... **brought** the Mizen Topsail, Yard and all, **down** with it, (*CS* 155) / [he] had attempted to **knock** one of the white Servants Brains **out** with a Hand-spike; (*CJ* 130) / [I resolv'd to] **send** the old Savage and this *Spaniard* **over** to them to treat: (*RC* 245)

[seven words]
[as a gerund] *Friday* was for **burning** the Hollow or Cavity of this Tree **out** to make it for a Boat. (*RC* 227)
[with a prepositional phrase] he filled them all with Gun-Powder, stopping strong Plugs bolted cross-ways into the Holes, and then **boring** a slanting Hole of a less Size **down** into the greater Hole, (*CS* 212)

[eight words]
[with a prepositional phrase] they had **thrown** all the small Arms, Powder, Shot, Swords, &c. **in** to the Sea, (*CS* 158)

153

[nine words]

[with a prepositional phrase] I began to work my Way into the Rock, and **bringing** all the Earth and Stones that I dug down **out** thro' my Tent, I laid 'em up within my Fence in the Nature of a Terras, (*RC* 60)

[ten words]

[the Gentleman] **took** the Cloth, and the Remains of what was to Eat, **away**; (*Rox* 63)

As the relatively long objects consisting of the six to nine words show, the VOP pattern tends to be followed by a prepositional phrase. Especially, the use of the nine-word noun phrase as the object of *bring out* is of great interest, in that the object contains another phrasal verb in the relative clause (i.e. *that I dug down*). As for the ten-word noun phrase, Defoe's aim and intention in employing such a long (i.e. the longest) phrase as the object of *take away* will be examined in the final section of this chapter (2.10).

2.2.4 The Division of Object by the Particle: As Special Cases of the VOP Pattern

In his employment of the VOP pattern, Defoe several times divides noun phrases as an object into two parts and puts them before and after the particle, as in *they ... began to fasten the Hatches to* **keep** *them* **down** *who were below*, (*RC* 271). The pronoun *them* is an antecedent of the relative clause *who were below*; consequently, *them who were below* as a cohesive unit is divided by the particle *down*. Such special cases are all collected here in this section.

There is a very similar case, in which *every Thing that could be hung up* as a cohesive unit is sepatated:

Chapter 2 The Syntactic Structure of Transitive Phrasal Verbs

> I plac'd Shelves, and knock'd up Nails on the Posts to **hang** every Thing **up** that could be hung up, (*RC* 75)

Next comes the case in which a noun phrase including a reflexive pronoun, *my self and my Family*, is divided into two parts by the particle *up*:

> Dr. Heath ... earnestly perswaded me to **lock** my self **up** and my Family, (*JPY* 77) / I took my Friend and Physician's Advice, and **lock'd** my self **up**, and my Family, (*JPY* 80).

In the following passages, the object of the phrasal verb, which consists of three noun phrases "A, B and C" (e.g. *a Hat, a Shirt, and a Neckcloth*) is divided into "A" and "B and C":

> my Leader **had** a Hat **on**, a Shirt, and a Neckcloth; (*CJ* 19) / Then we unrigged our Top-masts, and cut them down, **hoisted** all our Guns **out**, our Provisions and Loading, and put them ashore in the Tents. (*CS* 193)

This syntax might suggest a desire to emphasize part of the object over the others: namely, the hat is noticed first, over the shirt and neckcloth, and the guns are more emphasized than the provisions and loading. It could also be a matter of chronology, with the first item coming before the others which then occur together, as in A then B and C.

In the following passages, noun phrases, such as *a little Necklace*, occur between the verb and the particle, but the object in this context virtually includes the additional words after *on*; "a little Necklace of Gold Beads" and "no other Cloaths but a Shirt" can be considered as a

155

cohesive unit:

> the Child **had** a little Necklace **on** of Gold Beads, (*MF* 194) / many times I could **bear** no other Cloaths **on** but a Shirt; (*RC* 134) / he **had** not a Rag of Cloaths **on**, but his Gown and Slippers, and Shirt; (*Rox* 143)

Defoe could have written, for example, *the Child **had** a little Necklace of Gold Beads **on***. Nevertheless, his choice of such a two-part divison by the particle suggests that Defoe perhaps wants to put emphasis on the noun phrases at the end, namely, *Gold Beads* and *a Shirt*.

2.3 The Fronting of the Particle: the Pattern "Particle (+ Subject) + Verb + Object" (PVO)

Particle fronting is a remarkable phenomenon in Defoe when he uses intransitive phrasal verbs (e.g. ***away** he **went*** ... (*CJ* 110)). However, in the employment of transitive phrasal verbs, only two instances are observable in *Moll Flanders*; interestingly, the two instances appear in the same page:

> to put you out of doubt of that, says my Gentleman, read this Paper, and **out** he **pulls** the License; (*MF* 183) / well, *said I*, do as you please; so **up** they **brings** the Parson, and a merry good sort of Gentleman he was; (*MF* 183)

In comparison with an intransitive phrasal verb, as for the usage of a transitive one, it seems to be far more difficult for the particle to

Chapter 2 The Syntactic Structure of Transitive Phrasal Verbs

be moved to the front position, mainly because of the attachment of the object and its heaviness. In this sense, the PVO pattern might be considered a variant of the VOP pattern rather than the VPO pattern, for it seems that *out* is easier to move as in the case of *he pulls the License **out***, as opposed to the case of *he pulls **out** the License*.

NOTES:
This pattern seems to be generally rare, in that *The Pilgrim's Progress*, Behn's fiction and *Pamela* have one instance each:

> [*PP*] So soon as the man overtook me, he was but a word and a blow, for **down** he **knocked** me, and laid me for dead. (70) / [Behn] but **out** he **led** Miss Majesty ere the third Act was half done; (135) / [*Pamela*] (Lady *Davers* says to Pamela) Come, my little Dear, pull off thy Gloves, I say; and **off** she **pull'd** my Left Glove herself, and spy'd my Ring. (387)

The above three instances by three authors other than Defoe are used in the past tense, while Defoe's are in the (dramatic) present tense. Moreover, in Defoe's second instance, a grammatical error (*they brings*) can be pointed out. Nevertheless, such an error no doubt leads to a unique feature of the language of *Moll Flanders* and, in consequence, Defoe's fiction.

2.4 The Pattern "Object (+ Subject *or To*) + Verb + Particle" (OVP)

Defoe sometimes puts the object before the verb and the particle, as in the three syntactic positions:

(i) in the main clause
(ii) in the subordinate relative clause
(iii) in the *to*-infinitive construction

2.4.1 The OVP in the Main Clause (e.g. <u>These two whole Days</u> *I* **took up** in grinding my Tools (*RC* 83))

This section presents the cases where the object precedes the subject and the verb plus particle in the main clause, as can be seen in the above instance.

The following are similar cases, in which a determiner (e.g. *the*, *this*, or *these*) is attached to the noun phrases:

> <u>The eldest</u> [of "my two Nephews"] having something of his own, I **bred up** as a Gentleman, (*RC* 305) / we had made both Mast and Sail for our two large Periagua's, and <u>the other</u> we **paddl'd along** as well as we could; (*CS* 31) [cf. *OED* s.v. periagua, 1. "A long narrow canoe hollowed from the trunk of a single tree"] / <u>these two Poles</u> they **set up** afterwards sticking them up in the Ground; (*CS* 38) / <u>This Plantation</u>, tho' remote from him, he said he did not **let out**; (*MF* 336) / <u>The last</u> I **begg'd off**, upon Condition of paying 300 Pieces of Eight for their Ransom, (*CJ* 280) / <u>This horrid Project</u> he **carried up** so high, (*CJ* 225), etc.

Interestingly, in the OVP pattern, the demonstrative pronouns *this* or *these* occur alone as the object of a phrasal verb, as in:

> <u>this</u> [= "a great Vessel made of Earth"] they **set down** for me, (*RC* 31) / <u>these</u> [= some of the smaller twigs] I **set up** to dry within my Circle or Hedge, (*RC* 107) / <u>all this</u> I had **found out** by enquiring the Night before into the several ways of

Chapter 2 The Syntactic Structure of Transitive Phrasal Verbs

going to *London*. (*MF* 265) / this she **carried on** with so much Government of her self, (*CJ* 190) / BUT this he **manag'd Away** by himself, (*CJ* 150)

A very long noun phrase with a relative clause (nine words) is found, as in:

all the Provisions which were in the *French* Ship he **took out** also. (*CS* 167)

2.4.2 The OVP in the Subordinate Relative Clause (e.g. *The Trees that I cut down, were lying to rot on the Ground.* (*RC* 129))
Another important aspect to be noted is the pattern "Object as a relative pronoun (+ S) + V + P," as in the above instance. Defoe makes frequent use of this pattern. The relative pronoun *that* is in a "restrictive" relative clause which "give[s] essential information in order to identify what / who [the narrator is] talking about" (Leech et al. 2001: 452), i.e. *the Trees* in this context.[10]

Other instances of the same type are:

this is the poor Man, says he, *that* you **knocked down** *with your Fork Yesterday*, (*MC* 212) / ... the most prosperous of our Circumstances in the wicked Trade that we had been both **carrying on**. (*MF* 332) / However he took out the 15 Guineas that he had **put in** at first, (*MF* 261) / this was the most uneasie Disguise to me that ever I **put on**. (*MF* 253) / It happen'd to be a Chance Coach that I had **taken up**, (*MF* 179) / for a good while I left off the wicked Trade that I had so newly **taken up**; (*MF* 198) / a Whore that he had **pick'd up**, (*CJ* 64) / in ten Year I shou'd double the 1000 *l. per Annum*, that I **laid by**; (*Rox* 167)

In restrictive relative clauses, *whom* and *which* are used as well:

> ... and so to buy off the *Scots* whom he cou'd not **beat off**. (*MC* 138) / I was most diverted that Day with viewing the Works which *Tilly* had **cast up**, (*MC* 93) / it was only intended to prevent the Flight of the Relations of certain Nobles whom the King had **clapt up**; (*CS* 246) [cf. *OED* s.v. clap, *v.*[1] 13. b. "*to clap up*: to make, settle, or concoct hastily (a match, agreement, etc.); 'to complete suddenly without much precaution' (J.). (Rarely without *up*.) *arch*." 1595~] / the Account which the Weekly Bills **gave in** was sufficient; (*JPY* 215)

The instances cited above all belong to the simple pattern. In the following passages, instances with prepositional phrases comes immediately after the particle:

> the Barrel of Powder which I **took up** out of the Sea, (*RC* 179) / I found three very good Bibles ... which I had **pack'd up** among my things; (*RC* 64) / besides taking about 2000 Musquets which they **brought back** to the Army. (*MC* 102) / then I show'd her the two Parcels of Silk which I told her I had from *Ireland*, and **brought up** to Town with me; (*MF* 198)

What or *whatever* can be also used as an object of phrasal verbs, as in:

> The Garrison had often surprized them by Sallies, and indeed had chiefly subsisted for some time by what they **brought in** on this Manner. (*MC* 233) / *said I*, we cannot restore what we have **taken away** by Rapine and Spoil. (*CS* 266) / Then I let him know what I had **brought over** in the Sloop, (*MF* 339) / we were very willing whatever she shou'd so **lay up**, (*Rox* 252)

160

The relative pronoun *what* sometimes functions as an adjective:

> we set forward for the Gold Coast, to see <u>what Method</u> we could **find out** for our Passage into *Europe*. (*CS* 136) / we wou'd see to Morrow Morning, <u>what Strength</u> we cou'd both **make up** in the World, (*Rox* 250)

In addition, there are cases in which a relative pronoun is omitted, as with *I found the Grapes I had **hung up** were perfectly dry'd* (*RC* 102). Others are:

> nor can I tell to this Day what Wood to call <u>the Tree</u> we **cut down**, (*RC* 227) / first he put on <u>all the carved Work</u> he had **taken off** before; (*CS* 254) / to make up <u>the Damage of the Cargo</u> I **brought away** with me, (*MF* 127) / as they do very young to <u>all the Children</u> they **carry about** with them, (*MF* 9) / they were Partners it seems in <u>the Trade</u> they **carried on**, (*MF* 208) / I was in <u>the good Agreement</u> we had always **kept up**, (*MF* 100) / in spite of <u>the forc'd Smiles</u> they **put on**; (*MF* 65) / <u>all</u> we could **make up** did not amount to above 800 Horse. (*MC* 260) / <u>the Retreat</u> I had **taken up**, wou'd have render'd it a hundred Thousand to one odds that he ever found me at-all; (*Rox* 225), etc.

On the other hand, a relative pronoun can be found in a "non-restrictive" relative clause, which "give[s] extra information, not essential for identifying what [the narrator is] talking about" (Leech et al. 2001: 453). In this clause, *who* or *whom* are used, though *which* is the most-typical pronoun. Cases in which a relative pronoun in the non-restrictive clause serves as an object of phrasal verbs are numerous:

The Parliament call for an Account of their Demands, which the *Scots* **give in**, amounting to a Million; (*MC* 268) / the Boat being on Shore with twelve Men, my self, *William*, the Surgeon, and one Fourth Man, whom we had **singled out**, (*CS* 262) / she [= the ship] had on board some Goods, which we **took in** as we lay about the *Philippine* Islands, (*CS* 254) / In these Parts Mr. *Knox* met his black Boy, whom he had **turned away** divers Years before. (*CS* 244) / by great good Luck I had an old silver Spoon in my Pocket, which I **pull'd out**, (*MF* 270) / ... an Amour, which he had now **carried on** so long; (*Rox* 98), etc.
[with a prepositional phrase]
the Lord *Hopton*, with the Remainder of his Horse, which he had **brought off** at *Torrington* in a very shattered Condition, retreated to *Lanceston*, (*MC* 262) / had we not given them a Month's time, which we **lingered away** at this fatal Town of *Gloucester*: (*MC* 187) [cf. *OED* s.v. linger, *v*. 6. *quasi-trans.* a. "**to linger away**: to waste (time) by lingering." 1550~] / I had about eight thousand Pounds reserv'd in Money, which I **kept back** from him, (*Rox* 260) / My Ink, as I observed, had been gone some time, all but a very little, which I **eek'd out** with Water a little and a little, (*RC* 133) / with three Women Servants, lusty Wenches, which my old Governess had **pick'd up** for me, (*MF* 340), etc.

The following instances can be observed when a phrasal verb follows a perception verb or a causative verb and its object:

she immediately perceiv'd it was the same Dress that she had seen me **have on**, (*Rox* 289) / THESE were the two Boxes of Ribbands, and Lace, which ... I had made my Wife **pack up**, (*CJ* 306)

2.4.3 The OVP in the *To*-Infinitive Construction (e.g. *I have no <u>Cloaths</u> to **put on**,* (*CJ* 126)) The most typical case of transitive phrasal verbs in the *to*-infinitive form is the "Common Noun + *to* + V + P" pattern, as shown in the above instance. This case is superficially similar to instances such as *I had no <u>Plow</u> to **turn up** the Earth,* (*RC* 118), in that both phrasal verbs modify the preceding nouns. From a structural point of view, however, they are completely different; the object of *to put on* is the preceding *Cloaths*, while that of *to turn up* is the subsequent *the Earth*. In this respect, these two types of instances must be strictly distinguished. Other instances similar to *Cloaths to **put on*** are presented below:

> we got <u>above 20 young Kids</u> to **breed up** with the rest; (*RC* 247) / I had <u>the loose Earth</u> to **carry out**; (*RC* 74) / I was loth to lose the Advantage of them [= "my little Herd of Goats"], and to have <u>them all</u> to **nurse up** over again. (*RC* 162) / I had <u>the Seiling</u> to **prop up**, (*RC* 74) / I had no <u>Spies</u> to **send out**. (*RC* 182) / such as Linnen to Make, and Laces to Mend, and <u>Heads</u> to **Dress up**, (*MF* 15) / I found that they had <u>a secret clandestine Trade</u> to **carry on**, (*CJ* 288) / then you had had <u>the Money</u> to **put out**; (*Rox* 169), etc.

Next are those cases where the relative pronouns are the object of *to*-infinitives, such as *my Servant <u>who</u> I had intended to **take down** with me, deceiv'd me;* (*JPY* 10). Others are:

> there was little left in her [= the ship] <u>that</u> I was able to **bring away** if I had had more time. (*RC* 58) / she had been Sued by a certain Gentleman who had had his Daughter stolen from him, and <u>who</u> it seems she had helped to **convey away**; (*MF* 197)

/ I did not foresee that this was my Harvest, in which I was to **gather up**, (*Rox* 75) / But there fell out a great Difficulty here, which I knew not how to **get over**; (*Rox* 326), etc.
[with a prepositional phrase]
there was seven or eight Pound Weight left, which was agreed to leave in his Hands, to work it into such Shapes as we thought fit to **give away** to such People as we might yet meet with, (*CS* 97) / there was a Suit of Cloths at one of our Houses of Rendezvous, which was left there for any of the Gang to **put on** upon particular Occasions, as a Disguise: (*CJ* 75), etc.

As well as in the predicate (e.g. these I **set up** to dry within my Circle or Hedge, (*RC* 107)), the demonstrative pronoun, *these*, as the object of *pick up* comes before not only the *to*-infinitive but also the subject and the predicate *we ordered them*, as in:

these we ordered them to **pick up**, (*CS* 77)

Finally, there are two interesting cases where the subject of the sentence (in which the demonstrative *these* and *those* are included) virtually acts as the object of the *to*-infinitive *bring in* and *put on*, as in:

these things wou'd be too tedious to **bring in** here; (*Rox* 185) / those [= "three Suits of Cloaths"] were for me to **put on**, when I went out of Mourning, (*Rox* 71)

The use of *to tell off* in the following, though lacking a copula, is of the same nature:

we had many pleasant Adventures with the Savages, too long to mention here, and some of them too homely to **tell off**; (*CS* 130)

2.5 The Pattern of "Verb + (Indirect) Object + Particle + (Direct) Object" (VOPO)

This section focuses on the manner by which Defoe employs two objects in the use of transitive phrasal verbs. The basic and most frequently used pattern is the VOPO, as seen in [*he*] ***gave*** *me* **back** *an exact Inventory of them* ... (*RC* 33); here *me* as indirect object is also called "dative." Moreover, the VOOP, VPOO and OVOP patterns can be recognized in Defoe's works as variants of the basic pattern.

2.5.1 The VOPO Pattern (e.g. [*he*] ***gave*** *me* **back** *an exact Inventory of them* ... (*RC* 33))

In terms of the position of the "dative" or indirect object, Jespersen (*MEG* III: 287) makes the interesting statement: "As a rule the indirect object is placed (after the verb) immediately before the direct object, only in rare cases separated from this by a commentary adverb" (my emphasis added); a single instance from Carlyle is given: "he sometimes *gave* *me* *up* his bedroom." In spite of Jespersen's remark, such a case is far from being "rare" in Defoe. As for his instance from *Robinson Crusoe* cited above, Defoe could have written, for example, *he **gave back** an exact Inventory of them **to** **me***. Therefore, Defoe's choice of the dative is of great interest, given the following remark (as already quoted in Section 2.2.2, p.143) by *the same* Jespersen (*MEG* III: 284) that the use of the dative in *I made me a large tent* is "frequent in Defoe."[11] Hence, Defoe is no doubt a *dative*-conscious writer. Such a consciousness seems to emerge in the use of transitive phrasal verbs.

As for the basic pattern "V + (indirect) O + P + (direct) O" as with [*he*] ***gave*** *me* **back** *an exact Inventory of them* (*RC* 33), this could be considered a derivation of the VPO rather than the VOP, in that the direct object (i.e. *an exact Inventory of them*) follows the particle.

The other two instances of *give back* are:

>we **gave** them **back** the Bows and Arrows, (*CS* 69) / My Comrade that **gave** me **back** the Bills, (*CJ* 41)

In the use of this pattern, *bring-* and *send*-phrasal verbs are also seen:

>[*bring*-phrasal verbs]
>he **brought** us **back** about three and thirty thousand Pieces of Eight, and some Diamonds; (*CS* 254) / He ... **brought** me **back** an Answer from her in writing; (*MF* 308) / She **brought** me **back** word, upon this second going, that ... (*Rox* 188) / they **brought** us **up** afterward, a Neats Tongue and a Ham, that was almost cut quite down, (*CJ* 237) / he would go out ten Miles at a time, and **bring** us **in** all the News of the Country; (*MC* 217) / if I would live on it, then it would be worth much more, and he believ'd would **bring** me **in** about 150 *l*. a Year; (*MF* 336) / [as *to*-infinitive] I found it a Difficulty how to dispose of it, so as to **bring** me **in** annual Interest; (*Rox* 164) / my good Steward the Captain had laid out the Five Pounds ... to **bring** me **over** a Servant under Bond for six Years Service, (*RC* 37)

>[*send*-phrasal verbs]
>The Lieutenant **sent** me **back** word the Post was taken by the Enemy, (*MC* 94) / I would **send** him **back** a general Release, (*MF* 125) / he had **sent** me **back** all the Goods that he had seiz'd for Rent, (*Rox* 32) / [I] **sent** him **over** the Value of 2000 *l*. at several times, with which he traded, and grew rich; (*Rox* 262) / I also **sent** him **over** a Wife; a beautiful young Lady, well-bred, an

Chapter 2 The Syntactic Structure of Transitive Phrasal Verbs

exceeding good-natur'd pleasant Creature; (*Rox* 263)

Other instances include *draw out, fetch up, find out, lay down, pay down, pull out*, and *put back*:

> he **drew** me **out** a Table, as he call'd it, of the Encrease, for me to judge by; (*Rox* 167) / [he] bad the maid, I think it was, **fetch** him **up** a Pint of warm Ale; (*JPY* 71) / my Governess **found** me **out** a very creditable sort of a Man to manage it, (*MF* 248) [Note: there are two more instances in *MF* and *Rox*.] / the next Morning he **laid** me **down**, on my Toilet, a Purse with 300 Pistoles: (*Rox* 96) / Then she pull'd out her Money, and **paid** him **down** an hundred and twenty Pounds, (*Rox* 195) / then he **pull'd** me **out** some old Seals, and small Parchment-Rolls, (*Rox* 258) [Note: there are two more instances in *MF* and *Rox*.] / yet it **put** him **back** near three Years in his coming into the World, (*Rox* 203)

The following instance of *cut out* is a variation of a set phrase *cut out work (for)*:

> they had retaken *Newcastle, Tinmouth, Durham, Stockton*, and several Towns of Consequence from the *Scots*, and might have **cut** them **out** Work enough still, (*MC* 219) [cf. *OED* s.v. work, *n*. 30. "to **cut out work** *for* a person: to prepare work to be done by him, to give him something to do"; 1619~]

Instead of the prepositional phrase "*for* a person" as suggested in the *OED*, Defoe chooses to use the dative *them* immediately after the verb *cut*.

The most-repeatedly used phrasal verb in this pattern is *take up*, in the sense of "to occupy the whole of, fill up (space, time, etc.)" (*OED* s.v. take, *v.* 93w), which occurs 19 times in total. Some of the instances are:

> the Attempt which I made in vain, to make a Wheel-Barrow, **took** me **up** no less than four Days, (*RC* 74) [Note: there are other 9 instances in *RC*.] / The Modelling the Parliament Army **took** them **up** all this Winter, (*MC* 239) / which way to do it, or to whom, was an inextricable Difficulty, and **took** me **up** many Months to Resolve; (*MF* 92) / this **took** us **up** about 10 Days, (*CJ* 297) / These Enquiries **took** us **up** three or four Weeks, (*Rox* 190) [Note: there are other 5 instances in *Rox*.], etc.

2.5.2 Additional Patterns: VOOP, VPOO and OVOP

Next, there are a few rare cases, which do not conform to the basic VOPO pattern; thus three additional patterns, VOOP VPOO, and OVOP are here offered by way of analysis.

When the direct object is the personal pronoun *it*, in the use of *give back*, the VOOP pattern occurs twice; this case could be regarded as a derivation of the VOP pattern, in that the direct object occurs before the particle:

> Then I pull'd out his Watch and **gave** it him **back**, (*MF* 155) / as he had remitted to me the Offer of a Thousand Pistoles, which I wou'd have given him for the Recompence of his Charges and Trouble with the *Jew*, and had **given** it me **back**; (*Rox* 160)

In the following use of *pay off*, the direct object *the 20 l.* though not functioning as a personal pronoun:

Chapter 2 The Syntactic Structure of Transitive Phrasal Verbs

I would **pay** him the 20 l. **off** of my Bill for each of us: (*CJ* 117)

Probably because the particle *off* is "closely connected" (*OED* s.v. of, *prep*. 1.c) with the following preposition *of*,[12] the choice of the VOOP pattern might have been necessary.

And on the contrary, when the indirect pronoun is *not* a personal pronoun in the use of *take up*, the VPOO pattern can be observed just three times:

> These Consultations **took up** our People no less than two or three Days, (*CS* 209) / it **took up** Amy almost a Month so entirely, to put off all the Appearances of Housekeeping, (*Rox* 211)

Finally, when *take up* occurs in the (restrictive) relative clause in the following passage, this case of the OVOP pattern could be considered a derivation of the OVP pattern (as observed in the previous section):

> for the prodigious deal of Time and Labour which it **took** me **up** to make a Plank or Board: (*RC* 67)

2.6 Passive Construction

Defoe often uses phrasal verbs in the passive voice. This section mainly looks into cases where the passive voice is used in the finite form like *his Cloths were **pulled off**,* (*JPY* 72). As well, discussed here are the three additional forms: (1) the *to*-infinitive form like *she had heard I was to be **Turn'd out**,* (*MF* 33), (2) the participial constructions like *the Ship being*

169

fitted out, ... *I went on Board in an evil Hour*, (*RC* 40), and (3) the past participial form (without *be*-verbs) after perception verbs or causative verbs, as in *we found the Fire all **put out** by a great Quantity of Water thrown upon it.* (*CS* 211), and *I had my Leg **wrap'd up** in a great piece of Flannel*, (*CJ* 270). Furthermore, the adjectival use in passive voice, as in *a meer **cast off** Whore*, (*MF* 56), will be discussed here. However, the gerund form like *upon the general Belief of my being **cast away***, (*RC* 280) is discussed separately (in Section 2.7).

The passive instances are generally divided into two types: instances with and without *be*-verbs. Cases with *be*-verbs are first presented.

2.6.1 With *Be*-Verbs

i) The Passive with *By*-phrase (e.g. *I was **knock'd down** by a Gyant like a German Soldier*, (*CJ* 219))

The most typical case of the passive construction is "S + *be* + PP [i.e. past participle of verb] + Particle + by + Noun Phrase" (as with the above instance). A noun phrase following *by* is an agent which corresponds to the subject of an active clause.

Other instances of this pattern are:

> I was **lifted up** by the Waves, (*RC* 45) / we were **driven back** again by a violent Storm ... (*CS* 10) / (she says) Are you sure, you was **Nurs'd up** by your own Mother? (*MF* 174) / the Major, a good Condition'd easy Boy, was **wheedled a way**, by a couple of young Rogues ... (*CJ* 13) [cf. *OED* s.v. wheedle, *v.* 1. *trans*. "To entice or persuade by soft flattering words; to gain over or take in by coaxing or cajolery." and 1. b. "with various preps. and advs., or with inf.: To bring into a specified condition by such action."; The *OED* cites this passage as the form ***wheedled away*** in the 1840

Chapter 2 The Syntactic Structure of Transitive Phrasal Verbs

edition.] / those that attacked him were **cut down** by his Men, (*MC* 117) / the *Spaniards* were **knocked down** by the *Scots* ... (*MC* 80) / some of our Men ... were often **picked up** by the Enemy; (*MC* 255) / the whole Families, ... were **carry'd off** by the Distemper: (*JPY* 120) [cf. *OED* s.v. carry, *v.* 51. **carry off**. a. *trans.* "To remove from this life, be the death of." *c* 1680~], etc.

Similar cases occur in relative clauses, in which the relative pronoun serves as the subject:

the City of *Mantua*, which was **block'd up** by the Imperialists. (*CJ* 216) / the Repentance which is **brought about** by the meer Apprehensions of Death, wears off ... (*Rox* 128)

In the passive use of *to*-infinitives of phrasal verbs with *by*:

Sir *Philip Stapylton*, ... was once in a fair way to have been **cut off** by a Brigade of our Foot, (*MC* 160) / [he] ask'd me how I could entertain such a Thought without horror as that of leaving my two Children (for one was dead) without a Mother, and to be **brought up** by Strangers, (*MF* 91), etc.

In the participial construction:

being **taken up** by some of the Parish Officers of Colchester, I gave an Account that I came into the Town with the Gypsies, (*MF* 9) / I fancy'd, they [= the ship's people] were all gone off to Sea in their Boat, and being **hurry'd away** by the Current ... (*RC* 187), etc.

In the following two passages, the preposition *by* does not introduce an agent, but rather functions as part of an idiomatic adverbial phrase:

> the Trees were **torn up** by the Roots, (*RC* 81) / the Duke of *Brandenburgh* was **brought in** afterward almost by Force. (*MC* 48)

The pattern "*be* + PP + Particle + *by* + NP" is sometimes followed by a preposition indicative of direction, e.g. *to*, plus noun phrase:

> when I was **brought back** by the Mob to the Mercer's Shop, (*MF* 241) / I was **hurried on** by an inevitable and unseen Fate to this Day of Misery, (*MF* 274), etc.

In the following passage, between the phrasal verb and the *by*-phrase, the subject complement (i.e. *Apprentice* and *Prisoner*) occurs:

> he was **put out** Apprentice, by the Kindness and Charity of his Uncle, (*Rox* 190) / the King was **carried away** Prisoner from *Newark*, by the Scots, (*MC* 274)

The complement of the subject is also shown in the prepositional phrase *as a Prisoner*, as in:

> he was **taken away** ... as a Prisoner, by a Pyrate Ship; (*CS* 143)

The following is the case of an exclamatory sentence in which the fronting of the *by*-phrase causes the inversion of *be* and subject:

Chapter 2 The Syntactic Structure of Transitive Phrasal Verbs

> by what secret differing Springs are the Affections **hurry'd about** as differing Circumstance present! (*RC* 156)

ii) "Agentless Passive"[13] (e.g. *the Masque was **thrown off**,* (*MC* 270))
As seen in the above instance, there are the cases where no word follows a phrasal verb in passive voice. Some instances are:

> when the two Ladders were **taken down**, (*RC* 162) / his Cloths were **pulled off**, (*JPY* 72) / by that time the Punch was **drunk out**, (*CJ* 110) / Some Houses were indeed, entirely **lock'd up**, (*JPY* 72) / When all the Dress was **put on**, I loaded it with Jewels, (*Rox* 247) / my Measure was not yet **fill'd up**. (*MF* 204) / till at length his Stratagem was **found out**, (*JPY* 169) / the Disease was, as I may say, only **frozen up**, (*JPY* 204) / the Infection was **handed on**, (*JPY* 207) / [Crusoe's reason says] Why were you **singled out**? (*RC* 63) / three of them [= the prisoners] were **eaten up**, (*RC* 207) / especially poor Maid Servants were **turn'd off**, (*JPY* 96) / this Hope of mine was soon **taken away**; (*RC* 19) / the Impression was not quite **blown off**, as soon as the Storm; (*Rox* 128), etc.

Such an agentless passive is also used in a relative clause:

> I had the biggest Maggazin of all Kinds now that ever were **laid up**, (*RC* 55) / all the Bodies that were **thrown in**, were immediately covered with Earth, (*JPY* 60) / he let him have an old Top-gallant Sail that was **worn out**, (*JPY* 127) / I told her, there was many a Ship in a Storm, that was not **cast-away**; (*Rox* 124) / I got Notice of two young Women who were newly **set up**, (*MF* 208), etc.

173

As well, in the *to*-infinitive form:

> It was to be a large Tree, which was to be **cut down**, (*RC* 115) / I expected every Day to be **swallowed up**, (*RC* 41) / the King ordered the Regiment to be **drawn out**, (*MC* 75) / tho' she lay then a League to Sea, and made such pitiful Moan to be **taken in**, (*CS* 15) / I expect to be **call'd down** next Sessions; (*MF* 275) / she was not fit to be **turn'd out**, (*MF* 44) / because it was rumour'd that an order of the Government was to be **issued out**, (*JPY* 8) / *said I*, and whether am I to be **sent away**. (*CJ* 126) / But she was not to be **put off** so: (*Rox* 303), etc.

In the participial construction:

> I perceived one of them immediately fell, being **knock'd down**, I suppose with a Club or Wooden Sword, (*RC* 201) / how many [earthen vessels] crack'd by the over violent Heat of the Sun, being **set out** too hastily; (*RC* 120) / but being **commanded away**, I had no Time, (*MC* 97), etc.

iii) The Passive with Prepositional Phrases (e.g. *all the In-side of the Ship was **choack'd up** with Sand*: (*RC* 84))

The prepositional phrase often comes immediately after the phrasal verb, as in the above instance. This strongly suggests that the particle in phrasal verbs is likely to co-occur with the preposition in the passive use as well. According to the types of preposition, passive instances can be grouped:

[*with*-phrases]
The Sea was all on a Sudden **cover'd over** with Foam and Froth, (*RC* 81) / before the Street is **block'd up** with the Crowd; (*MF* 204) / their Heads and Breasts were **dress'd up** with Flowers, (*Rox* 179) / for he was so **swallow'd up** with Joy, he could not speak. (*CS* 259) [cf. *OED* s.v. swallow, *v*. 10. d. "To occupy entirely, engross," 1581~] / those Lances [= "horse-soldiers armed with a lance" (*OED*, 4.a.)], ... were **mowed down** with their Shot, (*MC* 201) [cf. *OED* s.v. mow, *v*.[1] 1. c. *transf.* and *fig.* "To cut (*off, down*, etc.) with a sweeping stroke like that of a scythe; to destroy or kill indiscriminately or in great numbers." *c* 1430~], etc.

The following is the case where the (*even*) *to*-phrase indicating emphasis is inserted before the *with*-phrase:

their Ware-houses, in a few Months, were **piled up**, even to the Ceiling, with Chests of Pieces of Eight, and with Bars of Silver. (*CJ* 302)

Additional prepositional phrases are:

[*from*] by which great Quantities of Corn were **brought in** from *Yorkshire* and *Lincolnshire*: (*JPY* 218) / the Ground is **palisadoed off** from the rest of the Passage, (*JPY* 232) / [*to*] when his Sword was **put on** to him, (*MF* 60) / he was **carried off** to *Ingolstat*, (*MC* 91) / the poor Boy was **deliver'd up** to the Rage of the Street, (*MF* 212) / [*into*] he was **forced up** into the farthest Corner of *Cornwall*. (*MC* 259) / our two *Irish* Regiments were **drawn out** into the Field, (*CJ* 215) / [*on*] the Fort was effectually **block'd up** on the Land-side; (*MC* 77) / [*in*] the Knowledge of God, ... is so

plainly **laid down** in the Word of God; (*RC* 221) [cf. *OED* s.v. lay, *v.*¹ 51. h. "To establish, formulate definitely (a principle, rule);" 1493~] / one of them was, they said, **dress'd up** in Widow's Weeds, (*MF* 241) / [*for*] I was now **set up** for a *Guiney* Trader; (RC18) / as I had been long ago **given over** for dead, (*RC* 279) / I was **cry'd up** for a vast Fortune, (*Rox* 169) [cf. *OED* s.v. cry, *v*. 22. *trans.* "To proclaim (a thing) to be excellent; to endeavour to exalt in public estimation by proclamation or by loud praise; to extol." 1593~] / [other prepositions including *of*, *upon* and *under*] the Trouble was all **taken off** of their Hands. (*Rox* 153) / The Fore Yard was **lower'd down** upon the Forecastle, (*CS* 155) / The three poor distressed Men ... were however **set down** under the Shelter of a great Tree, (*RC* 254), etc.

In a relative clause as well as in a main clause, prepositional phrases follow the agentless passive, as in *he had two Sons and a Daughter which were **brought up** at Nimeugen in Holland*, (*Rox* 229). The elements of a prepositional phrase, namely the preposition and its object, are sometimes separated, as follows:

I look'd on it as a kind of Trade, that I was to be **bred up** to, (*CJ* 19) / it was the Business I might be said to be **brought up** to, (*CJ* 60)

Finally, in the case where a phrasal verb follows a causative verb and its object:

there the Constable resisted him again, and would not let them be **brought in**. (*JPY* 152) / there's the twenty Pound, *added she*, and pray let him be **fetch'd away**. (*Rox* 192) / so I **made** the House be, as it were, **shut up**; (*Rox* 67) / he said, what would you have me be **found out** and sent to *Bridewell*, (*CJ* 30)

2.6.2 The Passive Progressive (e.g. *his Children were breeding up*, (*Rox* 248))
In Defoe's use of phrasal verbs, the progressive form in the passive voice is included. However, the standard form in contemporary English, as seen in *we are being followed*, had not yet been established.[14] As far as the use of phrasal verbs is concerned, there are only three cases of the passive progressive among Defoe's seven works:

> The Bishop's Treasure, and other publick Monies not plundered by the Soldiers, was **telling out** by the Officers, (*MC* 73) / ... his Native Country, where his Children were **breeding up**, (*Rox* 248) / It was not above three Years that all the Ready-Money was thus **spending off**; (*Rox* 11)[15]

In the passages above, the highlighted subjects virtually play the role of the object, rather than an agent, of each of the phrasal verbs. The first instance, for example, implies an alternative expression in the active voice, such as *the Officers were telling out the Bishop's Treasure . . .*

2.6.3 Without *Be*-Verbs
From this subsection on, the passive instances without *be* are dealt with.

i) Ellipsis (e.g. *the Fire Engines were broken, the Buckets thrown away*; (*JPY* 35))
First, cases of an ellipsis of *be* shall be considered. As in the above

instance, when used in the preceding passage (i.e. *were broken*), *be* can be omitted. This pattern can help avoid redundancy in the text. Other instances are:

> the Gentlemen <u>are</u> in great Hurries, their Heads and Thoughts entirely **taken up**, (*CJ* 45) / he fought like a Lion, but <u>was</u> slain, and most of his Regiment **cut off**, (*MC* 62) / Papers <u>were</u> taken out, and others **put in**; (*CJ* 45) / his Master order'd him to <u>be</u> shut out, and the Doors **lock'd up**, (*CJ* 65), etc.

Although *be* is not used in the passage involved, the context sometimes suggests the omission of *be* due to the use of phrasal verbs:

> with that he shew'd me several Cabbins built up, some in the Great Cabbin, and some **partition'd off**, (*MF* 315) [Note: the *OED*'s first citation of *partition off* is from 1741.] / I wanted a Basket or a Wheel-barrow, ... having no such things as Twigs that would bend to make Wicker Ware, at least none yet **found out**; (*RC* 73), etc.

ii) *With*-Clauses (e.g. *with my Heart as well as my Hands* **lifted up** *to Heaven, ... I cry'd out aloud*, (*RC* 96))

With-clauses contain phrasal verbs in the passive sense, such as the above instance. In this pattern, *be* (or more precisely *being*) is thought to be omitted. Additional instances are:

> [they] turned round three times <u>with their Hands</u> **laid up** upon the Tops of their Heads. (*CS* 117) / <u>with his Hands</u> **lifted up**,

[that Clergyman] repeated that Part of the Liturgy of the Church continually; (*JPY* 103) / I observ'd a Man follow'd me, <u>with one of his Legs</u> **tied up** in a String, (*CJ* 203) / Sometimes I thought I saw her ... <u>with</u> her Head cut, and <u>her Brains</u> **knock'd-out**; (*Rox* 325), etc.

iii) The Use of Complement (e.g. *there stood <u>our Ladder</u> **haul'd up** on the Top of the Tree*, (*CS* 211))

In "passive" phrasal verbs without *be*, their use as a complement of either the subject or object seems most remarkable.

As for the complement of the subject, for example, in *there lay a Gun just by him, **fir'd off**,* (*RC* 300), *a Gun* is the subject in this sentence, and *fired off* serves as a complement of the gun; and it is construed that *a gun was* (or *had been*) *fired off*. Hence, this particular use of phrasal verbs adds specific details to the main clause. Some additional instances are:

<u>The Ship</u>, ... stuck fast, **jaum'd in** between two Rocks; (*RC* 191) [The *OED* cites this passage as its first illustration: (*OED* s.v. jam, $v.^1$ 1. *trans.* "To press or squeeze (an object) tightly between two converging bodies or surfaces;")] [cf. *OED* s.v. stick, $v.^1$ 11. *intr.* "To be set fast or entangled in sand, clay, mud, mire, and the like; similarly of a boat, to become fixed or grounded on sand, a rock, etc.; more explicitly *to stick fast*."] / I stood **drawn up** without the City with 800 [soldiers] more, (*MC* 223) / I became sincerely **given in** to the Interest of King *George*; (*CJ* 276) / I seemed so absolutely **given up** to what he had proposed, (*MC* 9), etc.

With the complement of the object, as in *I pull'd <u>a Paper</u> out of* *my Bosom,* **folded up***, but not seal'd, (Rox* 78)*, a Paper* is the object, and *folded up* can be regarded as the complement (of the object). This phrasal verb (as well as *but not seal'd*) contributes to a more-detailed description of the scene. Additional instances are given:

> Gentlemen, *said he,* here is the Book, and so pull'd it out **wrapt up** in a Dirty peice of a Colour'd Handkerchief, (*CJ* 53) / I kept the Hedge which circled it in, constantly **fitted up** to its usual Height, (*RC* 152) / they saw a Man go to and again, **mufled up** in a brown Cloak, (*JPY* 61) / as the Prince had held *Mantua* closely **block'd up** all the Winter, (*CJ* 216), etc.

iv) The Participial Construction (e.g. *These Fellows looked, when* **drawn out***, like a Regiment of Merry Andrews ready for Bartholomew Fair.* (*MC* 133))

Instances in this pattern, where *being* is omitted, are as follows:

> I was alone, circumscrib'd by the boundless Ocean, **cut off** from Mankind, (*RC* 156) / their whole Army appeared with them, making together an Army of 24000 Men, **drawn up** in View of our Forces, (*MC* 173) / she came into the Room I was in, **cloath'd** all **over** with my Things, (*CJ* 257) / for they were all open'd, taken out of the Bales, and separated, and being mix'd with other *European* Goods, which came by the Galeons, where **made up** in new Package, (*CJ* 300) / There was it seems, a Ship Bound Home to *France* from *Martinico*, **taken off** of Cape *Finisterre* by an *Englishman* of War, (*CJ* 182), etc.

v) Following a Perception Verb (e.g. *I saw the House* **shut up**; (*Rox* 89))

Instances in this pattern are presented according to usage.

Chapter 2 The Syntactic Structure of Transitive Phrasal Verbs

First, there are a few cases with the preposition *by* indicative of agent:

> we <u>found</u> the Fire all **put out** <u>by</u> a great Quantity of Water thrown upon it. (*CS* 211) / tho' I have <u>seen</u> many Armies **drawn up** <u>by</u> some of the greatest Captains of the Age; (*MC* 54)

In the cases of agentless passive:

> when he <u>saw</u> five Men upon him, and his Comrade **knock'd down**; (*RC* 265) / [I] Walking one Morning before the Gate of the *Louvre*, with a Design to <u>see</u> the *Swiss* **Drawn up**, (*MC* 16) / I resolv'd to go in the Night and <u>see</u> some of them **thrown in**. (*JPY* 61) / [he] said he would only <u>see</u> the Bodies **thrown in**, and go away, (*JPY* 62) / his Business was to <u>see</u> the Tobacco **pack'd up**, and deliver it either on Board the Sloops, or otherwise, (*CJ* 130)

[with a prepositional phrase]

> [I have <u>seen</u>] the People **driven away** <u>from</u> their Dwellings, like Herds of Cattle; (*MC* 168) / [I] had the Satisfaction, or the Terror indeed of looking out of the Window upon the Noise they made, and <u>seeing</u> the poor Creature **drag'd away** in Triumph <u>to</u> the Justice, (*MF* 221)

vi) Following a Causative Verb (e.g. *I <u>had</u> my Leg **wrap'd up** in a great piece of Flannel*, (CJ 270))

First come the cases with the preposition *by*, which introduces the agent of the action. Interestingly, in the second passage of the following two, the *by*-phrase comes immediately before the phrasal verb in the passive:

181

if possible I might <u>have</u> an Answer **brought back** <u>by</u> the same Hand, (*MF* 308) / I enter'd into some Measures to <u>have</u> my little Son <u>by</u> my last Husband **taken off**; (*MF* 198)

Agentless instances are given below:

I consented to have it be broken open, that is to say, to <u>have</u> the Lock **taken off**, (*MF* 265) / he would have <u>had</u> me **play'd on**, but it grew late, and I desir'd to be excus'd. (*MF* 261) / We <u>had</u> a fair Easterly Wind **sprung up** the third Day after we came to the Downs, (*MF* 319) / The Magistrates had enough to do to bring People to submit to <u>having</u> their Houses **shut up**, (*JPY* 183) / if you have a Mind to <u>have</u> your Money **brought over**, (*CJ* 148) / I doubt not, you should <u>have</u> all your Plantation **carried on**, (*CJ* 146) / he would <u>have</u> the said Writing **Seal'd up**, (*CJ* 52), etc.
[with a prepositional phrase]
Madam, that may take you and your Money together into keeping, and then you would <u>have</u> the trouble **taken off** <u>of</u> your Hands? (*MF* 132) / this Trade grew so open, and so generally practised, that it became common to <u>have</u> Signs and Inscriptions **set up** <u>at</u> Doors; (*JPY* 26) / it was an odd and new Thing at *New-England*, to <u>have</u> such a Quantity of Goods **bought up** there by a Sloop <u>from</u> *Virginia*, (*CJ* 292) / so that I <u>had</u> an extent of Ground **mark'd out** <u>to</u> me, (*CJ* 151), etc.

In the following passages, the object *it* is a formal object, while the actual object refers to the *that*-clause (e.g. *that I was a Fortune*):

I took care to make the World take me for something more than

I was, and <u>had</u> it **given out** that I was a Fortune, (*MF* 127) / I would be wholly within-Doors, and <u>have</u> it **given out**, that I was oblig'd to go to *England*, (*Rox* 67)

2.6.4 Adjectival Use (e.g. *House **shut up*** (from *JPY*) or *a meer **cast off** Whore* (from *MF*))

Transitive phrasal verbs are occasionally used as an adjective or modifier, apart from the adjectival use of the *to*-infinitive. In such a case, as with the two instances cited just above, the verb in the past participle plus a particle modifies the preceding (or following) noun or noun phrase, which is often called "the head-word." But the two-word restriction of "phrasal" verbs (and additional factors) seem to make it difficult for those verbs to premodify the head-word. Such cases where phrasal verbs are used as postmodifiers are first presented:

I liv'd just like <u>a Man</u> **cast away** upon some desolate Island, (*RC* 35) / <u>my Wife's account, or Invoyce</u> **drawn out** by my Tutor, and Manager, amounted to 2684 *l.* 10 *s.* (*CJ* 289)

In the above citations, *cast away* and *drawn out* postmodify *a Man* and *my Wife's account, or Invoyce* as the head-word, respectively. However, these phrasal verbs are closely bound to the subsequent prepositional phrases (i.e. *upon some desolate Island* and *by my Tutor, and Manager*). Hence, the postmodifiers in both passages consist of relatively "long" phrases; it seems difficult to place these verbs before the head-word.

Additional instances of phrasal verbs as a postmodifier are given below:

presently after we saw about a hundred [wolves] coming on

directly towards us, all in a Body, and most of them in a Line, as regularly as <u>an Army</u> **drawn up** by experience'd Officers. (*RC* 298) / how I was <u>a Prisoner</u> **lock'd up** with the Eternal Bars and Bolts of the Ocean, (*RC* 113) / We offered them no Uncivility of any kind, but gave them every one <u>a Bit of Silver</u> **beaten out** thin, (*CS* 116) / For <u>a little Bit of Silver</u> **cut out** in the Shape of a Bird, we had two Cows; (*CS* 28) / none of them ever suspected that I had any more Money in the World, having been known to be only <u>a poor Boy</u> **taken up** in Charity, (*CS* 20) / The Manner of its coming first to *London*, proves this also, (viz.) by <u>Goods</u> **brought over** from *Holland*, (*JPY* 194) / it will be <u>a Store</u> well **laid up** for them, (*Rox* 22) / [they] sat down on a *Safra*, that is to say, almost cross-legg'd on <u>a Couch</u> **made up** of Cushions laid on the Ground. (*Rox* 179), etc.

As for the use of a phrasal verb as a modifier, *shut up* in *A Journal of the Plague Year* is the case in point. *Shut up* in *JPY*, which occurs 123 times in total, is used as a modifier 12 times; all of the uses occur as a postmodifier. In addition, some are found in "solo" use, as in:

three of those Watchmen, were publickly whipt thro' the Streets, for suffering People to go out of <u>Houses</u> **shut up**. (*JPY* 57) / A great variety of these Cases frequently happen'd between the Watchmen and <u>the poor People</u> **shut up**, (*JPY* 157)

On the other hand, there are also some cases where adverbials occur between *shut up* and the head-word, as in:

What variety of Stratagems were used to escape and get out of <u>Houses</u> thus **shut up**, (*JPY* 156) / when they were willing to be remov'd either to a Pest-House, or other Places, and sometimes

Chapter 2 The Syntactic Structure of Transitive Phrasal Verbs

giving the well Persons in <u>the Family</u> so **shut up**, (*JPY* 156) / prudent cautious People ... burnt Perfumes, Incense, Benjamin, Rozin, and Sulphur in <u>the Rooms</u> <u>close</u> **shut up**, (*JPY* 242) / Complaints of the Severity of it, were also daily brought to my Lord Mayor, of <u>Houses</u> <u>causelessly, (and some maliciously)</u> **shut up**: (*JPY* 47)

A comparison of the following two passages reveals an interesting symmetry in the use of modifiers:

[a] But I come back to the Case of <u>Families infected, and</u> **shut up** by the Magistrates; (*JPY* 55)
[b] a Watchman who attended at <u>an infected House</u> **shut up**, promis'd to send a Nurse in the Morning: (*JPY* 119)

Here, the two modifiers, *infected* and *shut up*, are quite different in use. In [a], *infected* postmodifies *Families*, while in [b] it premodifies *Houses*. Yet, *shut up* postmodifies the head-word in both cases; though in [a] *shut up* is closely bound to the subsequent prepositional phrase *by the Magistrates*. Is such a postposition characteristic of phrasal verbs?

Concerning the use of adjectives, postmodification (or predicative use) tends to indicate a "temporary" characteristic, while premodification (or attributive use) presents a "permanent" characteristic (cf. Quirk et al. 1985: 1242; Declerck 1991: 346). Can such a tendency be observed in those cases where *shut up* or other phrasal verbs function as a postmodifer or a premodifier?

Quirk et al. (1985: 1328), giving examples such as "a *muttered* reply" and "a *drawn* sword," state that "The premodifying participle usually characterizes <u>a type rather than an instance</u>" (my emphasis

185

added). Considering the difference in passages [a] and [b]: *Families infected, and* **shut up** vs. *an infected House* **shut up**, in [b], the premodification of *infected*, along with the indefinite article *an*, suggests that the whole expression (i.e. *an infected House shut up*) stands for a "type." On the other hand, in [a] the postmodification of *infected* may turn the whole expression into a literal "instance."

In both cases, the postmodification of *shut up* leads to the supposition that multi-word verbs like phrasal verbs are less likely to premodify, unless the phrase is fully lexicalized (e.g. *shut-up*). In this sense, it seems worthwhile to investigate whether phrasal verbs in Defoe occur as premodifiers.

Only four uses of phrasal verbs as a premodifiers have been found. Of the four occurrences, three are instances of *cast off*, as follows:

> Thus he wrought me up, in short, to a kind of Hesitation in the Matter; having the Dangers on one Side represented in lively Figures, and indeed heightn'd by my Imagination of being turn'd out to the wide World, a meer **cast off** Whore, (*MF* 56) / as I had Money enough, and needed not fear being what they call *a* ***cast-off*** Mistress, (*Rox* 144) / so I came out blown, and look'd like *a* ***cast-off*** Mistress, nor indeed, was I any better; (*Rox* 182) [cf. *OED* s.v. cast-off, A *ppl. a.* "Thrown off, rejected from use, discarded: as clothes, a favourite, a lover, etc." 1746~]

As mentioned, undue emphasis should not be placed on the hyphenation in *Roxana*, because it is owing to "a quirk on the part of a compositor," rather than "Defoe's intention" (Furbank 2009: 293).

Secondly, the *OED* first citation of *cast-off* as an adjective dates from the year 1746. In this regard, the dictionary editors have seemingly overlooked these three instances in Defoe; *Moll Flanders* was first published in 1722, and *Roxana* in 1724. As for "Modern English word-formation," Adams (1973: 125) makes the interesting point that: "*Cast-off, dug-out, grown-up, left-over* ... seem likely have been attributives originally. But according to the *OED* [Note: the year of first-citation as a noun is 1741.], the head noun *cast-off* appeared a little before the attributive, ..." Thus, the doubt (or sense of strangeness) Adams might have had would have been cleared up—if she had been aware of these instances from Defoe.

Furthermore, the parenthetical phrase *what they call* in the second passage (from *Rox*) offers corroborating evidence that the whole phrase, *a cast-off Mistress*, was on people's lips in Defoe's time. Given the above discussion, both *a meer* (i.e. "mere") *cast off Whore* in *MF* and *a cast-off Mistress* in *Rox* may represent what Quirk et al. term a "type," rather than an "instance."

Finally, the remaining instance of a phrasal verb functioning as a premodifier, in this case *turn out* in *JPY*, is examined:

> It is true, some of the dissenting **turn'd out** Ministers staid, and their Courage is to be commended, (p. 236)

Two kinds of participles (i.e. present and past), *dissenting* and *turn'd* (out), premodify *Ministers*. Here, *dissenting* refers to something religious—nonconformist. Given the historical context that, by "dissenting" against the Church of England, "puritan" clergymen had been "dismiss[ed] or eject[ed] from office or employment" (*OED* s.v. turn, *v.* 76e) in the 1660s, the choice of premodification is considered appropriate.[16] This is because *the dissenting turn'd out Ministers* "characterizes a type rather than an instance."

2.7 Gerunds

Transitive phrasal verbs used as the gerund can be classified into two main groups: the group with a determiner (such as *the* or *his*) as in *I consider'd the **keeping up** a Breed of tame Creatures thus at my Hand*, (*RC* 153); and the group lacking determiners, as in *I entertain'd a Thought of **breeding up** some tame Creatures*, (*RC* 75). Concerning determiners, as seen in the first instance cited above, the use of the definite article, *the*, is of great interest.

On the topic of "Object after Gerund without *of*," Jespersen (*MEG* V: 118) states that "The object without *of* after the gerund preceded by the definite article is much more frequent than one would expect, as modern native grammarians are unanimous in condemning it"; he therefore tried to "give comparatively many quotations" in his grammar book. Among them, Jespersen, quoting an instance of "in the managing my household affairs" from *RC*, makes the important point that such uses are "frequent in Defoe" (p. 118). It would be possible to argue that the determiners added to the gerund serve as an index which makes the *-ing* form more nominal than the gerund form without determiners.

Next, instances of the gerund occurring in the patterns VPO, VOP, OVP, and Passive will be examined.

2.7.1 The VPO Pattern

i) The *-ing* Form with a Determiner (e.g. *the one was the **carrying on** my Business and Shop*; (*JPY* 8))

The nominal *-ing* phrase with a determiner is first presented. In the following passages, the gerund phrase acts as a subject or complement of the sentence:

the **delivering up** the King became a Consequence of the Thing unavoidable, and of Necessity. (*MC* 268) / the one was the **carrying on** my Business and Shop; (*JPY* 8)

Sometimes, the gerund phrase is used as the object of certain types of transitive verbs, as in:

I <u>consider'd</u> the **keeping up** a Breed of tame Creatures thus at my Hand, (*RC* 153) / the Earl of *Worcester*, ... <u>proposed</u> the **taking in** the Town of *Gloucester* and *Hereford* first: (*MC* 181) / But the great Number of Families and Houses ... obtain'd the Favour to have their dead be return'd of other Distempers to <u>prevent</u> the **shutting up** their Houses. (*JPY* 205)

Most of these cases occur after the preposition, seen in *as <u>to</u> her serving out her time with me*, (*CJ* 260). Similar cases are:

several Regulations and Conclusions <u>for</u> the **carrying on** the War, (*MC* 112) / the Time <u>of</u> their **shutting up** Houses, (*JPY* 69) / <u>UPON</u> his **calling out** stop the Horse, (*CJ* 93) / I might not be oblig'd to neglect his Business <u>for</u> the **carrying on** my own, (*CJ* 151) / *says I*, all the Pretence I can have <u>for</u> the **making-over** my own Estate to me, is, that ... (*Rox* 259) / All this was acted in the first Years <u>of</u> my **setting-up** my new Figure here in Town, (*Rox* 198) / it happen'd after I had laid my Scheme <u>for</u> the **setting up** my Tent and making the Cave, (*RC* 60), etc.

In the following passage, a noun phrase (i.e. *the Lady*) occurring after *of* is construed as the notional subject of the *-ing* phrase, and therefore as a determiner (i.e. *the Lady's*):

> he talk'd something merrily of <u>the Lady</u> **throwing away** her Maidenhead, ... upon an old Man; (*CJ* 226)

ii) The "VP *of* O" Pattern (e.g. *the **shutting up** of Houses* (*JPY* 167))

As a variant of the gerund form in the VPO pattern, the "VP *of* O" pattern, in which the nominal *-ing* plus particle combination is followed by *of* NP, is focused on here. It has been pointed out that the *-ing* form with *of* NP has more nominal characteristics than the pattern without it (cf. Declerck (1991: 497)). The typical instance in Defoe is *the **shutting up** of Houses* in *A Journal of the Plague Year*, which occurs 13 times; *the* is used 11 times, and *this* twice. In this case, *Houses* can be considered an object of *shutting up*. Some additional instances are given below:

> the **shutting up** of Houses was no way to be depended upon, (*JPY* 167) / But I return to the **shutting up** of Houses. (*JPY* 57) / During the **shutting up** of Houses, ... some Violence was offered to the Watchmen; (*JPY* 69) / This **shutting up** of Houses was a method first taken, (*JPY* 37)

Other than the *shutting up of*, an instance of the same kind is found in the following passage, where two *-ing* forms in the coordination pattern share both the determiner and the *of* phrase:

> upon the <u>building, and</u> **fitting out** of Ships; (*JPY* 95)

iii) The *-ing* Form Lacking Determiners (e.g. *I was immediately for*

selling off my Plantations, (*CJ* 268))
Next, the gerund form without a determiner is examined. In addition to cases with determiners, this case can also serve as either the subject or complement of a sentence. Four instances are given:

> [I] believ'd that **putting off** the Voyage wou'd have put an End to it all; (*Rox* 296) / as to marrying, which was **giving up** my Liberty, (*Rox* 146) / in this Case, **shutting up** the WELL or removing the SICK will not do it, (*JPY* 192) / Our principal Trade was watching Shop-Keepers Compters, and **Slipping off** any kind of Goods we could see carelesly laid any where, (*MF* 215)

This form is also employed as a concrete example of the foregoing (e.g. *three sorts of Craft* or *Absurdities*), as in:

> The Comrade she helped me to dealt in three sorts of Craft, (viz.) Shop-lifting, stealing of Shop-Books and Pocket-Books, and **taking off** Gold Watches from the Ladies Sides, (*MF* 201) / he acts Absurdities even in his View; such as Drinking more, when he is Drunk already; **picking up** a common Woman [= "a harlot" (*OED* s.v. common, 6b)], without regard to what she is, or who she is; (*MF* 226) [cf. *OED* s.v. pick, $v.^1$ 21. e. *spec.* "to form an acquaintance with (a person) casually or informally, esp. with the intention of having a sexual relationship." 1698~]

The most common use of the nominal *-ing* form occurs immediately after the preposition, as seen in *now they talked of* **cutting down** *his Woods*. (*MC* 238). Since there are numerous instances of this type, several are given below:

I was in some Degree settled in my Measures <u>for</u> **carrying on** the Plantation, (*RC* 36) / they advise the King to lay out his Money <u>in</u> **fitting out** the biggest Ships he had, (*MC* 138) / We ... did not much trouble our selves <u>about</u> **laying in** any Stores, (*CS* 218) / I acknowledge, that I was <u>for</u> **Manning out** the Boat, (*CS* 222) / I was upon the Point <u>of</u> **giving up** my Friend at the Bank, (*MF* 176) / I had, as I have said, no thoughts <u>of</u> **laying down** a Trade, (*MF* 269) / I was immediately <u>for</u> **selling off** my Plantations, (*CJ* 268) / *Amy* carried on the Affair <u>of</u> **setting-out** my Son into the World, (*Rox* 198) / he fancy'd I wou'd be <u>for</u> **taking-up** our Abode, (*Rox* 241) / [having + *pp*] now the *Scots* were sent Home, <u>after</u> having **eaten up** two Counties, (*MC* 142) [cf. *OED* s.v. eat, *v.* 18. **eat up**. b. "To devastate, consume all the food in (a country);" 1616~ ; the *OED* cites this passage in this sense.] / We were perfectly secured at *Bassaro*, <u>by</u> having **frighted away** the Rogues, (*CS* 263), etc.

Shutting up occurs twice after the preposition, as in the following:

> this was another of the Inconveniencies of **shutting up** Houses; (*JPY* 73)

It should be noted that after the preposition *shutting up of Houses* occurs four times here:

> this way <u>of</u> **shutting up** of Houses was perfectly insufficient for that End. (*JPY* 167)

In the following passage where *not* is put before the *-ing* form, the reflexive pronoun as the object of a phrasal verb occurs as the VPO

192

pattern:

> No Man of common Sense will value a Woman the less for <u>not</u> **giving up** <u>herself</u> at the first Attack, (*MF* 75)

As a rare case, the *-ing* form of a phrasal verb occurs after certain types of verb (i.e. *stop*):

> I happen'd to <u>stop</u> **turning over** the Book at the 91st *Psalm*, (*JPY* 12)

2.7.2 The VOP Pattern

As in previous sections, instances of the gerund in the VOP pattern are to be discussed on the basis of whether or not the object is a personal pronoun.

i) The *-ing* Form with a Determiner: [O is a *personal pronoun*] (e.g. *an order for <u>the</u> **taking** them **up**,* (*MF* 63))

When the object is a personal pronoun, instances such as the above are found. Similar instances (though there are not many) are cited:

> I will give you Credit for what ever is needful to you for <u>the</u> **carrying** it **on**; (*CJ* 151) / yet I did not design <u>the</u> **carrying** it **on** so far, (*CJ* 191) / He began with a kind of an Extasie upon the Subject of <u>his</u> **finding** me **out**; (*Rox* 225) / but I had a-mind <u>the</u> **putting** it **off** shou'd be at his Motion, not my own; (*Rox* 296)

Two *-ing* phrases (including two phrasal verbs) with the negative determiner *no* act as part of the idiomatic construction *there is no -ing*:

> I found there there was no **laying** them [= wild creatures] **up** on Heaps, and no **carrying** them **away** in a Sack, (*RC* 101)

There is just one instance of the "the + V-*ing* + *of* + O + P" pattern, in *Roxana*:

> [I resolved] to let any of the People that had the **breeding of** them **up**, know that there was such a-body left in the World, (*Rox* 188)

Jespersen (*MEG* V: 109), citing only this passage, states that "The gerund and adverb [i.e. "particle" in this study] may in rare cases be separated by an object" (my emphasis added).

ii) The -*ing* Form Without a Determiner: [O is a *personal pronoun*] (e.g. *I had no Gust to the Thought of **laying** it **down*** (*MF* 208))
Remarkable in this pattern are those cases where the -*ing* form follows the preposition, (as seen in the above instance). Additional instances are:

> [they] would swear to be faithful to him ... in **carrying** her **back** to *Jamaica*, (*RC* 264) / we would give them a full Account of our Business, by **taking** them **along** with us, (*CS* 169) / I went out into the Street to see if I could find any possibility of **carrying** it **off**; (*MF* 264) / you ought not to lose by your Kindness to him, more than the Kindness of **bringing** him **up** obliges you to; (*Rox* 192) / he had shew'd himself very good to me, in **conveying** me **away**, as above: (*Rox* 122) / because it did not secure the Girl from pursuing her Design of **hunting** me **out**; (*Rox* 315) / I went to a little Cabinet, and taking out some Money, which made a

Chapter 2 The Syntactic Structure of Transitive Phrasal Verbs

> little Sound in **taking** it **out**, offer'd to give him five Pistoles. (*Rox* 60), etc.

In the following passage, the combination of the *-ing* phrase (i.e. *bringing it out*) with the preposition *a* after the copula may be regarded as a variant of the progressive form; as *a* is an archaic form equivalent to *on*, rather than an indefinite article:

> He was, as I have said, long a-**bringing** it **out**, (*Rox* 141)

Reflexive pronouns are used as an object in the VOP pattern:

> they talk of **locking** themselves **up**, (*JPY* 122) / my Husband having so dexterously got out of the Bailiff's House by **letting** himself **down** in a most desperate Manner from almost the top of the House, (*MF* 63)

iii) The *-ing* Form with a Determiner [O is a *non-personal pronoun*] (e.g. the People of the Village oppos'd his **driving** the Cart **along**, (*JPY* 152))

In this pattern, noun phrases generally function as an object and are likely to be short, as seen in the above instance. Similar cases are:

> they [= baskets] were such as were very handy and convenient for my **laying** things **up** in, (*RC* 144) / in the **keeping** the People **in**; (*JPY* 164) / I wou'd not agree to his **having** the Child **away**, (*Rox* 229) / in short, there was no retreat; no **shifting** anything **off**; (*Rox* 278)

As well as in the other syntactic patterns previously discussed, a relatively long (eight-word) noun phrase occurs between the verb and the particle:

> at <u>their</u> **bringing** the dead Bodies of their Children and Friends **out** <u>to</u> the Cart, (*JPY* 178)

iv) The *-ing* Form Without a Determiner [O is a *non-personal pronoun*] (e.g. *The next Day I set him to work <u>to</u> **beating** some Corn **out**,* (*RC* 213))

This pattern also occurs most frequently after the preposition, as seen in the above instance. Additional instances containing short noun phrases are given:

> we thought he depended <u>upon</u> **shaking** the Bear **off**; (*RC* 296) / Pray let me ask you another Question: Are you in any Likelihood <u>of</u> **getting** your Ship **off**, if you refuse it? (*CS* 227) / ... which would at once have destroy'd all the possibility <u>of</u> **breaking** the Truth **out**, (*MF* 92) / However with all this, and all that I had secur'd before, I found <u>upon</u> **casting** things **up**, (*MF* 63) / the Power <u>of</u> **shutting** People **up** in their own Houses, was granted by Act of Parliament, (*JPY* 37) / at the Charge <u>of</u> **bringing** some of them **back** again, (*CJ* 221) / he had the greatest Dexterity <u>at</u> **Conveying** any thing **away**; (*CJ* 44), etc.

Cases where longer noun phrases occur between the verb and the particle are observed as well:

> I found myself so refresh'd <u>with</u> **having** a Pair of warm Stockings **on**, (*CJ* 15) / *Friday* was <u>for</u> **burning** the Hollow or Cavity of this Tree **out** to make it for a Boat. (*RC* 227)

Chapter 2 The Syntactic Structure of Transitive Phrasal Verbs

The *-ing* phrase in this pattern serves as the subject, as in:

> now I found that ... **breeding** some [goats] **up** tame was my only way, (*RC* 146)

After the particle of the VOP pattern, the prepositional phrases, which bear a close relation to it, sometimes occur, as in *I was angry at him heartily, for **bringing** the Bear **back** upon us, (RC 295)*. Similar instances are:

> it was a very unhappy thing to the King and whole Nation, ... and was the Occasion of **bringing** the *Scots* Army **in** upon us, (*MC* 172) / the King was for **drawing** *Essex* **on** to the *Severn*, in hopes to get behind him, (*MC* 153) / for fear of **bringing** the Infection **along** with them, (*JPY* 8)

As a final instance, the case of "V-*ing* + *of* + O + P" occurs only once, in *JPY*:

> I mention'd above **shutting** of Houses **up**; and it is needful to say something particularly to that; for this Part of the History of the Plague is very melancholy; but the most grievous Story must be told. (*JPY* 36)

As seen just above, *shutting of Houses up* seems rarer than the "rare" case of *the breeding of them up*, earlier observed in (i) of this section (see p.194), for the reason that *breeding of them up* can be considered a nominalization of the original verbal phrase, "breed them up" (this word order is normal), while *shutting of Houses up* can be traced back to either "shut up Houses" or "shut Houses up." The former case is used more frequently in a normal context; in actuality, instances of *shutting up of Houses* (as described above), are numerous in *JPY*. So why is this syntax chosen here?

It seems that the choice between the VPO and VOP patterns has much to do with semantic focus or information focus; as mentioned above, this issue is to be discussed in the final section. In addition, the VOP pattern tends to be more colloquial and emotive than the VPO pattern. In spite of the statement by Hiltunen (1994: 133) that in Early Modern English the VPO pattern is the "predominant one if the object is nominal," instances of the VOP pattern in "nominal" cases can often be observed in Defoe. This phenomenon relates directly to the genius of the language of Defoe, heretofore labeled as "colloquial." If so, the VOP pattern is in keeping with a representation of "emotive" aspects. It is fair to say that the syntax of *shutting of Houses up* in the passage above is inextricably linked with those contexts in which adjectival phrases denoting strong feeling and emotion, i.e. *very melancholy* and *the most grievous*, are used. As such, this unique gerund variant of a phrasal verb *shut up* indicates an emphatic, emotionally-charged expression.

2.7.3 The OVP Pattern (e.g. ... *a Plaster for the Maid, which he was to stay for the **making up**, (JPY* 51))

There are seven instances belonging to this pattern in total, each differing markedly from the next.

First, cases possessing a determiner will be examined. In the following passage, the *-ing* form, which occurs after the preposition in the relative clause, takes a relative pronoun *which* as an object:

Chapter 2 The Syntactic Structure of Transitive Phrasal Verbs

> ... a Plaster for the Maid, which he was to stay for the **making up**, (*JPY* 51)

The following two cases appear to be of the same nature:

> But never was any thing in the World of that Kind so unpleasant, awkard, and uneasy, as it was to me to wear such Cloaths at their first **putting on**. (*RC* 274) / he had been as careful of this, as of his own, and had made very little Difference in their **breeding up**; (*Rox* 193)

At first glance, these gerund phrases (lacking following nouns) might be considered an intransitive use. However, in both of the above cases, personal pronouns as the determiner *their* refer to "Cloaths [i.e. clothes]" and "children" in their respective contexts. As a result, these pronouns virtually serve as the direct objects of the phrasal verbs *put on* and *breed up*. On this point, these gerund expressions may then possess a passive meaning, as it seems that *their breeding up* is similar in nature to *his Children were* ***breeding up***, (*Rox* 248), (discussed as the passive progressive, in Section 2.6.2; p.177).

In the following passage, *the taking off* is more complex:

> (Crusoe says) Thou [= "this Money"] art not worth to me, no not the **taking off** of the Ground, one of those Knives is worth all this Heap, (*RC* 57)

This is a part of Crusoe's monologue on the uninhabited island after finding the "Money," more specifically, "about Thirty six Pounds value in Money, some *European* Coin, some *Brazil*, some Pieces of Eight,

199

some Gold, some Silver" (p. 57). Given that before *the taking off*, the adjective *worth* is doubtlessly omitted, the real object of this phrasal verb is the preceding *Thou*. As well, this instance may have a passive meaning.

Next, the *-ing* form lacking determiners will be discussed. In the following passage, the object of *taking away*, which comes after the adjective *worth*, is the foregoing (*no*) *one thing* as in:

> the Jonk that carry'd them had <u>no one thing</u> worth **taking away**, but a little Rice, and some Coffee, (*CS* 174)

Two *-ing* forms (including two phrasal verbs) follow the preposition *a*. The object of the phrasal verb *cut down* in the first *-ing* form is *This Tree*, at the beginning of a sentence:

> <u>This Tree</u> I was three Days <u>a</u> **cutting down**, and two more cutting off the Bows, (*RC* 115)

2.7.4 Passive Construction

Jespersen (*MEG* V: 112-114) mentions that "gerunds were originally indifferent to the distinction between active and passive meaning" (p. 112), but "To avoid ambiguity ... a new passive gerund developed from about 1600" (p. 114). Given this observation, the new "*being* + pp" form appears to have become common by Defoe's era.[17]

As far as the passive gerund in transitive phrasal verbs in Defoe is concerned, two main types are observed: the type with a determiner: *such as my being **taken up** by the Portuguese Master of the Ship* (*RC* 131), and the type lacking a determiner: *The fear of being **swallow'd up** alive, made me that I never slept in quiet* (*RC* 82). The type with a

Chapter 2 The Syntactic Structure of Transitive Phrasal Verbs

determiner will be examined next.

i) The Passive with a Determiner (e.g. *my being* **taken up** *by the Portuguese Master of the Ship*; (*RC* 131))
The passive gerund with a determiner is likely to occur after a preposition, as in:

> upon the general Belief of my being **cast away**, (*RC* 280) / except the Possibility only of their being **taken up** by another Ship in Company, (*RC* 187) / as to my being **brought over** by a legal Transportation as a Criminal; (*MF* 328) / he had a kind of Horror upon his Mind at his being **sent over** to the Plantations ... (*MF* 301) / I am speaking now of People made desperate, by the Apprehensions of their being **shut up**, (*JPY* 55) / as well after her being **turn'd away**, as before; (*Rox* 313)

The following passive-gerund phrase is used as an object of the transitive verb *prevent*:

> THE Count *de Tesse*, ... follow'd them close at the Heels to prevent our being **cut off**, (*CJ* 213)

In the following passage, the noun phrase *my Powder* represents the notional subject of the following *being* phrase, and serves as a determiner (i.e. *my Powder's*):

> I mean my Powder being **blown up** by Lightning, (*RC* 63)

Other instances of the same kind, though they all occur after a preposition, are next given:

likewise the Opinion of others, who talk of <u>infection</u> being **carried on** by the Air only, (*JPY* 75) / of <u>the Infection</u> being thus **carryed on** by Persons apparently in Health, (*JPY* 208) / When I speak of <u>Rows of Houses</u> being **shut up**, (*JPY* 17)

ii) The Passive Without a Determiner (e.g. *my Fears and Apprehensions of being* **swallow'd up** *by the Sea being forgotten* (*RC* 9))

Next, the passive gerund lacking a determiner is focused on. As with the above instance, all cases found occur after a preposition, and build up the prepositional phrases. Instances are:

I might run the same Risk <u>of</u> ... being **carry'd away** from it [= the island]; (*RC* 143) / my Imagination <u>of</u> being **turn'd out** to the wide World, (*MF* 56) / I was ... very hearty and sound in Health, but very impatient <u>of</u> being **pent up** within Doors without Air, (*JPY* 104) / most of the Persons infected would be stone dead, and the rest run away for Fear <u>of</u> being **shut up**; (*JPY* 166) / I had effectually secur'd myself <u>from</u> being **found out**, (*CJ* 199) / While I was dayly musing on the Circumstances <u>of</u> being **sent away**, (*CJ* 105) / at the Apprehensions <u>of</u> being **turn'd away**, (*CJ* 150) / the unfortunate Mother of that illegitimate Birth, has a dreadful Affliction, either <u>of</u> being **turn'd off** with her Child, ... (*Rox* 79), etc.

2.7.5 The Pattern Distribution in the Gerund Construction: Statistical Summary

Results of the four patterns discussed above are summarized in Table 6:

Table 6. Syntactic Distribution in the Gerund Construction

	RC	MC	CS	MF	JPY	CJ	Rox	total
VPO	12	11	7	16*	39	8	10	103 (52%)
VOP	12	3	4	8	10	11	12	60 (30%)
O = *personal*	(5)*	(0)	(2)	(6)*	(2)*	(8)	(10)	(33)
O = *non-personal*	(7)	(3)	(2)	(2)	(8)	(3)	(2)	(27)
OVP	3	0	1	1	1	0	1	7 (4%)
passive	7	0	2	3	9	4	2	27 (14%)
total number of the gerund	34	14	14	28	59	23	25	197

* One instance with a "reflexive pronoun" is added to the number.

Among the seven works, *JPY* shows the highest frequency of 59 occurrences (about 30%) of the gerund. Of the 59 instances, *shut up* is used 38 times. *Shut up* occurs 123 times in *JPY* and represents the most frequently used phrasal verb (including intransitive instances) in Defoe. In this respect, the relationship between the use of this phrasal verb and the theme or subject matter of the work is worth further investigation. This issue will be discussed in Chapter 3.

Finally, the frequency of the use of determiners, in particular the definite article *the*, is presented in Table 7:

Table 7. Distribution of Determiners in the Gerund Construction

	RC	MC	CS	MF	JPY	CJ	Rox	total
VPO	3 (3)	4 (4)	0	1 (1)	20 (17)*	4 (1)	2 (1)	34 (27)
VOP	5	0	1	1 (1)	3 (1)	3 (2)	5 (2)**	18 (6)
O = *personal*	3	0	1	1	0	3	3	11
O = *non-personal*	2	0	0	0	3	0	2	7
OVP	2 (1)	0	0	1	1 (1)	0	1	5 (2)
passive	4	0	1	2	5	1	1	14
total number of the gerund construction	14 (4)	4 (4)	2	5 (2)	29 (19)	8 (3)	9 (3)	71 (35)

The number in parentheses shows the occurrences of the definite article.
* Twelve occurrences of the variant form "*the* VP of O" like *the shutting up of Houses* are added to the number.
** One occurrence of the variant form "*the* V of OP" i.e. *the breeding of them up* is added to the number.

The instances of gerund with a determiner occur 71 times (36%) out of 197 in total. Among them, the use of *the*, occurring 35 times, accounts for about 50% in a variety of determiners. Out of these 35 occurrences, 27 are in the VPO pattern.

2.8 Adverbial Insertion: the "VP [adv] O" and "VO [adv] P" Patterns

In this section, the patterns in which adverbials are *internally* related to the structure of transitive phrasal verbs in Defoe are examined. Compared with the case of "adverbial insertion" in intransitive phrasal verbs, that of transitive phrasal verbs is more complicated, because adverbials occur in two main patterns: the "VP [adv] O" pattern and the "VO [adv] P" pattern. Needless to say, the former pattern is a variant of the VPO and the latter a variant of the VOP.

2.8.1 The "VP [adv] O" Pattern (e.g. *he cry'd out earnestly, O pray! O pray!* (*RC* 296))

In fact, in the VP [adv] O pattern there are only seven cases where an adverbial occurs between the particle and the object, as in:

> the Land **broke off** <u>a little</u> the Violence of the Wind: (*RC* 14) / [the Turkish rover] after returning our Fire, and **pouring in** <u>also</u> his small Shot from near 200 Men which he had on Board. (*RC* 18) / I contented my self ... to **write down** <u>only</u> the most remarkable Events of my Life, (*RC* 104) / We **took in** <u>also</u> a monstrous Quantity of Ducks, and Cocks and Hens, the same kind as we have in England, (*CS* 190) / so as if he **send away** <u>first</u> his Sound, he not after send thither the Sick, nor again unto the Sick the Sound. (*JPY* 42) / how justly may that Power, so disoblig'd, **take away** <u>again</u> his Wooll, (*CJ* 171) / we had **eaten up** <u>almost</u> every thing, and little remain'd, unless, (*Rox* 18)

Except for one instance of a "degree" adverbial *a little*, no adverbs that attract special attention are found in this pattern.[18]

However, in the use of some phrasal verbs as a reporting verb (cf. Section 2.1.2; pp.134-136), adverbial insertions, including a *-ly* "manner" adverb, occur before the actual speech as a direct object. In the following passages, *burst out* and *gape out* as well as *cry out* and *call out* could be regarded as a reporting verb introducing direct speech:

> I **cry'd out** <u>aloud</u>, *Jesus, thou Son of David*, (*RC* 96) / the Bellman **call'd out** <u>several Times</u>, *Bring out your Dead*; (*JPY* 49) / he **cry'd out** <u>earnestly</u>, *O pray! O pray!* (*RC* 296) / she **burst out** <u>at last</u>, is it *possible!* Are you the Man that has kill'd

205

the Marquis? (*CJ* 230) / *Amy*, saw it, and **gapes out** (<u>*as was her way*</u>) *Law'd Madam!* never be concern'd at it; (*Rox* 237) [cf. *OED* s.v. gape, *v.* 1. e. *trans.* "To open (the mouth) wide. †to **gape out**: to emit with open mouth. *rare*. 1608~]

The following insertion consists of two different elements of *tho' softly* and *two or three times*:

I was very Penitent too, for my former Sins; and **cry'd out**, <u>tho' softly, two or three times</u>, *Lord have Mercy upon me*; (*Rox* 126)

In the indirect speech, the *as if* clause is inserted:

so I let it go that Moment, and **cried out** <u>as if I had been kill'd</u>, that some body had Trod upon my Foot, (*MF* 211) / I **put in** <u>two or three times</u>, that she had a good Memory, (*Rox* 289)

Such adverbial insertions in the use of reporting phrasal verbs seem to serve as a stylistic elaboration which creates a sense of reality and immediacy in the following reported clauses (i.e. character utterances).

Next, apart from these cases, a prepositional phrase, which normally ought to be placed in the end position, occurs between the particle and the noun, as in *the Women ... **brought out** <u>to us</u> several Sorts of Food*, (*CS* 116). In this pattern, the object placed at the end, by a prior occurrence of a prepositional phrase, seems to be more highlighted than in the usual word-order. Among other 14 cases of the same pattern, some of them are given:

they **brought down** <u>to us</u> Victuals in Abundance, Cattel, Fowls,

Chapter 2 The Syntactic Structure of Transitive Phrasal Verbs

Herbs, Roots, (*CS* 27) / when she **counted out** to me, sixty two Guineas and a half; (*Rox* 181) / the Plague ... **carried off** in that Time thirty or forty Thousand of these very People, (*JPY* 98) / It seems, after he found I did not come, he **found out**, by his unweary'd Enquiry, where I had liv'd; (*Rox* 133) / [I gave humble and hearty Thanks] That he [= God] could fully **make up** to me, the Deficiencies of my Solitary State, (*RC* 112) / I ordered him publickly to keep the Money on board which he had, and to **buy up** with it a Quantity of Ammunition if he could get it, (*CS* 260) / the Merchants at *Leghorn* and at *Naples* ... sent again from thence ... to **bring back** in other Ships such as were improper for the Markets at *Smyrna* and *Scanderoon*. (*JPY* 214) / he began to **reckon up** to me some of the greatest Families in *France*, and in *England* also. (*Rox* 81), etc.

In addition, there are three cases in which two different elements, (e.g. *by Enquiry* and *to my particular Satisfaction*), are inserted between P and O:

When I came to *Lisbon*, I **found out** by Enquiry, and to my particular Satisfaction, my old Friend the Captain of the Ship, (*RC* 279) / I **brought over** with me for the use of our Plantation, three Horses with Harness, and Saddles; (*MF* 339) / [with a -*ly* adverb and a prepositional phrase] this drove the People from haunting the Doors of every Disperser of Bills; and from **taking down** blindly, and without Consideration, Poison for Physick, and Death instead of Life. (*JPY* 35)

A prepositional phrase is sometimes inserted between a reporting phrasal verb and its object (i.e. a character utterance), as in:

he **cries out** <u>to me</u>, *O Master!* (*RC* 230) / one of the Servants ... **call'd out** <u>to me</u>, *Sir, for Godsake open the Door*, (*CJ* 201)

Call out and *give out* take *that*-clauses or *to*-infinitives as an object, thus suggesting an indirect speech act:

[Captain *Wilmot*] **called out** <u>to me</u>, that *William* was right, (*CS* 148) / the Captain ... **call'd out** <u>to him in the Boat</u>, to yield, or he was a dead Man. (*RC* 265) / So *John* **called out** <u>to them</u> not to come to them, (*JPY* 141) / so he **gave out** <u>among his Servants</u>, that he was gone to —, where he often went a-Hunting, (*Rox* 68) [cf. *OED* s.v. give, *v.* 62. a *trans*. "To utter, publish; to announce, proclaim, report" *c* 1340~]

A long insertion can also occur (in which a phrase and a clause are combined such as *to me*, *in English*, and *as well as he could*), as follows:

Friday **call'd out** <u>to me in English, as well as he could</u>, *O Master!* (*RC* 251) / so he **calls out** <u>as loud as he could, to one of them</u>, *Tom Smith, Tom Smith*; (*RC* 267) / he **calls out** <u>to him [= a bear] again, as if he had suppos'd the Bear could speak English</u>; *What you no come farther*, ... (*RC* 295)

NOTES:

In four works by the authors other than Defoe, the "VP [+ prepositional phrase] O" pattern is commonly found:

[in *PP*]

They see that these fears tend to **take away** <u>from them</u> their pitiful old self-holiness, (143) / Then they **cast off** <u>by degrees</u> private Duties, (145) / That I may be Rich in good Works, **laying up** <u>in store</u> a good Foundation against the time to come, (214) / Then they **brought up** <u>in course</u> a Dish of *Butter* and *Hony*. (245), etc.

[in Behn]

The other told her then, that she must **write down** <u>to her Uncle</u> a Farewell-Letter, (196) / At which they **set up** <u>with one accord</u> a most terrible and hideous mourning and condoling, (41) / he **wore off** <u>in time</u> a great part of that chagrin, (32)

[in *GT*]

they **flung up** <u>with great Dexterity</u> one of their largest Hogsheads; (24) / But this I was not able to do till three Days after, which I spent in **cutting down** <u>with my Knife</u> some of the largest Trees in the Royal Park, (47) / after which Nature had **pointed out** <u>to them</u> a certain Root that gave them a general Evacuation. (262), etc.

[in *Pamela*]

I should never forgive myself, if I were not to **lengthen out** <u>to the longest Minute</u> my happy Time of Honesty. (137) / The intriguing Gentleman thought fit, however, to **keep back** <u>from her Father</u> her three last Letters; (92) / after I had **cast about** <u>in my Mind</u>, every thing that could make me hope, (172) / I should soon have the Pleasure of **sending back** <u>to you,</u> not only those Papers, but all that succeeded them to this Time, (280), etc. [cf. with a prepositional phrase and a temporal clause with a conjunction] we shall **make out** <u>between us, before we have done</u>, a pretty Story in Romance, I warrant ye! (32)

As for this pattern in *Pamela*, the object, through a detailed elaboration, tends to be very long, as in *not only those Papers, but all that succeeded them to this Time*. The following passage from the same work contains a very long noun phrase made up of 29 words (i.e. *all the Cloaths and Things ... by my Lady*):

> he **brought down**, <u>in a Portmanteau</u>, all the Cloaths and Things my Lady and Master had presented me, and moreover two Velvet Hoods, and a Velvet Scarf, that used to be worn by my Lady; (120)

The tendency to place a long elaborate object at the end leads to Richardson's preference for the VPO pattern over the VOP pattern in *Pamela*. This problem will be examined more in depth in the final section (Section 2.10).

In conclusion, abundance of such instances suggests that the "VP [pp] O" pattern serves as an effective variation of the VPO pattern.

2.8.2 The "VO [adv] P" Pattern and the "V [adv] P" Pattern (e.g. *The violence of the blow **beat** the old Gentleman <u>quite</u> **down**, (CJ 56) and she is **brought** <u>sadly</u> **down**; (JPY 108)*)

Usually when Defoe inserts adverbials between V and P in the use of transtive phrasal verbs, the "VO [adv] **P**" pattern is used with the active voice while the "**V** [adv] **P**" pattern with the passive voice. These two patterns could be considered *more internally* related to the structure of a transitive phrasal verb than the "**VP** [adv] O" pattern in the previous subsection (2.8.1) because the "core" part of a phrasal verb (i.e. V and P) is separated; on the other hand, the "core" part in the "**VP** [adv] O" pattern remains unseparated.[19]

Table 8 shows the distribution when "adverbial insertion" occurs in any of the four syntactic patterns, VPO, VOP, OVP, and Passive:

Table 8. Syntactic Distribution in the "VO [adv] P" Pattern and the Passive "V [adv] P" Pattern

	RC	*MC*	*CS*	*MF*	*JPY*	*CJ*	*Rox*	total
V [adv] PO	1	0	0	0	0	0	0	1
V [adv] OP	0	0	0	0	2	0	2	4
VO [adv] P	13	6	8	15	5	18	22	87 (81%)
OV [adv] P	1	0	1	0	0	0	0	2
V [adv] P (passive)	4	0	2	0	4	3	1	14 (13%)
total	19	6	11	15	11	21	25	108

Thus, whether adverbials occur between V and P might reveal certain characteristics in the VPO and VOP patterns, such as the range or limit of expressiveness unique to each pattern.

In the "V [adv] PO" pattern, there is only one instance of the insertion, but this sole case is exceptional:

> the Captain then **calls** himself **out**, You *Smith, you know my Voice*, (*RC* 267)

The inserted word, *himself*, is a reflexive pronoun, not an adverb. The pronoun here cannot be taken as the object of a reporting phrasal verb *call out*; the reported clause, or the actual utterance is the object. In thise sense, the use of *himsef* is probably emphatic. If this case were to be excluded, there would be no instances in the VPO pattern.

In the "V [adv] OP" pattern, four instances are found, but no special adverbials are used; they function as a modifier to the following noun phrase:

... where they had **sent** perhaps their Wives and Children **away**; (*JPY* 85) / they would ... **take** even the Cloths **off**, of the dead Bodies, (*JPY* 83) / and she **had** not many Cloaths **on**, (*Rox* 46) / he **had** not a Rag of Cloaths **on**, but his Gown and Slippers, and Shirt; (*Rox* 143)

Instead, the "VO [adv] P" pattern takes over the role for adverbial insertion (this accounts for 81% of instances). In this pattern, a variety of adverbials come between O and P, as with *it* [= the wind] ***blew** the Ebb further **out** than usual*, (*CS* 230), or *a Woman **gave** herself entirely away from herself*, (*Rox* 147).

The 103 occurrences of adverbials used in the patterns "VO [adv] P," "OV [adv] P," and "V [adv] P" are listed and categorized:

i) The "degree" adverbials: ***quite* (15)**, (*so*) *clean* (2), *clear* (2), *entirely* (2), *tollerably* (1), *almost* (1), *wholly* (1), *well* (1), *so much* (1), *a little* (1). (*The number in parentheses indicates that of occurrences.) [10 types]

ii) The "space and distance" adverbials: *farther* (3), *a vast Way* (2), *close* (1), *further* (1), *short* (1), *bottom* (1), *home* (1), *a good way* (1), *a little way* (1), *one way* (1), *about a League in my Way* (1). [11 types]

iii) The "time and frequency" adverbials: *first* (1), *once* (1), *still* (1), *then* (1), *continually* (1), *the sooner* (1), *at once* (1). [7 types]

iv) The "manner" adverbials: *directly* (3), (*very* or *all*) *carefully* (2), (*so* or *also*) *effectually* (2), *chearfully* (1), *faithfully* (1), *sadly* (1), *very gently* (1), *handsomely, tho' privately* (1), *in a most butcherly manner* (1). [9 types]

v) Others: ***all* (36)**, *safe* (1), *thus* (1), *so* (1), *for him* (1), *as it were* (1). [6 types]

In accordance to the following five categories, each adverbial is surveyed:

i) In the list of "degree" adverbials, as well as in the "intransitive" case, the intensive adverb *quite* is used very frequently (15 times). Among them, the 12 instances occur in the "VO [adv] P" pattern, and the two in the "V [adv] P" in the passive, as in:

> [in the "VO [adv] P" pattern]
> *Friday*, a lusty strong Fellow, **took** the *Spaniard* quite **up** upon his Back, (*RC* 240) / this our Carpenters undertook, who first **palisadoed** our Camp quite **round** with long Stakes ... (*CS* 99) / The violence of the blow **beat** the old Gentleman quite **down**, (*CJ* 56) / I **thrust** my Hand quite **up** to my Elbow, (*CJ* 25) / I began indeed, to **give** *Amy* quite **over**, (*Rox* 317) / I frequently resolv'd to **leave** it [= "a frightful Spectre"] quite **off**, (*MF* 120), etc.
> [in the "V [adv] P" in Passive]
> they brought us up afterward, a Neats Tongue and a Ham, that was almost **cut** quite **down**, (*CJ* 237) / 'tis supposed they were roll'd off by Thieves, stoln, and **carried** quite **away**. (*JPY* 83)[20]

In emphasizing the meaning of transitive (as well as intransitive) phrasal verbs, the intensifier *quite* proves to be a very useful word for Defoe.

Only one of the 15 *quite* instances occurs in the "OV [adv] P" pattern; two instances in total of the "OV [adv] P" pattern are cited below:

> [fifteen Ton of Elephants Teeth] which he made others [of the savages] **bring** with him quite **down** to our Camp. (*CS* 133) / The 7th, 8th, 9th, 10th, and Part of the 12th. (for the 11th was

Sunday) I **took** wholly **up** to make me a Chair, (*RC* 72)

As for the use of *quite* in the above passage, a prepositional phrase (i.e. *with him*) is also inserted, while the other passage contains another intensifier, *wholly*.

With other "degree" adverbials, *clean* and *clear* as intensifiers are used twice respectively; one instance of *clean* is reinforced by an attachment of another intensifier *so*:

> I run to get hold of it, and gave it a quick snatch, **pulled** it clean **away**, and run like the Wind down the *Cloyster* with it, (*CJ* 56) [cf. *OED* s.v. clean, *adv.* 5. "Without anything omitted or left; without any exception that may vitiate the statement, without qualification; wholly, entirely, quite, absolutely."] / I took care to **convey** the gold Watch so clean **away** from the Lady *Betty*, (*MF* 258) / I went boldly in and was just going to lay my Hand upon a piece of Plate, and might have done it, and **carried** it clear **off**, (*MF* 269) [cf. *OED* s.v. clear, *adv.* 5. a. "Completely, quite, entirely, thoroughly; = clean *adv.* 5."] / I thought myself happy when he got another Man to **take** his Brewhouse clear **off** of his Hands; (*Rox* 10)

ii) In the list of "space and distance" adverbials, *farther* or adverbials using "way" (e.g. *a vast Way*) are chiefly employed. As in the case of the "intransitive" adverbial insertion, *farther* has a close relationship with *off*:

> This **drove** me farther **off**, (*CJ* 24) / ... where the Thing was done, but have **carried** them farther **off**. (*Rox* 115) / till that Wave having driven me, or rather **carried** me a vast Way **on** towards

Chapter 2 The Syntactic Structure of Transitive Phrasal Verbs

> the Shore, (*RC* 44) / [with another adverbial of a prepositional phrase *for something*] then **sending** him for something a good way **off**, I seriously pray'd to God ... (*RC* 219) / in this Fright I went to her, and **lifted** her a little way **up**, (*Rox* 125) / This Eddy **carryed** me about a League in my Way **back** again directly towards the Island, (*RC* 140) / [passive] I should be **carry'd** a vast Way **out** to Sea, (*RC* 190) / I might judge whether if I was **driven** one way **out**, (*RC* 190), etc.

iii) In the list of "time and frequency" adverbials, unlike the recurrent use of *immediately* in the "intransitive" insertion, each adverbial is used just once. In the following passages, adverbial phrases indicative of speed, e.g. *the sooner* and *at once*, are used:

> so they advanced the hastier to get within our great Guns, and consequently out of their Danger, which **brought** the Fight the sooner **on**. (*MC* 201) / When the Poor Woman had taken up all, she was so weak, she could not **carry** it at once **in**, (*JPY* 109)

iv) In the list of "manner" adverbials, a variety of *-ly* adverbs are used:

> Sir *John* without any Ceremony **carries** me directly **up** to the King, (*MC* 57) / I **gave** my self chearfully **up** to her Management, (*CJ* 271) / if he liv'd to see any of them **serve** their Time faithfully **out**, (*CJ* 120) / [passive] *Poor Woman!* says he, *she is* **brought** sadly **down**; (*JPY* 108)

In the following passages, an intensifier is added to *-ly* adverbs:

> Early in the Morning we marched, and **kept** our Scouts very

215

carefully **out** every Way, (*MC* 213) / We **took** it [= "the Earth"] all carefully **up**, and washing it in the Water, (*CS* 96) / I **lifted** them [= "earthern ugly things"] very gently **up**, (*RC* 120) / I have often thought, that had such a Thing befallen a Man, ... after having **given** it so effectually **over**. (*CJ* 26)

Two -*ly* adverbs are inserted:

I found he appointed the Children a settled Allowance, ... which was sufficient for **bringing** them handsomely, tho' privately, **up** in the World; (*Rox* 80)

A prepositional phrase *in a most butcherly manner* is inserted as follows:

they came sweating and blowing into the Shop, ... **dragging** the poor Creature in a most butcherly manner **up** towards their Master, (*MF* 243)

When a three-word noun phrase as the object, *the poor Creature*, is combined with the inserted adverbial, there arises a very long (eight-word) distance between V and P (i.e. *dragging* and *up*). Through this distance, in consequence, the *action* of dragging up the poor person seems to be highlighted, rather than *who* or *what* they are dragging up.

v) In the list of "others," *all* is the by far most frequently used "word" (36 times in total: 32 at the "VO [adv] P"; 4 at the "V [adv] P"). As for its use at the "VO [adv] P", *all* always appears when the object is a personal pronoun, as with *we might ... build a Bark large enough to carry us all away* (*RC* 244). The personal pronouns involved in this

Chapter 2 The Syntactic Structure of Transitive Phrasal Verbs

pattern are *us*, *them*, and *it*. Thus, *all* might be construed as a kind of "reflexive" pronoun, i.e. "*all* of us," but it seems that this word is used as an intensive adverb like *quite*, in the sense of "Wholly, completely, altogether, quite" (*OED* s.v. all, *adv.* 2).

In addition, what seems particularly interesting is that the use of *all* becomes more frequent in Defoe's later works. Notice the change of frequency in the seven works: *RC* (twice), *MC* (once), *CS* (4 times), *MF* (5 times), *JPY* (twice), *CJ* (9 times), and *Rox* (13 times). several instances from the last two works, *CJ* and *Rox*, are given below:

> [VO [adv] P]
> all the Offence I ought to have punish'd him for, had been that of stealing a Bottle of Rum, and **drinking** it all **up**; (*CJ* 135) / from that Moment I **gave** them all **up** as lost, and meditated nothing but how to escape from them, (*CJ* 265) / so he **pours** it all **out** into my Hat; (*CJ* 44) / another Accident had like to have **blown** us all **up** again. (*Rox* 283) / they **carried** them all **away** to one of their Aunts. (*Rox* 19) / He look'd at them a-while, and then **handed** them all **back** again to me; (*Rox* 259) / she **reckon'd** them all **up** by Name, (*Rox* 308) / She **set** them all **down** at the Door before she knock'd, (*Rox* 20) / but I perceiv'd he **took** them all **out**, (*Rox* 257), etc.
> [Passive]
> it [= "fine China Dishes and Plates"] was **set** all **up** in a large Glass-Cupboard in the Room I sat in, (*Rox* 177) / she came into the Room I was in, **cloath'd** all **over** with my Things, (*CJ* 257)

Whatever the word class or part of speech of *all* is, its use no doubt enhances the meaning of the phrasal verbs plus the object, e.g. *drinking it all up* and renders the passages cited above more dynamic and vivid.

Through an observation of the uses of *quite* and *all*, it could be appreciated that the VOP pattern provides a form far more appropriate for emphasis than the VPO pattern. In this sense, the evidence suggests that the VOP pattern might convey a particular colloquial and emotive flavour than the VPO pattern.

2.9 The Composite Pattern of "V and VPO" or "V and VOP"

Among instances of transitive phrasal verbs in Defoe, there are several cases where a phrasal verb shares the same object with another verb. In the case of *we had very happily **found out** and stopp'd the worst and most dangerous Leak that we had* (*CS* 231), it can be construed that *find out* as well as *stop* takes the *Leak* as an object. Such coordinated use of a phrasal verb with another verb phrase will be discussed in Chapter 3. This section focuses on the cases where a phrasal verb seems to share the same particle as well as the same object with another verb.

In the following passages, from the structural viewpoint of transitive phrasal verbs, the "V and VPO" pattern can be observed:

>we kill'd sixteen Cows, and pickled and **barrelled** up the Flesh as well as we could be supposed to do in the Latitude of eight Degrees from the Line. (*CS* 215) / when I had it [= a lame goat] Home, I bound and **splinter'd up** its Leg which was broke, (*RC* 75) [cf. *OED* s.v. splinter, *v*. 2. "To bind, fix, or secure by means of a splint or splints;" Also with *up*. *Obs.* 1594-1720; The *OED*'s last instance is from Defoe's *Captain Singleton*, i.e. As to his arm, he found one of the bones broken; .. and this he set, and **splintered** it

up, and **bound** his arm in a sling."]

In the two passages, *barrel up* and *splinter up* ought to be treated as phrasal verbs. However, seen from a broader perspective, *pickle and barrel* and *bind and splinter* seem to function as a single unit consisting of two transitive verbs respectively, in that both take the same objects *the Flesh* and *its Leg*. It follows that the first verb (i.e. *pickle* and *bind*) seems to share the particle *up* indicating the completion or finality of the action as well as the object in the context, at least at the semantic level. If so, this case might be called "composite" pattern in transitive use, in the same sense as the *intransitive* "V + -ing + P" pattern (e.g. *he came running back*) has been called such in Chapter 1. Namely, two phrasal verbs *pickle up* and *barrel up* co-exist at the deep structure level. Although both describe a sequence of actions, the coordination of *pickle and barrel* suggests a "chronological" sequence, while the two verbs in *bind and splinter* can be considered more cohesive, or rather synonymous to each other, given the *OED* definition of *splinter* and another citation from *Captain Singleton*.

A similar case, in which *call out* as a reporting verb is coordinated with *cry* in a participial construction, is given; the direct utterance *Rise, and let in the Constable here* serves as an object:

> I ... was immediately Rouz'd with Noise of People knocking at the Door, ... and <u>Crying and **Calling** out</u> to the People of the House, <u>Rise, and let in the Constable here</u>, (*CJ* 73)

As has been examined in Section 2.1.2, *cry out* as well as *call out* are often used as reporting verbs in Defoe. Hence, *cry and call out* could be seen as a case where two phrasal verbs (*cry out* and *call out*) are combined, probably for the sake of emphasis.

Next, the "V and VOP" composite pattern, in which the first verb shares both the object and the particle with the second verb, is examined:

>the Throng was so great, and the Coaches, Horses, Waggons and Carts were so many, driving and **dragging** the People **away**, (*JPY* 183) / the Shoemaker began to hale and **drag** me **a long** (i.e. along) as he us'd to do when I was a Boy. (*CJ* 70) [cf. *OED* s.v. hale, *v.*[1] 1. b. "To draw or pull along, or from one place to another, esp. with force or violence; to drag, tug."] / so I made it my Business to enquire, and **find** him **out**, and to give him notice of it. (*CJ* 81) cf. well, *says I*, Dame, **enquire** her **out** if you have Opportunity; (*CJ* 87) / he **enquir'd** the Name **out** immediately, (*CJ* 21) [cf. *OED* s.v. inquire, enquire, *v.* 6. *trans.* "To seek, search for, try to find. esp. with *out* (rarely *forth*):" *Obs.* 1390~] / this made them paddle and **shove** the Boat **away** as well as they could, (*CS* 236)

Among the above passages, in the third citation, since the comma is placed between *enquire* and *find*, there seems to be no strong relationship between these two verbs. Yet, *enquire out* as a phrasal verb is employed in the same text (*CJ*); note the definition of the *OED* as well. In this respect, this instance belongs to a "composite" pattern. The last and fourth instance contains the verb *paddle*. According to the *OED* (s.v. paddle, $v.^2$ 2a), the transitive use of this verb is from the year 1784, but through the coordination with *shove the Boat*, *paddle* strongly seems to have a transitive force as a composite pattern.

2.10 Distribution of Syntactic Patterns in Transitive Phrasal Verbs

This section summarizes the total use of transitive phrasal verbs, according to the six syntactic patterns. (Note: as for a treatment of the "composite pattern" in the previous section (2.9), the instance like *we ... pickled and barrelled up the Flesh* is counted as "VPO," one like [*the Throng*] *driving and dragging the People away* as "VOP," for convenience.) The following table, therefore, shows the pattern-distribution of *all* instances in both predicate and non-predicate categories:

Table 9. Distribution of Transitive Patterns

	RC	*MC*	*CS*	*MF*	*JPY*	*CJ*	*Rox*	total	*PP*	Behn	*GT*	*Pamela*
VPO	257 (34%)	200 (41%)	218 (44%)	197 (34%)	184 (34%)	167 (30%)	246 (39%)	1,469 **(36%)**	153 (44%)	132 (48%)	203 (50%)	269 (41.0%)
VOP	**306** **(41%)**	134 (28%)	186 (37%)	**243** **(41%)**	128 (24%)	**240** **(42%)**	247 (39%)	1,484 **(37%)**	107 (31%)	79 (28%)	98 (25%)	237 (36.1%)
(O = personal pron.)	205	95	122	157	70	176	191	(1016) (25%)	86	53	78	(166) (25.3%)
(O = reflexive pronoun)	24	4	8	27	23	10	13	(109) (3%)	2	6	2	(29) (4.4%)
(O = non-personal pron.)	77 **(10%)**	35	56 **(11%)**	59 **(10%)**	35	54	43	**(359)** **(8.9%)**	19 (5.5%)	20 (7.2%)	18 (4.4%)	(42) (6.4%)
OVP	53 (7%)	15 (3%)	21 (4%)	30 (5%)	11 (2%)	18 (3%)	21 (3%)	169 (4%)	13 (4%)	9 (3%)	17 (4%)	22 (3.3%)
VOPO*	12	4	3	8	1	4	**19**	51 (1%)	3	3	1	8 (1.2%)
PVO	0	0	0	2	0	0	0	2	1	1	0	1
passive	117 (16%)	134 (28%)	70 (14%)	103 (18%)	**209** **(39%)**	134 (24%)	99 (15%)	866 (21%)	67 (19 %)	51 (19%)	86 (21%)	119 (18.1%)
total	745	487	498	583	533	563	632	4,041	345	275	405	656

* Instances of additional patterns such as VOOP or VPOO are included.

It might not be fair to directly compare Defoe's "corpus" consisting of his seven works with "single texts" by Bunyan, Swift and Richardson (or a collection of Behn's "novellas"); for example, Defoe's 4,041 instances and Richardson's 656 [in *Pamela*]. However, such a comparison of these two "corpora" by Defoe and Richardson in Table 9 helps us to grasp distinct characteristics unique to each author in employing phrasal verbs. An examination of this table confirms the following four points:

i) Generally, the frequencies of the VPO and VOP patterns in Defoe and the other four authors (i.e. *PP*, Behn, *GT* and *Pamela*) are remarkably high. The combined percentage of these two patterns in each work ranges from about 70 to 80%, excepting only *JPY*, which has the lowest percentage (58%). The four texts other than Defoe's corpus show a higher frequency of the VPO over VOP respectively; especially *GT* shows a remarkable contrast (VPO 50% vs. VOP 25%). In this resepct, even a slight predominance of the VOP over the VPO in Defoe's total (VOP 37% vs. VPO 36%) attracts special attention. Focused on the VOP frequency in Defoe's works, in *RC*, *MF*, and *CJ*, the VOP pattern is more frequently used, while in *MC*, *CS*, and *JPY*, the VPO pattern is more frequent; *Rox* shows almost an equal balance between these two patterns.

ii) In *JPY*, unlike the other works, the relatively high-frequency use of the passive construction accounts for about 40% of the total. As mentioned above, this phenomenon is closely related to the 123 repetitive uses of *shut up* in this work.

iii) Concerning the use of OVP and VOPO patterns, which totally only account for some 5% of transitive patterns, *RC* shows a relatively higher frequency, but it is notable that the VOPO pattern is most frequently chosen in *Rox*.

iv) Examing the use of "non-personal pronoun" as an object in the VOP pattern, there are 359 instances (8.9%) in total. In *RC*, *CS*, and *MF*, this use accounts to more than 10% of the total. In comparison with the frequencies in the texts by the other four authors (and in terms of Hiltunen's survey on the VOP pattern ["Among the total of 851 examples [of the VOP pattern in Helsinki Corpus]], there were only 30 cases where a nominal object ... intervened between the verb and the particle" (pp. 133-134)), there is evidence that Defoe likes to use the pattern "V + *Non-personal Pronoun* + P" in his fiction.

2.10.1 Choice between VPO and VOP
With regard to VPO and VOP patterns, Quirk et al. (1985: 1154) state that "The particle tends to precede the object if the object is long," but whether the object is long or short is a matter of degree; it is difficult to decide whether, for example, a five-word noun phrase in *I **held** this wicked Scene of Life **out** eight Years*, (*Rox* 188) is "long" as an object. It seems that, as the instances described in Section 2.2.3 suggest, Defoe does not depend exclusively upon the length of the object, in choosing between the VPO and the VOP.

In the following passage, *bring out* in the participial form takes the second longest (nine-word) object (as here found in Defoe's seven works). It consists of a noun phrase, *all the Earth and Stones*, and a relative clause: *that I dug down* (in which another phrasal verb is used), as in:

I began to work my Way into the Rock, and **bringing** all the

Earth and Stones that I dug down **out** thro' my Tent, (*RC* 60)

Why has Defoe chosen this syntax? It is useful to consider the fundamental difference between the two patterns of VPO and VOP in the use of transitive phrasal verbs. The first topic to be discussed regarding this is the "euphonic" factor (van Dongen 1919: 330).[21] Referring to particles which are "monosyllabic and short (e.g. *on, up*)," van Dongen mentions, "Even when emphatic, these short adverbs (i.e. "particles" in this study) can hardly be put behind the noun and pronounced with emphasis without spoiling the elegance of the sentence" (p. 334).[22] Based upon this explanation, the use of *bring out* in the passage cited above might be regarded as deviant.

It rather seems preferable to assume that Defoe's choice of the VOP pattern is related to "means of achieving semantic focus" (Bolinger 1971: 54). Visser explains the opposition: "he took his shoes off" / "he took off his shoes" in a straightforward manner: "Here the difference in wordorder (*sic*) may perhaps be accounted for by assuming that in the first of the two statements it is the taking *off*, and in the second the *shoes* on which the attention of the speaker is *mainly* focused, so that the first sentence might be seen as an answer to the question, 'What happened to the shoes?' and the second as an answer to the question, 'What did he take off?'" (1984 [1963]: 602).

If the theory of such a semantic focus is applicable to Defoe's use of *bring out*, the focus of the VOP is on the bringing *out*. In other words, the instance of *bring out* used in the VOP pattern can be seen as an answer to the question, 'What happened to "all the Earth and Stones that *you* dug down"?'

Thus, in the choice between the VPO and VOP patterns, Defoe apparently takes advantage of the difference in semantic focus or

Chapter 2 The Syntactic Structure of Transitive Phrasal Verbs

"information focus" (Halliday 1994: 208).[23] Compare the uses of *pull out* and *wipe off*, in the following passage:

> as he saw the Tears drop down my Cheek, he **pulls out** a fine Cambrick Hankerchief, and was going to **wipe** the Tears **off**, but check'd his Hand, as if he was afraid to deface something; (*Rox* 108)

Here *pull out* occurs in the VPO, while *wipe off* appears in the VOP. The information focus in the VPO instance is on "a fine Cambrick Hankerchief" as newsworthy, while in the VOP instance the focus is on the action of wiping *off*, not "the Tears" which is given information, as the reader already knows "he saw the Tears drop down" the heroine's cheek.

The way Defoe uses both patterns in the same context can best be exemplified in the two uses of *take away*:

> The Wine being out, he call'd his Gentleman again, to **take away** the Table, who, at first, only **took** the Cloth, and the Remains of what was to Eat, **away**; (*Rox* 63)

Since *take away the Table* in the VPO pattern obviously means "To clear the table after a meal" (cf. *OED* s.v. take, v. 85(f)) in this context, the longest (ten-word) object in the VOP, *the Cloth, and the Remains of what was to Eat*, showing the details of "the table" to be cleared, can be contextually considered assumed and thus given information. Through the use of the two types of VPO and VOP, Defoe's minute and accurate delineation of the scene can be appreciated.

In the same vein, the VOP pattern, by emphasis on the particle placed in the end position, tends to highlight a dynamic "action" inherent in the phrasal verb. On the other hand, the VPO pattern, focusing on the object in the end position, makes up a less action-based but, as it were, more object-based description. As far as the use of the transitive phrasal verbs is concerned, more action-based descriptions abound in *Robinson Crusoe*, *Moll Flanders*, and *Colonel Jack*; on the contrary, *Memoris of a Cavalier*, *Captain Singleton*, and *A Journal of the Plague Year* contain more object-based descriptions.

NOTES:

The most frequently used transitive phrasal verb in *Pamela* is *put on* (35 occurrences in total). Among them, as many as 29 instances (83%) occur in the VPO pattern; as for the rest, two instances in the VOP, one in the PVO and the VOPO respectively, two in the passive.[24] Some of the VPO instances are given below:

> As soon as I have din'd, I will **put on** my new Cloaths. (54) / There I trick'd myself up as well as I could in my new Garb, and **put on** my round-ear'd ordinary Cap; (55) / I will, I think, open the Portmanteau, and, ... **put on** my best Silk Night-gown. (259) / He **put on** a clean Shirt and Neckcloth, (290) / Her Ladyship instantly **put on** her Hood and Gloves, (425), etc.

In this epistolary novel, Pamela, the eponymous heroine, (and Richardson, the author) likes to write down the details of her (or others') clothes in her letters or journals. The VPO pattern serves as a word-order suitable for her (and the author's) predilection, since the noun phrases placed in the end position tend to be highlighted. In other words, Richardson wants to focus on "what did Pamela (or other

Chapter 2 The Syntactic Structure of Transitive Phrasal Verbs

persons) put on?," *not* "what happened to the clothes?" In this respect, it is of great importance to notice that in the use of *put on*, personal pronouns are *never* employed, like *I put them on*.

Finally, the only instance of the OVP pattern deserves comment:

<u>A plain Muslin Tucker</u> I **put on**, <u>and my black Silk Necklace</u>, instead of the *French* Necklace my Lady gave me, (55)

In the above passage, the object of *put on* is virtually a long noun phrase *A plain Muslin Tucker and my black Silk Necklace*. Through a unique syntax by which this noun phrase is divided into two parts, Pamela's strong concern about clothing is emphasized.

notes

[1] Generally, many verbs (except "pure" intransitive verbs such as *go* or *come*) can be used either intransitively or transitively. In this connection, in Defoe the type of verb such as *she **opened** the door* tends to be more variable than the type such as *the door **opened***.

[2] In comparison with the data of intransitive verbs in the same work (out of 88 verbs, 195 types including composite types such as *come running back* are generated), transitive phrasal verbs have a wider variety of use than intransitive verbs.

[3] As its subtilte "A military Journal of the Wars ..." suggests, *MC* (i.e. *Memoirs of a Cavalier*) is rather different from Defoe's other fictional works, in that it is full of a variety of military terms.

[4] As well, Kennedy (1967 [1920]: 31) states that "In a few instances the impersonal pronoun *it* intervenes, but is itself so colorless that the unity of the verb-adverb combination is hardly affected at all." He gives several examples like *to hit it off* 'to agree' or *to stick it out* 'to persevere.'

[5] In *Captain Singleton* or other works by Defoe, the boat or ship is conventionally referred to as a feminine pronoun "her," as in:

the high Tide had **floated** her [= the ship] **off** to Sea. (*CS* 156) / ... into a little Cove, or Inlet, where a small Brook came into the main River,

227

we **laid** her [= "our Frigate"] **up** for those that came next, (*CS* 67) / Upon this we prepared to **pour in** a Broadside upon her [= the ship]. (*CS* 156) / how to **get** her [= "another Boat"] **off** into the Sea, was a doubtful thing; (*RC* 43) / they might not **carry** her [= the boat] **off**; (*RC* 259), etc.

[6] *Lay down* is also used intransitively in Defoe, as follows:
so the poor Creature **laid down**, and went to sleep. (*RC* 205) / I **lay down** and slept heartily: (*MC* 212) [cf. *OED* s.v. lay, $v.^1$ 43. a In intransitive uses, coinciding with or resembling those of lie $v.^1$; c 1300~]

[7] Jespersen (*MEG* III: 325) goes on to mention that "the tendency is towards getting rid of the cumbersome *self*-pronoun whenever no ambiguity is to be feared; thus a modern Englishman or American will say *I wash, dress, and shave*, where his ancestor would add (*me*, or) *myself* in each case."

[8] This phrasal verb is used twice (as *to*-infinitive) in the VOP pattern, in the same work:
without which they would never be able to **give** themselves **up**, (*MF* 174) / the greatest of Spirits, ... are subject to the greatest Dejections, and are the most apt to Despair and **give** themselves **up**. (*MF* 315)

[9] The *OED* first-citation of the reflexive *give up* is from Shakespeare's *Othello* in 1604: "He hath deuoted, and **giuen vp** himselfe to the Contemplation ... of her parts and graces" (*OED* s.v. give, *v*. 64d). Of particular interest is the evidence that this instance appears in the pattern of VPO. In passing, other instances of the VPO pattern in the reflexive use are:
In like manner, at another House in the same Lane, a Man having his Family infected, but very unwilling to be shut up, when he could conceal it no longer, **shut up** himself; (*JPY* 169) / [as *to*-infinitive] To fight them with their Foot would be Desperation, and ridiculous; and to retreat, would but be to **coop up** themselves in a narrow Place, (*MC* 262)

[10] Parrott (2010: 406), giving the instance "*I like working with students **who** appreciate what I do*. / *with appreciative students*," remarks that "Relative clauses are similar in function to adjectives." In this sense, phrasal verbs in the restrictive relative clause can be said to serve as part of a modifier.

[11] Further, in referring to "a tendency to place a weakly stressed pronoun as near to the verb as possible," Jespersen (*MEG* III: 288) pays special attention to "the two word-orders [in which] the weak pron. is placed before the heavier sb. [i.e. noun]" in Defoe's *MF*: "they often gave me money, and I gave it my old nurse."

[12] The *OED* records *off of* as a set phrase. See *OED* (s.v. of, *prep*. 1.c).

[13] Leech (2006: 11) refers to this as "a passive construction that has no agent."
[14] According to Jespersen (*MEG* IV: 205), "The construction *is* (*was*, etc.) *building* in a passive sense, ... was frequent from the 16th to the 18th century."
[15] Jespersen (*MEG* IV: 208) cites this passage in explanation of the passive progressive form under discussion.
[16] In the Penguin edition of *JPY*, editors Anthony Burgess and Christopher Bristow have changed *turn'd out* into the more palpable adjective-form *turned-out* (Penguin Classics 1986: 244).
[17] Jespersen (*MEG* V: 114) also notes that Shakespeare "has perhaps only three instances," and as "literary quotations" gives a few instances of the "new passive gerund" from Defoe.
[18] When -*ly* adverbs occur in the VPO pattern, they tend to precede V, as with *I thankfully* **laid down** *the Book*, (*RC* 157), or following O, as in *I* **took up** *the second Piece immediately*, (*RC* 28). Additional instances are:
    we immediately **poured in** our Broad-Side, (*CS* 151) / I stood ready, and presently **felt out** the Bag of Money, (*CJ* 58) / it had certainly **blown-up** the whole Affair, (*Rox* 280) / then the QUAKER unhappily, tho' undesignedly, **put in** a Question, (*Rox* 286), etc.

Or:
    ... by which we **lengthen'd out** our Provision considerably; (*CS* 88) / [the umbrella] **kept off** the Sun so effectually, (*RC* 135) / he **wrote down** the words distinctly, (*MF* 102) / [we] **cut off** their Retreat so effectually, (*CJ* 213), etc.

[19] As noted in Chapter 1, it is necessary to reconsider the linguistic insights by Quirk et al. (1985) and Palmer (1987)—namely that the more idiomatic a phrasal verb becomes, the less likely the verb and particle are to be separated.
[20] This adverb is used only twice in the VPO, though it comes before V, as in *till at last I quite* **lay'd aside** *the Thoughts of it* (*RC* 16).
[21] According to van Dongen (1919: 330), "playing a more or less important part [in the VOP pattern], is *euphony*, especially *rhythm*."
[22] In van Dongen's material, among "270 cases of inseparableness of *verb* and *up*, only 20 cases occur where the two are sundered. In the case of *out*, these numbers are respectively, 144 and 18" (p. 334).
[23] Concerning the syntax of a transitive phrasal verb with a personal pronoun, Halliday (1994: 209) suggests that the main reason why "*they called it off*" rather than "*they called off it*" occurs is that "a pronoun is hardly ever newsworthy."
[24] Instances of the VOP and VOPO patterns are given for reference:
    [VOP] I bid him ask Mr. *Colbrand* to walk up; and he came; but neither

of them would sit, nor **put** their Hats **on**. (246) / [VOPO] I'll **put** thee **on** a Gown and Cassock, and thou'lt make a good Figure in his Place! (69), etc.

Chapter 3
Semantic and Stylistic Analysis of Phrasal Verbs: Six Aspects

The syntactic features of phrasal verbs were the main focus of Chapters 1 and 2. In this Chapter, semantic and stylistic features of phrasal verbs in Defoe will be investigated. There are six main topics which will be addressed: (1) coordinated use with other verbs, (2) inversion and particle fronting for stylistic effect, (3) the function of particles in psychological contexts, (4) descriptions of the sea, (5) the "redundant" use of particles, and (6) repetition and synonym.

3.1 Coordinated Use with Other Verbs: the "A and B (and C ...)" Pattern

As instances of the transitive "composite pattern" in Section 2.9 (e.g. [*we*] *pickled and* ***barrelled up*** *the Flesh*) show, phrasal verbs in Defoe's fiction have a strong tendency to be coordinated with another verb through the coordinate conjunction *and*, as in *we* ***sat down*** *and considered*, (*CS* 33). This section investigates such cases including all types, both intransitive and transitive, and attempts to generalize their characteristic features.

3.1.1 Cohesive Relation in the "A and B" Coordination (*e.g. we sat down and considered, (CS 33)*)
In the instance cited here, *we **sat down** and considered*, two verbs, one

of which is a phrasal verb, are linked by the coordinator *and*. Such a coordination pattern often suggests not only a chronological sequence of two actions, but also a very close relationship in meaning.[1] That is, the coordination of two different actions makes up an integrated and cohesive whole, or what Quirk et al. (1985: 943-944) suggest a "single combined activity."[2] Let us examine the following case:

>I **stood up**, and humbly thank'd his Highness, (*Rox* 59).

Stand up and *thank* in coordination semantically complement each other, in that the description of the (humble) behavior of "thanking" a man of higher rank is somehow incomplete without the action of "standing up." Thus, a sense of unity arises from the two-verb coordination including a phrasal verb. Furthermore, the coordinated use of *kneel down* in the following passages is of the same nature:

>I **kneel'd down** and pray'd to God to fulfil the Promise to me, (*RC* 94) / he **kneel'd down** and pray'd with me. (*MF* 287) / immediately I **kneel'd down** and gave God Thanks aloud, (*RC* 96) [cf. *OED* s.v. kneel, *v. intr.* "To fall on the knees or a knee; ... as in supplication or homage"]

The verb phrases coordinated with *kneel down* are *pray to God* and *give God thanks*. *Kneel* (*down*) expresses not merely a physical movement but a gesture of "supplication or homage" (*OED*). Thus, these two-verb phrases are fully complementary to each other. Seen in this light, coordinated instances such as *stand up and thank* and *kneel down and pray* can function as a single unit, such as "hendiadys," which is a figure of rhetoric, meaning: "one thing by two" (from Greek), e.g.

Chapter 3 Semantic and Stylistic Analysis of Phrasal Verbs: Six Aspects

bread and butter, and *nice and warm*.
In the coordination pattern under discussion, transitive phrasal verbs are used as well. Consider *pull out* in the following passages:

> he first of all **pull'd out** a Deer skin Bag, and gave it me, with five and fifty Spanish Pistoles in it, (*MF* 336) / with that, he **pull'd out** a silk Purse, which had threescore Guineas in it, and threw them into my Lap, (*Rox* 42) / one of the Men **pulled out** a Knife and shewed them, (*CS* 22) / [in the use of "dramatic present"] with that he **pulls out** a silk Purse, with an Hundred Guineas in it, and gave it me; (*MF* 28) / so he **Pulls out** a peice of Paper, and throws it to me, (*CJ* 148), etc.

Since *pull out* is used in the VPO pattern, the objects such as *a Deer skin Bag* or *a silk Purse* are likely to be more highlighted than in the case of the VOP; note that the objects, introduced by an indefinite article, are all newsworthy. Based on syntactic features of the VPO, the coordination between *pull out* and another verb such as *give* or *throw* seems to form a strong, cohesive unit, for the goal of "pulling out (something)" is achieved exclusively by the action of the following verb phrase.

In addition to the phrasal verbs discussed above, all of which occur in the place of A in the framework "A and B," other similar cases are given:

> [intransitve phrasal verbs]
> he **stood up** and made his Bow, (*MF* 251) / Immediately all the House **rose up**, and paid me a kind of a Compliment, (*Rox* 175) / [after the causative verb] *says I*, let me **go back** and fetch my Linnen, (*CJ* 106) / [after verbs of perception] it was about that

233

Time that I heard him and his two Men **go out** and shut the Yard-Gates after them. (*Rox* 12), etc.

[transitive phrasal verbs]
so they **Mann'd out** their Boat, and sent to us with a Flag of Truce. (*CS* 216) / at which the Man enraged **took up** his Fuzee [= "A light musket or firelock" (*OED*)], and shot the Negro through the Heart. (*CS* 52) / I **pull'd off** my blue Apron, and wrapt the Bundle in it, (*MF* 239) / [VOP] I **took** Captain *Wilmot* **aside**, and began to talk to him about it; (*CS* 183), etc.

In the following passages, a sense of unity arises, mainly because a transitive phrasal verb shares with the second verb the preceding object (i.e. the demonstrative pronoun *that* or the relative pronoun *which*):

[OVP] that [= "a very good Necklace of Pearl"] he **pull'd out**, and ty'd about my Neck; (*Rox* 257) / Here they pitched their little Camp, which consisted of three large Tents or Hutts made of Poles, which their Carpenter, ... **cut down** and fix'd in the Ground in a Circle, (*JPY* 140) / ... the Letters, which the Merchant himself only **read over**, and Sign'd, (*CJ* 303)

Phrasal verbs also occur in the position of B in the "A and B" framework such as *we weighed, and* ***stood away*** *South*, (*CS* 173). Other similar cases are given here:

[intransitive phrasal verbs]
Come, come, says she, *be thy self, and* ***rouze up***, (*Rox* 222) / But she cry'd and **took on** like a distracted Body, (*MF* 283) [cf. *OED* s.v. take, *v.* 86. j. "To 'go on' madly or excitedly; to rage, rave; to be greatly agitated; to make a great fuss, outcry, or uproar;" *c* 1430~] /

Chapter 3 Semantic and Stylistic Analysis of Phrasal Verbs: Six Aspects

[in the form of *to*-infinitive] poor *Xury* cryed to me <u>to weigh the Anchor and</u> **row away**; (*RC* 26) / [after verbs of perception] in three Minutes we <u>saw</u> all the Men <u>hurry into the Boat, and</u> **put off** (= "To leave the land" (*OED*)); (*CS* 263), etc.

[transitive phrasal verbs]
[VPO] so she <u>put her Hand in her Pocket, and</u> **pulls out** her Purse. (*Rox* 191) / the Small-Pox, a frightful Distemper in that Country, <u>broke into my Family, and</u> **carry'd off** three of my Children, and a Maid Servant; (*CJ* 249) [cf. *OED* s.v. carry, *v.* 51. a. *trans*. "To remove from this life, be the death of." *c* 1680~] / [VOP] we ... <u>lower'd the Top-Sail</u> upon the Cap, <u>and</u> **clewed** them **up** that we might lye as snug as we could, (*CS* 147) [cf. *OED* s.v. clew, *v.* 3. *Naut*. "*to clew up*: to draw the lower ends or clews (of sails) up to the upper yard or the mast in preparation for furling or for making 'goose-wings'." *a* 1745~] / I <u>threw open the Bed, and</u> **thrust** her **in**. (*Rox* 46), etc.

In the following passage, a phrasal verb *bring down* shares with another verb *fetch* the same object (i.e. a relative pronoun *which*) as well as *to* as an infinitive marker:

besides about fifteen Ton of Elephants Teeth, <u>which</u> he had, ... obliged the Savages of the Country <u>to fetch, and</u> **bring down** to him from the Mountains, (*CS* 133)

In both A and B slots, two different phrasal verbs can occur, as with *I* **went in** <u>and</u> **sat down** *in my Tent*, (*RC* 81). Additional instances are given:

[the coordination of two intransitive phrasal verbs]

235

and with that he **rose up** and **brush'd off**. (*MF* 47) [cf. *OED* s.v. brush, *v.*¹ 3. *intr.* "To burst away with a rush, move off abruptly, be gone, decamp, make off." 1690~] / I **got up** out of my Cabbin, and **look'd out**; (*RC* 12) / [after verbs of perception] When *Amy* saw me **come back**, and **sit down** without speaking, (*Rox* 123), etc.

[the coordination between a transitive phrasal verb and an intransitive phrasal verb]
Amy **pack'd up** her Alls, and **march'd off**, (*Rox* 313) / the Fellow ... **puts on** a Ploughman's Habit, and **went away** immediately with a long Pole upon his Shoulder; (*MC* 88) / he **pulls off** his Hose and **goes in**, (*MC* 88) / Her Mother ... **threw down** her Candle, and **shriekt out** in such a frightful Manner, (*JPY* 56), etc.

Note that in this coordination pattern, a transitive phrasal verb is likely to occur in the VPO pattern.

[the coordination between an intransitive phrasal verb and a transitive phrasal verb]
[VP and VPO] But we **went on** with our Business, and **lay'd out** 12000 Pieces of Eight, (*CJ* 293) / I **push'd on** for another Voyage, and **laid up** a Stock of all sorts of Goods ... (*CJ* 297) / I could easily perceive that the Goats had **gone in** and **eaten up** the Corn, (*RC* 145) / I told him he should **go back** again, and **choose out** five of them, (*RC* 270) / [VP and VOP] We **drank on**, and **drank** the Punch **out**, (*CJ* 110) / the Cart **fell in** and **drew** the Horses **in** also: (*JPY* 180), etc.

[the coordination of two transitive phrasal verbs]
[VPO and VPO] I **threw down** the Piece, and **took up** the

Chapter 3 Semantic and Stylistic Analysis of Phrasal Verbs: Six Aspects

Fowling-Piece, (*RC* 234) / he **burnt down** the Tree and **stopt up** the Entrance into the Cave. (*CS* 213) / our Negroes **took down** the Tent, and **pull'd up** the Stakes, (*CS* 85) / [in the participial use] Now *Friday*, says I, **laying down** the discharg'd Pieces, and **taking up** the Musket, (*RC* 234), etc.

[VPO and VOP] he **pull'd out** his Letter Case, and **laid** it **down**, (*CJ* 31) / I **put away** all her Servants, and almost **lock'd** her **up**; (*CJ* 242) / But I **rous'd up** my Judgment, and **shook** it **off**, (*Rox* 277) / Then he **pull'd out** his Grandmother's Will, and **read** it **over** to me, (*MF* 336) / I **reach'd out** my Hand, ... and **threw** one of the Candles **off** of the Table; (*Rox* 297) / [as *to*-infinitive] This furnish'd me with an Excuse to my Spouse, to **break off** the Discourse for the present, and **call** *Amy* **down**; (*Rox* 297) / he was to **lock up** the Outer-Door of the House, and **take** the Key **away** with him; (*JPY* 50) / he was very busy **Writing down** the Sums, and **putting** it **up** in several Bags; (*CJ* 43), etc.

[Passive] a whole Family was **shut up** and **lock'd in**, (*JPY* 51) / they [= the dead people] were always **clear'd away**, and **carry'd off** every Night (*JPY* 103), etc.

In the "VPO and VPO" pattern, e.g. *I threw down ... and took up ...* (*RC* 234), the contrastive use of the particles, *down* and *up*, creates a sense of unity in a sequence of dynamic actions. Nevertheless, in the coordination of two transitive phrasal verbs, it is taken for granted that the first verb tends to occur in the VPO and the second in the VOP, as in *he pull'd out his Letter Case, and laid it down*, (*CJ* 31); in terms of information focus, the first object is new and the second one given.

In the following passage, two transitive phrasal verbs, *bring in* and *thrash out*, share the same object *above 220 Bushels*:

from our 22 Bushels of Barley, we **brought in** and **thrashed out** above 220 Bushels; (*RC* 247)

In Defoe's fiction, a phrasal verb is sometimes coordinated with two or more verbs, like *So he **went in**, and fetched a pail of Water, and set it **down** hard by the Purse;* (*JPY* 105). When coordinating three or more words and phrases (including nouns as well as verbs), as in the instance cited, Defoe prefers to use *and* in each case.[3] Among instances of such a three (or more) verb coordination, through a chronological sequence of different actions, a cohesive relation can be observed.

In the following passages, through sharing the infinitive marker *to*, a coordination of three verbs (note the first one contains two intransitive phrasal verbs *turn about* and *walk away* as well as the transitive *take up*) creates a sense of unity:

> I took my opportunity to **turn about** and **take up** what was behind me and **walk away**: (*MF* 196) / so I was fain to **sit down** again, and take it out of my Shoe, and carry it in my Hand, (*CJ* 23)

In the following passage, however, the actions described by three verbs (including one phrasal verb) seem to be occurring simultaneously rather than successively:

> THE poor Captain stamp'd, and danc'd, and **roar'd out** like a mad Boy; (*CJ* 12)

Finally, as a very rare case, five verbs, *go, dress, come, smile*, and *be*, are employed in coordination. However, examined closely, the first two phrases (including *go up*) and the other three (including *come down*)

238

seem to serve as separate units respectively, in a dialogic context:

> you, Madam, *says he* to me, **go up** and dress you, and **come down** and smile and be merry; (*Rox* 27)

3.1.2 Synonymous Relation in the "A and B" Coordination

As another type of the coordination under discussion, the use of *make off* from *JPY* is examined:

> he, with the sound part of his Servants and Family, **made off** and escaped; (*JPY* 169) [cf. *OED* s.v. make, *v*. 89. d. *intr*. "To depart or leave a place suddenly, often with a disparaging implication; to hasten or run away; to decamp, 'bolt'." 1709~]

The phrasal verb *make off* in the passage cited above is most probably employed in the sense of "to leave a place" or "to run away" (*OED*). In this case, the coordination of *make off* and a single-word verb of Romance origin, *escape*, suggests a synonymous relationship rather than a sequence of two separate actions—probably in order to enhance the meaning.[4]

In the following passage, *look back* and *reflect* seem to share not only the infinitive marker *to* but the preposition *upon*, for *look back upon*—this form is frequently used in Defoe (as seen in the instances of *upon* in Section 1.4.1; pp.86-87). In this case, two verbs can be; considered synonymous in this context:

> I recommend it to the Charity of all good People to **look back**, and reflect duly upon the Terrors of the Time; (*JPY* 236)

In the same text (*JPY*), *put off* is coordinated with two different verbs of Romance origin, *delay* and *dismiss*, respectively:

> It would make the stoutest Heart bleed to hear how many Warnings were then given by dying Penitents, to others not to **put off** <u>and delay</u> their Repentance to the Day of Distress, (*JPY* 104) [cf. *OED* s.v. put, v.¹ 46. c. "To postpone to a later time; to defer." 1398~] / this occasion'd <u>the</u> **putting off**, <u>and dismissing</u> an innumerable Number of Journey-men, and Work-men of all Sorts, (*JPY* 223) [cf. *OED* s.v. put, v.¹ 46. f. "To <u>dismiss</u>, put away: ... (b) from one's service or employment." *Obs. c* 1400 ~ *a* 1713]

The coordination pattern serves to make the meaning of polysemous (and therefore rather ambiguous) phrasal verbs such as *put off* more specific. Thus, Defoe makes good use of phrasal verbs within the syntactic framework of "A and B." In addition, it is of great interest to note that such a synonymous coordination is used almost extensively in the rather non-fictional *JPY*.

In the coordination pattern, a single verb of Romance origin occurs prior to a phrasal verb, as in:

> they would always have Preservatives in their Mouths, and about their Cloths to <u>repell and</u> **keep off** the Infection. (*JPY* 209) / [I have been speaking] of the wretched inhuman Custom of their <u>devouring and</u> **eating** one another **up**, (*RC* 166) / [cf. in the use of *or*] it seems they found means to <u>Bribe or</u> **buy off** some of those who were expected to come in against them, (*MF* 295)

In this case, a phrasal verb (e.g. *keep off*) partly serves to "define" the preceding verb (e.g. *repel*).

3.1.3 Coordinated with Words or Phrases of Different Word Class

In very rare cases, a phrasal verb in the passive voice is coordinated with a pure adjective; in this case, the coordinated phrase seems to serve as a subject complement:

> [I] sat still upon the Ground, greatly **cast down** and disconsolate, not knowing what to do: (*RC* 81) [cf. *OED* s.v. cast, *v.* 76. d. "To deject in spirits, disappoint, dispirit. Chiefly in *pa. pple.* = downcast." 1382~] / Heartless, and **tired out** with continual ill News, and ill Success, I had frequent Meetings with some Gentlemen, (*MC* 260) / This Part of the Country almost unpassable, and **walled round** with Hills, was indifferent quiet, (*MC* 215)

In these cases, *cast down*, *tired out*, and *walled round* are all assumed to have an adjectival status, rather than a verbal one.

In the following passage, an adverbial phrase, *very gravely to me*, is coordinated with an *-ing* participle clause including *pull off*:

> said one of them *very gravely to me, and* **pulling off** his Hat at the same time to me, (*RC* 254)

In this context, *pulling off* has no doubt an adverbial status.

NOTES:
In Bunyan's *The Pilgrim's Progress* and Behn's fiction, especially in the former, phrasal verbs are frequently used in the coordination pattern, but there seem to be far fewer cases where a cohesive relation between two verbs as seen in Defoe's cases can be observed; most of the cases show exclusively a temporal sequence:

[in *PP*]

[intransitive phrasal verbs] for a while he **sat down** and wept, (44) / they [= "*Fiends*"] **gave back,** and came no further. (63) [cf. *OED* s.v. give, *v.* 55. b *intr.* "To retreat, fall back." 1548~ ; The *OED* cites this passage as an instance in this sense.] / Then they **went away** and sang. (119) / [A and B and C] When the Gate was opened he would **give back,** and give place to others, and say that he was not worthy. (234) / So they **went in** and spake to the men, and called each by his Name, (278), etc.
[transitive phrasal verbs] but his Lord and ours did **gather up** his Tears, and put them into his Bottle, (177) / [Then said the *Gyant*] thou **gatherest up** Women and Children, and carriest them into a strange Countrey, (229) / It [= a *Monster*] would also **carry away** their Children, and teach them to suck its Whelps. (258), etc. / [A and B and C] And with that she **pluck'd out** her Letter, and read it, and **said** to them, What now will you say to this? (173) / Then he took her by the hand, and **led** her **in**, and said also, (179) / Then he took her again by the hand, and **led** her gently **in**, and said, (180), etc. / [A and B and C and D] So he [= Mr. *Great-heart*] smote him [= *Slaygood*, a giant] and slew him, and **cut off** his Head, and **brought** it **away** to the *Inn*. (249)
[phrasal verb and Romance one] The *Interpreter* answered, This fire is the work of Grace that is wrought in the heart; he that casts Water upon it, to extinguish and **put** it **out**, is the *Devil*; (32) / even as we see the Dog that is sick of what he hath eaten, ... he vomits and **casts up** all; (144) [cf. *OED* s.v. cast, *v.* 83. b. "To vomit." *Obs.* or *dial.* 1484~]

[in Behn]

[intransitive phrasal verbs] They **sat down**, and ask'd for something to relish a Glass of Wine, (133) / At last, one of the Nuns **came up**, and told Dame Katteriena, (154) / When the

242

Chapter 3 Semantic and Stylistic Analysis of Phrasal Verbs: Six Aspects

fellow found himself so wounded he **wheeled off** and cried, (86) [cf. *OED* s.v. wheel, *v.* 4. a. *intr*. "To turn so as to face in a different direction; to turn round or aside, esp. quickly or suddenly. Often with *round, about,* †*off.*" 1639~], etc. / [A and B and C] I fancy he **got up**, and took this poor Man, and has occasion'd his Death: (188) / he **came up** to Parham, and forcibly took Caesar, and had him carried to the same post where he was whipped; (72)

[transitive phrasal verbs] at last she **drew** it **out**, and gave him a pistole, (81) / When we had eat, my brother and I **took out** our flutes, and played to 'em, (54) / He **took off** his perrywig and **put on** a white, satin cap with a holland one done with point under it, (116) / [passive] All the windows were **taken down** and filled with spectators, (106) / [A and B and C] At that, he **ripped up** his own belly, and took his bowels and **pulled** 'em **out**, with what strength he could; (70)

As the above instances show, it has been found that the coordination pattern is not unique to Defoe; the "A and B and C" pattern is also used by Bunyan and Behn. Hence, such coordination seems to have been useful for composing fictional narratives and story-telling.[5]

As seen in the first instance in *PP* and Behn respectively, *sit down* tends to be used in the "A and B" coordination pattern. This tendency is further developed in Richardson's use of it. The use of *sit down*, the most recurrently (94 times) used phrasal verb in *Pamela*, can be characterized with two distinct features inherent to the novel: the "social" *sit down* and the "mental" *sit down*. The former appears in the context where a character tries to develop a relationship with others, while the latter can be seen when a character faces a mental or emotional dilemma and is not able to "stand" any more:

[the "socal" *sit down* in *Pamela*]
>He **sat down**, and look'd at me, (57) / He **sat down** on the Bed-side, and interrupted me, No need of your foolish Fears; (221) / So my Lady **sat down** with me half an Hour, and told me how her Brother had carryd her a fine Airing, and had quite charm'd her with his kind Treatment of her; (440), etc.

[the "mental" *sit down* in *Pamela*]
>[A and B and C] So I **sat down**, and was quite sick with the Hurry of my Spirits, and lean'd upon her Arm. (399) / Her Ladyship **sat down**, and leaned her Head against my Bosom, and made my Neck wet with her Tears, holding me by my Hands; (433) / She [= Lady *Davers*] **sat down**, and fann'd herself, and burst into Tears, (419), etc.

3.2 Inversion and Particle Fronting for Stylistic Effect

In the use of phrasal verbs, Defoe sometimes changes the "normal" word order concerning the relationship between a verb and a particle, or these two words and a subject. The most typical case is the phenomenon of "fronting of the particle" (e.g. ***away he went***, (*RC* 239)), which has been closely examined in terms of its syntax in Section 1.1.1. This section, however, focuses on *why* such cases are employed. Probably, most of them are used for some stylistic effect based on Defoe's artistic intentions.

"Inversion," in which a phrasal verb itself precedes the subject, occurs exclusively in the use of intransitive phrasal verbs, at least, in Defoe's fiction.[6] Defoe's texts (the seven works mentioned) contain only 10 cases of "inversion" with *Memoirs of a Cavalier* and *A Journal of the Plague Year* having no instances. First examined are three

Chapter 3 Semantic and Stylistic Analysis of Phrasal Verbs: Six Aspects

instances of inversion with *there* fronted:

> ... there **came in** four French Gentlemen, (*RC* 290) / but there **rose up** a little Cloud of Fowls, (*RC* 116) / But there **fell out** a great Difficulty here, (*Rox* 326)

The "Verb + Particle + Subject" word order seems to be in full accordance with the principle of end-focus. Namely, the focal point in the above instances is the subject, and each of the instances would be the answer to each of the following questions, *who came in there?*, *what rose up there?*, or *what fell out there?* rather than *what happened* (e.g. *to four French Gentlemen*, etc.)?

Thus, Defoe seems to employ such a pattern of inversion to create a sort of suspense in the context, by delaying the information which the reader expects to find. Among the rest (the other seven cases), three cases are selected for scrutiny.

In *Moll Flanders* the inverted subject is a very long (i.e. fourteen-word), detailed noun phrase; in this case, the "S + V + P" word order would be rather unusual. In consequence, the whole expression consisting of a phrasal verb plus a subject describes the heroine's inner struggle:

> WITH these Reflections **came in**, of meer Course, severe Reproaches of my own Mind for my wretched Behaviour in my past Life; (*MF* 287)

As this case suggests, some of phrasal verbs contribute to the characters' psychological expressions in Defoe's fiction (which will be further discussed in the following section (3.3)).

245

In *Colonel Jack* an inversion of "*come up* plus a subject" occurs after a series of four phrasal verbs:

> We **drank on**, and **drank** the Punch **out**, and more was **brought up**, and he **push'd** it **about** a pace; then **came up** a Leg of Mutton, and I need not say that we eat heartily, (*CJ* 110)

Here, through an intensive use of spatial particles, *on, out, up, about,* a boisterous banquet is vividly and dynamically described; the context indicates that the inverted subject *a Leg of Mutton* is an eagerly-awaited dish.

Captain Singleton has a sole occurrence of inversion in the nonfinite use:

> we perceived **standing in** for the Shore, an *English* Man of War of Thirty six Guns: (*CS* 145)

In the passage cited above, immediately after *perceive*, a perception verb, follows the participial construction *standing in*, not the object *a man of war*, which would normally occur. This reverse word order might provide some sort of suspense and a realistic feel for the reader; the reader can feel something like a ship moving (because *stand in* is a nautical term), but does not realize what it is until the end.[7]

In the category of inversion under discussion, there are two cases where an intransitive phrasal verb occurs in the "Verb + Subject + Particle" pattern, as in:

> While I said thus, pretty boldly to the Fellow, **comes** a Woman **out**, (*CJ* 27) / ... and presently **comes** *William* **up** to me; (*CS*

152)

These two instances can be regarded as a stylistic variation of the inversion discussed above; the word order of "V + S" agrees with the definition of inversion. In addition, this pattern seems to have more immediate and lively impact than the pattern of the normal inversion, probably because the end position of the particle puts more emphasis on the action of the phrasal verb than the subject. Furthermore, note that the "dramatic" present tense, *comes*, is used in the above passages.

In spite of such observations, Defoe's seven works contain no more than 12 occurrences of inversion (including two variants) in total, while, as shown in Section 1.1.1, there are far more cases of particle fronting such as ***away he went***, (*RC* 239). This suggests that particle fronting is a much more appropriate tool for Defoe's stylistic purposes.

In most of the instances of particle fronting, the subject is "human," namely personal pronouns (referring to the real persons like *he* or *she*) or a common noun (e.g. ***away runs*** *the Maid*; (*MF* 205)) and a proper noun (e.g. ***away runs*** *Friday* (i.e. Crusoe's servant), (*RC* 294)). However, there are four exceptions in total. These four instances are to be investigated from both stylistic and contextual viewpoints.

First, the "neuter" personal pronoun *it* is used three times as a subject, as in:

> [a] they will presently say, there's something else in it, and then **out** it **comes**, that I am Marry'd already to somebody else, (*MF* 35)
> [b] ... and then **out** it [= "a Pocket-book"] **came** again, ... and then **in** it **went** again, (*CJ* 45)

In [a], *it* functions as a formal subject (in fact, *that*-clause is a real subject). In [b], the two instances of the particle fronting, which complement each other in the same page from *Colonel Jack*, are of particular significance. Here, *it* refers to a "Pocket-book" ("a book-like case of leather or the like, having compartments for papers, banknotes, bills, etc." (*OED*)). The description in which an inanimate thing seemingly "comes in" and "goes out" by itself seems quite strange. The truth of the matter is that it is the owner of the pocket-book who moves it. This can be confirmed from a wider context:

> I saw two Gentlemen mighty Eager in Talk, and one pull'd out a Pocket-book two or three times, and then slipt it into his Coat-pocket again, and then **out** it **came** again, and Papers were taken out, and others put in; and then **in** it **went** again, and so several times, (*CJ* 45)

The use of the fronting pattern in this passage leads to an interpretation that the narrator and protagonist *I*, as a pickpocket, is paying close attention to the pocket-book (and its contents) as a game; he takes no notice of the owner of the book. In this respect, these are stylistically marked expressions.

Next, it is necessary to pay special attention to the only case in which an inanimate and intangible noun (*the kind*) *Motion* ("a proposal" (*OED* 7a)) is used as a subject, in *Roxana*. The effect of the inversion in this case must be construed from a wider context:

> the QUAKER cou'd not help saying, *Mine was just such a-one*; and after several other Similitudes, all very vexatious to me, **out comes** the kind Motion to me, *to let the Ladies see my Dress*; (*Rox* 291)

The passage cited above, as the adjective *vexatious* suggests, describes the heroine's (and narrator's) mental conflict. The Quaker, her friend, is asking her to show the ladies her dress, in an innocent way. But the heroine is very nervous lest a showing of the dress from her days as a courtesan should ruin her. Hence, the use of the epithet *kind* is considered ironic, because the proposal by the Quaker is really annoying her. It is worth noting that the use of particle fronting occurs in psychologically tense situations.

NOTES:
The Pilgrim's Progress contains nine instances of the "V + P + *Subject*" inversion, (plus two variants of "V + *Subject* + P"), some of which are given below:

> So *Watchful* the *Porter* rang a Bell; at the sound of which, **came out** at the door of the House, a Grave and Beautiful Damsel, named *Discretion*, (47) / there **comes down** from *Broad-way Gate*, a Lane called *Dead Man's Lane*; (121) / There **came out** also at this time to meet them, several of the Kings Trumpeters, (152) / out thence [= from the cave] **came forth** *Maull* a Giant. (229), etc.
> ["V + *Subject* + P"] Then **went** the Jury **out**, (94) / Then **ran** *Innocent* **in** (for that was her name) and said to those within, (187)

On the other hand, in Behn's fiction, *Gulliver's Travels*, and *Pamela*, inversion with phrasal verbs never occurs, while the particle fronting occurs, to a greater or lesser extent, in each of the other three works (see the materials recorded in NOTES of Section 1.1.1).

3.3 The Function of Particles in Psychological Contexts

Phrasal verbs in "physical" descriptions are closely related to seemingly incompatible "psychological" expressions. In identifying psychological aspects in Defoe's fiction, a remark on *Robinson Crusoe* made by McKillop (1967: 23) is illuminating: "Even though Defoe does not use elaborate psychological notation, Crusoe's anxiety and anguish are vividly presented ... His strongest feelings are translated into physical reactions"; as an example, McKillop quotes "I walked about on the shore, lifting up my hands, and my whole being, as I may say, wrapt up in the contemplation of my deliverance, making a thousand gestures and motions."

As seen in the use of ***lifting up*** *my hands* cited above, Defoe employs dynamic phrasal verbs to describe characters' mental or inner states. Another example is the use of *look back (upon)* as used in *Now I **look'd back** upon my past Life with such Horrour*, (*RC* 97); a rather figurative sense of "To direct the mind to something that is past" (*OED* look, 32b) is strongly associated with the literal and physical sense of "To turn and look at something in the direction from which one is going or from which one's face is turned" (*OED* look, 32a).

The syntactic difference between intransitive and transitive phrasal verbs brings about two types of psychological expressions, "unconscious" and "conscious" in a way, different in quality, which are separately discussed.

3.3.1 The Function of Particles in Intransitive Phrasal Verbs

Defoe often employs intransitive phrasal verbs to represent an involuntary and unconscious movement of strong emotions or feelings,

Chapter 3 Semantic and Stylistic Analysis of Phrasal Verbs: Six Aspects

especially negative ones, into the mind of protagonists or other characters. In the following passages from *Roxana* and *Moll Flanders*, the use of *in* implicitly suggests the movement of *dark Reflections* and *severe Reproaches of my own Mind* intruding "into" the heroine's "psyche" or mental self:

> there was, and would be, Hours of Intervals, and of dark Reflections which **came** involuntarily **in**, (*Rox* 48) / [in the case of inversion] WITH these Reflections **came in**, of meer Course, severe Reproaches of my own Mind for my wretched Behaviour in my past Life; (*MF* 287)

Instead of a more explicit prepositional phrase *into my mind*, the use of an implicit particle *in* gives more simplified and context-dependent descriptions. At the same time, the use of intransitive phrasal verbs such as *come in* in such a psychological context might make the reader feel as if negative thoughts serving as a subject were a living thing, from an analogy with, for example, the following case: *my Maid Amy came in, and brought with her a small Breast of Mutton*, (*Rox* 18).

In the following passage, an abstract noun, *Avarice*, is combined with a phrasal verb, *step in*. This combination can be regarded as a psychological as well as allegorical representation of avarice; here *in* also implies "into the heroine's mind":

> Avarice **stept in** and said, go on, go on; (*MF* 203)

The pattern of "verb + *in* + *upon*" is of the same nature; note the use of the preposition *upon* indicating the target of the "attack" (already mentioned in Section 1.4.1; pp.86-88), as in:

251

conscious Guilt began to **flow in** upon my Mind (*MF* 281)) / All these Thoughts, and many more, **crowded in** so fast, I say, upon me, that I wanted to give Vent to them, and get rid of him, (*Rox* 230) / Conscience will, and does, often **break in** upon them at particular times, (*Rox* 49)

As a case similar to the above instances, the use of a transitive verb with a reflexive pronoun is given here:

These things **pour'd** themselves **in** upon my Thoughts in a confus'd manner, and left me overwhelm'd with Melancholly and Despair. (*MF* 274)

In the representations in which negative thoughts (which already entered) are incessantly on the heroine's head or mind, particles *round* or *about* play a major role:

while these Thoughts **run round** in my Head, (*MF* 180) / 'tis impossible to express the anxious Thoughts that **rowl'd about** in my Mind, (*Rox* 317) / my Head flash'd, and was dizzy, and all within me, as I thought, **turn'd about**, (*Rox* 277)

And, in the descriptions where strong feelings, including not only negative ones such as *Fear* but positive ones like *Repentance*, gradually disappear on their own, *wear off* is employed, as in:

all the Sense of my Affliction **wore off**, (*RC* 89) / the Fear of their Coming **wore off**, (*RC* 243) / whereas all the Regret, and Reflections **wear off** when the Temptation renews it self; (*MF* 237) / and so the Thought in time **wore off**, (*CJ* 87) / the Repentance which is brought about by the meer Apprehensions of Death, **wears off** as those Apprehensions **wear off**; (*Rox* 128) / *Amy*'s Repentence **wore off** too, as well as mine, (*Rox* 129), etc.

Compared with a more neutral verb such as *disappear*, the choice of *wear off* suggests that the directional force of *off* creates a more tangible image where strong feelings change from "on" to "off," (i.e. out of consciousness), through "fad[ing] by gradual loss" (*OED* s.v. wear, $v.^1$ 13a).

3.3.2 The Function of Particles in Transitive Phrasal Verbs

When transitive phrasal verbs describe a given character's mentality, they are likely to represent his or her "will," or intentional act of thinking as with *I cast about innumerable ways in my Thoughts how this might be done*, (*MF* 327).

As far as the particles are concerned, the use of *off* first attracts attention, in that this particle seems appropriate for describing physical (but actually metaphorical) actions to overcome negative thoughts—as seen in *the serious Thoughts did, as it were endeavour to return again sometimes, but I shook them off*, (*RC* 9). Additional instances of *shake off* are:

I **shook** them [= "many sad Reflections"] **off**, and still flatter'd myself that something or other might offer for my Advantage. (*MF* 106) / But I rous'd up my Judgment, and **shook** it **off**, (*Rox* 277) / Well, well, *says he*, if that be all your Grief, I hope you will soon **shake** it **off**; (*Rox* 324), etc.

As other phrasal verbs, *throw off* and *cast off* are also likely to evoke clear images similar to a real dynamic action, as in *did not I **drag** your Cloaths **off** of your Back*, (*Rox* 48):

> I **threw off** all Thoughts of him; (*Rox* 93) / I **threw** those Thoughts **off** again as much as I cou'd. (*Rox* 214) / I **cast off** all Remorse and Repentance; (*MF* 207)

Another particle evoking a dynamic image is *aside*, as in *come, says he, **lay aside** these melancholly things*, (*Rox* 31). The combination of *lay aside* with *thought(s)* as an object serves as a figurative representation indicating the character's mental states:

> till at last I quite **lay'd aside** the Thoughts of it, (*RC* 16) / I fell on my Knees and gave God Thanks for my Deliverance, resolving to **lay aside** all Thoughts of my Deliverance by my Boat, (*RC* 141) / we agreed to **lay** that Thought **aside**, (*CS* 93), etc.
> cf. Being thus prevailed upon by our own Reason to **set** the Thoughts of that Voyage **aside**, we had then but two things before us; (*CS* 29)

Phrasal verbs with an intensifier *up*, in combination with the subsequent prepositional phrases containing nouns such as *Memory*, *Heart*, and *Thoughts*, serve as psychological expressions:

> as I have **gather'd** them **up** in my Memory, (*CJ* 5) / But I **lay'd up** all these things in my Heart. (*CJ* 8) / [I] **laid up** all the rest in my most secret Thoughts, (*CJ* 290)

3.3.3 Orientational Metaphors: *Down* and *Up*

Among the instances discussed above, the directional force of the particles, as seen in *come in, wear off, lay aside, shake off*, serves in part to characterize the metaphorical meaning of each psychological expression. In this connection, the concept of "orientational metaphor" proposed by Lakoff and Johnson (2003 [1980]: 14) is useful in examining some instances of phrasal verbs used in psychological contexts.[8] The use of phrasal verbs with the particles *down* and *up* is of great interest, when viewed in light of Lakoff and Johnson's metaphorical concept of "HAPPY IS UP; SAD IS DOWN" (p. 14).

Among phrasal verbs with *down* in "sad" contexts are *sink down, fall down*, and *knock down*. As mentioned in introductory part of Chapter 1, *sink down* and *fall down* are "redundant" phrasal verbs, in that both the verb and the particle denote "downward" movement. However, such redundancy seems to create some sort of synergy effect in psychological contexts:

> I **sunk down** when they brought me News of it, (*MF* 282) / I was so surprised, that I **fell down** in a Swoon. (*RC* 12) / I began to be a little chearful; but I was **knock'd down** again as with a Thunder-Clap, (*Rox* 279)

Although these instances are "factive" statements (i.e. the "actual performance" of the action), Defoe often does describe the mere "potentiality" for action, as in:

> I was at first <u>ready to</u> **sink down** with the Surprize. (*RC* 273) / [I] was <u>at the very point of</u> **sinking down** out of the Chair I sat in:

(*MF* 38) / I thought I shou'd have **sunk down** at the very Words; (*Rox* 272) / the very thought frighted me so that I was ready to **drop down**, (*MF* 194)

In the passages cited above, *I*, as the hero or heroine, did *not* "sink down" or "drop down," owing to the preceding phrases: *ready to, at the very point of,* and *shou'd have*.

Among phrasal verbs with *up* in "happy" contexts are *lift up, pluck up, work up, rouse up, swallow up,* and *feed up*; interestingly enough, all of them are transitive:

I forgot not to **lift up** my Heart in Thankfulness to Heaven, (*RC* 273) / my Spirits were **lifted up** to a Degree I had not been us'd to, (*Rox* 30) / **plucking up** my Courage, I took up a great Firebrand, (*RC* 177) / he bade me **pluck up** a good Heart, (*Rox* 30) / With these Reflections I **work'd** my Mind **up**, (*RC* 132) / But I **rous'd up** my Judgment, and shook it off, (*Rox* 277) / for he was so **swallow'd up** with Joy, he could not speak. (*CS* 259) [cf. *OED* s.v. swallow, *v.* 10. d. "To occupy entirely, engross," 1581~] / my Vanity was **fed up** to such a height, that I had no room to give Way to such Reflections. (*Rox* 74)

3.4 Descriptions of the Sea: With Special Reference to Nautical Terms

Certain phrasal verbs develop into topically technical terms. Defoe often uses phrasal verbs connected to "nautical" terms in his fiction. Since nautical terms consist overwhelmingly of descriptions of the sea, such phrasal verbs frequently occur in *Robinson Crusoe* and *Captain Singleton*, the latter of which contains an abundance of descriptions of

Chapter 3 Semantic and Stylistic Analysis of Phrasal Verbs: Six Aspects

navigation and scenery, with the use of "intransitive" phrasal verbs.

3.4.1 Descriptions of Navigation

As a formative element of nautical phrasal verbs, there are some cases where the verb itself can usually be taken as transitive. In the following two passages, *put* is a case in point:

> [a] praying to God to direct my Voyage, I **put out**, and Rowing or Padling the Canoe along the Shore, (*RC* 189) [cf. *OED* s.v. put, *v*.[1] 48. j. (a) *Naut*. "To send or take (a vessel) out to sea. *rare*. (b) *intr*. To go out to sea; to set out on a voyage." 1590~]
>
> [b] Here I **put in**, and having stow'd my Boat very safe, (*RC* 142) [cf. *OED* s.v. put, *v*.[1] 45. f. *intr. spec*. (a) *Naut*. "to enter a port or harbour, esp. by turning aside from the regular course for shelter, provisions, repairs, etc."; the *OED* cites this passage.]

Both passages cited above describe the movement of a canoe or a boat. Taking into consideration the definition of the *OED*, *put out* in [a] would be construed as the case in which the object as an inherently transitive verb (i.e. "put out the canoe") is omitted. Likewise, the use of *put in* in [b] is of the same nature as that of [a].[9] Thus, intransitive phrasal verbs employed as nautical terms can be analyzed as an absolute use of transitive verbs with the object assumed.

On the other hand, there are numerous cases in which inanimate subjects, such as a ship or vessel, co-occur with intransitive phrasal verbs. An example is the use of *stretch away*, a phrasal verb which can be also used transitively:

> the Boat began to **stretch away**, (*RC* 140) [cf. *OED* s.v. stretch, *v*. 11. *Naut*. "To sail (esp. under crowd of canvas) continuously in one

257

direction. Also with *advs*." The *OED* cites this passage.]

Normally, the description of the movement of a boat with use of such an intransitive phrasal verb gives the impression that the boat is sailing on its own, and could be regarded as a sort of personification of the boat but may also represent a longstanding convention regarding (inanimate) ships, in terms of language use.

As its full title, "The life, Adventures, and Pyracies of Captain Singleton" suggests, *Captain Singleton* is full of phrasal verbs employed as nautical terms. Instances of such verbs have been collected, as seen below. In those cases where the description of ship navigation refers to a human subject, *CS* contains the following phrasal verbs (arranged in alphabetical order):

edge down, in (which occurs once in this work; the latter, *edge in*, is employed in the "composite" pattern described in Section 1.3; p.75):

> when we got him upon our Quarter we **edg'd down**, and received the Fire of five or six of his Guns; (*CS* 151) / they ... **stood edging in** for the Shore, (*CS* 216)

haul away, up (once respectively):

> we **hall'd away** Southward under the Lee of the Island, (*CS* 44) / so they immediately **haul'd up** on a-Wind on t'other Tack, (*CS* 216) [cf. *OED* s.v. haul, *v*. 3. a. *Naut*. (*intr*.) "To trim the sails, etc. of a ship so as to sail nearer to the wind (also ***to haul up***); hence more generally, to change or turn the ship's course; to sail in a certain course." 1557~]

luff up (once):

> all which time we **luffed up**, (*CS* 151) [cf. *OED* s.v. luff, *v*. orig. *Naut*. 1. *intr*. "To bring the head of a ship nearer to the wind; to

Chapter 3 Semantic and Stylistic Analysis of Phrasal Verbs: Six Aspects

steer or <u>sail</u> nearer the wind; to <u>sail</u> in a specified direction with the head kept close to the wind. Also with advs., †*by, in, off, to, up*, etc." 1390~]

ply away, about (once respectively):
we **plied away** from them to Windward, (*CS* 149) / We **ply'd about** here in the Latitude of [22 Degrees] South for near a Month, (*CS* 154) [cf. *OED* s.v. ply, $v.^2$ II. In nautical and derived uses. 6. *intr.* "To beat up against the wind; to tack, work to windward." 1556~ ; 6. b. with *about, off and on, to and again, up and down*, and the like. *c* 1595~]

put back (twice):
we were forced to **put back** to *Laconia*, (*CS* 197) [cf. *OED* s.v. put, *v.* 40. f. *intr. Naut.* "To reverse one's course; to return to the port which one has left." The *OED*'s first citation is from 1771.]

sail away (twice), *back* (once), *along* (once), *on* (4 times):
We **sailed away** for the Cape of *Good Hope*, (*CS* 168) / Friend, says he, I understand the Captain is for **sailing back** to the *Rio Janiero*, (*CS* 153) / We **sailed along** there, not in Sight of the Shore, (*CS* 189) / we resolved to **sail on** along the Coast, (*CS* 46)

slant away (once):
so we might **slant away** North West, (*CS* 112) [cf. *OED* s.v. slant, *v.* 3. a. "Of persons: To travel, move, <u>sail</u>, etc. <u>in an oblique direction;</u> to diverge from a direct course." 1692~]

stand on (once), *over* (once):
we **stood on** upon the *Brasil* Coast, (*CS* 149) [cf. *OED* s.v. stand, *v.* 98. c. *Naut.* (See sense 36.) "To keep one's course, continue on the same tack." 1666~] / so we concluded to **stand over** directly, (*CS* 44) [cf. *OED* s.v. stand, *v.* 100. a. *Naut.* (See sense 36.) "To leave

one shore and <u>sail</u> towards another." 1699~]

steer away (5 times):

[we] got out of the Wake of the Island, and **steer'd away** North, (*CS* 173) [cf. *OED* s.v. steer, $v.^1$ 2. c. "Of a navigator: To guide a vessel in a certain direction; <u>to sail </u>or row towards a specified place." 1340-70~]

stretch away (3 times), *off* (once), *over* (once):

we **stretcht away** to the Westward, to get the Wind of him. (*CS* 214) / the Wind shifting very often, and at that time coming to the E.S.E. we **stretcht off**, (*CS* 220) / as soon as we had, with a kind of a Land Breeze, **stretched over** about 15 or 20 Leagues, (*CS* 36) [cf. *OED* s.v. stretch, *v.* 11. *Naut.* "<u>To sail</u> (esp. under crowd of canvas) continuously in one direction. Also with advs." 1687~]

tow up (once):

We **tow'd up** as far as ever our Boats would swim, (*CS* 72) [cf. *OED* s.v. tow, *v.* 4. *intr.* or *absol.* "To advance or proceed by towing or being towed." 1612~ ; The *OED* cites this passage.]

Next are presented those cases where the subject is a ship or vessel: *bear down* (twice), *hale in* (once), *lay up* (once), and *stand off* (twice) are cited:

bear down (upon) (twice):

the Ship was within a League of us, and, as we thought, **bore down** to engage us; (*CS* 216) [cf. *OED* s.v bear, *v.* 37. a. esp. in *Nautical* phraseology: "To sail in a certain direction" 1605~] / we being unmoor'd, and our Fore Top-Sail loose for sailing, when we spy'd <u>a large Ship</u> to the Northward, **bearing down** directly <u>upon</u> us; (*CS* 216) [cf. *OED* s.v. bear, *v.* 37. b. *Naut.* and *gen. to*

260

Chapter 3 Semantic and Stylistic Analysis of Phrasal Verbs: Six Aspects

bear down upon: "to proceed (esp. with force) towards." 1716~]

hale in (once):
> she [= the ship] **haled in** to keep the Land aboard, (*CS* 186) [cf. *OED* s.v. hale, *v.*[1] 4. *intr.* "To move along as if drawn or pulled; to move with force or impetus, hasten, rush; <u>spec. of a ship</u>, to proceed before the wind with sails set, to <u>sail</u> (cf. 1 a). Also *fig. Obs.*" 13.. ~ 1727]

lay up (once):
> I told them, I would run the venture of their *Dutch* Power from *Batavia*, but I would not have the News come there before me, because it would make <u>all their Merchant Ships</u> **lay up**, and keep out of our Way. (*CS* 189) [cf. *OED* s.v. lay, *v.*[1] 60. g. "To put away (a ship) in dock or some other place of safety. Also *intr.* for *pass.* or *refl.*" 1667~]

Finally, the following cases are those where the subject is used in both (i.e. human and non-human) types.

stand away (25 times), *off* (4 times), *out* (6 times) *in* (10 times):[10]
> [human] we **stood away** for *China*. (*CS* 197) [cf. *OED* s.v. stand, *v.* 87. b. *Naut.* "To <u>sail</u> or steer away (from some coast, quarter, enemy, etc.) (See sense 36.)" 1633~] / [we] resolved to **stand off** to Sea, (*CS* 146) [cf. *OED* s.v. stand, *v.* 96. e. *Naut.* "To sail away from the shore." 1625~] / we weighed Anchor the same Tide, and **stood out** to Sea, (*CS* 140) / we **stood in** for the Shore with all the Sail we could make. (*CS* 37)
>
> [nonhuman] the Ship **stood away** to the South-East, (*CS* 21)[11] / the Ship **stood off** to Sea, (*CS* 147) / she proved an excellent Sailer ('a ship or vessel' (*OED*)), and **standing out** to Sea, we saw plainly she trusted to her Heels, (*CS* 147) / In two Hours

after, we saw our Game, **standing in** for the Bay with all the Sail she could make, (*CS* 148) [cf. *OED* s.v. stand, *v.* 95. e. *Naut.* "To direct one's course towards the shore. (See sense 36.)" *c* 1595~]

put off (4 times):

[human] the Men that enter'd out of the other Boat, ... jump'd all back again into their Boat, and **put off**, not knowing what the Matter was. (*CS* 156) [cf. *OED* s.v. put, *v.* 46. n. (a) *intr. Naut.* "To leave the land; to set out or start on a voyage; also, to leave a ship, as a boat." 1582~]

[nonhuman] in a few Minutes more we perceived their Boat **put off**; and as soon as the Boat **put off**, the Ship struck, and came to an Anchor, as was directed. (*CS* 217)

Concerning transitive phrasal verbs,[12] *beat up* and *lead away* are next presented:

beat up (twice):

We were at Sea above two Months upon this Voyage, **beating** it **up** against the Wind, (*CS* 197)

lead away (once):

we **led** it **away**, with the Wind large, to the *Maldivies*, (*CS* 185)

As pointed out in Section 2.2.1 (pp.140-143), the use of the personal pronoun *it* in the instances of two phrasal verbs might be considered "empty" place holders.

In order to better grasp the meaning of the phrasal verbs cited above, the *OED* definitions have been added. The verb elements in those phrasal verbs collected here, by themselves, are used transitively rather than intransitively; these include *lay, put, tow, hale*. Therefore,

Chapter 3 Semantic and Stylistic Analysis of Phrasal Verbs: Six Aspects

combinations of such verbs with particles are rather ambiguous in the determination of type, whether intransitive or transitive, in that the use of these verbs can be analyzed as absolute uses of transitive verbs (note the usage labels such as "*intr.* or *absol.*" or "*intr.* for *pass.* or *refl.*" in the *OED* definitions).[13]

In addition, in defining the phrasal verbs instanced above, the *OED* editors tend to use the verb "sail" (e.g. *stretch away*, *luff up*, *slant away*, *stand away*, *bear down*, *hale in*, etc). Among these phrasal verbs, the definition of *haul* (*up*) is of special interest, as the editors suggest that this verb in its original and specific sense of "To trim the sails" is used in the more general sense of "to sail in a certain course." Given this evidence, the verb *sail* is no doubt one of the most "general" words to describe how a ship moves. In fact, as instanced above, *sail* is used eight times as a phrasal verb in *Captain Singleton*, though there are not many occurrences of it, in comparison with a variety of other phrasal verbs, including *stand*. Thus, instead of overly relying on the generic term *sail*, Defoe makes extensive use of more specific phrasal verbs (many are used only once) in describing vessel movements in some detail. This tendency reflects, at least to some extent, Defoe's strong preference for realistic representations.

3.4.2 Descriptions of Scenery
In Defoe's era, the wind was essential for navigation of ships. Furthermore, the sailors of the day were required to be familiar with other "products of nature," as well as a variety of winds. In this regard, the scope of descriptions of the sea is expanded to include descriptions of natural scenes such as wind, tide, or shore. Descriptions of scenery are no doubt related to the narrative style of the novel.[14]

As for phrasal verbs used in descriptions of natural scenes, *chop about* in the description of the wind is a case in point:

> if the Wind had **chopt about** any where, they must have gone with it. (*CS* 155) [cf. *OED* s.v. chop, $v.^2$ 6. *intr.* esp. *Naut.* "Of the wind: To change, veer, or shift its direction suddenly; usually with *round, about (up,* obs.)". *a* 1642~]

Additional phrasal verbs used in the description of the wind might also be related to nautical terms, though not recorded as *Naut.* in the *OED*, as in:

> the Wind **came off** like a Land Breeze, (*CS* 36) / when a Gale **sprung up**, we took her in Tow. (*CS* 31) / the Northern Monsoons being perhaps by that time also ready to **set in**. (*CS* 198) [cf. *OED* s.v. set, $v.^1$ 46. f. "Of a current or <u>wind</u>: To flow or <u>blow towards the shore</u>."], etc.

In a similar vein, phrasal verbs used in descriptions of scenery from *Robinson Crusoe* and *Captain Singleton* may belong to or be closely related to nautical terms:

> I <u>saw</u> the Land **run out** a great Length <u>into the Sea</u>, (*RC* 31) [cf. *OED* s.v. run, *v.* 77. f. "To extend or project; to protrude, jut out." 1565~] / At length we <u>saw</u> a great Head-Land (= "a cape or promontory" (*OED*)) **lye out** far South <u>into the Sea</u>, (*CS* 221) [cf. *OED* s.v. lie, $v.^1$ 27. a. "To stretch out, extend. *Obs.*" 1601~] / I <u>found</u> a great Ledge of Rocks **lye out** above two Leagues <u>into the Sea</u>, (*RC* 137) / we <u>found</u> at a great Distance, a large Promontory, or Cape of Land, **pushing out** a long Way <u>into the Sea</u>; (*CS* 33)

Chapter 3 Semantic and Stylistic Analysis of Phrasal Verbs: Six Aspects

> [cf. *OED* s.v. push, *v.* 5. b. *intr*. "To stick out, project."; the *OED* cites this passage as its first illustration.] / [without the use of a perception verb] we came off at the Head of a Promontory or Point of Land that lies about the Middle of the Island, and that **stretches out** West a great way into the Sea; (*CS* 36)

Followed by dynamic phrasal verbs, such as *run out*, are all "inanimate" products of nature which cannot move by themselves: *the Land, a great Head-Land, a great Ledge of Rocks*, and *a large Promontory*. Hence, such an expression as *the Land run out* might be understood as a sort of personification or animate metaphor. In addition, these four instances, connected with the subsequent prepositional phrase *into the Sea*, occur after perception verbs like *see* or *find*. A combination between a human subject plus a perception verb (e.g. *I saw*) and a dynamic movement of surrounding nature (e.g. *the Land* **run out** ... *into the Sea*) no doubt creates a realistic "illusion" offering the reader a wider panorama of the scene; these instances contribute to describing an entirely different, marvelous world, far from England. In particular, in *we found a large Promontory ... pushing out ... into the Sea*; (*CS* 33), the use of present participle *pushing* makes the scene more vivid.

Similar instances are given for reference:

> I found the Point of the Rocks which occasioned this Disaster, **stretching out** as is describ'd before to the Southward, and casting off the Current more Southwardly, (*RC* 141) / the Land **trended away** to the West, (*CS* 108) / the Shore **falls off** to the Westward towards *Cromer*, (*RC* 13-14) [cf. *OED* s.v. fall, *v.* 92. d. *Naut.* "Of a coast-line: To trend away."; the *OED* citing this passages.] / the Shore of the Island **fell off** again above 200 Miles to the East, (*CS* 36) / we were surprized to see the Shore **fall**

265

away on the other Side, (*CS* 33), etc.

In the following passage, two phrasal verbs are employed in the coordination pattern of "A and B."

> at length we <u>found</u> <u>the Land</u> **break off**, and **go trending away** to the West Sea, (*CS* 205) [cf. *OED* s.v. trend, *v.* 4. *intr.* "to run, stretch, incline, bend (in some direction), as a river, current, coast-line, mountain-range, territory, stratum, etc." 1598~]

The latter of the two phrasal verbs, *go trending away*, is, as investigated in Section 1.3, an instance of the "composite" pattern, in which two phrasal verbs, (i.e. *go away* and *trending away*) are contained in the deep structure. In that light, it turns out that Defoe attempts to make a dynamic, detailed description of natural wonders.

3.4.3 The Role of Absolute Participial Construction

Finally examined are the cases in which phrasal verbs are used as an "absolute" participial construction (or absolute clause) as in *The Road winding about, we saw them a great way*, (*CJ* 90). Some of them are closely related to descriptions of sea-scenery.

According to a suggestion by Jespersen (*MEG* V: 45ff), since the period of Modern English, the absolute participial construction has been much more frequently used than expected by certain grammarians and linguists.[15] In this regard, it is of some significance to describe instances of the absolute construction in Defoe, examining the significance of its use. In his fiction, when the subject is non-human, Defoe tends to employ the absolute clause mainly for two stylistic purposes: (1) time-presentation and (2) background-presentation. In

Chapter 3 Semantic and Stylistic Analysis of Phrasal Verbs: Six Aspects

(1), the following instances, many of which include *come on*, are given only for reference:

> the Night **coming on**, the Armies only viewed each other at a Distance for that time. (*MC* 200) / but Night **coming on**, and we being very Weary, we thought we should not find the way; (*CJ* 92) / the fair Weather **coming on**, we began just as he directed, to search about the Rivers for more Gold; (*CS* 135) / Winter **coming on**, it was proper to think of coming to *Paris* again, (*Rox* 84) / the Season for curing the Grapes **coming on**, I caused such a prodigious Quantity to be hung up in the Sun, (*RC* 247) / the Time **spinning out**, the King's Commissioners demanded longer Time for the Treaty; (*MC* 228) [cf. *OED* s.v. spin, *v*. 6. g. *intr*. "To run out; to extend; to last out." The *OED* cites this passage as its first illustration.], etc.

As far as instances of (2) are concerned, some of them occur in descriptions of the sea:

> the Tide **coming in**, I was oblig'd to give over for that Time. (*RC* 84) / a strong Current or Tide **running up**, I look'd on both Sides for a proper Place to get to Shore, (*RC* 51) / and which, the Water being **ebb'd out**, I could see; (*RC* 191) / the Tide soon after **ebbing out**, they found it lay dry upon the Sands, (*CS* 178) / the Tide being **coming in**, as they call it, that is running West-ward, he reached the Land not till he came about the Falcon Stairs, (*JPY* 162) / We had a strong Gale of Wind at S.W. by W. and the Ship had fresh Way, but a great Sea **rolling in** upon us from the N.E. which we afterwards found was the Pouring in of the Great Ocean East of *New Guinea*. (*CS* 194)

Descriptions through the absolute construction (as seen in the citations) add greater detail to the background of the narrative, situation, or surroundings in which the protagonists (such as Crusoe) are placed.

Moreover, in the absolute clause, *being* as an auxiliary verb is used in two grammatical functions. One of these functions is to indicate the perfect tense,[16] as in:

> [a] the Water <u>being</u> **ebb'd out**, (*RC* 191)
> [cf. the Horse <u>being</u> thus **gone off**, (*MC* 246) / the Caravans <u>being</u> not **come in**; (*CS* 261)]

The second function is to indicate the progressive tense, as in:

> [b] the Tide <u>being</u> **coming in**, (*JPY* 162)
> [cf. the *Brasil* Fleet <u>being</u> just **going away**, (*RC* 287) / the Throng <u>being</u> still **moving on**, (*MF* 212)]

In [b], for example, *the tide **being** coming in* can be regarded as a more time-specific (and therefore realistic) expression than an alternative, such as *the tide coming in* (as in this citation from *RC*), which is more ambiguous as to tense.

NOTES:

Participial construction in the use of intransitive phrasal verbs in the seven works is summarized in Table 1:

Chapter 3 Semantic and Stylistic Analysis of Phrasal Verbs: Six Aspects

Table 1. Adverbial Participial Clauses: Frequency of Occurrence

	RC	MC	CS	MF	JPY	CJ	Rox	total
occurrences of participial clauses	45 (6.8%)	34 (6.1%)	29 (5%)	26 (4.3%)	20 (5.1%)	28 (4.1%)	20 (3.5%)	202 (5%)
(including absolute clauses)	(9)	(12)	(6)	(7)	(6)	(6)	(6)	(52)
total occurrences of intransitve phr. vbs	661	561	582	608	397	675	568	4,052

On the whole, the use of the participial clause becomes gradually less frequent in the transition from *RC* to *Rox*. This phenomenon might have something to do with the nature of the narrative in each work; e.g. how each narrator attempts to describe the situation where he or she is.

What may be of greater interest here is the constant use of the absolute clause. Even *JPY*, which has the smallest number of instances of intransitive phrasal verbs among the seven works, six occurrences of the absolute clause are found. Thus, there seems no correlation between the use of participial clauses and the use of the absolute. As mentioned above, the absolute clause serves to elaborate the background of the narrative.

3.5 The "Redundant" Use of Particles

According to Hampe (2002: 33-61), many English "verb-particle constructions" in present-day English contain a "redundant" particle. When the meaning between *finish* and *finish off* (or *finish up*) for example is "roughly similar," *off* (or *up*) can be considered "redundant." Hampe, at the same time, points out that the addition of such a "redundant" particle to a verb "can function as an index of an emotional involvement of the speaker" (p. 101),[17] and terms the "verb plus redundant particle" constructions "superlative verbs."

In a short pamphlet titled *A New Test of the Church of England's Loyalty* (1702) written by Defoe in his journalist days, there is interesting evidence concerning the absence and/or presence of a particle in the use of phrasal verbs. A case in point is *take up Arms*, which consists of the transitive phrasal verb "take up" and its object "Arms." This three-word verb phrase, meaning "to get weapons and fight," is treated as an idiom or a set-phrase in many current English dictionaries.[18] Nonetheless in this work by Defoe the particle "up" seems entirely optional. All instances of *take up Arms* (and **take Arms*) are cited here, in order of appearance:[19]

1 [the Dissenters] never took **up** Arms against their Prince. (p. 63)
2 the Whigs in 41. to 48. took **up** Arms against their King; (p. 65)
3 We did take **up** Arms, but we did not kill him: (p. 65)
4 'tis lawful ... to take **up** Arms against the King; (p. 67)
5 it is not Lawful upon any Pretence whatsoever to take **up** Arms against the King; (p. 68)
* I do abhor that Traiterous Position of taking Arms by his Authority against ... (p. 68)
6 You have taken **up** Arms against, ... (p. 68)
* they have both of them, in their Turn, taken Arms against, and depos'd their Rightful and Lawful Kings. (p. 70)
* not in taking Arms, (p. 70)
7 Apostates ... have Sacrilegiously and Traiterously taken **up** Arms against their Prince, (p. 71)

Chapter 3 Semantic and Stylistic Analysis of Phrasal Verbs: Six Aspects

    8 Sir Thomas Wyatt, ... took up Arms against their Lawful Prince, (p. 74)
    * once [they] took Arms against her after she was Queen; (p. 74)
    * At last they took Arms; (p. 74) [cf. *OED* s.v. arm n^2. 4. c. **to take up arms**: "to arm oneself, rise in hostility defensive or offensive, to draw the sword"]

In total, *take up Arms* appears eight times and *take Arms* five times. It seems unlikely that Defoe carelessly omits the particle *up*. Rather, such an alternative use seems both intentional and stylistic. If so, an interesting observation made by Hampe seems directly applicable to Defoe's alternative use of "take (up) Arms" in the early eighteenth century. At the same time, arguably this three-word expression has not been established as an idiom; therefore, the collocation of the verb *take* with the particle *up* in accompanying the object *arms* appears to have been more flexible in Defoe's day. This can be confirmed from the *OED* citations (cf. *OED* s.v. arm, $n.^2$ 4c), to some extent. In treating the phrase *take up arms*, the following four passages are cited—here presented in chronological order:

    c 1590 Marlowe *Massac. Paris* iii. i, The Guise hath **taken arms** against the King;
    1602 Shakes. *Ham.* iii. i. 59 To **take Armes** against a Sea of troubles;
    1769 Robertson *Charles V*, V. iii. 329 Obliged to **take arms** in self-defence;
    1831 *Newton* (1855) II. xiv. 2 Newton **took up arms** in his own cause.

Note that the first three instances from the 16th to 18th centuries are *take arms*, while the last in the 19th century is *take up arms*. The *OED* editors seem to suggest that the phrase *take up arms*, developing from the simple form *take arms*, was later established as an idiom or a set-phrase in the 19th century.

As a result, it is fair to say that Defoe takes advantage of an existing linguistic flexibility. That is to say, depending on the context, he intentionally adds the particle to emphasize his statement, or omits it to adopt a more objective tone. As Dobrée (1990 [1959]: 50), quoting a certain passage from this pamphlet, mentions: "you can almost hear a voice from a platform"; here might be witnessed in one phrase an excellent example of Defoe's writing skill as a journalist or pamphleteer, pertaining to oratorical style.

It is more difficult to discover such an emphatic use of the particle, or more precisely, Defoe's (intentional) differentiation between the absence and presence of a particle, in his fiction (in comparison with his short, non-fiction works). Two obvious cases (all the same, concerning *take up*) have been observed. The first case reveals the differentiation between *take up short* and *take short* in *Moll Flanders* and *Roxana*:

> [*take up short*]
> I saw clearly that I should lose nothing by being backward to ask, so I **took** her **up** short; (*MF* 111) / But I **took** him **up** short, I protested I had never suffer'd any Man to touch me since my Husband died, (*MF* 236) / I **took** him **up** short, and told him I hop'd he did not understand by my speaking, (*MF* 303) / I **took** him **up** short at the first of these; (*Rox* 146) [cf. *OED* s.v. short, *a.* 5. b. ***to take (a person) short.*** (b) "To interrupt with a reply; not to allow to complete his speech or offer explanations. Often with *up*." 1565~]

[*take short*]
She took me short, and told me, that was none of her Business, (*MF* 162) / Nay, says *the Alderman*, taking him short, now you contradict yourself, (*MF* 271) / I took him short there; Look you, Sir, said I, you have an Advantage of me there indeed, (*Rox* 151) / he took me short, and with more Warmth than he had yet us'd with me, tho' with the utmost Respect; (*Rox* 157) / I took him short again, What need you, says I, send me out of your Way? (*Rox* 239)

Another case is the use between *take up for* and *take for* in *MF*:

[*take up for*]
[I told him] That to be **taken up** for a Thief was such an Indignity as could not be put up, (*MF* 251) [cf. *OED* s.v. take, *v*. 48 "*to take ... for*. To suppose to be, consider as; often, with implication of error, to suppose to be (what it is not), to mistake for" *c* 1435~]

[*take for*]
I should be taken for an impudent Creature that had forg'd such a thing to go away from my Husband, (*MF* 97) / I might be taken for such a Creature, (*MF* 251)

In both cases of *take* (*up*) *short* and *take* (*up*) *for*, as the *OED* suggests, the forms lacking the particle *up* can be regarded as standard. A comparative examination of those instances with and without the particle suggests that when using the particle *up* the characters may be more "excited."[20]

3.6 Repetition and Synonym: the Case of *Shut Up*

As referred to in Chapter 2, *shut up* in *A Journal of the Plague Year* is by far the most frequently-used phrasal verb in Defoe's seven works (123 instances). This final section examines the repetition of *shut up*, and the use of its synonyms. Why might *shut up* occur so frequently in this work? *JPY* differs from Defoe's other fictional works, in that he (through the narrator, "H.F.") provides a detailed document of the Great Plague of 1665; as a result, Defoe's text contains numerous descriptions of isolate, infected cases, as well as quarantined houses—apparently to prevent the spread of the plague. Within such descriptions, *shut up* is recurrently used as a transitive phrasal verb, often taking grammatical objects such as "houses" and "people." In this regard, the use of *shut up* is intimately related with what Hiltunen (1994: 135) refers to as "text-specific features."[21]

JPY also presents a unique textual structure, in which the actual bills issued in 1665, known as "Orders Conceived and Published by the Lord Mayor and Aldermen of the City of London, concerning the Infection of the Plague" (henceforth *Orders*), are quoted almost in their entirety.[22] In the quotation (spanning nine pages of the text: pp. 38-46), some 13 instances of *shut up* can be observed. Such an intensive use of *shut up* in the *Orders* likely explains its high frequency in *JPY*. It seems that Defoe is (or more precisely, Defoe has the narrator H.F. be) so obsessed with scrutinizing the consequences of the *Orders* put into practice that he does not alter the topic of shutting up people, or houses. This is surely part of the reason why *shut up* is incessantly repeated.

Thus, *shut up* can be regarded as one of the keywords or key phrases relevant to the main subject in *JPY*. An examination of the

Chapter 3 Semantic and Stylistic Analysis of Phrasal Verbs: Six Aspects

repetition of this phrasal verb may shed light on significant aspects of Defoe's style.

3.6.1 Repetition of *Shut Up*

The syntactic use of *shut up* can be classified into three main categories: (1) active constructions, (2) gerund, and (3) passive constructions. The occurrences of *shut up* in these categories are shown in the following Table:

Table 2. Occurrences of *Shut Up* in Three Syntactic Categories*

	JPY	H.F.'s narrative	the *Orders*
(1) 'Active' *shut up*	21	21	0
(2) 'Gerund'	34	32	2
shutting up of NP	(19)	(18)	(1)
shutting up NP	(13)	(13)	(0)
others	(2)	(1)	(1)
(3) 'Passive' *shut up*	68**	57	11
with *be*	(46)**	(38)	(8)
without *be*	(22)	(19)	(3)
total	123	110	13

*As the text of *JPY* substantially consists of H.F.'s narrative (including dialogues by other characters) and the *Orders*, the frequency of *shut up* in each part is given separately.
** For descriptive purposes, five instances of the "passive gerund" such as *the Apprehensions and Terror of being **shut up**,* (*JPY* 73) are included in "Passive" categories.

Of the 123 instances of *shut up*, this phrasal verb is used 21 times (17%) in the active voice, while 34 instances (28%), including two in the *Orders*, occur as a gerund construction (i.e. *shutting up*). Among these, there are 19 cases of "shutting up of House(s)." Furthermore, the case with the definite article *the* occurs 11 times, as follows:

275

> But I return to the **shutting up** of Houses. (*JPY* 57) / During the **shutting up** of Houses, as I have said, some Violence was offered to the Watchmen; (*JPY* 69) / It is true, as I have mentioned, that the **shutting up** of Houses was a great Subject of Discontent, (*JPY* 155), etc.

What is common in this type is that the agent (i.e. of *who* shut(s) up the houses) is not mentioned. Coupled with the "timeless" and "voiceless (or moodless)" character of the gerund (cf. Jespersen (*MEG* V: 112); Tajima (1982: 111)), the agentless nominalization of *shutting up* serves as a concise representation of the topic.

Sixty-eight instances (55%) of *shut up*, including 11 from the *Orders*, are used in the passive. In addition, except for two instances (as in "the Case of Families infected, and **shut up** by the Magistrates" (*JPY* 55)), all the rest, 66 instances, are agentless. Some instances are given below:

> A House in *White-Chapel* was **shut up** for the sake of one Infected Maid, (*JPY* 158) / when a House was **shut up** in the City, and any one had died of the Plague, (*JPY* 197) / in the infected Houses which were **shut up**, (*JPY* 52), etc.

As Table 2 shows, the passive use (55%) of *shut up* is the most-frequent of the three categories; the gerund use (28%) is more frequent than the active use (17%). The frequent use of the (agentless) passive, as often seen in descriptions of scientific experiments,[23] "is presumably to give an illusion of objectivity" (Dixon 2005: 355). At the same time, a consistent use of the (agentless) nominalization of *shutting up* suggests Defoe's reportorial manner of rendering the inherently dynamic action "static."[24] Defoe's strong preference for such agentless expressions of *shut up* clearly reflects a distinctive feature of the documentary style of (fictional) reportage in *JPY*: what can be considered a "static and impersonal objectivity."

(a) "Internal Deviation" in *Shut Up*
There are certain cases where *shut up* is apparently *not* used in the "normal" context (as discussed above). Instances to be recognized relate to what Leech and Short (2007: 44) term "internal deviation," [25] for example in:

> the Trade with *London* was as it were entirely **shut up**; (*JPY* 217)

The combination of *shut up* with *the Trade* seems to deviate from the phrasal verb's norm of use in *JPY*. This is evident from the addition of the parenthetic phrase *as it were*. With the help of the *OED* explanation (*OED* s.v. as, B. 9c), this collocation may be "practically right" though "perhaps not formally exact."

The following three uses of *shut up* are strongly connected to each other. Each is used in the episode of three men among the homeless escaping from London into the countryside:

> [a] *John*. ... We wonder how you could be so unmerciful!
> *Const*[*able*]. Self-preservation obliges us.
> *John*. What! to **shut up** your Compassion in a Case of such Distress as this? (*JPY* 138)
> [b] On the other Hand, says *John*, if you will **shut up** all Bowels of Compassion and not relieve us at all, we shall not extort any thing by Violence, (*JPY* 143)

[c] This, in the first Place intimated to them, that they would be sure to find the Charity and Kindness of the County, which they had found here where they [= the "County" people] were before, <u>hardned and **shut up**</u> against them [= strangers like John]; (*JPY* 148)

In [a] and [b], *shut up* is used in the dialogue between John, one among the three men, and a constable. The combination of *shut up* with (*Bowels of*) *Compassion*, bearing a metaphorical meaning, denotes a lack of mercy, or cruelty.[26] In order to represent the unmerciful attitude of (certain) country people towards homeless Londoners, Defoe has *John* draw an analogy with that of the shutting up houses or people.

In [c], the coordination with *hardned* ("Rendered unfeeling or callous" (*OED* s.v. hardened, 2)) makes the meaning of *shut up* (which is similar with that in [a] and [b]) more explicit and clear.

The three instances in the passages cited above are qualitatively different from the mainstream use of *shut up* in *JPY*, at least on the surface. Therefore, Defoe's obsessive image of "shutting up" appears to act as a leitmotif, which articulates negative ideas in the text.

3.6.2 Synonyms for *Shut Up*

Despite the repetitive use of *shut up*, Defoe does not exclusively use this phrasal when describing "shutting up" in this work. As Halliday (1994: 331) suggests, if "we depart from straightforward repetition, and take account of cohesion between **related** (*sic*) items," "synonyms of the same or some higher level of generality" (e.g. *snake* vs. *python*) must be considered.

In terms of synonyms for *shut up* used with *Houses*, a case in point is a different phrasal verb, *lock up*, which is used 14 times, as in:

Chapter 3 Semantic and Stylistic Analysis of Phrasal Verbs: Six Aspects

>It is true, that the **locking up** the Doors of Peoples Houses, and setting a Watchman there Night and Day, to prevent their stirring out, (*JPY* 47)

In comparison with *shut up*, *lock up* is more specific and detailed, as evident from the dictionary definition "To shut up or confine with a lock" (my emphasis added) (*OED* s.v. lock *v*. 2), as well as taking a more specific object *the Doors* (of houses). Hence, strictly—and semantically—speaking, *lock up* is a "hyponym" for *shut up*, rather than a synonym; *shut up* is the "superordinate" term.[27]

In a similar vein to *lock up*, the verbs *padlock* and *nail* (over) in the following passage seem broadly synonymous with *shut up*:

>Some Houses were indeed, entirely **lock'd up**, the Doors **padlockt**, the Windows and Doors having Deal-Boards **nail'd** over them, (*JPY* 72)

Padlock is used as a phrasal verb, though only once:

>the Officers afterwards had Orders to **Padlock up** the Doors on the Outside, (*JPY* 50)

Phrasal verbs in Defoe's writings are not always idiomatic and fixed expressions. Rather, depending on the context, particles (especially *up*) are flexibly attached to the verbs, in order to enhance descriptions; this is a similar case to the "redundant" use of particles, (e.g. *take* (*up*) *arms*) in the previous section (3.5).

Synonyms for *shut up* used with animate objects will next be examined. Although there are uses of phrasal verbs such as *pen up* ("To enclose so as to prevent from escaping ... Often with *up*;" *OED* s.v. pen *v*.[1] 2), as in [*I was*] *very impatient of being* **pent up** *within Doors without Air* (*JPY* 104), what attracts more attention here is the use of the Latinate verb *confine*, which occurs 17 times in total, as in:

> no Care was taken to shut up Houses, and **confine** the sick People from infecting others; (*JPY* 155)

The verb *confine* is here likely to occur in the same context as that in which *shut up* is used. Thus, the act of shutting up the houses and the act of confining people are two sides of the same coin, at least in *JPY*. In addition, Defoe uses a stylistic device. After a colloquial, a vivid phrasal verb such as *shut up*, the phrasal verb is then followed by a more formal and neutral verb, such as *confine*. Such coexistence and differentiation between phrasal verbs and their more formal single-word synonyms must not be overlooked as one of the significant features of Defoe's style.[28]

Next, the verb *imprison*, occurring only four times, can be regarded as a context-dependent synonym for *shut up*. Its first occurrence from the *Orders* is used in the literal sense of "to put into prison" (*OED* s.v. imprison *v*. 1):

> no Neighbours nor Friends be suffered to accompany the Corps to Church, or to enter the House visited, upon pain of having his House shut up, or be **imprisoned**. (*JPY* 42)

Following the quotation of the *Orders*, Defoe uses this verb three times with different shades of meaning in the H.F. narrative, as in:

Chapter 3 Semantic and Stylistic Analysis of Phrasal Verbs: Six Aspects

here were just so many Prisons in the Town, as there were Houses shut up; and as the People shut up or **imprison'd** so, were guilty of no Crime, only shut up because miserable, (*JPY* 52)

Here, as a paraphrase of *shut up*, *imprison* is clearly used in the transferred or figurative sense of "To confine, shut up" (*OED* s.v. imprison *v*. 2). Hence, it is easy to fully appreciate Defoe's idea of imagery that the houses shut up are the very prisons.[29]

notes

[1] In the case of *we **sat down** and considered*, (*CS* 33), cited as a typical instance of the coordination pattern, current English dictionaries are likely to regard the "sit down and do" pattern as an idiomatic phrase. For example, according to *Oxford Advanced Learner's Dictionary* (7th ed.: 2006), "**sit down and do sth** (= something)" is defined and instanced as follows: "to give sth time and attention in order to try to solve a problem or achieve sth: *This is something that we should sit down and discuss as a team.*"

[2] As regards the issue of ellipsis and simple coordination, Quirk et al. (1985: 943-944) remarks: "To understand the verb phrase coordination of *Peter washed and dried the dishes, . . . washed and dried* is typically interpreted as a single combined activity (*What are you doing to the dishes? I'm washing and drying them*), rather than as two separate activities."

[3] A similar phenomenon has been noticed by Jespersen (1992 [1924]: 26-27), through comparison with these two similar passages:

    (1) There I saw Tom Brown, and Mrs. Hart, and Miss Johnstone, and Colonel Dutton.
    (2) There I saw Tom Brown, Mrs. Hart, Miss Johnstone, and Colonel Dutton, —

Jespersen points out that the construction (2) "is more appropriate in the written language," and that construction (1) is more appropriate "in ordinary speech." Jespersen cites an instance from Defoe, i.e. "our God made the whole world, and you, and I, and all things," (*RC*2). This instance is (partly) used as evidence for his argument that "Defoe is one of the great examples of colloquial diction in English literature" (p. 27: on the same page).

Note that generally accepted syntax is also used, as in:
> they <u>withdrew</u>, <u>paid</u> their Compliment to me, (for I was Queen of the Day) <u>and</u> **went off** to undress. (*Rox* 179) / upon which he <u>ran down</u> to the Still-yard Stairs, **threw away** his Shirt, <u>and plung'd</u> into the *Thames*, (*JPY* 162) / with that, I <u>sat her down</u>, **pull'd off** her Stockings and Shoes, and all her Cloaths, Piece by Piece, <u>and led</u> her to the Bed to him: (*Rox* 46), etc.

[4] Seen from a historical perspective, phrasal verbs "have often been used to translate Latin verbs (*to putte downe ... calare, deponere: Catholicon Anglicum*, 1483) and to define verbs of Latin origin in English (*abrogate ... take away*: Cawdrey, *Table Alphabeticall*, 1604)" (McArthur 1992: 773).

[5] It is rather difficult to determine the origin of the coordination pattern "A and B and C (and D ...)" but the King James Bible (Authorized Version in 1611) seems to contain ample instances. The following passages show the "A and B and C and D" pattern:
> And he [= Samson] <u>found</u> a new jawbone of an ass, <u>and</u> **put forth** his hand, <u>and took</u> it, <u>and slew</u> a thousand men therewith. (*Judg* 15: 15) / But the Philistines <u>took</u> him, <u>and</u> **put out** his eyes, <u>and</u> **brought** him **down** to Gaza, <u>and bound</u> him with fetters of brass; (*Judg* 16: 21), etc.

[6] Two cases in passive voice of a transitive phrasal verb *wrap up* seem to have an effect similar to "inversion":
> I found there three great Bags of Pieces of Eight, ... and in one of them, **wrapt up** in a Paper, <u>six Doubloons</u> [= "A Spanish gold coin" (*OED*)] <u>of Gold</u>, (*RC* 193) / there was a Silver Porringer of a Pint, a small Silver Mug and Six Spoons, some other Linnen, a good Smock, and Three Silk Handkerchiefs, and in the Mug **wrap'd up** in a Paper <u>Eighteen Shillings and Six-pence in Money</u>. (*MF* 192)

Although the texts in which the two instances occur are different, the two descriptions are quite similar. The past participial phrase *wrap'd up in a paper* occurs before the subject in passive voice of *wrap up* (in effect, the object of the phrasal verb), i.e. *six Doubloons of Gold* and *Eighteen Shillings and Six-pence in Money*, both of which are coins, whatever the difference between their values is.

[7] The other four cases of inversion are given for reference only:
> Just as the insolent Rogue was talking thus to the Constable, **comes back** Mr. *William* and Mr. *Anthony*, (*MF* 243) / WHILE these things were in agitation, **came on** <u>the Invasion of the *Scots*</u>, (*CJ* 250) / came

Chapter 3 Semantic and Stylistic Analysis of Phrasal Verbs: Six Aspects

over a transported Felon, from *Bristol*, (*CJ* 157) / Then **came in** my Share, the Lady *Roxana*; (*Rox* 312)

[8] According to Lakoff and Johnson (2003 [1980]: 14), "Orientational metaphors give a concept a spatial orientation; for example, HAPPY IS UP. The fact that the concept HAPPY is oriented UP leads to English expressions such as "I'm feeling *up* today. Such metaphorical orientations are not arbitrary. They have a basis in our physical and cultural experience."

[9] It is necessary to note, in passing, that neither *put out* nor *put in* have transitive (i.e. with an object) use in this sense in *RC*.

[10] As for the use of *stand*-phrasal verbs in *CS*, which occur 52 times in total, those instances unassociated with nautical terms, such as *William* **stood up** *in the Stern of the Pinnace* (*CS* 225), are not presented here.

[11] Of the total 25 occurrences, the subject in 22 instances is the personal pronoun, *we*; the other three instances present non-human subjects.

[12] Both those which have something to do with navigation, e.g. *clew up*, and those which do not, e.g. *man out*, are given:

> we ... lower'd the Top-Sail upon the Cap, and **clewed** them **up** that we might lye as snug as we could, ... (*CS* 147) [cf. *OED* s.v. clew, *v.* 3. *Naut.* "*to clew up*: to draw the lower ends or clews (of sails) up to the upper yard or the mast in preparation for furling or for making 'goose-wings'." *a* 1745~] / so they **Mann'd out** their Boat, and sent to us with a Flag of Truce. (*CS* 216) [cf. *OED* s.v. man, *v.* 1. a. *trans.* (orig. *Mil.* and *Naut.*) "To furnish (a fort, ship, etc.) with a force or company of men to serve or defend it." c 1122~]

[13] In this study, such cases have been treated as belonging to the "intransitive" type.

[14] Watt (1957a: 17-18) points out that two aspects "of especial importance in the novel" are "characterization, and presentation of the background." He goes on to specify that "the novel is surely distinguished from other genres and from previous forms of fiction by the amount of attention it habitually accords both to the individualization of its characters and to the detailed presentation of their environment" (my emphasis added).

[15] In the treatment of the "absolute participle," Jespersen expresses sharp disagreement with statements by Onions and Sweet. Onions (1993 [1971]: 76) states: "In general prose, spoken or written, the absolute participial construction is almost limited to conventional phrases like 'weather permitting', 'God willing', ..." And Sweet (1955 [1898]: 124): "The absolute participle-construction is not only uncolloquial, but is by many felt to be un-English, and to be avoided in writing as

well."

[16] As an auxiliary verb denoting the perfect tense, *having* is also used in the absolute clause, as in:
>the Crowd having **gathered about**, (*MF* 186) / one of the Women having **swoon'd away**; (*CJ* 252)

[17] Hampe goes on to suggest that "the postulation of semantic redundancy is generally motivated by the observation that the meaning of the verb-particle construction is *roughly similar* (original italics) to that of the corresponding verb" (p. 33).

[18] For example, the *Oxford Dictionary of English* (2003) treats *take up arms* as an idiom, while the *Oxford Advanced Learner's Dictionary* (7th ed.) (2005) also refers to the following prepositional phrase, as in *take up arms (against sb)*.

[19] Citations from *A New Test of the Church of England's Loyalty* are based on W. R. Owen ed., Volume 3: DISSENT from *Political and Economic Writings of Daniel Defoe* (General Editors: W. R. Owens and P. N. Furbank), 8 vols. (Pickering & Chatto 2000).

[20] Hampe (2002: 139) suggests that "Redundant phrasal verbs can occur when speakers are very excited about a topic ..."

[21] Hiltunen goes on to mention that "one and the same combination may be repeated several times in succession. Usually this is due to the subject matter of the text" (p.135). In addition, *The Storm* (1704), Defoe's first full length work, contains many more occurrences of *blow down*, 173 times in the 61,972 word text, in comparison with the 123 times, *shut up* is used in the 93,929 word *JPY*. As *The Storm* is a written documentary on the "storm" of 26-27 November 1703 which devastated Southern and Central England and Wales, the frequent use of *blow down* is also considered to be one of "text-specific features." See Murata (2007) in details.

[22] According to Rynell (1969), between the original *Orders* in 1665 and the quotation by Defoe, there are just a few differences. Perusal of the differences pointed out by Rynell reveals no alteration as regards the use of phrasal verbs.

[23] Interestingly, Richetti (2008: 136) points out that "*A Journal of the Plague Year* is a kind of laboratory experiment, an extreme instance of the problem of narrative realism."

[24] Wales (1989: 321) states that "the effect of a consistent use of a nominalizing STYLE is to render static the potentially dynamic or active, ..."

[25] According to these authors, "features of language within [a] text may depart from the norms of the text itself: that is, they may 'stand out' against the background of what the text has led us to expect. This is the phenomenon of

Chapter 3 Semantic and Stylistic Analysis of Phrasal Verbs: Six Aspects

INTERNAL DEVIATION, ..."

[26] This phrase has biblical overtones. See I *John* 3: 17, "But whoso hath this world's good, and seeth his brother have need, and **shutteth up his bowels** *of compassion* from him, how dwelleth the love of God in him?" (from the King James Version). Defoe also uses this phrase in his last novel, *Roxana* (p. 23).

[27] As for a synonymous relationship between two words, Leech (1981: 93) states that "The more specific term is called *hyponym* of the more general, and the more general is called the *superordinate* term."

[28] In Defoe's *The Shortest Way with the Dissenters* (1702), as observed in the Introduction, *root out* is effectively employed with satirical intention. Nevertheless, this short pamphlet contains some interesting instances of synonyms for *root out*. Based on the *OED* definition of "root (out)," as recorded in the citations of *root out* (see p. 9), the verbs "extirpate," "exterminate," and "destroy" may be called synonyms of "root (out)" in a figurative sense. What is of great interest is that two of the three verbs, *extirpate* and *destroy*, are employed in the same pamphlet; the former is obviously more formal and learned than the latter:

> we had, once, an opportunity to serve the Church of England, by **extirpating** her implacable Enemies, (103) / I answer, 'tis cruelty to kill s Snake or a Toad in cold Blood, but the Poyson of their Nature makes it a Charity to our Neighbours, to **destroy** those Creatures, (104)

[29] This imagery develops as follows: "every **Prison**, as we may call it, had but one Jaylor" (p. 52) / "It is to be consider'd too, that as these were **Prisons** without Barrs and Bolts, which our common **Prisons** are furnish'd with," (p. 53).

Conclusion

The present study explored the structure of Defoe's phrasal verbs so as to grasp the genius of his language of fiction. Since phrasal verbs can be used both intransitively and transitively, all instances of these verbs occurring in Defoe's seven fictional works were classified into these two syntactic categories. Before looking into how "phrasal" verbs are used, "verbs" and "particles" as essential elements in forming phrasal verbs were examined within each category.

Many of the intransitive phrasal verbs Defoe employs tend to be made up of "pure" intransitive verbs, such as, *go* and *come*. In fact, *go away* (54 times in *Rox*) or *come up* (60 times in *MC*) are among the most frequently used phrasal verbs. Also of great interest are *fall* and *stand* in *MC* and *CS* respectively, both of which mainly build military and nautical terms unique to these two works (especially *fall in* 32 times and *stand away* 25 times in each). As for transitive phrasal verbs, *bring* acts as the most prolific verb element, co-occurring with ten different particles in *MF*, but *take* is far more frequently used owing to a semantically versatile *take up*, which always shows the highest (or the second highest) frequency in each of the seven works. However, *shut up* in *JPY*, in close relation to the subject matter of this work, is the most frequently used phrasal verb (123 times) in Defoe's fiction, even including intransitive verbs.

The distribution of the particles with intransitive phrasal verbs is relatively *even*, while that in transitive verbs is much more *variable*. *Up* is the most frequent and versatile particle employed in forming transitive phrasal verbs. That is, Defoe uses this particle not only to provide literal meaning, but also in an intensifying or aspectual sense of meaning. In addition, as seen in the instances of *take (up) short* (examined in Section 3.5), it was found that this particle can be used "redundantly." On the other hand, particles such as *forth, across,* and *around* very rarely occur, whether in intransitive or transitive uses.

Chapters 1 and 2 attempted to disclose the structures of intransitive and transitive phrasal verbs, respectively. In Chapter 1, which dealt with intransitive phrasal verbs, the simple pattern of "Verb + Particle" is mainly used as in *the Indians **fled away**, (CS* 207), but there are 88 cases in total where the particle is instead fronted, probably with the aim of making the description more vivid and dynamic. The "P + *Subject* + V" pattern such as ***away** he went*, (*RC* 239) is used 75 times (85%), while the "P + V + *Subject*" pattern such as ***out rushed** three monstrous Wolves*, (*RC* 292) 13 times (15%). The choice between the two patterns depends on the nature of the subject. Namely, when the subject is a personal pronoun, PSV is chosen, but when the subject is a non-personal pronoun, PVS is used. In this respect, three deviant cases in *MF* like ***away came** I with my Bundle*; (*MF* 206) appear to have been intentionally employed by Defoe. When the particle is fronted, *away* is used the most frequently (69 times: 78%). Further, particle fronting is used 28 times (32%) as the "dramatic" present tense in past tense narrative, as in *he came out to me, ... and **away** he **Scours***; (*CJ* 43).

There are 160 cases where an adverbial occurs between the verb and the particle. Adverbials used to indicate "degree," "space (and distance)," "time (and frequency)," "manner," etc. are wide and varied. As seen in *I resolv'd to **run** quite **away** from him.* (*RC* 6), adverbial insertion is intended to give the phrasal verb a more nuanced or shaded meaning, especially for emphasis or force. When such an insertion occurs, *come-* or *go-*phrasal verbs are likely to be used; occurrences

Conclusion

of both types of verbs inserted account for 50% or more in all works except *RC* (45%). The statistics of *RC*, showing the widest variety (namely 40 cases of adverbial insertion, 24 types of adverbials and 28 types of phrasal verbs inserted), suggest that Defoe might have attempted to write his first fictional work elaborately and expressively. On the other hand, *Rox*, his last work, has only 13 cases of adverbial insertion, but the 13 adverbials are each different. One of them is a long *-ing* clause as in *he **walk'd**, talking with another Man of the same Cloth, **back** again, just by me*; (*Rox* 85).

There are 29 cases of the "composite" pattern of "V + *-ing* + P." The *-ing* present participle here looks just like an inserted adverbial such as with *talking* in *he **walk'd**, talking ... **back***, cited above, but is completely different in structure and function. In [*wolves*] ***went bleeding off***, (*RC* 298), in which, I argued, two phrasal verbs, *go off* and *bleeding off*, exist in the deep structure. This pattern contributes to a more dynamic and realistic rendition than its *rough* equivalent (e.g. *wolves bled, and went off*). In this pattern, *come* and *go* are basically used as "V," but the former is far more frequently employed than the latter (15 types *vs.* 3 types), probably because of descriptions of "extraordinary scenes"; the composite pattern is more intensively used in *CS* (13 occurrences and 10 types), which contains a unique instance of [*they*] ***stood edging in** for the Shore*, (*CS* 216), than in any other work.

The cases where an intransitive phrasal verb is followed by a preposition like *we **came back** to our Castle*, (*RC* 208) are too numerous to count. Among them, it was found that there are instances of a three-word verb which could be paraphrased by a one-word "transitive" verb like *About three in the Afternoon he **came up** with* (= "overtook") *us*, (*RC* 18) or instances of "hybrid formation" like *she*

fell in among *a Gang of Thieves*, (*CJ* 258), in which the adverb *in* is inserted ad hoc between the verb and the preposition of the already-existing phrase *fall among*; it could be also construed that *fall among* is contextually mixed with another prepositional verb *fall into*.

There are 159 cases where phrasal verbs are employed as a gerund. The presence or absence of the determiner (e.g. *my*, *the* or *a*) significantly affects the deep structure of phrasal verbs; the former case occurs 83 times while the latter 76 times. As seen in *the constant* ***rushing in*** *of the Water* (*RC* 191), adjectives such as *constant* occur exclusively in cases with a determiner. More than half (87 cases: 55%) of gerund constructions consist of *go*- and *come*-phrasal verbs; *go*-phrasal verbs are used 54 times and *come*-verbs 33 times. Finally, there are several cases where phrasal verbs are used as a completely different word class, including an instance of nonce-use like *we were awaken'd in the Dead of the Night* with ***come out*** *here*, (*CJ* 10) or the cases prior to the *OED* earliest citation (from the year 1814), such as *I gave a great* **Cry-out**, (*Rox* 97).

In Chapter 2, in order to reveal the structure of transitive phrasal verbs, the placement of the object, an essential element, was the primary focus. Apart from the conventional dichotomy between VPO and VOP (e.g. *I* ***sold off*** *most of my Goods*, (*MF* 190) and *I* ***barr'd*** *it* [= the door] ***up*** *in the Night*, (*RC* 208)), it was found that the sub-patterns of OVP and VOPO (e.g. *This horrid Project he* ***carried up*** *so high*, (*CJ* 225) and [*he*] ***gave*** me **back** an exact Inventory of them, (*RC* 33)) serve as variants of the two main patterns. Added to these four patterns is the passive construction, such as, *the Masque was* ***thrown off***, (*MC* 270), the subject of which (i.e. *the Masque*) is virtually the object of the transitive phrasal verb *throw off*.

The VPO pattern is likely to have a long object, for example, containing a relative clause, such as *I **left off** the wicked Trade that I had so newly taken up*; (*MF* 198). In our discussion of the VPO, as seen in *I **cry'd out**, Lord be my Help*, (*RC* 91), the case where a reporting verb is followed by uttered words was counted as an instance of the VPO, given that *Lord be my Help* can function as the direct object of *cry out*. The VOP pattern was examined according to three categories in which the object can be (1) a personal pronoun, (2) a reflexive pronoun, or (3) anything except these two. When the object is a personal pronoun, the VOP is *always* (100%) chosen, but a reflexive pronoun does not always occur in the VOP; seven cases in total are observed in the VPO, like *I **gave up** myself to a readiness of being ruined without the least concern*, (*MF* 26). When the object is anything except these two, the VOP is employed less frequently than the VPO, but the choice of the VOP does not depend upon the "length" of the object, as evidenced in the longest (ten-word) noun phrase in [*the Gentleman*] ***took** the Cloth, and the Remains of what was to Eat,* ***away***; (*Rox* 63). Further, it was found that there are several cases where a noun phrase as the object is divided by the particle, like *the Child* ***had** a little Necklace **on** of Gold Beads*, (*MF* 194). Though in only two cases, the pattern "P (+ Subject) + V + O" (PVO), or transitive "particle fronting," is employed in *MF*, as in ... *and **out** he **pulls** the License*; (*MF* 183); it was argued that this pattern is a variant of the VOP, rather than the VPO.

The OVP pattern has been observed to occur in the following three syntactic positions: (1) in the main clause (e.g. *These two whole Days I **took up** in grinding my Tools*, (*RC* 83)), (2) in the subordinate relative clause (e.g. *Pieces of the Sails, which I **cut out**;* (*RC* 56)), and (3) in the *to*-infinitive construction (e.g. *I have no Cloaths to **put on**,* (*CJ* 126)). When Defoe employs two objects in the use of transitive phrasal verbs, the VOPO pattern, "V + *indirect* O + P + *direct* O," is basically employed as in we **gave** <u>them</u> **back** <u>the Bows and Arrows</u>, (*CS* 69). This basic pattern is, according to the nature of the object, can be made into three additional patterns: (1) VOOP like *Then I pull'd out his Watch and* **gave** <u>it</u> <u>him</u> **back**, (*MF* 155); (2) VPOO like *These Consultations* **took up** <u>our People</u> <u>no less than two or three Days</u>, (*CS* 209); (3) OVOP like *for the prodigious deal of Time and Labour* <u>which</u> it **took** <u>me</u> **up** *to make a Plank or Board*: (*RC* 67).

In comparison with these two sub-patterns of OVP (169 cases in total: 4%) and VOPO (51 cases, including three additional patterns: 1%), the passive construction (e.g. *I was* **knock'd down** *by a Gyant like a German Soldier*, (*CJ* 219)) is used much more frequently (866 cases in total: 21%). Among them are included three cases of the passive progressive such as *his Children were* **breeding up**, (*Rox* 248). Phrasal verbs in the passive voice are also used as adjectives, with a few cases being premodifiers, instead of the more usual postmodifiers, such as *a* **cast-off** *Mistress* (*Rox* 144) and *the dissenting* **turn'd out** *Ministers* (*JPY* 236).

There are 197 cases where transitive phrasal verbs are used as gerunds. Cases with a determiner occur 71 times (36%) as in *I consider'd* <u>the</u> **keeping up** *a Breed of tame Creatures thus at my Hand*, (*RC* 153). Cases lacking determiners are employed more frequently (126 times: 64%) as in *I entertain'd a Thought of* **breeding up** *some tame Creatures*, (*RC* 75). Among the 71 cases with a determiner, the definite article, *the*, is used 35 times. When all the 197 cases were classified into the five syntactic categories, it was found that the 103 cases (52%) are employed in the VPO pattern, while the VOP pattern is used 60 times (30%), the passive 27 times (14%), the OVP pattern 7 times (4%); the VOPO pattern is not used as a gerund. Twelve occurrences of the form "*the* VP of O" such as *the **shutting up** of Houses* (*JPY*) were, as a variant of the VPO, added to the total number (i.e. 103 occurrences) of VPO. Furthermore, among seven cases of the OVP, as seen in <u>their</u> (= children's) ***breeding up***; (*Rox* 193), it was found that gerund expressions possess a passive meaning, as the determiner functions as the object of the phrasal verb.

As for "adverbial insertion" in the transitive use, the "VP [adv] O" pattern was first examined. This pattern can be well observed in the case where a prepositional phrase as an adverbial occurs prior to the object, as in *the Women ... **brought out** <u>to us</u> several Sorts of Food*, (*CS* 116). When an adverbial occurs between V and P, two patterns are mainly employed: the "VO [adv] P" pattern such as *The violence of the blow **beat** the old Gentleman <u>quite</u> **down***, (*CJ* 56) and the passive "V [adv] P" pattern such as *she is **brought** <u>sadly</u> **down***; (*JPY* 108). The former occurs 87 times (81%) and the latter 14 times (13%) of the total 108 cases. Through frequent uses of intensifiers such as *quite* or *all* in the "VO [adv] P" pattern, it was argued that the VOP pattern provides a form far more appropriate for emphasis than the VPO pattern.

A closer examination of how transitive phrasal verbs are exploited has led to the detection of the "composite" pattern in which two transitive verbs share a particle as well as an object, as seen in the "V and VPO" pattern such as *we kill'd sixteen Cows, and <u>pickled and</u> **barrelled** up the Flesh ...* (*CS* 215) or the "V and VOP" pattern such as *this made them <u>paddle and **shove**</u> the Boat **away** as well as they could*, (*CS* 236). These patterns, making descriptions of a sequence of events more concise and condensed, might be called "innovative" novel-writing techniques pioneered by Defoe.

Finally, as for the pattern-distribution of transitive phrasal verbs, it was found that the frequencies of both the VPO and VOP patterns account for 73% (VPO 37% and VOP 36%) of total occurrences. Defoe does prefer the VOP to the VPO, even in comparison with his contemporaries; in particular, *RC*, *MF*, and *CJ* strongly show this tendency. It was concluded that the fundamental difference between these two patterns is that the VOP contributes to more action-based descriptions, while the VPO to more object-based descriptions.

Chapter 3 focused on six aspects of semantic and stylistic features as opposed to syntactic features of Defoe's phrasal verbs: (1) coordinated use with other verbs, (2) inversion and particle fronting for stylistic effect, (3) the function of particles in psychological contexts, (4) descriptions of the sea, (5) the "redundant" use of particles, and (6) repetition and synonym. These six modes of expression, though seemingly unconnected, are closely related to one another. Synonyms (examined in Section 3.6), for example, have been already mentioned in their coordinated use with other verbs (in Section 3.1.2), such as *he ... **made off** and escaped*; (*JPY* 169). If another example is needed, nautical terms (as seen in Section 3.4) are sometimes used in psychological contexts (in Section 3.3). In the following passages from *Roxana*, phrasal verbs with adverbial particles belonging to the nautical terms *aground* and *adrift*, both of which are beyond the scope (i.e. of the 16 particles) of the present study, describe the characters' mental deterioration in their figurative uses; these are instances of, as it were, "synthetic" expressions:

> Here she **run** me **a-ground** again; (*Rox* 289) [cf. *OED* s.v. aground, *adv.* 2. "**to run aground**: to run into a place where the ship lodges on the bottom." 2 b. *fig.* 1665~] / as for her, we was not a-going to **turn** her **adrift**, (*Rox* 249) [cf. *OED* s.v. adrift, *adv.* 1. "In a drifting condition, drifting, at the mercy of wind and tide." 2. *fig.* 1690~]

Conclusion

This research was undertaken as there had not yet been a thorough examination of the relationship between Defoe's language of fiction and his use of phrasal verbs. The results obtained in the previous three chapters, I hope, demonstrate that Defoe's phrasal verbs serve as one of the most concrete and convincing examples capturing the very essence of his language which helped create a "new" fictional prose. The instances described in the present study are directly associated with what Watt (1957a: 29) refers to as "physical" closeness (of his descriptions), concerning Defoe's writing style in his novels. Moreover, Defoe's phrasal verbs are often employed to dynamically describe scenes and actions in his seven fictional works in a sort of "kinematographic comprehension" (Jespersen 2010 [1960]: 594).

As a final note, from the viewpoint of social history, it is worth mentioning that Trevelyan (1982 [1942, 1944]) selects Defoe as an author particularly representative of the period 1700-1740 (Chapter 10 in his book is subtitled "Defoe's England"). The reason for this selection is that Defoe "was one of the first who saw the old world through a pair of sharp modern eyes" (pp. 308-309). Aspects of "modernity" concerning Defoe's views on society should be reflected in his use of language. That is, when first attempting to write a fictional work, Defoe intentionally chose more colloquial and easier-to-understand phrasal verbs, instead of more formal and learned Latinate verbs (*put off* vs. *postpone*), for a large reading public, and employed these verbs with great diversity (as observed in the previous chapters). This intentional use of language as a "strategy" by Defoe the novelist helps us to appreciate his "modernity."

Appendices

APPENDIX I: Types of Intransitive Phrasal Verbs in Six Works Other Than *Robinson Crusoe* (The notation is the same as that of *RC*, pp. 24-25.)

1. Types of Intransitive Phrasal Verbs in *Memoirs of a Cavalier*:
    break *off, out, in* (3); burst *out*; call *out*; charge *in*; clap *in*; clutter *away*; coast *round*; come *away, back, down, off, out, up, in, on, over* (9); cry *out*; draw *down, off, out, up* (4); drop *away*; dwindle *away*; face *up, about* (2); fall *down, off, out, in, on* (5); flee *away, up* (2); fly *away, over* (2); follow *in*; gallop *up*; get *away, back, down, off, out, up, over, in* (8); give *over*; go *away, back, down, off, out, up, about, along, round, in, on, over* (12); hang *back*; hold *out*; hop *away*; jog *on*; keep *off, on* (2); leap *down*; leave *off*; lie *down, in* (2); look *back, out, about, on* (4); make *back, off, up* (3); march *away, back, off, out, up, by, on* (7); pass *on*; pierce *in*; pour *in*; press *back, on* (2); push *on*; put *off*; ride *away, back, off, out, up* (5); roll *about*; rove *about*; run *away, back, down, off, in* (5); sally *out*; scape *away*; send *away, up* (2); set *down, out* (2); shift *away*; sit *down*; spin *out*; stand *out, up by* (3); start *up*; step *up*; stir *out*; swim *over*; take *up*; thrust *in*; turn *away, back about* (3); wade *over, in* (2); walk *about*; wear *off*; wheel *off, about* (2); [out of 61 types of verbs **129 types** of phrasal verbs]
    composite type: come galloping *away, in* (2); come swiming *over*; [**3 types**]
    [132 types in total]

2. Types of Intransitive Phrasal Verbs in *Captain Singleton*:
    adventure *over*; bear *down*; beat *about*; break *off, in* (2); chop *about*; clamber *up*; clear *up*; come *away, back, down, off, out, up, along, round, in, on, over* (11); cruise *away*; crumble *down*; cry *out*; draw *up*; dress *up*; drive *about*; drop *away*; dry *up*; ebb *away, out* (2); edge *down*; face *about*; fall *away, down, off, out, in* (5); fire *in*; flee *away*; fly *away, back,* (2); get *away, back, down, off, up, in* (6); give *over*; go *away, back, down, off, out, up, about, along, in, on, over* (11); grow *up*; hale *away, up, in* (3); hold *out*; huddle *down*; jog *on*; jump *back, up, aside* (3); keep *up, on* (2); kneel *down*; launch *off, out* (2); lay *down, up* (2); lead *away*; leap *up*; leave *off*; lie *away, down, off, out, by* (5); live *on*; look *down, out, up* (3); luff *up*; make *off, up, in* (3);

march *back, off, up* (3); mount *up*; move *off, on* (2); pass *over, by* (2); pile *away*; plunge *in*; ply *about*; point *up*; pour *in*; push *out, on* (2); put *away, back, off, out, in* (5); rear *up*; rise *up*; roll *in*; row *away, in* (2); run *away, back, down, out, up, along, in* (7); sail *away, back, along, on* (4); search *about*; seek *out, about* (2); set *out, forth, in* (2); sheer *off*; shift *off*; shoot *out*; shrink *away*; sink *away*; sit *down*; slant *away*; spring *up*; stand *away, off, out, up, in, on, over* (7); start *up*; stay *out*; steer *away*; step *out, in* (2); stir *away, out* (2); stoop *down*; stretch *away, off, out, over* (4); swim *off, over* (2); tack ab*out*; tend *away*; tow *up*; travel *up*; trend *away*; turn *out, about, round* (3); venture *off, out, up, over* (4); walk *off, out, about* (3); wear *off*; wind *away*; [out of 91 lexical verbs, **179 types** of phrasal verbs]

composite type: come flying *out*; come roaring *out*; come running *down, up, in* (3); come thundering *back*; go trending *away*; run scream *away*; stand edging *in*; cf. run staring and howling about [**10 types**]

[189 types in total]

3. Types of Intransitive Phrasal Verbs in *Moll Flanders*:

break *off, out, in* (3); brush *off*; burst *out*; call *down, out* (2); clap *in*; come *away, back, down, off, out, up, along, by, in, on, over* (11); cry *out*; drive *away*; drop *down*; faint *away*; fall *off, out, in* (3); flow *in*; fly *out*; gather *about*; get *away, off, out, up, over* (5); go *away, back, down, off, out, up, about, along, round, by, in, on, over* (13); grow *up*; hang *back*; hold *out*; hurry *on*; jump *out*; kneel *down*; launch *out*; lay *down*; leave *off*; lie *down, in* (2); look *back, out, up, about, round, in, on* (7); make *off*; move *on*; pass *by, over* (2); play *on*; put *off, in* (2); ramble *about*; reach *up*; rise *up*; roar *out*; run *away, down, out, up, round, in, on, over* (8); scream *out*; send *away*; set *out, up* (2); sin *on*; sink *down*; sit *down, up* (2); sleep *over*; slip *out*; stand *off, up, by* (3); start *up*; stay *out*; step *up, in* (2); swoon *away*; take *up, on* (2); throw *out*; turn *away, about, round* (3) walk *away, off, out, about* (4); wander *about*; wear *away, off, in* (3); write *back* [*out* of 57 lexical verbs, **117 types** of phrasal verbs]

composite type: come running *out*; [**1 type**]

[118 types in total]

4. Types of Intransitive Phrasal Verbs in *A Journal of the Plague Year*:

break *off, out, in* (3); call *out*; clear *up*; come *away, back, down, out, up, about, along, by, in, on, over* (11); cry *out*; die *off*; drive *away*; drop *down*; fall *down, in* (2); fill *up*; flee *away, out* (2); fly *away*; get *away, out, up, in* (4);

Appendices

go *away, back, down, off, out, up, about, along, by, in, on, over* (12); grow *on*; help *out*; hurry *away*; keep *off, on* (2); lie *up*; look *back, out, up, on* (4); make *off*; pass *along, by, over* (3); read *on*; rise *up*; rove *about*; row *up*; run *away, down, out, up, about, in, on* (7); sally* *out*; scream *out*; set *out, up, in* (3); shift *away*; shoot *out*; shriek *out*; sit *down*; slip *away*; stare *up*; start *out*; stir *out*; swim *back, over* (2); take *up*; travel *away, on* (2); turn *away, out, round* (3); venture *out, in* (2); walk *away, out, up, about* (4); wander *away, about* (2); work *on* [out of 46 lexical verbs, **97 types** of phrasal verbs]
composite type: go piping *along*; [**1 type**]
[98 types in total]

5. Types of Intransitive Phrasal Verbs in *Colonel Jack*:
bear *away, down* (2); beat *up*; break *off, out, in* (3); burst *out*; call *out*; clap *in*; clear *up*; come *away, back, down, off, out, up, about, along, by, on, over, in* (12); cross *back*; crowd *away*; cry *out*; die *away*; draw *up*; drink *on*; face *about*; fall *down, out, in* (3); fly *out, in* (2); gallop *away*; get *away, down, off, out, up, over, in* (7); go *away, back, down, off, out, up, about, alongby, on, over, in* (12); grow *up*; hang *down, out, up, about* (4); hanker *about*; hasten *away, on* (2); hold *on*; hollow *out*; hop *about*; hurry *away, on* (2); jog *away*; jump *off, about* (2); keep *up, on* (2); kneel *down*; knock *down*; lay *on*; leave *off*; lie *down, by, in* (3); loiter *about*; look *back, down, out, up, about, on, in* (7); lug *out*; lurk *about*; make *down, in* (2); march *on*; pass *by, over* (2); plump *up*; push *on*; put *out, up, in* (3); reach *over*; ride *away, out,* (2); rise *up*; roar *out*; run *away, up, about, on, in* (5); scour *away*; scream *out*; set *out, up* (2); shuffle *along*; shut *in*; sink *down*; sit *down, up* (2); skulk *about*; slip *away, down* (2); snatch *away*; spread *about*; stand *away, off, up, by, on, over, in* (7); start *up*; steer *away*; step *back, up, in* (3); stir *out*; stretch *away*; stroll *away, about* (2); swim *over*; swoon *away*;tumble *out*; turn *away, back, off, in* (4); vanish *away*; venture *out*; walk *away, off, out, up, about, on, over* (7); wander *about*; wear *off*; wind *about*;
[out of 79 lexical verbs, **158 types** of phrasal verbs]
composite type: come riding *by*; come trotting *on*; go spooning *away*; [**3 types**]
[161 types in total]

6. Types of Intransitive Phrasal Verbs in *Roxana*:
break *off, out, up, in* (4); burst *out*; call *out*; clap *in*; come *away, back, down, out, up, along, in, on, over* (9); crowd *in*; cry *out*; dance *in*; draw *back, out,*

in (3); drive *back*, *out* (2); drop *away*; faint *away*; fall *back*, *down*, *out* (3); flock *over*; flow *in*; flush *up*; fly *out*, *up* (2); get *away*, *down*, *off*, *out*, *up*, *over* (6); go *away*, *back*, *down*, *off*, *out*, *up*, *about*, *along*, *in*, *on*, *over* (11); grow *up*; hang *back*, *down*, *on* (3); hasten *on*; jump *out*; keep *away*; leave *off*; lie *in*; live *up*, *on* (2); look *back*, *out*, *up*, *in* (4); march *off*; pass *back*, *off*, *on*, *over* (4); pull *back*; put *in*; remove *back*; ride *out*; rise *up*; roll *about*; rouse *up*; run *away*, *down*, *out*, *up*, *in*, *on* (6); saunter *about*; send *over*; set *down*, *out*, *up* (3); sin *on*; sink *down*; sit *down*, *up* (2); skulk *about*; slip *out*; stand *away*, *out*, *up*, *by*, *over* (5); start *up*; steer *away*; stir *off*; swoon *away*; take *up*, *on* (2); turn *away*, *back*, *about*, (3); walk *away*, *back*, *in* (3); wear *off*; [out of 55 lexical verbs, **113 types** of phrasal verbs]

composite type: come riding *by*; come running *in*; [**2 types**]

[115 types in total]

Appendices

APPENDIX II: Types of Transitive Phrasal Verbs in Six Works Other Than *Robinson Crusoe* (The notation is the same as that of *RC*, pp. 120-121.)

1. Types of Transitive Phrasal Verbs in *Memoirs of a Cavalier*:
   bear *down*; beat *back, down, off, out, up, in,on* (7); block *up*; break *off, up* (2); bring *away, back,down,off, out, up, in, on, over* (9); buy *off, up* (2); call *back, off, out, up, in* (5); carry *away, off, up, on* (4); cast *up*; choose *out*; command *away, up* (2); compass *about*; coop *up*; cry *out, up* (2); cut *down, off, out* (3); deliver *out, up* (2); disperse *about*; draw *away, down, off, out, up, on* (6); dress *up*; drink *up, round* (2); drive *away, back, out, up* (4); eat *up*; fetch *away, off, about, round, in, over* (6); fight *out*; fill *up*; find *out*; fit *out*; fold *up*; force *off, up* (2); fright *away*; frighten *away*; get *over*; give *out, up, in, over* (4); hasten *away*; have *out*; hearten *up*; help *off, out, up* (3); hem *in*; hold *out*; huddle *up*; hurry *away*; issue *out*; keep *back, down,off, out, up* (5); knock *down*; lay *down, out, up, aside, in* (5); lead *up, on* (2); leave *out*; lengthen *out*; let *in*; lift *up*; linger *away*; lock *up*; make *out, up* (2); mark *out*; mow *down*; order *away*; pack *up*; pass *over*; persuade *off*; pick *up*; pour *in*; puff *up*; pull *down, off, out, over* (4); push *on*; put *away, off, up, by, on* (5); raise *up*; restore *back*; run *down*; seek *out*; send *away, back, out, round, over* (5); set *down, up, on* (3); shed *down*; ship *over*; shut *up*; single *out*; spike *up*; spin *out*; store *up*; swallow *up*; swell *up*; take *away, down, off, up, round, in* (6); tell *out*; throw *away, down, off, out, up* (5); thrust *in*; tie *up*; tire *out*; trip *up*; trod *down*; turn *off, about* (2); wall *round*; wheel *off*;
   [out of 91 lexical verbs, **172 types** of phrasal verbs]

2. Types of Transitive Phrasal Verbs in *Captain Singleton*:
   barrel *up*; beat *off, out, up* (3); bind *up*; blow *out, up* (2); bore *down*; breed *up*; break *off, up* (2); bring *away, back, down, out, up, in* (6); burn *down*; burst *out*; buy *up*; call *out, up* (2); carry *away, back, off, up, along, round, on* (7); cast *away, off* (2); clap *up*; clew *up*; cry *out*; cut *down, off, out* (3); deliver *up*; do *over*; drag *about*; draw *up*; dress *up*; drive *away, back, off* (3); dry *away*; eat *up*; eke *out*; fetch *away, back, off* (3); fill *up*; find *out*; fit *out, up* (2); fling *down*; float *off*; force *down, out* (2); fright *away*; gather *up, in* (2); get *away, down, off, out, up* (5); give *away, back, up, over* (4); hang *out, up* (2); haul *down, up* (2); have *out*; hearten *up*; heave *in*; heel *over*; help *out*; hew *away*; hoist *out, up* (2); hold *out, up* (2); hurry *away*; invite *in*; jam *in*; keep *off, out, up, on* (4); knock *down, out* (2); lay *down, up, aside, in* (4); lead *away, back, out, about* (4); leave *off*; lengthen *out*; lift *up*; load *back*; look

out; lower *down*; make *out, up* (2); man *out*; mix *up*; paddle *along*; palisado *in, round* (2); pick *up*; pickle *up*; pile *up*; pour *in*; pull *out, up* (2); put *back, off, out, up, in, on* (5); raise *up*; read *over*; ride *out*; root *out*; run *up*; salt *up*; scare *away*; search *up*; send *away, back, down, forth, off, out, up, over* (8); set *down, out, up, aside, in* (5); shave *off*; shore *up*; shove *away*; shrink *up*; shut *in*; single *out*; sit *down*; smoke *out*; snatch *up*; spin *out*; spirit *away*; splinter *up*; split *off, up* (2); spot *over*; spring *up*; squander *away*; starve *out*; stick *up*; stock *up*; stop *up*; swallow *up*; sweep *away*; take *away, down, off, out, up, aside, along, in* (8); tell *off*; throw *away, down, out, up,* bout, *in* (6); thrust *in*; tie *down*; tow *along*; travel *out*; tread *down*; turn *away, off, out* (3); wallow *up*; wash *away*; work *down*;

[out of 116 lexical verbs, **197 types** of phrasal verbs]

3. Types of Transitive Phrasal Verbs in *Moll Flanders*:

bear*back*; beat *down, off* (2); bind *over*; block *up*; blot *out*; brazen *out*; break *down, off, out, up* (4); breed *up*; bring *away, back, off, out, up, about, along, in, on, over* (10); build *up*; buy *off, in* (2); call *away, back, down, out, up, in* (6); carry *away, back, down, off, out, about, on, over* (8); cast *away, down, off, up, about, on* (6); clear *up*; convey *away*; cry *down, out* (2); cut *down*; debauch *away*; deliver *up*; drag *away, up, along* (3); draw *out, in* (2); dress *up*; drink *away*; drive *away, out, along, on* (4); drop *out*; eke *out*; enquire *out*; fetch *away, up* (2); fight *out*; fill *up*; find *back, out* (2); force *out*; get *away, off, out, in* (4); give *back, out, up, in, over* (5); have *up, on* (2); heap *up*; hear *out*; help *off, up* (2); hold *out*; hurry *away, on* (2); invite *over*; keep *off, up, in* (3); knock *down*; lay *down, out, up, aside, in* (5); lead *back, on* (2); leave *off*; lengthen *out*; let *down, out, in* (3); lift *up*; lock *up*; look *over*; lose *back*; make *out, up* (2); melt *down*; muffle *up*; muster *up*; nurse *up*; pack *up*; partition *off*; pick *out, up* (2); pickle *up*; place *out*; play *back, on* (2); pour *out, in* (2); pull *away, back, off, out, up, in* (6); push *back, on* (2); put *away, off, out, up, by, in, on, over* (8); reach *out*; read *over*; reckon *up*; return *back*; roll *up*; run *out*; sell *off*; send *away, back, out, in, over* (5); set *down, off, out, up, in, on* (6); shake *off*; sham *off*; shift *off*; ship *off*; shut *up, in* (2); single *out*; sit *down*; slip *away, off, out, up* (4); sort *out*; spring *up*; sue *out*; take *away, back, off, out, up, aside, in* (7); talk *up*; throw *down, off, out, up* (4); thrust *away, down* (2); tie *up*; turn *away, out, up, about* (4); wear *off*; work *up, about* (2); wrap *up, about* (2); write *down*; yield *up*;

[out of 99 lexical verbs, **203 types** of phrasal verbs]

Appendices

4. Types of Transitive Phrasal Verbs in *A Journal of the Plague Year*:
beat *back*; block *up*; blow *up*; break *down, up* (2); bring *back, down, off, out, up, along, in, over* (8); burn *down, up* (2); call *away, out* (2); carry *away, back, down, off, out, along, in, on* (8); cast *off, up* (2); choose *out*; clear *away*; convey *away*; cry *down, out* (2); cut *down, off, out* (3); dig *up*; direct *out*; drag *away*; draw *up, in* (2); drive *back, along* (2); enquire *out*; fetch *away, back, out, up* (4); fill *up*; find *out*; fit *out*; force *back*; freeze *up*; get *out, on, over* (3); give *out, up, in, over* (4); grow *up*; hand *about, on* (2); have *on*; help *down*; hold *down, up* (2); issue *out*; keep *off, out, up, in* (4); lay *down, out, up, along, aside, by, in* (7); lead *away, out* (2); leave *off*; let *down, out, in* (3); lift *up*; lock *up, in* (2); make *away, out, up* (3); muffle *up*; pack *up*; padlock *up*; palisado *off*; pass *back*; pen *up*; pick *up*; plaster *over*; pluck *up*; point *out*; pull *down, off, out* (3); push *down*; put *down, off, out, in, on, over* (6); raise *up*; reckon *up*; remove *off*; roll *off*; scum *off*; send *away, out, up, about* (4); set *down, off, up* (3); shake *out*; shoot *out*; shut *up, in* (2); stop *up*; stretch *out*; strip *off*; sweep *away, off* (2); take *away, down, off, out, up, in* (6); throw *away, down, out, in* (4); thrust *in*; tie *up*; turn *away, back, off, out, round, over* (6); wall *about*; wear *out*; wind *up*; wrap *up*; write *down*;
[out of 79 lexical verbs, **154 types** of phrasal verbs]

5. Types of Transitive Phrasal Verbs in *Colonel Jack*:
bear *down*; beat *back, down, off, out, up* (5); beg *off*; bind *up*; block *up*; blow *up*; break *off, out, up* (3); breed *up*; bring *away, back, down, off, out, up, in, on, over* (9); bully *away*; burst *out*; call *out, up, in, over* (4); carry *away, back, down, off, up, along, in, on, over* (9); cast *away, up* (2); clear *off, up* (2); clothe *over*; convey *away*; cry *down, out* (2); cut *down, off* (2); deliver *up*; drag *out, along* (2); draw *off, out, up, in* (4); dress *up*; drink *out, up* (2); drive *back, down, off* (3); endorse *off*; enquire *out*; feel *out*; fetch *off*; fight *out*; find *out*; fish *up*; fit *out, up* (2); gather *up*; get *away, down, off, out, over* (5); give *away, back, out, up, in, over* (6); hale *about, along* (2); hang *out*; have *on*; hedge *up*; help *out, on* (2); hold *out, up, on* (3); hurry *away*; keep *down, off, up* (3); knock *down, off, out* (3); lay *down, out, up, on* (4); lead *out*; lean *back*; leave *off, out* (2); let *down, in* (2); lift *up*; load *back*; lock *up, in* (2); look *out, over* (2); lug *out*; make *out, up* (2); manage *away*; mark *out*; pack *up*; pass *by, over* (2); pay *off*; pick *out, up* (2); pile *up*; post *up*; pour *out*; pull *away, off, out* (3); push *about, on* (2); put *away, back, off, out, up, in, on* (7); read *over*; receive *back*; reckon *up*; root *out*; run *out*; seal *up*; sell *off*; send *away, back, down, out, up, over* (6); serve *out*; set *down, up* (2); ship *back*,

303

off, along, over (4); shoot *away*; shut *out, in* (2); single *out*; sit *down*; slip *back, out* (2); snatch *up*; spirit *away*; steal *away*; strike *up*; take *away, down, off, out, up, aside, in* (7); talk *up*; tell *out, over* (2); throw *away, down, off, in* (4); thrust *away, off, up, in* (4); tie *up*; tire *out*; tumble *over*; turn *away, back, off, out, in* (5); wear *out*; wheedle *away*; whip *away*; wrap *up*; write *down*;
[out of 102 lexical verbs, **203 types** of phrasal verbs]

6. Types of Transitive Phrasal Verbs in *Roxana*:

blow *off, up* (2); break *off*; breed *up*; bring *back, down, off, out, up, about, along, in, over* (9); call *down, out, up, in* (4); carry *away, back, down, off, out, up, on* (7); cast *away, off, up* (3); catch *back*; choke *up*; clear *up*; close *up*; convey *away*; count *out*; cry *out, up* (2); cut *off*; delude *away*; dig *up*; drag *off, over* (2); draw *out, in* (2); dress *up*; drink *up*; drive *away, over* (2); dry *up*; eat *up*; enquire *out*; feed *up*; fetch *away, out* (2); fill *up*; find *out*; fit *up*; fold *up*; force *back*; fright *away*; gape *out*; gather *up*; get *away, out, over* (3); give *away, back, out, up, in, over* (6); hand *back*; hang *up*; have *away, on* (2); heal *up*; help *off, out* (2); hoard *up*; hold *out, up, on* (3); hunt *out*; keep *back, off, up* (3); knock *down, out* (2); lay *down, out, up, aside, by* (5); lead *out, up* (2); leave *off, out* (2); let *down, out, in* (3); lift *up*; look *over*; make *away, out, up, over* (4); muffle *up*; pack *off, up* (2); pass *away*; pay *down, off* (2); pick *up*; pin *down*; pluck *up*; point *out*; pour *in*; press *on*; puff *up*; pull *off, out* (2); put *back, off, out, up, by, in, on* (7); reach *out*; reckon *up*; repeat *over*; roll *up*; rouse *up*; run *down*; sell *off*; send *away, back, out, up, in, over* (6); set *down, forth, off, out, up* (5); shut *up*; single *out*; sit *down*; shake *off*; shift *off*; slip *on*; snatch *up*; spend *off*; squander *away*; stir *up*; sum *up*; swallow *up*; take *away, down, off, out, up, along, in* (7); talk *up, over* (2); throw *away, back, down, off, out* (5); thrust *by, in* (2); tie *up*; trace *out*; turn *away, off, out, in* (4); usher *in*; wear *out*; weigh *down*; wipe *off, out* (2); wring *up*; yield *up*;
[out of 101 lexical verbs, **185 types** of phrasal verbs]

References

Adams, V. (1973) *An Introduction to Modern English Word-Formation*. London: Longman.

Adamson, S. (1989) "With Double Tongue: Diglossia, Stylistics and the Teaching of English," in M. Short (ed.) *Reading, Analysing and Teaching Literature*. Harlow: Longman. 204-240.

Akimoto, M. (1999) "Collocations and Idioms in Late Modem English," in L. Brinton and and M. Akimoto (eds.) *Collocational and Idiomatic Aspects of Composite Predicates in the History of English*. Amsterdam: John Benjamins. 207-238.

Beal, J. C. (2004) *English in Modern Times: 1700-1945*. London: Arnold.

Biber, D., S. Johannsson, G. Leech, S. Conrad & E. Finegan (1999), *Longman Grammar of Spoken and Written English*. Harlow: Longman.

Blake, N. F. (2002) *A Grammar of Shakespeare's Language*. London: Palgrave.

_____ (2004) *Shakespeare's Non-Standard English: A Dictionary of His Informal Language*. Bristol: Thoemmes Continuum.

Blewett, D. (ed.) (2001) *Passion and Virtue: Essays on the Novels of Samuel Richardson*. Tronto: University of Tronto Press.

Bolinger, D. (1971) *The Phrasal Verb in English*. Massachusetts: Harvard University Press.

Brinton, L. J. and E. C. Traugott (2005) *Lexicalization and Language Change*. Cambridge: Cambridge University Press.

Cambridge Phrasal Verbs Dictionary (2nd ed.) (2006 [1997]). Cambridge: Cambridge University Press.

Charleston, B. (1960) *Studies on the Emotional and Affective Means of Expression in Modern English*. Bern: Francke Verlag.

Claridge, C. (2000) *Multi-word Verbs in Early Modern English*. Amsterdam: Rodopi.

Collins COBUILD Phrasal Verbs Dictionary (3rd ed.) (2012 [1989]). Glasgow: HarperCollins Publishers.

Cowie, A. P. and R. Mackin (1975) *Oxford Dictionary of Current Idiomatic English,* Volume 1: *Verbs with Prepositions and Particles*. Oxford: Oxford University Press.

Davis, L. (1983) *Factual Fictions: The Origins of the English Novel*. New York:

Columbia University Press.

Declerck, R. (1991) *A Comprehensive Descriptive Grammar of English*. Tokyo: Kaitakusha.

Denison, D. (1998) "Syntax," in S. Romaine (ed.) *The Cambridge History of the English Language*, Vol. IV 1776-1997. Cambridge: Cambridge University Press. 92-329.

Dixon, R. M. W. (2005) *A Semantic Approach to English Grammar* (2nd ed.). Oxford: Oxford University Press.

Dobrée, B. (1949) "Some Aspects of Defoe's Prose," in J. L. Clifford and L. A. Landa (eds.) *Pope and his Contemporaries: Essays presented to George Sherburn*. Oxford: Clarendon Press.

———— (1990 [1959]) *The Early Eighteenth Century 1700-1740: Swift, Defoe, and Pope*, repr. Oxford: Clarendon Press.

Eaves, T.C. D. and B. D. Kimpel (1967) "Richardson's Revisions of *Pamela*," *Studies in Bibliography* 20. 61-88.

Fraser, B. (1976) *The Verb-Particle Combination in English*. New York: Academic Press.

Furbank, P. N. and W. R. Owens (1986) "Defoe and the 'Improvisatory' Sentence," *English Studies*, 2: 157-166.

———— (2009) "Textual Notes," in P. N. Furbank (ed.) *The Fortunate Mistress* (1724). London: Pickering & Chatto (Publishers) Ltd.

Gordon, I. A. (1966) *The Movement of English Prose*. London: Longman.

Greenbaum, S. (1996) *The Oxford English Grammar*. Oxford: Oxford University Press.

Halliday, M. A. K. (1994) *An Introduction to Functional Grammar* (2nd ed.). London: Arnold.

Hampe, B. (2002) *Superlative Verbs: A Corpus-based Study of Semantic Redundancy in English Verb-particle Construction*. Tübingen: Gunter Narr Verlag Tübingen.

Hiltunen, R. (1994) "On Phrasal Verbs in Early Modern English: Notes on Lexis and Style," in D. Kastovsky (ed.) *Studies in Early Modern English*. Berlin: Mouton de Gruyter. 129-140.

———— (1999) "Verbal Phrases and Phrasal Verbs in Early Modern English," in L. J. Brinton and M. Akimoto (eds) *Collocational and Idiomatic Aspects of Composite Predicates* in the History of English. Amsterdam/Philadelphia: John Benjamins. 133-165.

Hornby, A. S. (1954) *A Guide to Patterns and Usage in English*. London: Oxford University Press.

References

Huddleston, R. & G. K. Pullum (2002) *The Cambridge Grammar of the English Language*. Cambridge: Cambridge University Press.

Ito, H. (1980) *The Language of the Spectator: A Lexical and Stylistic Approach*. Tokyo: Shinozaki Shorin.

_____ (1993) *Some Aspects of Eighteenth-Century English*. Tokyo: Eichosha.

James, E. A. (1972) *Daniel Defoe's Many Voices: A Rhetorical Study of Prose Style and Literary Method*. Amsterdam: Rodopi.

Jespersen, O. (1909-1949) *Modern English Grammar*, Vols. I-VII. London: George Allen & Unwin.

_____ (1992 [1924]) *The Philosophy of Grammar*, repr. Chicago: The University of Chicago Press.

_____ (2010 [1960]) *Selected Writings of Otto Jespersen*, repr. Abingdon, Oxon: Routledge.

Kennedy, A. G. (1967 [1920]) *The Modern English Verb-Adverb Combination*, repr. New York: AMS Press.

Kumamoto, S. (1999) *The Rhyme-Structure of The Romaunt of The Rose-A: In Comparison with Its French Original Le Roman De La Rose*. Tokyo: Kaibunsha Ltd.

Lakoff, G. and M. Johnson (2003 [1980]) *Metaphors We Live By*. Chicago and London: The University of Chicago Press.

Lannert. G. L. (1920) *An Investigation into the Language of Robinson Crusoe as Compared with That of Other 18th Century Works*. Uppsala: Almovist & Wiksells.

Leech, G. (1981) *Semantics* (2nd ed.). Harmondsworth: Penguin Books.

_____, B. Cruickshank, and R. Ivanic (2001) *An A-Z of English Grammar & Usage* (2nd ed.). Harlow: Pearson Education Ltd.

_____ (2006) *A Glossary of English Grammar*. Edinburgh: Edinburgh University Press.

_____ and M. Short (2007) *Style in Fiction* (2nd ed.). London: Pearson Education Ltd.

Lindelöf, U. (1937) *English Verb-Adverb Groups Converted into Nouns*. Societas Scientiarum Fennica. Commentationes humanarum litterarum, Tomus IX. 5 (Helsinki).

Masui, M. (1964) *The Structure of Chaucer's Rime Words: An Exploration into the Poetic Language of Chaucer*. Tokyo: Kenkyusha.

McArthur, T. (1992) *The Oxford Companion to the English Language*. Oxford: Oxford University Press.

McCarthy, M. and F. O'Dell (2004) *English Phrasal Verbs in Use: Intermediate*.

Cambridge: Cambridge University Press.

_____ (2007) *English Phrasal Verbs in Use: Advanced*. Cambridge: Cambridge University Press.

McIntosh, C. (1986) *Common and Courtly Language: The Stylistics of Social Class in 18th-Century British Literature*. Philadelphia: University of Pennsylvania Press.

_____ (1998) *The Evolution of English Prose, 1700-1800*. Cambridge: Cambridge University Press.

McKillop, A. D. (1967) *The Early Masters of English Fiction*. Lawrence: University of Kansas Press.

Mullan, J. (1998) "Swift, Defoe, and Narrative Forms," in S. N. Zwicker, (ed.) *The Cambridge Companion to English Literature 1650-1740*. Cambridge: Cambridge University Press. 250-275

Murata, K. (2000) "On the Verb-Adverb Combination in Defoe's *Captain Singleton*: With Special Reference to Nautical Terms," *Research Reports of the Ariake National College of Technology* 36: 151-160.

_____ (2001) "Some Observations on Phrasal Verbs in Defoe's *A Journal of the Plague Year,*" *Research Reports of the Ariake National College of Technology* 37: 153-160.

_____ (2002) "Some Syntactic and Semantic Observations on Defoe's Phrasal Verbs," *Kumamoto Studies in English Language and Literature* 45: 87-112.

_____ (2003) "Richardson's Revision of *Pamela* and the Use of Phrasal Verbs," *Studies in Modern English*. Tokyo: Eichosha. 443-455.

_____ (2007) "Some Observations on Phrasal Verbs in Defoe's *The Storm*: From a Stylistic Point of View," *Kumamoto Studies in English Language and Literature* 50: 67-86.

_____ (2009) "Phrasal Verbs in Defoe's Non-fictional Writings and their Stylistic Significance," in M. Hori, T. Tabata, and S. Kumamoto (eds.) *Stylistic Studies of Literature: In Honour of Professor Hiroyuki Ito*. Bern: Perter Lang. 17-32.

_____ (2010) "On the Pattern "Verb + Adverb + Preposition" in Defoe: Does His Text Contain "Phrasal-prepositional Verbs," *Kumamoto Studies in English Language and Literature* 53: 1-22.

_____ (2012) "Notes on Defoe's Style and the Use of Phrasal Verbs" (in Japanese), *Research Reports of the Ariake National College of Technology* 48: 1-18.

_____ (2013) "Investigating Defoe's Style: As Seen in the Use of SHUT UP in *A Journal of the Plague Year,*" *Kumamoto Studies in English Language and*

Literature 56: 1-24.

_____ (2014) *The Structure of Defoe's Phrasal Verbs: An Exploration into Defoe's Language of Fiction* (A doctoral dissertation submitted to Kumamoto University, Japan).

Nevalainen, T. (1999) "Early Modern English Lexis and Semantics," in R. Lass (ed.) *The Cambridge History of the English Language*, Vol. III 1476-1776. Cambridge: Cambridge University Press. 332-458.

Onions, C. T. (1993 [1971]) *Modern English Syntax*, repr. London: Routledge.

Palmer, F. R. (1987) *The English Verb* (2nd ed.). London: Longman.

Parrott, M (2010) *Grammar for English Language Teachers* (2nd ed.). Cambridge: Cambridge University Press.

Partridge, A. C. (1969) *Tudor to Augustan English*. London: André Deutsch.

Quirk, R., S. Greenbaum, G. Leech and J. Svartvik (1985) *A Comprehensive Grammar of the English Language*. London: Longman.

Richetti, J. (2005) *The Life of Daniel Defoe*. Oxford: Blackwell Publishing.

_____ (2008) "Defoe as Narrative Innovator," in J. Richetti (ed.) *The Cambridge Companion to Daniel Defoe*. Cambridge: Cambridge University Press. 121-138.

Rissanen, M. (1999) "Syntax," in R. Lass (ed.) *The Cambridge History of the English Language*, Vol. III 1476-1776. Cambridge: Cambridge University Press. 187-331.

Rogers, P. (1972) *Daniel Defoe: The Critical Heritage*. London: Routledge.

Rynell, A. (1969) "Defoe's *Journal of the Plague Year*, the Lord Mayor's *Orders* and *O.E.D.*," *English Studies* 50, 452-464.

Simpson, J. A. and E. S. C. Weiner, prepared (1989) *The Oxford English Dictionary*, Second Edition on CD-ROM Version 4.0 (2009). Oxford University Press, Oxford.

Sinclair, J. (1991) *Corpus, Concordance, Collocation*. Oxford: Oxford University Press.

Smith, L. P. (1947 [1925]) *Words and Idioms*, repr. London: Constable & Company Ltd.

Sørensen, K. (1988) "Phrasal Verb into Noun," in M. Powell and P. Preisler (eds.) *English Past And Present: A selection of Essays by Knud Sørensen Presented to Him His Sixtieth Birthday*. Aarhus: Aarhus University Press. 148-159.

Starr, G. A. (1974) "Defoe's Prose Style: 1. The Language of Interpretation," *Modern Philology*, 71: 277-294.

Sweet, H. (1955 [1898]) *A New English Grammar: Part II Syntax*. Oxford: Clarendon Press.

Tajima, M. (1985) *The Syntactic Development of the Gerund in Middle English.* Tokyo: Nan'un-do.

Thim, S. (2012) *Phrasal Verbs: The English Verb-Particle Construction and its History.* Berlin/Boston: De Gruyter Mouton.

Trevelyan, G. M. (1982 [1942, 1944]) *English Social History: A Survey of Six Centuries Chaucer to Queen Victoria.* Harmondsworth: Penguin Books.

van Dongen, W. A. (1919) "He Put On His Hat and He Put His Hat On," *Neophilologus* 4, 322-353.

Visser, F. T. (1984 [1963]) *An Historical Syntax of the English Language*, Vol. I. Leiden: E. J. Brill.

Wales, K. (1989) *A Dictionary of Stylistics.* London: Longman.

Watt, I. (1957a) *The Rise of the Novel: Studies in Defoe, Richardson and Fielding.* London: Chatto & Windus.

_____ (1957b) "Defoe as Novelist," in B. Ford (ed.) *From Dryden to Johnson: A Guide to English Literature* Vol. IV. London: Cassell & Campany Ltd. 195-208.

Index

absolute 95, 257, 263, 266, 269, 283
adjective 113, 139, 183-187, 241
adverbial insertion 48-66, 204-217, 288, 289, 293
adverbial particle 1, 4, 12, 14, 50, 94, 294
Behn 77, 117, 157, 209, 221, 222, 242, 243
Bunyan 4-6, 17, 44, 222, 243
Captain Singleton 75, 219, 226, 228, 246, 256, 258, 263, 264, 297, 301
causative verb 33, 37, 131, 162, 176, 181, 233
cohesive 89, 154-156, 219, 231-239, 241
colloquial 2, 17-18, 198, 218, 280, 282, 295
Colonel Jack 96-99, 114, 117, 226, 246, 248, 299, 303
complement 49, 59, 139, 140, 172, 179, 180, 188, 191, 241
composite 24, 66-78, 99, 218-221, 227
connotation 98
context 3, 6, 12, 17, 43, 76, 79, 86-88, 97, 98, 114, 117, 124, 125, 128, 140, 141, 155, 159, 178, 187, 198, 219, 225, 239, 241, 243, 245, 246, 248, 251, 272, 277, 279, 280
conversion 112-115, 118
coordination 143, 144, 190, 219, 220, 231-244, 266, 278, 281, 282
coordinated 87, 144, 218, 219, 231, 232, 238, 240, 241, 294
deep structure 7, 219, 266, 289, 290
deviant 40, 41, 70, 148, 224, 288
direct speech 134, 135, 205
Early Modern English 18, 20, 94, 140, 148, 198

eighteenth century 1-2, 11, 16, 50, 73, 271, 306
ellipsis 177, 281
"empty" *it* 140-142, 262
fiction 26, 32, 33, 37, 41, 45, 48, 67, 77, 86, 87, 116, 117, 157, 223, 231, 238, 241, 244, 245, 249, 250, 256, 266, 272, 283, 287, 295
fictional 1, 2, 4, 18, 28, 33, 41, 227, 240, 243, 274, 277, 287, 289, 295, 308
figurative 10, 20, 66, 85, 250, 254, 281, 285, 294
focus 69, 70, 116, 198, 224, 225, 226, 237, 245, 290
free combination 10, 63
fronting (of the particle) 17, 37-48, 76, 156, 157, 231, 244, 247-249, 288, 291, 294
gerund 32, 92, 99-112, 115, 143, 147, 153, 170, 188-204, 275, 276, 290, 292, 293
Gulliver's Travels 4, 5, 17, 45, 209, 222, 249
hybrid 93-99, 289
idiom 2, 18, 19, 66, 88-93, 270-272, 284
idiomatic 2, 10, 15, 18, 20, 50, 63, 66, 69, 79, 139, 172, 193, 229, 279, 281
imagery 9, 281, 285
indirect speech 37, 134-136, 206
infinitive 32, 33, 36, 37, 49, 50, 80-85, 103, 109, 130, 132-134, 137, 141, 146, 147, 150-152, 158, 163, 164, 166, 169, 171, 174, 183, 208, 228, 235, 237-239, 291
informal 4, 11, 12
intensifier (or intensive adverb) 51, 52, 66, 213-215, 254, 293
inversion 17, 40, 172, 231, 244-249,

311

251, 282, 294
Jespersen   2, 9, 20, 43, 44, 143, 145, 165, 188, 194, 200, 228, 229, 266, 276, 281-283, 295
Journal of the Plague Year   5, 17, 21, 147, 184, 190, 226, 244, 274-281, 284, 298, 303
Latinate   280, 295
literal   10, 20, 63, 66, 69, 125, 128, 250, 280, 288
Memoirs of a Cavalier   5, 17, 87, 112, 227, 244, 297, 301
metaphor   9, 10, 19, 255, 265, 283
metaphorical   8, 253, 255, 278, 283
military terms   30, 88, 89, 125, 227, 287
modifier   183-187, 211, 228
Moll Flanders   1, 5, 17, 18, 27, 40, 41, 47, 147, 156, 157, 186, 226, 245, 251, 272, 298, 302
monosyllabic   3, 9, 11, 26, 87, 121, 128, 224
native   3, 11, 26, 121
nautical terms   30, 40, 75, 82, 142, 143, 246, 256-268, 283, 287, 294
nominalization   197, 276
nonce-use (*or* formation)   94, 98, 114, 290
novel   1, 2, 4, 6, 9, 16, 19, 23, 30, 98, 112, 117, 226, 243, 263, 283, 285, 295
Pamela   4-6, 17, 45-48, 78, 92, 93, 116, 157, 209, 210, 221, 222, 226, 227, 243, 244, 249
participial   32, 33, 36, 59, 107, 131, 138, 151, 169-171, 174, 180, 219, 223, 237, 246, 266, 268, 269, 282, 283
participle   1, 3-7, 10-17, 23, 32, 36-38, 49, 66-69, 72-74, 77-99, 107, 115, 137, 141, 170, 183, 185, 187, 241, 265, 283, 284, 289
passive   7-9, 92, 93, 129, 169-187, 188, 199-204, 210, 211, 213, 215, 217, 221, 222, 226, 229, 237, 241, 243, 275, 276, 282, 290, 292, 293
passive progressive   177, 199
perception verb   32, 33, 72, 131, 162, 170, 180, 246, 265
personification   88, 258, 265
phrasal-prepositional verb   10-12, 14, 21, 78, 89
Pilgrim's Progress   1, 4, 5, 17, 44, 77, 102, 108, 117, 157, 170, 172, 208, 221, 222, 241-243, 249
postmodification   115, 185, 186
prepositional verb   10-12, 14, 20, 21, 50, 95, 96, 290
premodification   185-187
redundant   17, 26, 115, 145, 231, 255, 269-273, 279, 284, 288, 294
repetition   17, 28, 42, 63, 135, 231, 274-278, 294
reporting verb   134-136, 205, 219, 291
Richardson   1, 2, 4, 6, 15, 46, 47, 78, 116, 222, 226, 227
Robinson Crusoe   1, 5, 17, 24, 27, 116, 143, 165, 226, 250, 256, 264, 297, 301
Romance verb   11, 26, 121, 239, 240, 242
Roxana   1, 5, 17, 71, 94, 147, 186, 187, 194, 248, 251, 272, 285, 299, 304
semantic   1, 12, 16, 72, 74, 117, 125, 198, 219, 224, 231, 284
structure   2, 6, 7, 16, 23, 27, 32, 74, 78, 80, 93-95, 97, 105, 107, 119, 128, 204, 210, 219, 266, 274, 287-290
style   2, 11, 16-19, 28, 41, 47, 111, 263, 272, 275, 277, 280, 284, 295
stylistic   1, 8, 16, 18, 40, 87, 95, 206, 231, 244, 247, 248, 266, 271, 280, 294
synonym   17, 54, 99, 231, 274, 278-281, 285, 294
synonymous   219, 239, 240, 279, 285
syntax   18, 38, 106, 155, 198, 224, 227, 229, 244, 282

Index

Swift 4, 5, 17, 18, 20, 222
word-formation 187